D0356420

Praise for Candace Camp

"Alex and Sabrina are a charming pair."
—*BookPage* on *His Sinful Touch*

"Those who have not discovered Camp's Mad Morelands are in for a treat… Camp is a consummate storyteller whose well-crafted prose and believable characterization ensure that this intriguing mystery… will utterly enchant readers."
—*RT Book Reviews* on *His Sinful Touch*

"From its delicious beginning to its satisfying ending, Camp's delectable [story] offers a double helping of romance."
—*Booklist* on *Mesmerized*

"[Camp] is renowned as a storyteller who touches the hearts of her readers time and time again."
—*RT Book Reviews*

"A smart, fun-filled romp."
—*Publishers Weekly* on *Impetuous*

"A clever mystery adds intrigue to this lively and gently humorous tale, which simmers with well-handled sexual tension."
—*Library Journal* on *A Dangerous Man*

"Delightful."
—*Publishers Weekly* on *The Wedding Challenge*

"The talented Camp has deftly mixed romance and intrigue to create another highly enjoyable Regency romance."
—*Booklist* on *An Independent Woman*

"A truly enjoyable read."
—*Publishers Weekly* on *Mesmerized*

CANDACE CAMP

HER Scandalous PURSUIT

HQN

HQN

ISBN-13: 978-1-335-04144-9

Her Scandalous Pursuit

Copyright © 2020 by Candace Camp

This edition published by arrangement with Harlequin Books S.A.

For questions and comments about the quality of this book,
please contact us at CustomerService@Harlequin.com.

HQN
22 Adelaide St. West, 40th Floor
Toronto, Ontario M5H 4E3, Canada
www.Harlequin.com

Printed in U.S.A.

Recycling programs
for this product may
not exist in your area.

HER Scandalous PURSUIT

HER
Scandalous
PURSUIT

PROLOGUE

London
December 1556

A WOMAN RAN down the narrow street, staying close to the wall beneath the overhang of the buildings. There was no time. She was ahead of them—thank God one of Jamic's urchins had slipped her the message—but she knew they were not far behind. Now that he had the writ for her arrest, he would waste no time.

Hatred burned in her heart for the man who sought to destroy her. Hal told her it was only her invention the man wanted, but Hal was a good man, too ready to assume that quality in others. He didn't know, as she did, the heart of darkness.

Ducking into the court, she pulled open their door and barred it behind her. "Hal! They're coming."

She hurried through her workroom into the family's living area. A fire burned low in the small fireplace, a pot hanging from the metal arm above it. They had thought to eat before they left, but it was too late now. She ran up the narrow stairs to the level above, where the sleeping quarters lay. Jutting out over the street, it was a larger area than below, with a wide, enclosed room for her and Will, and a smaller one for the children. It was a commodious house, a point of pride for her. She had done well, risen above her former station.

And now they were reduced to fleeing the city like common thieves.

Hal was in the children's room, filling a sack, and he jumped to his feet, leaving the remainder of the belongings lying on the floor. Guy, the eldest, also turned from his task, his face pale in the dim flicker of the rushlight.

"Are they here?" Hal asked, his voice tight.

"Not yet. But they'll not be far behind. We must hurry."

He nodded and snatched up Guy's cloak to place around the boy's shoulders. She went to the crib and lifted the little one. The baby didn't wake, merely turned her head and snuggled into her mother's warmth.

"Alice," she whispered, brushing her lips against the dark curls. "Beloved." Swallowing back her tears, she wrapped the baby's blanket more tightly around her, pulling down one corner to protect Alice's head from the cold.

When she turned back to Hal, she saw he had already donned his own cloak. As she held out the baby to him, he grasped her arm. "Come with us, love."

"I cannot. Thou knowest I cannot." Her voice shook. "I must destroy it."

His usually pleasant face darkened. "That wicked thing. I wish—"

"I know. I wish it, as well. But you must get the children to safety. And I must undo the evil I've created." She handed Alice to him and leaned in to kiss each cheek, then his mouth. His free arm lashed around her and he squeezed her to him.

"Follow me. Promise me you will follow."

"I will."

He kissed her then, hard and fast, and went down the stairs.

She kneeled before Guy, straightening the tie on his cloak and drinking in her son's face. "Be strong. Help your father."

He nodded sharply. "I will. I'll keep them safe."

"I know." This one was like her, perhaps too much so; he wasn't the sort to look back or give in. He'd charge ahead. Tears sparkled in her eyes, but she blinked them away and kissed him in the same ritual, a peck on each cheek and one on his mouth, then hugged him to her in a last embrace. "Take care."

She stood up. He looked at her solemnly. "I shan't see thee again, shall I?"

"I'll be with thee always."

He ran down the stairs, and she followed. The baby lay in the chair, still asleep, Hal's bundle on the floor. Hal had shoved aside the small chest and now he lifted the hatch in the floor. Cold, dank air rushed in from below.

Hal picked up the sack and pulled the strap over his head, adjusting the sack on his back. She went to the cupboard and grabbed her journal, as well as the athame in its scabbard that sat atop it. Going to him, she shoved them into the sack.

"That!" He pulled away. "No. Take it out. I want no part of it."

"Thou must. Else *he* will have it. Guard it. Keep it. Promise me."

His eyes flickered with heat and for an instant she thought he would refuse, but then he jerked his hand, as if throwing aside his thoughts. "I promise." He bent down to pick up the baby. She lit the wick of the fat tallow candle inside the pierced tin lamp and handed it to him. He held the lamp above the dark hole. "Come, son."

Guy looked back at her, and for an instant the scared little boy showed in his face, but then he started down the ladder. Hal bent to hand the boy the lamp. Straightening, he looked at her. He did not speak; his gaze said everything.

She felt as if she might drown in the sorrow rising in

her chest. But she nodded, summoning up a smile. "God-speed, my love."

Then her family was gone, leaving only the gaping black hole. For an instant she could not move, everything in her screaming to follow them. But she pushed down that craven impulse and rushed to lower the door. She dragged the small chest back in place.

Whatever she had promised, she knew she would not be following them. She was not about to lead her enemies straight to her family. No one would bother to hunt them down; it was her they wanted. Her and her creation.

She swung the pot out from the fire, then hurried to her workroom. She pulled out bottles of herbs and a small cellar of precious salt. It would be better if she could light her brazier and work at the table, but there wasn't time. She must trust that the rough fire in her fireplace would do. After pulling over a stool, she climbed up and inserted a key in the highest cabinet and opened it.

Reaching in, she pulled out a small object wrapped in velvet. Even through the cloth, she could feel the warmth of it in her hand. The pulse of power. This was hers. The culmination of her life's work, the fruit of her knowledge and skill. And she must destroy it.

Returning to the fire, she kneeled and unwrapped the instrument. It gleamed in the firelight, but she would not let herself look at it. She tossed in a handful of herbs, one after the other. She was not even sure this would work, but she had to try.

She had sought knowledge, but somehow the path she had created to take her to wisdom had changed, leading her into power. It had been heady, seductive, but at the core of that power lay evil. It must be destroyed; she could only hope it was not too late. With one hand she clasped the pendant that hung around her neck, drawing on its strength. With the other hand, she picked up the infernal device.

She turned to the fire and stretched out her arm. She tried to call up the Latin words, but they would not come out. Her hand shook. Outside, thunder rumbled. She realized her own creation was fighting her now. Outside there was the sound of booted feet and a low barked command. *His* voice.

A knock thudded on the door. She gripped the instrument more tightly; it cut into her skin, but she scarcely noticed it. The familiar tingling began to creep up her arm. A siren call whispered in her ear: she could stop them. If she turned this instrument against her attackers, she'd be safe. She could be with her family.

But no. She must not give in to the temptation. Using it only strengthened it, made it more difficult to give up. She had sworn to stop using it. Sworn to prevent anyone—especially him—from ever using it.

Something far harder than a knock thudded against the door. Again. And again. The door crashed open. She jumped to her feet and whirled to face the intruders. The bishop's men charged in, drawing their swords. Behind them, she saw *him*. The man who had once been her mentor. The man she had trusted. The man who had given her up to the authorities.

Hatred pulsed in her, and without thought, she flung her arm out toward them, holding the instrument she had created. "Halt!"

Wind rushed in through the open door, swirling through the room, sending the papers in her workroom flying. Lightning illuminated the scene, and she felt the hair at the nape of her neck rise. The air between her and the men crackled with energy, lights sparkling and popping.

The soldiers stopped as suddenly as if they'd run into a wall, their hands frozen on the hilts of their swords. Fear flooded their faces as they realized that they could not move and were held powerless by the sizzling, stinging energy.

She knew their fear would turn to terror if they knew the full extent of the power she could wield with her creation. People whispered that she could speak to the dead. They said she could raise the dead. Pull death from a dying man. What they didn't realize was that she could send death to a living man just as readily.

Her smile was lethal, and she began to chant under her breath. She should not have done it, should not continue to use it, but she couldn't stop. Didn't want to stop. Pleasure filled her as she felt the power pour out of her toward them. She saw the horror in their faces as their hearts jolted and the shocks began to sizzle through their limbs. She increased the energy, watching them pale as the life began to leach from them.

She looked at the man who had once been her mentor and was now her sworn enemy. It wasn't fear she saw in his face; it was greed and envy. He coveted her power, yearned to hold the device. He would do anything to seize it, including accusing her of heresy and sending her to her death. His soul had been blackened by his lust for power.

As hers would be if she continued. She must stop. She must rid the world of this evil. But the darkness inside herself called seductively: use it and she would be free. Use it and she could do as she wished.

With a cry, she pulled out of its thrall and whirled. She heard him bellow, "No!" and saw him throw himself forward, but it was too late. She flung her creation into the fire.

CHAPTER ONE

London
December 1868

THISBE THOUGHT THE lecture at Covington Institute would be informative. She didn't expect it to change her life.

A few minutes after the talk began, there was an odd tingle at the nape of her neck, and she turned her head to look back. A young man stood in the doorway of the crowded lecture hall, his eyes on her. He quickly looked away, and Thisbe swiveled back to face the lecturer. All week, she had looked forward to this lecture, but now she had trouble focusing on the speaker's words. Her mind was preoccupied with the man in the doorway.

Being a woman working in a man's world, she was accustomed to being the object of others' gazes—from leers to astonished looks to baleful glares at her audacity—and she usually ignored them. But this man... She wasn't sure why he was so different from everyone else, but he intrigued her.

There was an odd burst of awareness in her chest that she had never felt before. It wasn't recognition; she was positive she'd never seen the man before in her life. Nor was it like the vague, pervasive sense she felt for her twin, Theo. It was more a rush of excitement and discovery, similar to the quiver of anticipation when an experiment was unfolding. But this time, a sense of certainty mingled with the anticipation, though she had no idea what she was certain of.

She started to glance back again, but just then he slid into the seat beside her. He had his head bowed and didn't look at her, just sat down, took out a small pad and stubby pencil and began to scribble. Amazingly, the peculiar feeling in her grew and warmed as she watched him. What was it about this man that made her feel this way?

She could see only his profile, and even that not well, given the way he was hunched over his notes, but what she could see appealed to her. He was young, maybe a bit older than she. His hair was thick and dark brown, a little too long and shaggy; it looked as if he'd hacked it off himself. What color were his eyes? She wished she could get a better look at him. He was tall and slender, his long legs taking up all the space between the rows. His fingers, too, were long and mobile, moving swiftly across the paper. The sight of them tugged at her midsection.

She faced the lecturer again, not wanting her neighbor to catch her studying him. She had apparently missed a good deal, for the man was now talking about atomic numbers. She returned to taking notes, though not with the speed or volume of the man next to her. No doubt that swiftness contributed to the fact that his handwriting was largely illegible. How did he ever read what he'd written down?

He neither turned to her nor spoke, but from the corner of her eye, she caught him looking at her time and again, his glances brief and almost furtive. Was he shy? That seemed possible, though shyness was a quality she was somewhat unfamiliar with, given the nature of her family. Or perhaps he was appalled by the presence of a woman at a scientific society's meeting.

Thisbe turned her head, watching him, so that the next time he glanced at her, he met her gaze. His eyes widened a little, and pink blossomed along his cheekbones before he jerked his eyes back to his note taking. Yes, that was it; he was shy. And his eyes were a warm, chocolate brown. A lovely color.

She was acutely aware of the man beside her. She could feel the heat of his body and smell his scent, a faint blend of man and cologne. That, too, caused a little pull deep inside her.

There was applause around her, and Thisbe realized the lecture had ended. Belatedly, she clapped and stood up, as everyone around them was doing. Her neighbor also popped to his feet, dropping his pad and pencil in the process, and he bent to retrieve them. His pencil rolled over toward Thisbe and stopped by the hem of her skirt. He picked up the pad and straightened, glancing back down at the pencil. He shifted a little and stuck the pad back into his pocket, sending another longing look at the pencil.

He would have to speak to her now. Thisbe waited, tucking her own pad and pencil back into her reticule. The applause had stopped, and all around them people were turning to leave. The man shuffled his feet, then started to move away. Obviously, it would be up to her if she wanted to talk to him.

"Sir!" She picked up the pencil. He was walking away. "Sir." Thisbe followed, reaching out to touch his arm.

He whipped back around so quickly that she almost ran into him. "Oh. Ma'am. Miss. I, um…"

"I believe this is yours," Thisbe went on, holding out his pencil. His face was very nice, too, and those deep brown eyes were surrounded by thick fringes of black lashes.

"Oh!" Red began to stain his cheeks again. "I, um, thank you." He took the pencil from her, his fingertips brushing her skin, which sent a tingle all through her. He dropped the pencil into his pocket, but continued to stand there, looking at her. "I, uh, it was a very nice talk, wasn't it?"

Thisbe knew a flash of triumph. He wanted to talk to her, as well. But clearly she would have to carry the burden of finding a topic. "Yes. The Covington Institute often has interesting lectures. Mrs. Isabelle Durant gave a very nice talk on botany last month. Of course, not all the discussions are scientific."

"*Mrs*. Durant?" He looked surprised.

"Yes. She's been an avid collector and illustrator of wildflowers for some time. She's published several books."

"Oh. I see. I'm sorry… Botany is not a field I'm especially familiar with. I'm afraid I've never, um, heard of her."

"Few have, unfortunately. Her work is largely ignored by her fellow scientists because she's a woman. The Covington Institute is quite forward thinking." She smiled. "Women can belong to it, speak at it and attend its lectures. That's why I come here so often." Thisbe didn't add that Covington was her mother's maiden name and her mother had endowed the institution to further the goal of female education. She had found over the years that it was better not to bring up her family. No one ever acted the same after they learned Thisbe was the daughter of a duke. Especially since he was a duke with a reputation for oddity.

"I'm glad you do." He smiled, and her heart wobbled in her chest.

"I noticed you were late."

"That's an understatement." His smile lingered. "I wasn't able to leave work earlier. I'm sorry—I hope I didn't disturb you." He seemed more relaxed now and as uninterested in walking away as Thisbe, though around them the lecture hall was emptying out.

"No. You didn't disturb me at all." That was a lie, of course, but the disturbance he had caused was of a far different nature than he meant. "I thought you might want to borrow the notes I made before you arrived." She pulled her notepad from her reticule and offered it to him.

"Are you sure?" he asked even as he reached for it. "Won't you want them yourself?"

She shrugged. "You can return it when you're done. Do you plan to come to the next lecture?"

"Yes," he answered promptly, his hand closing around the narrow pad. This time, Thisbe was certain that his fingers brushing hers was not an accident.

"I'm not sure what the topic is."

"It doesn't matter. I mean, I'm sure whatever they have will be interesting."

"You can return the notes to me then." A month seemed a very long time. She brightened as another thought struck her. "Or…do you plan to attend the Christmas lectures at the Royal Institution? I will be there, as well. Mr. Odling is speaking on the chemistry of carbon."

"Yes. It starts on Boxing Day, doesn't it?"

She nodded. "I think there are several lectures."

"Excellent. Though one has to wonder how one can spend several days on the properties of carbon."

"Ha! I can see that chemistry is not your field."

"Not especially. I take it you are interested in chemistry."

"It's my life's work," Thisbe said simply. "I've been studying it since I was seventeen. Well, earlier than that, really, but at seventeen, I made it my focus."

"Really? Where have you—" He quickly covered the amazement in his voice. "I mean, ah, you have been studying it?"

Thisbe let out a little laugh. At least he had tried to cover up his astonishment. "My family is quite keen on education, you see, for all of us—the boys and the girls. I learned alongside my brothers. After that, I went to Bedford College. They didn't allow women to read for examination at London University until this year, I'm afraid."

"The school for women. I see. How interesting." He looked as if he meant it, which was not usually the case. "I always thought it seemed unfair that Oxford and Cambridge won't admit women." He made a wry face. "Not that they would have taken me, either. No menial laborers' sons need apply."

Yes, it had been a good idea to conceal her connections to aristocracy. "They are rather hotbeds of snobbery."

"I attended London University. Well, for two years. There really are very few classes in scientific subjects."

"Exactly." It was one of Thisbe's greatest grievances against English education, right after its prejudice against women. "England lags far behind other countries in recognizing the importance of scientific research."

He nodded. "It's still considered a gentleman's hobby. There's far too much emphasis on philosophy and dead languages."

"Yes." She and her father had had a few heated discussions about that. "That's why I went to Germany to study under Herr Erlenmeyer."

"Emil Erlenmeyer! Are you joking?"

"No. You've heard of him?"

"Of course. His theory regarding naphthalene was brilliant!"

They launched into an animated discussion of naphthalene, fused benzene rings and experimentation that lasted several minutes. It wasn't until Mr. Andrews appeared at the open doorway and gave a subtle clearing of his throat that Thisbe realized that everyone else had left. There wasn't even a noise from the outer lobby.

"Oh. I believe Mr. Andrews would like to close the lecture hall." Of course, Andrews would let them stay if she asked, but there was no reason to make the poor man remain here just on her whim.

"Oh." He glanced around. "I hadn't realized…"

"Neither had I."

They trailed over to the doorway. Andrews bowed and said, "Good day, miss."

Thank goodness he hadn't called her "my lady," as he had in the past. She had managed to break him of the habit, but every now and then he slipped. It was clearly painful for him. He could not bring himself to address her as "Miss Moreland" and he apparently was unable to call her mother anything but "Your Grace."

They lingered in the lobby. It would take Andrews a while to straighten up in the lecture hall, so they had a few more minutes. Wanting to keep the conversation going, she said, "I'm sorry, we have been talking about my interests all this time. I haven't even asked what your field is."

"Oh. Well." He looked a trifle wary. "I have been working on a project with Professor Gordon."

"Archibald Gordon?" Thisbe stared. "The one who believes in ghosts?"

He let out a sigh. "That is all anyone says about him. He's a well-respected scientist."

"He *was* well-respected until he started dabbling in frauds like spirit photography," Thisbe retorted, then blushed. "I'm sorry—that was rude. Everyone says I am too blunt. I didn't mean to—to disparage your beliefs. If you are a Spiritualist…" It would be beyond disappointing, but, of course, she couldn't say that.

To her great relief, he grinned. "Don't worry. I'm not offended. Nor am I a Spiritualist. I don't believe in superstitions or legends. They are rife in Dorset, where I was raised, and my aunt used to spin me tales of ghosts and magic and such—a bullock's heart pierced with thorns in the chimney to keep a witch from coming down it and that sort of thing. I knew they were nonsense. However, one cannot ignore that people have seen spectral images—and I don't mean those claiming to witness Lady Howard in her ghost carriage riding across the moors. I'm talking about people who awakened to find a loved one standing beside their bed."

"Those are dreams. Everyone has peculiar dreams from time to time."

"But dismissing it offhand is ignoring evidence. Personally, I doubt that spirit photography actually captures the images of ghosts, but one has to consider the proof that's offered. Mr. Gordon saw the pictures—saw them taken and could see no sign of chicanery—so he believes in it. You have to admit that no one has come up with an explanation for how spirit photographers get the ghostly image on the photographic plate."

"Perhaps not, but didn't a woman in Boston say that the ghost in one of the photographs was actually a picture of her that she had had taken at that same studio? I would say that's conclusive proof."

He nodded. "That is why I find it difficult to believe in it. But if we accept that woman's words as proof, how can we then refuse to believe the people who have sworn that the images are of their loved ones? Surely a mother would recognize her own child."

"It is my opinion that grieving relatives want so much to believe it's the person they've lost that they imagine the features are much more like their loved one than they really are. The images are pale and vague, are they not? One baby in a christening gown and cap looks a good deal like any other, and if the face is a little blurry, it is easy to see what you long to see."

"What if you saw it? What if you had the evidence right in front of your face?"

"I would still be skeptical."

He laughed. "I have no doubt of that."

"But," she went on, "yes, if you could absolutely, incontrovertibly prove it, I would have to believe it."

"That is the very thing we are trying to do." His face lit with enthusiasm. "We are experimenting. My goal is to prove or disprove the presence of a spirit that exists even after death. It doesn't really matter to me which is correct. It's the exploration that's important. There are so many things in this world that we don't know, things we cannot see. Much we know now would have been deemed impossible fifty, even twenty, years ago. Telegraphy, for instance. Who would have thought one could send a message to someone miles and miles away in just a moment? Or photography. Electricity. Those principles were always there—we just could not see them."

Thisbe thought investigating ghosts was scarcely science, but she warmed to the joy in his eyes, the passion for learning and exploration. It was what she had felt all her life, that eager thirst for knowledge, the excitement of discovery. She had liked this man the moment she saw him, but now, in this instant, she knew that he was *important*.

"But how do you propose to prove the theory?" she asked.

"We have to find the right tools. Think of all the stars we could not see until the telescope was invented. All the minute things that were invisible until we had microscopes. What if people's spirits are right here with us all the time, and we just don't have the capability to see them?"

"You want to invent a tool with which we can see them?"

"That's my hope. Spirit photography was based on the idea that a camera might be able to catch what we couldn't see, what was too fast or too faint. What I am working on are the properties of light. Light isn't visible to our eyes as colors until one uses a prism. But William Herschel discovered that there was another kind of light, infrared, which we cannot see even with a prism."

Thisbe nodded. "Yes, I've read about it. He used a prism to separate the colors, then put a thermometer under each color to see which heated faster. But he found that the thermometer outside the spectrum increased the most. So there had to be another part of the spectrum that exists but is invisible to us."

"Exactly. And then Ritter found another band on the blue end—ultraviolet."

"So you think a spirit is something that exists in another band of light?"

"That can be *seen* in another band. Can we create an instrument that will allow us to see the invisible bands in the way that the prism allows us to see the separate colors?" He shrugged. "That's one of the things we're working on. There are others."

"We? You and Mr. Gordon?"

"And a few other fellows. Professor Gordon has a patron who's very interested in his research, so he is able to provide us with a laboratory and materials. It's quite nice. Perhaps you could see it sometime. I mean, well, if you have any interest, of course."

"That would be—" she began just as Andrews reappeared, carrying her cloak.

"I took the liberty of bringing you your wrap, La— Miss Moreland. I hope you don't mind."

"No, of course not. Thank you." There was nothing to do then, but leave. She spent some time tying her cloak and pulling on her gloves, but that could only last so long.

"Well, um…" She turned to her companion.

"I suppose we should leave." He shuffled his feet. "I, ah… It's been terribly nice speaking with you. It was most generous of you to lend me your notes." He patted his pocket, where he had stuck her small tablet. "I promise I'll take good care of them and return them to you. At the Christmas lecture, perhaps?"

"Yes. That sounds perfect." Thisbe held her hand out to him. "Excuse me. I should have introduced myself. My name is Thisbe Moreland."

He clasped her hand. Thisbe wished she hadn't already donned her gloves. "Miss Moreland. It's a pleasure to meet you. I'm Desmond Harrison."

"Mr. Harrison." With a last smile, she turned toward the door, and Desmond leaped to open it for her.

He followed her down the steps, then said, "Please, allow me to walk you home."

Thisbe cast a glance down the street, where the Moreland town carriage sat waiting for her. John, the coachman, who was standing at the head of the horses, saw her and climbed into the carriage. But she turned her back to him. "That would be very nice of you, Mr. Harrison. Thank you."

She heard the carriage begin to rattle up the street toward them. She started off with Desmond in the opposite direction. Holding one hand behind her back, she waved the coachman away. John would understand... Well, not understand exactly, but the servants were accustomed to the Moreland oddities.

Apparently, John caught her meaning, for the clip-clop of the horses stopped for a moment, then continued at a much slower pace. Hopefully, Desmond would not glance back and see the carriage creeping along after them.

She glanced over at Desmond, strolling along beside her, hands in his pockets. "Mr. Harrison! Where is your coat? And gloves. And hat." She started to turn back. "Did you leave them at the Institute?"

"No. I fear I forgot them," he told her sheepishly. "I was late and I ran out without my coat and cap. I lost the gloves last week." He looked faintly puzzled. "Somewhere."

"You sound like Theo. He can never hold on to a pair of gloves."

"Theo?" He looked at her sharply.

"Yes, my brother. My twin, actually."

"Ah." His face relaxed. "You have a twin. Twins are fascinating—though it's better if they're identical, of course." He glanced at her. "I'm sorry—naturally I didn't mean better. It's just, well, in terms of studying... That is to say..." He trailed off, his face reddening again.

Thisbe began to laugh. "It's all right. I know what you mean. I have two younger brothers who are identical twins—one can hardly tell one from the other. They are certainly...interesting."

"You must have several siblings." His voice sounded faintly wistful.

"I have four brothers and two sisters. Do you have siblings?" She wondered about the odd tone in his voice.

He shook his head. "I had a sister. Sally. She died several years ago."

"I'm sorry."

"Thank you. She was older than I by several years, but I was close to her. She helped my aunt raise me. Mother died, you see, right after I was born."

"How awful." Thisbe laid her hand on his arm. "I am so sorry. Is your father…?"

He hesitated, then said, "No, he is gone, as well."

"What about Christmas? Do you have other family here? You could come to our house." She'd have to reveal her family situation, of course, which wasn't ideal, but it pierced her heart to think of him alone on the holiday.

He smiled at her. "You're very kind, but you needn't worry about it. I spend Christmas with Mr. Gordon."

"I'm glad." Thisbe realized that she still had her hand on his arm and reluctantly pulled it back. "You're shivering. You must be freezing. There's really no need for you to walk me home. I've done it many times alone, and it's perfectly safe."

"I'm fine. I frequently lose track of my coat or cap or… well, any number of things." He gave her a rueful smile. "So I often find myself in such a situation."

She couldn't let him walk her home. Eventually, of course, she would have to let him know about her family, but not just yet. One look at Broughton House would be enough to frighten anyone away.

"It's a long way," she began. Ahead of her, she saw the answer to her dilemma. "I have to take the omnibus, you see." She pointed to a cluster of people waiting for the public vehicle. "If you walk me to the stop, I'll be fine from there."

He agreed to that, though he insisted on lingering until the vehicle actually arrived and she had boarded before he left. Thisbe watched him through the window of the omnibus as he jogged out of sight. Unfortunately, she was trapped for however long it took to reach the next stop. She had no idea where she was headed. She would have to get off at the first opportunity and walk back to her coach, which, she saw, was trundling along after them. She began to chuckle. No doubt this would make another excellent story about the Moreland madness for the driver to regale the other servants with at their meal tonight.

She didn't care. This evening had been worth far more than an embarrassing story about her making the rounds of the servants. She felt something tonight that she had never known before. For the first time, she had met a man who could make her forget all about science.

CHAPTER TWO

DESMOND RAN MOST of the way home—he was cold, but also bursting with energy. Thisbe—it was a delightful name. Unique and lovely, just like her. He had noticed her the moment he had walked into the hall simply because she was the only woman in the room. She had intrigued him. That was why he had chosen that chair instead one of the other empty ones.

Then he had seen her up close, and his entire chest had seized up. She was beautiful. Not the china-doll beauty of blond hair, blue eyes and a simpering smile. Her hair beneath her bonnet was jet-black, darker even than his own, and her eyes were a startling shade of bright green. She was so tall that he had not had to lean down to talk to her, and she was slender as a reed. Her willowy form was not the hourglass ideal achieved by cinching one's waist until it cut off her air, but it was more appealing to him. She moved with grace and ease, unlike the stiff posture of a corseted woman. And her face… Well, there was no adequate way to describe her face—even featured and feminine yet strong, with a squarish shape and a determined chin, all softened by her curving mouth, with its plump lower lip. Heavens, that lip; it was almost shocking how much he longed to feel it beneath his own mouth.

But it wasn't merely her looks that had turned him into a tongue-tied, clumsy wretch. She was just so—so…utterly different. There were her clothes—a small hat with no more than a plain ribbon to decorate it, a small-hooped skirt unadorned by even one ruffle and half boots that were more sturdy than fashionable. More than that, there was the way she talked—directly, even bluntly; the way she walked—with long, quick, purposeful strides; the way she looked at someone—straight on and confident. There were no demurely downcast gazes with her, no giggles or fluttering lashes or flirtatious glances. Thisbe was simply...herself.

He, of course, had acted like a dolt, sneaking glances at her as he wrote—he hated to think of the state of the notes he'd taken—then dropping his pad and pencil when he stood up. He couldn't pick it up with it touching her skirt; that seemed too forward to do without asking. Yet he'd also been too embarrassed to ask her. He was a trifle shy usually, but not that paralytically shy. He'd been so gripped by fear that he would bungle it all that he had been unable to talk at all.

Another man, someone like his friend Carson Dunbridge, say, would have talked to her and smoothly made a jest about dropping his pen. Desmond had seen Carson talk to women—he was relaxed and assured, and charmed them with a smile. But then Carson was a gentleman's son, trained from infancy in correct behavior and social ease. He was accustomed to dealing with ladies.

And it was clear Thisbe was a lady, though her plain clothes and bonnet suggested that she was not a wealthy one. Proper English could be taught—after all, hadn't Desmond himself learned to use proper grammar and speak with only a trace of a Dorset accent? But Thisbe had that unteachable, indefinable air of gentility. The manager of the Covington Institute had obviously recognized it, given the respect with which he spoke to her.

Desmond, however, was very much not one of the gen-teel class. He had not lied exactly about his father—the man was gone—but his answer had been an equivocation at best. His father had been a laborer and sometime thief whenever he couldn't find honest work; he'd ended up being shipped off to the penal colony in Australia.

Desmond's education had been largely self-taught, with the generous aid of the village vicar, who had recognized the intelligence and thirst for knowledge in him. It had been lack of funds as much as lack of scientific classes that had cut short his career at London University. Unlike Carson and the others in Gordon's laboratory, he had no stipend from parents and therefore had to work in a shop to support himself.

He would never have dreamed that a woman like Thisbe might start a conversation with him. Yet she had. It was then that he had discovered how truly fascinating Thisbe was. Once they began talking, it had been easy. Desmond had always had trouble talking to women, as they found deadly dull most of the things he was interested in. To be fair, most men found them deadly dull, as well.

But it had been entirely different with Thisbe. Even when she disagreed with him, it was friendly and enjoyable, even invigorating, to discuss the matter. She hadn't even seemed to find it peculiar that Desmond could be so absentminded as to forget his coat or lose his gloves, which, perplexingly, seemed to happen often.

He had been worried when she brought up Theo. It seemed unlikely that a woman as special as she would not already have a beau—he had already checked her hand to see that she wore no wedding ring. It had been a relief to find out the man was her brother. Because, as unlikely and impossible as it would be to win her, Desmond wanted this woman.

His chances of success were low; he was well aware of that. But for the moment he wasn't going to think about that fact. He was going to let himself dream. He would concentrate on the thought that he'd see her again in only a few days.

He couldn't retrieve his coat, which he had left in the workshop, now locked for the night, so he went straight to the laboratory. It was located in the basement of a building, reached by a set of stairs leading down from the street.

Inside the laboratory the light was low, having only the two high windows aboveground, and the rough stone walls of the narrow room were old and often damp. But it was well-equipped and spacious, being long as well as narrow, and none of the men who worked there noticed the musty smell or the lack of a view.

Desmond opened the door to find Professor Gordon and the other workers clustered together in the wide space between the worktables and the professor's desk, all talking in excited tones. His mentor looked over at him first and said, "Desmond. There you are. You're rather late this evening."

"Yes, I went to a lecture after we closed." He was reluctant to say anything about Miss Moreland. There was no reason to keep it a secret, but still, he'd rather keep it close to him, savor it, for the moment. "What's happened? You look—"

"Excited? That's because we are, my boy." Gordon beamed, his round face flushed. He gestured to Desmond. "Come here, come here, and see. I received a letter from Mr. Wallace. It's the most wonderful news."

"More money?" Desmond guessed, walking over. The

room was warm from the Franklin stove, thank goodness, and he was starting to have feeling in his fingers again.

"Better than that." Gordon's eyes twinkled.

Whatever it was, Desmond was glad to see his mentor in such good spirits. More and more these days he seemed sunken in gloom; the damage to his reputation weighed on him. Years ago, when Desmond first came to London, Gordon had been one of the leading lights of science in the city, his opinion sought after. Desmond had deemed himself fortunate indeed that Gordon was a friend of the vicar and had, as the vicar asked, taken Desmond under his wing. But now, having attached himself to the search for proof of the existence of the spirit after death, Gordon was ridiculed by his peers. It pained Desmond to see him grow more and more despondent.

"What's the news?" Desmond smiled, glancing around at the others. "Tell me."

"Mr. Wallace has located the Eye of Annie Blue," Gordon said triumphantly.

"What?" Desmond's eyebrows shot up. "Really?"

"Yes!"

"See, I told you Anne Ballew was real," Carson said in his careless way, leaning back, elbows propped on the high laboratory table, his mouth curved in a lazy smile. Carson never used the nickname given to the woman by the crowds.

"I knew she was real. And that she was burned at the stake as a heretic." Desmond had dug up all the history he could find on the woman—though at the time he had been trying to disprove his aunt's wild stories about her. "I will even accept that she made an instrument called the Eye. But I've never seen any evidence that it actually worked. Or that it survived her downfall. There's been no sign of the Eye since Anne Ballew. There were rumors it was burned."

"And there were rumors that it was saved from the fire," Carson pointed out.

"But we have proof of it now." Gordon waved the paper in his hand. "Mr. Wallace is certain he's found it."

Desmond made no comment. He would never dispute his mentor, but Gordon had more faith in his patron's expertise than Desmond did. Mr. Wallace was no scientist or scholar, but a wealthy man who was immensely eager to prove that ghosts existed. And as Thisbe had pointed out a few minutes ago, it was very easy to believe in something when one wanted to badly enough.

"Right here, you see." Gordon tapped the paper and began to read. "'I have seen with my own eyes a letter from a man named Henry Caulfield, written in 1692. In the letter, Mr. Caulfield describes a visit to the home of one Arbuthnot Gray, in which he states that Gray showed him Annie Blue's "devilish instrument."'"

"So Mr. Wallace now plans to track down what happened to the Eye after that?"

"No." Gordon fairly vibrated with excitement. "Mr. Wallace already knows where it is. He is convinced it remained in the possession of the Gray family, passed down from generation to generation. There is a will, written by this Arbuthnot's granddaughter, in which she bequeaths to *her* daughter 'the collection of antiquities, oddities and mystical curiosities given to me by my mother.' They're clearly family heirlooms—they would keep them even if they shut them away in a trunk somewhere. That's how the aristocracy is. Mr. Wallace is certain that it is now in the possession of her descendant, the Dowager Duchess of Broughton."

Despite his doubts, Desmond could not help but feel

a thrill of excitement. "Does Mr. Wallace intend to purchase it?"

Gordon's face fell. "He's tried. He said he has written three letters to her and received no reply. He hoped to actually have it in his possession before he told me of it, but he is at such an impasse, he felt he had to let me know. Perhaps he hoped we would have some idea how to obtain the Eye. Though I'm at a bit of a loss to see how I could persuade a duchess when he could not."

"Steal it," Carson suggested lightly.

Desmond rolled his eyes. "Don't be daft."

"I'm serious," Carson protested. "Mr. Wallace seems to think there is no hope of getting the thing from this woman."

"Yes, he did explain that the duchess is odd and difficult to deal with. Apparently she is an avid collector. Never gets rid of anything."

"Then she won't even notice it's gone," Carson said. "It's easy."

"It's illegal," Desmond responded.

"Well, if you think about it, it doesn't really belong to this duchess now, does it?" Benjamin Cooper said from his perch on a stool behind Gordon. "I mean, Anne Ballew was the true owner—she created it. It was undoubtedly stolen from her when they hauled her off to jail."

"That's true," Gordon said thoughtfully, nodding.

"Anne Ballew was an alchemist, the scientist of that day and age. She was dedicated to knowledge and discovery, just as we are," Albert Morrow, the other scientist in the room, chimed in. "Don't you think she would prefer that we have the Eye so we can study it, learn from it, instead of it lying about gathering dust in some old duchess's attic?"

"Yes, I'm sure she would." Professor Gordon's eyes gleamed. Over the years, Anne Ballew had become something of an obsession with him. "It would actually be a reclamation of something lost to science."

"Be that as it may," Desmond said wryly, "most of the world would call it theft."

"Come, come, Dez." Carson's eyes danced with mischief. "Don't be such a spoilsport. Wouldn't it be grand to take something from the ruling class for once instead of the other way around?"

"I hate to remind you, but you're part of the ruling class," Desmond retorted.

"I'm not *really* one of them," Carson said lightly. "My family hasn't the name or fortune to be important. I'm only on the fringes—you know, a bachelor one can invite to even out the numbers or fill out a party."

"You aren't serious about this, are you?" With Carson, it was always hard to tell. Desmond glanced around at the others.

The professor heaved a sigh. "No, you're right, of course. We can't take it, no matter how little she deserves to have it. It's just... I hate to think that it's right there, and we can't get it."

"Why don't you write this duchess?" Desmond suggested. "She probably looks on Mr. Wallace as just another wealthy gentleman. But you are a man of science. You want to study the Eye. What's important to you is discovering its mysteries, not possessing the thing. She could be more willing to *lend* the Eye to a man of science for a noble purpose than she is to sell it to another collector. Or she might allow you to study it at her home if she doesn't want to let it out of her hands."

"Mmm. You might be right. Especially if she thought she might receive some acclaim for it."

"That's the reason most gentlemen give to sponsor a project," Carson agreed.

"Yes. And I know how to flatter them—Lord knows, I've had to do it often enough." Gordon went to his desk at the far end of the room. Everyone else returned to their worktables—though from the continued murmuring among the tablemates, more speculation than experimentation was getting done.

Desmond sat down at his usual place beside Carson and pulled out Thisbe's notepad, as well as his own. Her handwriting, like her, was neat and crisp. He flipped to today's lecture, resisting the temptation to look back through it to find what else she had recorded there. Of course, she would hardly have given it to him if there was anything in it she minded him seeing.

"Lost your coat now, too, have you?" Carson turned on his stool to face Desmond. Carson always found amusement in Desmond's forgetfulness.

"No. Just rushed off without it. I was late to a lecture."

Carson chuckled and shook his head. "I must admit, I admire your single-mindedness. Sad to say, I am rarely careless about my comfort." He paused, then asked, "Was it worth it?"

"What?" Desmond glanced up sharply, then realized Carson meant the lecture, not meeting Thisbe. There was no way he could possibly have known about Thisbe. And, Desmond realized, he had no desire to tell the other man about her. Carson was something of a friend, but Thisbe Moreland was a subject Desmond meant to keep to himself, too precious to let others pore over it. "Oh. Yes. It was very interesting." Though he couldn't remember half of it. "I'll probably attend the next one."

Carson turned back to his experiment, and Desmond began to copy the notes. After a moment, though, Desmond stopped and turned to the other man. "You weren't serious, were you? About stealing the Eye?"

Carson grinned. "Only halfway. I don't suppose I'd go so far as to steal it, but the Eye shouldn't be locked up with some old lady who knows nothing about it or Anne Ballew." He gave Desmond a shrewd look. "You're still skeptical about the whole thing, aren't you?"

"It's all based on Mr. Wallace's suppositions being true—that this 'devilish instrument' really was the Eye and that the present heir still maintains possession of it. No one has actually seen the thing, let alone used it. We don't even know what it looks like. What it consists of."

"That's the best part. We get to explore all that. Doesn't it interest you?"

"Of course it does. I'd love to find out if she'd discovered the secret of seeing spirits. To see how it works, how to replicate it. It's just..." Desmond shrugged. "There are no drawings, no descriptions, no explanations. Only stories. It's the stuff of legends—'the great witch Annie Blue.' My aunt told me all the tales of Anne Ballew and her magical abilities. That she was a sorceress, that she could see the dead and speak to them.

"She also told me that if you see a hare run down a street, a house on that street will burn. I am willing to believe it could be possible that there is a spiritual world around us that we cannot see. But I don't believe in magic. There's no proof of the Eye. Fantastical folktales don't make the basis for proper science."

"Ah, but they'd make for public acclaim if it turned out to true."

There were times when Carson's cynicism grated on him. "You think—" His voice rose somewhat in indignation, and he glanced over at their mentor, then continued in a lowered voice, "You think Professor Gordon is doing it for public acclaim?"

"Not entirely. He truly wants to know—he wants to see the spirits. But it sweetens the pot a good deal to think he could toss it in the faces of all those who reviled him."

"They have been very unfair," Desmond said. "He has the same intelligence, the same probing mind, the same dedication to science that he did before."

Carson shrugged. "He shouldn't have announced it so loudly. He said he could prove the existence of the spirits among us, when the only thing he had were some questionable photographs. You're too close to him—your reverence for him muddies your vision."

"I owe him a great deal. He took the word of a country vicar that I was capable of doing the work, that I deserved a chance. But he went far beyond what would be expected of his friendship with the vicar. He helped me get into the university. He tutored me despite my lack of finances. He even recommended me to the optical shop."

"I know. And you've repaid him by turning your interests in spectrometry to the field where Professor Gordon needs help. I'd think astronomy would be a more pragmatic choice than exploring the spiritual realm."

"Spectrometry is useful in a number of fields. What I discover here can be applied to astronomy or chemistry or physics."

"Yes, but you aren't a true believer," Carson pointed out. "You're scornful of tales of the supernatural."

"Aren't you?" Desmond asked.

"I think there are important kernels of truth that can be found in stories handed down from generation to generation."

"Monsters and gremlins?"

"No, not those." Carson grimaced. "But spirits who

linger after their time is gone? Are all those stories concocted? Weren't they based on something? That shiver one gets quite out of the blue, the spot of cold in a hall, a curtain moving without any breeze…"

Desmond thought of that moment when he had awakened with a start and there was his dead sister, Sally, standing by his bed and smiling at him in that familiar way. The involuntary shiver that ran down his spine when Aunt Tildy talked about Desmond's curse. "I know that one can see things, feel things that seem impossible. I can be convinced. But tales are not enough to do it." He paused. "What about you? You're a cynical sort most of the time. Do you believe in such things?"

"I believe in Anne Ballew. I know she lived. I know people feared her and revered her. I know she was ahead of her time. I believe she created the Eye."

"Do you believe that she saw the dead through it?"

"Ah, well." The corner of Carson's mouth twitched up, and his eyes began to twinkle. "That's what we'll have to find out, won't we?"

His words were innocuous, but they seemed to hang in the air, and Desmond could not deny the chill that touched his back like a cold breath.

CHAPTER THREE

THISBE SAILED INTO the house, bursting with the need to talk to someone. As always, there were noises from all over the house, magnified by the huge, marble-floored entry hall. The buzz of her mother and the followers of her latest cause coming from the red drawing room. The pounding of small feet on the floor above, accompanied by shrieks of maniacal laughter from the twins, Con and Alex. A heavy thud from the back of the house, followed by her own twin's voice letting out a string of heartfelt curses.

Usually it was Theo to whom she turned, but he was not the one she needed for this conversation, especially given his apparent mood. Nor was it her father, hovering over two servants opening a large wooden crate at the end of the long gallery. Papa's answer, no matter the question, was usually a soothing "Yes, dear, that's good," after which he would ask her to admire his newest Minoan pot or statue or whatever else he had just received.

No. This discussion called for her sister. Thisbe started toward the stairs, but at that moment someone struck a chord on the piano in the music room, followed by a rollicking tune and female laughter. Thisbe turned and headed toward the music.

It was Kyria who was at the piano, her fingers flying and her head bobbing in time, the words she was singing unintelligible through her giggling. Her color was high, and a few stray tendrils of her auburn hair, loosened by her forceful pounding of the keys, trailed down from her upswept hair. She looked, of course, quite beautiful. A few feet away from Kyria, Olivia sat sideways in a chair, her legs draped over one arm and her back against the other, a book lying open and unread on her chest, as she waved her arms dramatically in time to the music and bellowed in a German accent, "*Nein, nein*, Fräulein Moreland. The pace! The pace! *Ach, mein Gott!*"

"I take it you've been harassing your music teacher again," Thisbe said, raising her voice to be heard over the music.

"Thisbe!" Olivia bounded up from her chair, her brown braids swinging. "It was Herr Schmidt who was harassing me! 'Fräulein, you must put the feeling into your music. It's art! It's passion!'"

"I was showing her how it's done." Kyria swung around on the bench to face her sisters.

Thisbe laughed. "It sounded more like the music hall than Mozart."

"It was." Kyria grinned. "Reed taught it to me. I told Livvy to play it for Herr Schmidt next time."

"Please don't. The poor man would probably have apoplexy," Thisbe replied.

"Yes, he loves only Beethoven." Olivia dropped down onto the bench beside Kyria. Only a little more than two years apart, the girls looked as if they were separated by much more. Kyria, making her debut this Season, was dressed in a ruffled white dress in the latest fashion, her hair swept up in an intricate style, pearl earrings in her earlobes. Olivia, at fifteen and still in short skirts with her brown hair done in plain braids, showed no desire to leave the world of the schoolroom.

"Where have you been?" Kyria asked. "No one seemed to know."

"I told Papa." When Olivia let out a hoot of derision, Thisbe went on, "Yes, I know. I should have told Smeggars, but he wasn't there when I left. I went to a lecture at the Covington."

"Oh." Kyria wrinkled her nose. "I hoped you were doing something exciting."

"I found it exciting," Thisbe said.

"Wait." Kyria jumped up. "I saw that smile. What happened? You look—"

"All aglow," Olivia interjected. "Like Kyria when she returns from a ball."

"Well…" Thisbe's grin grew. "I met someone."

"A man!" Kyria drew in a sharp breath and grabbed her older sister's arm. "That's why you're glowing."

Thisbe's cheeks colored. "Don't be silly. I'm not glowing."

"You are," Olivia told her. "And your eyes are sparkling."

"Who is he? Do we know him?" Kyria persisted.

High-pitched laughter suddenly filled the hall outside, and a moment later two toddlers dressed in their nightclothes burst into the room, their nanny in hot pursuit. The boys were mirror images of each other, with hair as dark and eyes as green as Thisbe's own. Their chubby cheeks were flushed from running and their eyes were bright with mischief. They glanced from one sister to another, then, after apparently deciding Thisbe had the most authority as the oldest sister, they flung themselves at her.

"Thisbe!" They split and ducked behind her, clutching her skirts. "Read to me. Read to me," they jabbered, first Con, then Alex, as they jumped up and down, seemingly choreographed to create the most noise and movement possible.

"I like that." Kyria put her hands on her hips in mock indignation. "You think only Thisbe can save you?"

The boys stopped and looked each other. Alex abandoned Thisbe and darted to Kyria, throwing his arms around her legs dramatically. "Kyria!"

Then, with a screech of glee, they began to run dizzyingly around all three sisters, weaving in and out, until finally Thisbe reached out and scooped up one as he darted by. "Con. Enough."

Con beamed at her and laid his head upon her shoulder, wrapping his arms around her neck. Drawing out his voice, he said pleadingly, "Thisbe. Pwease." Con was still having a little trouble with his *l*'s.

"You little dramatist." Thisbe laughed and kissed the top of his head.

Pleased with the word, Con repeated it. "Dramatist."

"Will you?" Alex asked from his perch in Kyria's arms. He liked to have a definitive answer. "Kyria, too."

"And Wivvy." Con pointed to Olivia.

"Livvy, too," Alex agreed.

"We might as well," Thisbe told her sisters. "Otherwise we'll never have any peace."

More important, it would give the nanny a rest. Thisbe looked over at the twins' weary keeper. Right now she looked as if she might turn in her notice tomorrow, which would make her the fourth one this year.

Carrying the twins—it was always better to have them in one's grip—the sisters trooped up the stairs and down the hall to the twins' rooms. Con regaled them with an account of his and Alex's day, punctuated now and then by insertions from his brother and an occasional disagreement over who had been the first to swipe the biscuits from under Cook's nose, or climbed the highest, or jumped over the most steps.

The pair had a suite of rooms: Con and Alex in one bedroom, their nanny in another, with the schoolroom in between. The schoolroom looked as if it had been hit by a hurricane, its usual condition by the end of the day. The nanny headed straight for her room—either to take a much-needed rest or pack her things, Thisbe wasn't sure which, and the sisters tucked the boys into their beds.

Thisbe read them a fairy tale, after which they wheedled their favorite story from Olivia, the one about a polar bear, a monkey—geographical limitations did not exist in the twins' stories—and the boy who saved them both with his cleverness. That was a mistake, as it left them more wide-awake than before, and Kyria had to quiet them with a lullaby before they closed their eyes.

As they left the room, Kyria grabbed Thisbe's elbow and hustled her off to Kyria's bedchamber. "Now." Kyria settled herself on the bed, legs tucked under her. "Tell us everything. This is so exciting."

Thisbe was surprised to feel a blush spreading across her cheeks. "Well…perhaps you won't find it all that interesting."

"You must be joking. You and a man? It's practically world-shaking."

"Yes," Olivia agreed, perching on the other end of the bed. "Who is he? Where did you meet him? Did he sweep you out of the way of a runaway carriage or rescue you from a footpad or—" Olivia was a great reader of novels.

"He sat beside me at a lecture."

"That's disappointing." Olivia looked deflated.

"Don't be silly." Kyria rolled her eyes at her younger sister. "Thisbe's not stupid enough to step in front of a speeding carriage. Nor does she carry anything worth stealing. Go on. Did he come to sit beside you or vice versa?"

"You really do want to know everything." Thisbe climbed onto the bed as well, taking the center, and the others turned to face her. It was a scene that had been enacted many times—the three of them settling in for a long chat—but tonight it felt different, as if imbued with a certain importance, a...well, yes, a glow. "He took the seat beside me. To be fair, he came late, and there weren't many available."

"Even if there were only two, it's significant that he chose *you*."

"I suppose it does mean something—most men seem afraid to sit by me."

"What's his name? Do I know him?" Kyria asked.

"I doubt it. He doesn't move in your circle. He works in a shop."

"He's a shopkeeper?" Even Kyria looked discouraged at this news. "Is he *old*?"

"Papa will be sorry to find he isn't a scholar," Olivia said.

Thisbe laughed. "Papa would find him perfectly acceptable... Well, as acceptable as a man can be who doesn't know an Etruscan vase from a Roman olive jar. Desmond is a scientist and very smart. And he's not old. He doesn't own the shop—he merely works there to support himself. Anyway, Papa's approval is hardly an issue. It's not as if I'm planning to marry the man."

"I wouldn't be so sure. He's the first man I've ever heard you talk about, except for some crusty old scientist who is usually dead," Kyria told her. "Desmond." She rolled out the word experimentally. "That's a good name."

"I'm glad you approve."

"What does he look like? What's special about him?" Olivia asked, pressing for details.

"He's quite tall, as tall as Theo—maybe even taller, though he's more slender. Not as muscular."

"That's fine," Kyria decided. "A scientist hardly needs to be able to paddle up the Amazon."

"His hair is dark, and it's rather too long and shaggy, and all mussed, though that might be because he was late and hurrying. It kept falling in his face as he talked, and he'd push it back with his hand, like this, which only made it messier." Thisbe smiled at the memory. "His face is more oval than square, and his chin is firm. His mouth is perfect, not too wide or too narrow. He has a lovely smile, though most of the time he looks very serious. His eyes are deep brown, like chocolate, and his lashes so thick and dark it's really unfair that a man has them." She had been gazing off into space as she talked, remembering the details about Desmond, and when she looked back at her sisters, they were staring at her, mouths ajar.

"I have never heard you describe anyone so thoroughly," Olivia said.

"Last week you couldn't even remember whether Mr. Barlow was blond or brown-haired," Kyria added.

"Who's Mr. Barlow?"

Kyria leaned her head back and laughed. "That's what I mean. He was here last week, but you scarcely recall him."

"I don't recall him at all," Thisbe retorted. "I don't keep track of your beaux, Kyria. It would take up entirely too much space in my brain."

"Tell me this, then—what color are Willis the footman's eyes?" Kyria challenged.

"I, um, brown?"

"They're blue," Kyria said triumphantly. "And he has

been here for years. You see him every night at the supper table. You don't pay the slightest attention to anyone's looks."

"I'm usually more interested in what they have to say."

"Yet you remember every last detail of how this man looked. Quickly—what did he wear?"

"An ordinary jacket and trousers—grayish. His shoes were black and rather scuffed." She grinned. "He forgot his coat and hat, and he'd lost his gloves."

"Shades of Papa!" Olivia cried, and all three of them broke into laughter.

"No wonder you said Papa would approve of him," Kyria said. "That's good because *you* are seriously smitten."

"Smitten? Is that what I am?" Thisbe smiled faintly. "I wondered what to call it. It was the strangest thing. I felt this—this zing all through me when he looked at me. And a—a connection, I guess, almost as if I knew him, only I didn't, of course, but it was as though, just looking at him, I *knew* him. Does that make any sense?"

"Not a bit, but then I've never been in love," Kyria told her. "I like various men just fine, some more than others. I wish I could dance with Howard Buckley more than two times at a ball, but that's because he's an excellent dancer, and Lord Highsmith makes me laugh. But I haven't the slightest inclination to fall in love with any of them." Her brow clouded. "Do you suppose there's something wrong with me?"

"Nothing except an overabundance of suitors," Thisbe replied. "How could you find anyone special among all that lot? This is your first Season, and it has barely begun. I don't imagine you have to find love as soon as you come out."

"True." Kyria grinned. "In fact, I think it would probably put a damper on the fun."

"Oh, who cares about your Season?" Olivia said, reaching over to poke Kyria in the leg. "I want to hear more about Thisbe's beau."

"I do, too," Kyria said, though she paused to pinch Olivia's arm in return before she went on. "What did he say when you met?"

"Nothing. I was the one who started the conversation. I had to grab his arm to get his attention."

"He didn't notice you?" Kyria asked, her eyebrows rising.

"Oh, he noticed me." Thisbe chuckled. "He kept glancing at me the whole time he was taking notes, like this." She demonstrated.

"That's good." Kyria nodded sagely.

"But he didn't say a word. I think he's a bit shy—he even blushed a little."

"That's sweet," Olivia said.

"So I asked him if he'd like to borrow my notes, and he did, and after that it became much easier to talk."

"What did you talk about?"

"Oh, school and Herr Erlenmeyer's theory about naphthalene."

"Naphthalene!" Kyria gaped at her. "Really, Thisbe, you talked about chemistry?"

"And spectrometry and, oh, spirit photography—we disagreed a bit about that."

"You quarreled with him?"

"Not quarreled, exactly. It was more a spirited discussion. It was actually quite invigorating. He's working with Professor Gordon, you see, which is too bad because I cannot think it will further his career to be associated with him. But he did have a point about keeping an open mind to scientific discovery."

"Thisbe…" Kyria groaned. "Do not tell me you talked about science the entire time."

"Oh, no, we talked about his family and such as he walked me to the omnibus."

"What omnibus? Didn't Thompkins take you in the carriage? I'm confused," Olivia said.

"Yes, Thompkins was right there, but I had to ignore him. You see, I didn't tell him about…you know—who we are."

"Oh," her sisters said in unison, understanding.

"It's better," Kyria agreed. "It's terribly hard to know whether a man flirts with you because he likes you or your money."

"No, it's not that. Desmond would make the world's worst fortune hunter."

"You didn't want him to know you were a Moreland because everyone thinks we're peculiar?" Olivia suggested.

"Did you know that they call us the 'Mad Morelands'?" Kyria said, anger flaring.

"Yes, Theo told me several years ago. That was why he got sent down from Oxford that time—he punched someone who called us that."

"Really? I always wondered what happened," Kyria mused.

"Theo was sent down?" Olivia asked. "I didn't know that. Why didn't anyone tell me?"

"You were too young. It never happened again. I think no one else wanted to get knocked down." Thisbe continued, "But none of that was the reason I said I was just plain Thisbe Moreland. I didn't want… Oh, you don't know how they act when they know who I am. They try to ingratiate themselves with me, wanting research money, or they think I'm only dabbling in science or that I've been favored by lecturers because my father is a duke."

"You thought he would do one of those things."

"I didn't want to find out. I wanted him to see me as me. Besides, I didn't want to frighten him away. I know he hasn't any money—he said his father had been a laborer, and he has to work in a shop to support himself. It doesn't matter to me, but I'm afraid it will to him."

"You're right. He might feel intimidated," Kyria told her. "But he's bound to realize when he comes to call on you— Wait, how will he call on you if he doesn't know who you are? How will you see him again?"

"I'll see him again the day after Christmas," Thisbe replied, a trifle smugly. "He's going to the Christmas lectures, and so am I. There are several of them between Christmas and Twelfth Night."

"By then he'll be so captivated that it won't matter who you are," Olivia assured her.

"I don't know about that." Thisbe laughed.

"I want to see him," Kyria announced. "We could come with you to the Christmas lectures. I'm sure it will be deadly dull, but—"

"No!" Thisbe said in alarm. "If you're with me, we'll be swarmed by every young single man in the place— and likely some of the old married ones, too. It will disrupt everything. I'll hardly have a chance to talk to him."

"We can sit somewhere else in the hall," Olivia offered.

Thisbe fixed them with a stony glare. "Don't. You. Dare."

"Oh, very well." Kyria gave in. "We won't spy on you." She brightened. "But I can help you dress for it.

You can wear one of my frocks. We're much the same size. I'll do your hair."

Thisbe looked wary. "I don't know. He's already seen how I look."

"But he hasn't seen how you look in something attractive."

"What's wrong with my clothes?" She looked down at her dress. "This is perfectly acceptable."

"It's perfectly plain."

"So am I. I don't want to be…sparkly."

"Please, Thisbe?" Kyria begged. "It will be such fun, and I promise I won't make you look 'sparkly.'"

The idea was tempting. Thisbe had never been concerned with the way she looked, but now she couldn't help but think how nice it would be to see Desmond look at her with the same sort of admiration with which other men gazed at Kyria.

"I won't make you look like a princess," Kyria bargained. "It won't make him suspect you're an aristocrat."

"No ruffles?"

"No ruffles. Well, maybe just one."

"No huge hoop and petticoats."

"No huge hoop. That's going out of style, anyway."

"No feathers or bangles. Or beading."

"None of those." Kyria nodded firmly.

"No flowers in my hair."

"Nary a one."

"Very well," Thisbe agreed. "I'll do it."

"Hoorah!" Kyria rubbed her hands together in anticipation. "Your Desmond doesn't stand a chance."

THISBE STOOD IN DARKNESS; walls of stone surrounded her. It was too small, too close. Her breathing hastened, her heart pounded. The stones began to dissolve into a thick gray fog. Her stomach turned; her head swam. The blanketing fog was more frightening than the prison of stone—a sightless, unending nothingness.

Something lurked out there. Someone. She could not see it or hear it; she was helpless against it. But she was certain it lay in wait. Tendrils of mist curled around her, brushing over her skin like a breath. A sound vibrated through the fog, low and indistinct—a moan? A sob?—and the very air seemed filled with yearning.

It wanted her. It sought her, reached for her. She sucked in a breath sharply, fear racing through her nerves like a bolt of lightning. She tried to run, to turn away, but she could not. The fog boiled, thick and pressing, encompassing her like a shroud. She would smother. The air would stop in her lungs, and she would be trapped in this endless nothingness, caught forever...

And still it reached for her, reached for her. A hand clamped around her leg, fingernails digging into her flesh. And pain—horrific, incredible pain—slammed through her...

THISBE SHOT UPRIGHT in her bed. Her muscles were clenched, her lungs burning; pain lit every inch of her body. For an instant she remained frozen, lost in the shadows between nightmare and fact. She panted, her senses gradually restoring her to reality. Everything was familiar; everything was known. She was in her own bed in her own room, surrounded by her family.

If she cried out, if she was in danger or pain, any of them—indeed, all of them—would come to her rescue. She wondered if her father would come as he had when she was a child, and she smiled faintly, thinking of him rushing in, candle in hand, nightcap askew on his now-graying head. And somehow that vision, more than anything, calmed her.

She relaxed her muscles and drew longer, steadier breaths. The pain seeped out of her. What a strange dream—the fog, that enclosed feeling, the fear of the murky unknown. That hand that grasped her leg, followed by that moment of agony.

Thisbe slipped out of bed, pulling on her dressing gown against the chill of the room. She lit a candle and settled down in her chair. There was no hope of going back to sleep just yet. Besides, she wanted to think about this dream.

It had been so peculiar, so unexpected. She would have thought her dreams would be pleasant tonight, given the sweetness of the day. Instead, she'd had a nightmare— and a peculiar one, at that. She'd dreamed before of being chased or of getting lost, but this wasn't quite like either of those things. But that wasn't the only oddity. It had been so clear, so vivid; even though the world around her had been gray and the threat unseen, there had been none of the vagueness usually found in dreams. It had been sharp and crystal clear. Nor had pieces of it immediately slipped from her memory; every detail, every moment, was stamped in her mind.

Strangest of all, though, had been the end. In other nightmares, the dream ended before the bad thing, whatever it was, actually happened. She fell but did not hit the ground. She saw the knife, but didn't feel it slice into her. She experienced the fear, but she didn't feel the physical pain.

Yet tonight, her whole body had been flooded with pain. She remembered the fingers grasping her legs, the nails sinking into her. She shivered at the memory and reached down to rub her calf. It was as if it had really happened. Which was, of course, ridiculous. She pulled up her gown as if to prove it to herself.

On the pale skin of her calf were five small red marks—the size and crescent shape of fingernails.

Thisbe froze, staring at the indentations. Her mind whirled with horrific thoughts. But only for a moment. The ideas were not only fear-invoking, but they were also impossible. There must be a logical explanation. There always was.

A hand digging into her in a dream world couldn't create an actual physical mark. There was no one else in the room when she awoke. Therefore…she had done it herself.

Of course! In the throes of her vivid nightmare, she had clutched at something in desperation, and the only thing within reach was her own limb. She had dug her fingers in with such fervor that they had left indentations on her flesh. And that explained the sensation of pain, as well—she had felt it because it was real. It all made sense now.

Satisfied, Thisbe blew out the candle and climbed back into bed.

CHAPTER FOUR

A FEW DAYS LATER, Thisbe sat in front of the mirror while Kyria worked on her hair. Thisbe wondered if it had been a mistake to agree to her sister's offer. The dress was lovely, and it *did* make her eyes even greener. All the fringe was gone, as Kyria had promised, and the skirt was narrower and slightly flatter in the front, so she wouldn't be bumping into everything around her. It was just that...well, she was attractive, but she didn't quite look like herself.

Of course, right now she looked like a witch—albeit a well-dressed one—for Kyria had separated her hair and pulled it into big hanks in several different places, each tied with a bow. "Are you sure you know how to do this?"

"Don't worry," Kyria reassured her as she twisted one of the sections of hair into a neat knot on the crown of Thisbe's head. "Joan taught me."

"And she practiced it on me," Olivia said from her perch on the end of the bed. "It looked splendid...at least, it did until I started playing with Alex and Con."

Thisbe snorted. "I can imagine."

"Alex had to take it apart to see how it was made, and he was most disappointed, I can tell you, that I couldn't put it back together."

"Which can also be said for the grandfather clock in Papa's study," Kyria added.

"Thisbe!" a deep, masculine voice said from the open

doorway. "Good Lord. What's Kyria roped you into now?"

"Hello, Theo." Well, that put the cap on it. Now here was her twin; much as she loved him, he was sure to tease her. Or, even worse, adopt his protective big-brother pose. And, by the way, he was *not* her big brother, having arrived in the world four minutes after Thisbe.

"What's going on?" Reed stuck his head around the door curiously.

"Why are you here?" Kyria asked in annoyance. "It's Boxing Day. Don't you have presents to give?"

"Already did," Theo answered.

"Well, then, chums to visit? Wassail to drink?"

"Bit early for that." Reed grinned. "Besides, what could be more enjoyable than spending time with our sweet-tempered sisters?"

"Go away. Both of you."

"Why? What are you up to?" Theo asked. Tall, with the same black hair and green eyes as his twin sister, he leaned casually against the doorjamb, arms crossed, and grinned at them.

"Why are you doing that to Thisbe? Are you angry at her?" Reed slid into the room. He was a slightly younger, less powerfully built version of his older brother. His hair was dark brown rather than black and his eyes were gray, but there was no mistaking the Moreland jaw or the lively intelligence in his eyes, which was a hallmark of the whole clan.

"No, I'm not angry at Thisbe. But I'll be angry at you if you don't stop bothering us."

"We're not doing anything," Theo pointed out.

"Kyria is dressing Thisbe's hair," Olivia told them.

"But why? And why like that?"

"Because it's pretty." Kyria swung around to face the

two young men, hands on her hips and a dangerous glint in her eyes.

"I see," Theo said dubiously.

"Well, it will be once I'm done, which would be much easier without your presence." Kyria swung back to continue her braiding and pinning.

"But why?" Theo and Reed glanced at one another, their suspicion aroused, and Thisbe braced herself for more questions.

She sent a pleading glance to Kyria in the mirror. But it was Olivia who saved the day. "Thisbe lost a bet. She said if Kyria won, she'd let Kyria choose her dress and do her hair for the Christmas lecture."

"Ah." A challenge was something their brothers understood.

"Thisbe said I was uneducated and couldn't name all the English monarchs from William the Conqueror on, and I said I could do it backward," Kyria said, enlarging the fabrication. "And I did." Deftly, she wound the braids and pinned them, tucking the last visible end under the knot. "There! You see? It's beautiful."

"You're right. It is. You look stunning, Thiz," Theo told her.

"You needn't sound so shocked," Thisbe retorted crisply, taking the hand mirror Kyria gave her and turning her head to look at her image from all angles.

Her hair was wound into an intricate array of thick braids, all of them twisted and tucked into an arrangement that seemed to have no beginning and no end, and so smooth and sleek that it drew the eye without seeming to call for attention. There were no ribbons, no ornaments, no fussy curls—just a thick, lustrous frame for her face.

"It's lovely, Kyria. I look so—so…"

"Gorgeous?" Kyria suggested.

"Different." She turned back to the mirror, tilting her head.

"Don't be silly. Theo, tell her she doesn't look different."

"But she does," Theo responded. At Kyria's glare, he went on hastily, "Not in a bad way. You look really pretty." He stopped. "Not that you don't always look pretty. I mean…"

Kyria rolled her eyes, and Reed chuckled, then said, "Better stop before you dig yourself any deeper."

"You look dressed up," Theo concluded lamely.

"Elegant," Reed declared. "Stunning."

"Much better." Kyria gave him an approving nod.

Theo hesitated, then said, "Should I, um…? Do you want me to escort you to the lecture?"

"No!" Thisbe yelped, then turned to her twin and, seeing his expression, began to laugh. "No need to look like you're about to climb the scaffold, Theo. I appreciate your offer, but I wouldn't ask you to make such a sacrifice." Her brother was as intent on discovery as Thisbe herself, but his explorations were aimed at the wonders of the physical world, not those of scientific research.

"Thanks." Theo grinned at her. "Come on, Reed, let's talk to Coffey about the expedition. You might decide to join us."

Reed followed his brother into the corridor, then looked back at his sisters, shook his head and said, "I won't."

"Reed's thinking of going to the Amazon with Theo?" Olivia asked.

"No," Kyria said decisively. She was the closest in the family to Reed, barely two years younger than he, and, like him, had the reputation of being the most "normal" of the Morelands. "Theo probably had to drag Reed away from working on that problem about Papa's factory."

"The one he keeps because he met Mother there?"

"Yes. Only Papa would find it romantic that she invaded his office and threatened to chain herself to the door," Kyria giggled.

"What amazes me is that Papa was actually *in* his office."

"He was young. I suppose he was trying to assume his duties as the new duke. Now—" Kyria firmly turned Thisbe back to face the mirror "—back to business." Kyria tilted her head. "You must wear one of my hats. Yours will hide all my work. I brought just the one."

The "one" turned out to be a small piece of felt little larger than a saucer, with a green ribbon and a sprig perched on the front. Thisbe laughed. "That is the most impractical hat I've ever seen. It couldn't possibly keep the sun from your eyes or warm your head."

"Of course not. Philippina's hats are works of art."

"How will it even stay on?"

"Hat pins, my dear." Kyria held up two long, lethal-looking pins.

"At least I'll have a weapon if I run afoul of any of Olivia's footpads."

Kyria positioned the hat at the front of Thisbe's head so that it tilted up in the back to touch the elaborate coil of hair at the crown of her head and dipped to her forehead in front. Then she plunged hat pins on either side, deep into the mass of braided and coiled hair. "Charming."

"It is!" Olivia agreed, jumping off her seat on the bed to admire her sister more closely. "Your Mr. Harrison will be overcome."

"It's lovely, Kyria. Thank you." Thisbe's words were heartfelt. The silly, minuscule hat was adorable, and the dress and hairstyle were flattering. But she could not help but worry all the way over to the lecture hall.

What if she looked too different? Too rich? Too aristocratic? She wasn't sure how one looked aristocratic, but perhaps others could recognize it. Or maybe Desmond would assume she was trying to ensnare him. Would he think she liked him? Was attracted to him?

But she did like him, and she was attracted to him, so there was no rational point in concealing that, was there? It seemed the reasonable thing to do. Yet she was also certain that Kyria never wanted the men who courted her to know if she preferred one or another.

It was all most confusing. Thisbe didn't know enough about feminine wiles. Perhaps she should have paid more attention to Miss Crabtree's lessons in deportment instead of reading books. Kyria seemed to *know* these things without having to learn them.

By the time she reached the lecture hall, Thisbe's stomach was in knots. She had the coachman set her down a block away from the Royal Institution and walked the rest of the way. After all her machinations to conceal the carriage last time, it would be silly to give it away now.

Of course, it was unlikely that Desmond would walk up at that precise moment or be loitering outside, especially this early. Thisbe had arranged to get there a good thirty minutes early so that she would be seated before he arrived. It was important that Desmond be able to choose whether or not to sit beside her. She also wanted to find just the right place so that it would be easy for him to reach, and she must save a seat for him in a way that wasn't obvious. Perhaps it was all unnecessary, but Thisbe didn't like to have variables.

She didn't meet him as she walked to the building,

nor was he waiting outside for her, which was a little disheartening, even though she knew that was illogical. She walked into the hall to survey the room. And there he was. He'd arrived even earlier than she; the audience was still quite sparse. Thisbe noted that he'd chosen one of the seats she would have picked and draped his coat over the seat beside him, which made her smile despite the roiling nerves in her stomach. She felt a sudden, unfamiliar shyness.

Desmond twisted around, searching the hall, and when his eyes fell on her, he jumped to his feet, grinning. The cold lump in Thisbe's stomach vanished, and she smiled back just as exuberantly. As she drew closer, she could see the look in his eyes, and it was everything she had hoped for.

She took off her gloves as she approached and extended her hand, aware of an urge to touch him. "Mr. Harrison."

"Miss Moreland." His hand, warm and slightly calloused, enfolded hers. He looked at her the way Kyria's beaux looked at her, as Thisbe had wanted, but it was somehow more, something deeper and more intense. "You look beautiful."

Thisbe felt heat rise in her cheeks. She was not used to compliments such as this. It made her chest swell with happiness, but she didn't know how to respond. "So do you." She blushed even more. She was fairly certain *that* was not the sort of thing she was supposed to say. "I mean, handsome. That is, um, you look very nice today."

"Thank you."

She hadn't noticed that he was still holding her hand until he released it. "I wasn't sure that you would come," she told him.

"I wouldn't have missed it." Desmond whisked up his

coat from the other chair, and they sat down, turning toward each other. "My employer is a good chap. He lets me leave early if I come into work earlier."

"I'm glad. Though it does seem too bad that you have to spend your days on that when you could be pursuing science."

"I'd prefer it," he admitted. "But my work is in the realm of my interests."

She cast about for something to keep him talking. It was hard to think, sitting so close to him. "What is it you do?"

"We deal in optical instruments and parts—lenses, thermometers and so on. Primarily, I work with kaleidoscopes."

"Kaleidoscopes? You make them?"

He nodded. "And I experiment on advancements in the area—using different sorts of objects or using them in various ways. Developing new ideas. In particular, I'm interested in combination kaleidoscopes."

"What are those? I'm not familiar with them." Her first inquiry had come more from a desire to talk to him, but now her curiosity was piqued.

"You know how a kaleidoscope works—there's a box containing various bits of colored crystals in different sizes and shapes and so forth. It's connected to the tube, with an eyepiece on the other end."

She nodded. "Light comes through the box, and mirrors at various angles create the effect."

"Exactly. What combination kaleidoscopes do is take away the little objects and instead make patterns in the same way, but using objects around you. A flower, for instance, is fractured, creating patterns. As you turn the box, the patterns shift, making it appear entirely different."

"That's fascinating." Thisbe leaned forward a little. "I'd like to see it."

"I'll show you," he offered. "Unfortunately, I don't have one on me." His gaze shifted to his hands as he went on. "Perhaps, if you'd like to see it, you could come to the shop, um, after the lecture. I'm sure it's not the sort of place you would go normally, but there won't be anyone there." He glanced up sharply, his face reddening. "That is I meant, you know, you wouldn't be embarrassed by going into a shop full of men. But I didn't think— that's no more proper. I didn't mean anything untoward. I wasn't trying to lure you, um, into a…an indelicate situation. I hope you will not—"

His expression was so stricken, so earnest, that Thisbe laid her hand on his arm. "It's quite all right. I knew what you meant, but you needn't have any concern in that regard. Anyone who knows me would tell you that I am not easily embarrassed. I am accustomed to the company of men. I have four brothers, after all, and I am often the only female at a lecture." She smiled, a dimple popping into her cheek, her eyes beginning to twinkle. Good heavens, she thought she was actually flirting.

Apparently he thought so, too, for his eyes gleamed, and his answering grin was as much flirtation as relief. "I'm glad you didn't take offense."

"Nor do I think you have wicked designs on my virtue. I hope I am a better judge of character than that. I would very much like to see your shop and your kaleidoscope."

In fact, she was delighted to have an excuse to extend her time with him, though she wouldn't tell him that— she was not that bold. Of course, there was the problem of her driver and carriage. She had tried to persuade Thompkins not to pick her up from the lecture, but he'd stubbornly refused. He took his orders from the duke, not her, and even her absentminded father insisted on her taking the carriage on her solitary excursions. But she managed to get Thompkins to agree not to approach her until she hailed him. Thisbe had confidence he would be able to follow unobtrusively, given how successfully he'd done it last time.

"Will your family worry if you're not home on time?"

"No, they are all occupied with their own interests, and everyone is used to my ways. In any case, I'm well armed." She reached up and pulled out one of Kyria's hat pins, holding it up to show him.

"That should certainly discourage any ungentlemanly urges I might have." He looked at her hat. "I wondered what held it in place. It's rather small."

"I told Kyria it was utterly useless," Thisbe agreed.

"Perhaps so, but it's charming."

"Then Kyria is proven right. It is her hat, you see."

"Kyria is your sister? A friend?"

"Well, both, I'd say. She is younger than I and not like me. She has no interest in science or books, really. In that way, she's like Theo."

"Your twin."

She nodded. "Theo and I are similar in some ways— I guess you'd say in our character. We're both single-minded and stubborn, and others sometimes—often—say we are too blunt. But he has never liked studies or reading. Theo wants to travel. To explore. He wants to see everything—I want to know everything."

"What of the others? You said there was another set of twins."

"Yes. The babies… Although, I guess they are not really babies anymore. They'll soon be three. Their names are Alexander and Constantine—we call them the Greats."

"For the emperors?" Desmond laughed.

"Yes, and they can be quite imperious, too. They're absolute terrors."

He chuckled. "You sound very fond of these terrors."

"I am. Fortunately, they're as lovable as they are lively. It's fascinating to watch them. They have their own language."

"You're joking."

"No. Really. When they were first learning to speak, even before they started talking to us, they communicated with each other. We had no idea what they were saying. They still do it sometimes, but what is even more eerie is that they'll just look at each other and then act in concert, as if they had planned it."

"You think that they can send thoughts to one another… that they pass through the air unheard?"

"It sounds a bit mad, I suppose," Thisbe admitted.

"No more mad than thinking it's possible there are spirits around us who cannot be seen or heard," he replied, his eyes twinkling.

Thisbe burst into laughter. "Very well. You have me there. I will strive to have a more open mind. Though I cannot imagine how you will go about proving or disproving it."

"I'll show you our laboratory one day. You could see what I'm working on."

"I should like that." They were making plans together, an assurance of seeing one another again. What the other day had seemed only a possibility was gaining substance.

"Tell me about the rest of your family. You said your father was an antiquarian?"

"Yes. And Uncle Bellard, who lives with us, is a dedicated historian. He's terribly bright and very shy. But if you ask him something about history, he'll talk for hours."

They continued to chat as the lecture hall filled up around them, oblivious to the rest of the room. Their conversation ranged from Mr. Odling, who was set to give the lecture, to carbon, the stated subject of his presentation, and on to the recent discovery of a new element named helium. Thisbe was almost sorry when the speaker stepped up to the podium, though she had been looking forward to the talk for days.

She had difficulty keeping her mind on the presentation, too aware of Desmond beside her. The Christmas lectures were always well attended and the seats were smaller and closer together than at the Covington in order to accommodate the crowd. There, he had been inches from her; here, his shoulder almost brushed hers. If either of them shifted in their seats, their arms were likely to touch. It was difficult to maintain a calm and attentive expression when every time his arm brushed hers, it sent a sharp dart of excitement all through her.

After the lecture was over, they walked to Desmond's shop, taking an omnibus part of the way. Her driver followed at a distance, but Desmond never glanced back. The shop was small, tucked in between two other larger buildings, and a sign across the door read Barrow and Sons. By the time they reached it, the light was fading and the shop was closed, but Desmond pulled a key from his pocket and opened the door. Lighting a candle, he ushered Thisbe inside.

The space was small, containing only a short counter and behind it a wooden cabinet. "We don't have wares out as typical shops do. People generally come to us for something in particular, and often it has to be custom-made,"

Desmond explained, crossing to a door to the side of the counter and opening it.

Here, obviously, was the real place of business. Thisbe had never been in a workshop before, and she looked around her with great interest. Shelves of supplies lined the walls on both sides of the long, narrow room. There were several tables, each with a set of two or three stools, most of them holding what looked to be works in progress. Desmond led her to the last worktable and turned on the gas lighting above it. Unlike many of the others, his section of the workspace was tidy, with tools to one side in a shallow tray.

He squatted down to rummage through a box beneath the table and came up holding out a kaleidoscope. Thisbe took it and looked into it, turning the other end to bring up other patterns. "It's beautiful. The colors are so brilliant."

"Thank you." He smiled. "Our lenses are the best. I always like to use vivid colors." He took out another kaleidoscope. "This is a combination kaleidoscope. Here— use it to look at something on this table." He set the tools and his key directly under the light. "It's what I've been working on recently."

Thisbe held the instrument to her eye. "Oh! It doesn't look like a key at all." She turned it from one station to the next. "This is wonderful." She lowered the instrument and smiled up at him.

He was watching her, a faint smile on his lips. "I'm glad you like it."

"Oh, I do." She raised the kaleidoscope again, focusing on something else. "This would be wonderful in full daylight, wouldn't it? You could look at flowers or a scene in the distance or, well, just about anything."

"Take it."

"What?" She lowered the kaleidoscope and turned to him.

"It's yours. I'm giving it to you."

"Oh, but… No, I didn't mean… I wasn't hinting that you should give me one. This must be intended for someone."

He shook his head. "No. It's mine—something I've been doing on my own."

"But I mustn't take yours." She held out the kaleidoscope to him.

"No, I want you to have it." He covered her hand on the instrument, pushing it gently back toward her. "Please, keep it."

He was so close, and he was gazing at her in such a way that it made her breath catch in her throat. Thisbe swayed toward him, and he did the same. Then he kissed her.

CHAPTER FIVE

No DOUBT IT was only fitting, Thisbe thought, that her first kiss should happen in such a mundane setting as a workshop. But there was nothing mundane about the kiss. It lasted only a moment, but it made her feel as if her heart would burst out of her chest.

Desmond lifted his head, his eyes a little hazy. Then he stiffened. "Oh, my God. I'm sorry." His hands, which had come up to curve around the sides of her waist, dropped away, and he took a half step back, his words tumbling out. "I shouldn't have— I never meant— I told you I wouldn't take advantage, and here I— I'm sorry."

Thisbe looked into his eyes and said, "I'm not." She stepped forward and kissed him, winding her arms around his neck.

He made an odd little noise, and his arms went around her tightly. Desmond's lips were soft on hers, warm and supple, their pressure increasing as the kiss deepened. Thisbe held on tightly, almost dizzy with sensations. How hard his arms were around her, the way his hands spread over her, that indefinable scent of him in her nostrils, and his mouth—oh, his mouth! It was moving on hers, opening her lips to him, his tongue slipping inside. Yes, well, *that* was a trifle startling and made everything inside her jump, but then—then she was melting into him, pressing up into his long, hard body.

It seemed forever before Desmond broke off their kiss,

yet she hated for it to end. He raised his head and gazed down into her face, his eyes dark and deep. "Thisbe."

How could it be so arousing to hear him say her name? It was such a pleasant thing that she returned the gesture. "Desmond." She reached up to brush back the strands of hair that had fallen across his forehead, and his face changed subtly in response. How odd, how exciting that her touch should have an effect on him. Experimentally she laid her hand against his cheek, and this time she could feel the rise of heat on his skin.

Desmond laid his hand atop hers, holding it to him for a moment, then took her hand and lifted it, turning to place a soft, sweet kiss upon her palm. "I—we—should probably leave."

"No doubt you're right."

He nodded, but he didn't step back. Instead he bent his head and kissed her another time, slowly, lingeringly, before he pulled away and thrust his hands into his jacket pockets. He was quiet as they walked through the shop and out the door. Thisbe was, too. There was nothing and at the same time entirely too much to say, the emotion between them too fragile to break with words.

Desmond walked her to the omnibus, where she went through the same charade, finally ending up back in her carriage, heading home. She hugged the knowledge of Desmond's kiss to herself all the way home. This moment was too private, too new, to share, even with her sisters. Later, perhaps, she would analyze it, consider what it meant. But right now she wanted only to revel in it.

When she walked through the door of Broughton House, Thisbe found her mother standing beside the foyer table, frowning down at a sealed letter on the table. Tall and ramrod straight, one had only to look at the duchess to know what Kyria would look like in middle age. The flame-red hair was now sprinkled with gray, and her figure had thickened a little around her middle, but the bone-deep beauty was still there. She was the most intimidating woman Thisbe knew. Stalwart in her beliefs and firm of purpose, Emmeline rarely let anything get in her way. It was unusual, therefore, to see her looking indecisively, even warily, at a simple letter.

"Mother? Is everything all right?"

"It's the dowager duchess."

"Ah." Thisbe understood now. The duke's mother was an irregular correspondent, and she rarely wrote her daughter-in-law except to criticize or deliver unwanted advice, usually both. She was also the only person Thisbe had ever met who could fluster Emmeline. "You may as well get it over with."

"I know." The duchess sighed and broke the seal. "It was just that today has been so pleasant. Kyria and Olivia spent much of the afternoon chasing Alex and Con around the grounds in back and thoroughly wore out the boys so that they went straight to bed after their supper. It may have saved me having to hire a new nanny. But now here is this letter."

"At least it's brief," Thisbe pointed out as her mother unfolded the single piece of paper.

"There is that," her mother agreed, holding her hand out a little farther to read the missive. It was one of the duchess's few vanities; she had so far resisted acquiring spectacles for close work. "She wishes us all a merry Christmas, and then, yes, I knew this would be the case… She bemoans the fact that she was all alone in Bath for the holiday." Emmeline grimaced and looked over at her daughter. "As if I were the one who made her stay there. I invited her to join us in the city. Thank goodness she didn't come."

"Grandmother likes a bit of drama. I'm sure she had a grand time with all her cronies."

"Of course she did. Oh! Oh, blast!" Emmeline stared at the piece of paper in horror. "She has changed her mind."

"She's coming here? I thought she hated the city."

"She does. Its air is 'insalubrious.' Well, to be fair, one cannot deny that. But look!" The duchess waved the note at Thisbe. "It's worse. She's coming for the Season! I didn't invite her for the entire *Season*."

"Oh, my."

"She is positive Kyria is not being properly brought out, given my 'inexperience in social activities.' As if Lady Jeffries wasn't one of the leading lights of the *ton* as well as a generous supporter of my campaign against child labor. It was quite considerate of Lady Jeffries to offer, and Kyria adores her. I am sure she is doing a far better job of introducing Kyria to society than the dowager duchess, who will, mark my words, alienate half of them within days after arriving."

"Kyria will hate it," Thisbe agreed. "I'm sure Grandmother will carp at everything she does."

"Of course she will. That is her intent. With the added advantage of making my life more difficult," Emmeline added darkly. "I am able to deal with her, but your poor father... She never fails to upset Henry. If it's not complaining about his shirking his duties as duke to 'play with his pots,' it's comparing him to his 'sainted' father—of whom she is a good deal more fond now that he's dead than she ever was when he was alive. She always finds some opportunity to point out to him that he married beneath him. That never fails to put your father in a temper, and you know how he dislikes being angry."

"Uncle Bellard will bolt as soon as she arrives."

"Yes. He'll probably hide the entire time in his rooms. Poor man, he's dreadfully scared of that woman. I don't know what he thinks she can do to him—she is only his sister-in-law."

"I think it was her saying Uncle Bellard was mad as a hatter and ought to be locked away in the attic."

"Yes. It was most unkind of her, but Uncle Bellard must know that Henry would never allow that. Even the old duke would have balked at it, no matter how much Cornelia complained. Henry is convinced that his father was always flitting off chasing this cure or that because it was the only way to get away from her." The duchess heaved a sigh. "I am sorry, dear. I should not criticize your grandmother to you. She loves all of you. In her own way."

"I know. Especially Theo. He and Reed can keep her out of Papa's hair a good bit. And the twins will be happy to see her again."

Emmeline chuckled. "True. She doesn't intimidate them."

"Little does. They love the multitude of shiny things she wears. It's Olivia she frightens, with all her talk of Olivia inheriting Grandmother's 'gift.'"

"Yes, Olivia will probably join Uncle Bellard in his books-and-battles room. But you know Livvy—she'll be happy doing that. And she can make sure that Uncle Bellard doesn't skip his meals."

Thisbe went up the stairs, pausing when she reached her twin brother's door. Theo was seated at the small writing desk in the corner, a book open before him as he scribbled on a piece of paper. She watched him for a moment.

All her life, Theo had been the person closest to her; it wasn't that she loved him more than the rest of her siblings, for each of them was essential to her life. But there was an additional bond with Theo, a certain unspoken awareness and understanding. However different Theo's interests were from hers, she was able to share what she felt and the other way around. She hadn't any desire to travel to Egypt, but last year when Theo went, she had understood and felt his excitement. And if an experiment failed, she could tell Theo and know that he would take some of that disappointment on himself.

But now, here was this new man edging into her life, and for the first time, she was keeping something important from her twin. It was disquieting, and she could not help but feel somewhat guilty. But she knew her brother; however much enlightenment their mother had instilled in her sons, the normally friendly and easygoing Theo was very protective of his sisters. Kyria had finally refused to go to any party if Theo would be there, glowering at her suitors and asking them pointed questions. Thisbe suspected that Theo might be even more suspicious about any man's intentions toward his twin sister. He would doubtless want to meet Desmond, and the last thing she wanted was for Theo to interrogate the poor man.

Theo glanced over and saw her. Looking not at all displeased to be interrupted at his task, he tossed down his pencil and stood up. "Hallo, Thiz. How was the lecture?"

"Wonderful." She walked over to him.

"What did he talk about?"

"The properties of carbon."

"Mmm-hmm. Wonderful, indeed." He made a wry face.

"I have other, less than happy news. Grandmother is coming to visit."

"Soon?" he asked warily. "Perhaps I'll already be gone."

"You aren't that lucky. She sounded as if she intended to come soon."

Theo groaned. "Now I'll have to escort her to the opera. Plays. Everything."

"You don't *have* to."

"Ha! If I don't, she'll go on and on at me about my duties as the heir."

"That's your punishment for her liking you best," Thisbe retorted.

"Because I'm the heir. I wish *you* could be the heir. You were four minutes older than I."

"Me? No, thank you. That is one area where I am glad they don't allow women to participate. I would be terrible at it, anyway."

"What do you think I'll be?" He frowned, seemingly thinking about his fate. "Reed would be excellent at it. He should be the one who inherits."

"I suspect he *will* be the one who does all the work," Thisbe teased, which brought a sheepish chuckle from her twin. She glanced toward his desk. "What were you doing? Don't tell me you're writing a letter."

"God, no." Theo's dislike of letter writing was well-known. "I was making notes on what I should take on the expedition. We've set a date."

"Is that why you went to meet that man at the Cavendish Museum today?"

He nodded, excitement in his eyes. "Yes. He's found a fellow to lead it. He's had a devil of a time finding someone who knew anything about the Amazon. We're to leave in another month."

"So soon?" Thisbe felt a little clutch at her heart. "You're leaving in winter?"

"Well, you know, it's the opposite down there."

"Yes, of course. I wasn't thinking. Oh, Theo!" Impulsively, she threw her arms around him. "I will miss you."

"Aw, Thiz—" He hugged her, patting her back. "It'll be all right. I'm not going away forever."

"I know." She stepped back and gave him a smile, albeit a rather watery one.

"I've gone on jaunts before. That one last year to Egypt."

Thisbe nodded. "I know. And the time you went down the Danube. Your tour of the Continent."

"There, you see? It'll be like that."

"This one is so very far away. And it seems so—so mysterious and strange. The jungle."

"Yes." His eyes shone, as they did whenever he talked about an adventure. "I can't wait to see it. They say there are parrots of all colors. Monkeys. And vines as big around as my arm."

"Snakes as big as your arm, too," she pointed out. "Don't they have fish that can eat people?"

"Yes," he replied cheerfully. "It's going to be grand."

Thisbe shook her head in mock exasperation. "I swear, Theo, I don't know how you can be so excited at the prospect of danger."

"Well, you know, Aunt Hermione always said I hadn't any more sense than a goose."

"Just remember that I love you, and I shall be extremely angry with you if you get yourself killed."

"I won't—I promise. And I'll be back before you know it." He reached out and drew her into the circle of his arm. "I'll miss you, too."

Thisbe sighed, leaning into him. "It's a little hard, isn't it? Growing up? Moving on?"

"Yes, but nothing can really separate us. And think of what's ahead. I can't wait to find out. Can you?"

"No." She pulled away and smiled up at him. "It's going to be a grand adventure."

OVER THE COURSE of the next week and a half, Thisbe continued to meet Desmond at the Christmas lectures. There were three more talks, and each time, they arrived early, then walked together afterward, talking. They strolled aimlessly up and down streets or went to a park, eating hot roasted chestnuts from a bag. And they talked.

They talked about all sorts of things—the ethics of scientific research, the problems of funding, the failure of equipment, the possibilities opening up all around them in the world of science.

"I was interested in photography at first," Desmond told her.

"Spirit photography?"

"No, the regular kind. I thought I might like to become a photographer. That was why the vicar recommended me to Professor Gordon. He knew of Gordon's interest in the subject—and I think he hoped I'd go to the university and be attracted to something more intellectual."

"I take it you were."

"Not the sort of thing the vicar was thinking of, philosophy or theology."

"You were interested in entering the clergy?"

"No. The vicar just wanted me to be." He gave her a rueful smile.

"Why did you decide against photography?"

"Once I'd learned the process—how to coat the glass with collodion and bathe it in silver, how to take the picture and develop it, and so on—I saw that that was exactly what it would continue to be. Always. I could perfect my skill, perhaps, or create a useful device, but mostly I would be doing the same thing. And I realized that what I had wanted wasn't *taking* daguerreotypes—it was *learning* how to do it."

"You want to discover things, find new knowledge," Thisbe said.

"Exactly. While I was at the university, I found work at Barrow and Sons, and that led to prisms and the properties of light. The possibilities for discovery and exploration—are there more bands of the spectrum invisible to the human eye?"

Thisbe loved to watch him when he talked this way—his enthusiasm for the subject lighting up his face. He moved his hands to illustrate his points, and his eyes fairly glittered—his whole wiry body was intense and focused.

Or perhaps it was simply that she loved to watch him talk about anything. She enjoyed just as much their quieter, more ordinary conversations, when they talked about themselves or their families, their favorite books, the silly extravagance of someone's hat or even mistakes they had made.

Thisbe related an experiment she's conducted a few years ago that exploded. "I expected a reaction, but I'd no idea it would be so enormous. It blew out the whole tank of water. Ruined all my notes. Of course, that was better than the time one of my experiments caught fire. It was only the draperies, but my mother was rather upset."

Desmond laughed and responded with a tale of one of his many mishaps when he had first moved to London. His laugh captivated her almost as much as his enthusiasm. His face would shift and his eyes danced with amusement and perhaps a bit of surprise. She had the impression that he was not accustomed to laughing. It made Thisbe want to say something else that would bring the sound from him. It also made her want to kiss him.

But there was little chance of that. They were in public the entire time, first in the lecture hall, then on the street. There was no chance of even holding Desmond's hand, let alone repeating their kiss. But once or twice, out of sight of others in the park, Desmond did pull her to him for a quick, hard kiss, their lips cold, but sparking a fire deep within.

She wanted to be alone with him. It would be nice, too, to be someplace warm. Most of all, the lectures would be over soon, and then how were they to meet? The obvious thing was for Desmond to call on her at Broughton House.

They couldn't be alone at Broughton House, either. Her mother was not the most constant or watchful chaperone, and there were simply too many people in the house, any of them likely to pop in at any moment. Now that Kyria was out, there was never an afternoon without at least one young man paying a call on her. Still, it would be more private than a park or public street or a lecture hall.

The problem was that once Desmond saw Broughton House, he would realize that she was an aristocrat, a fact that she had managed to conceal. She would have to tell him that her father was a duke. Desmond must know that she was a lady—her speech, her demeanor, her education on the Continent, the things her family did, would give that much away. But he was not aware that she was a Lady with a capital *L*. An upper-class scholar's daughter was a far cry from the daughter of a duke.

Of course, she ought to tell him who her family was. Indeed, she ought to have told him long before now. She hadn't lied to him, but she had certainly withheld the truth. Everything she said about herself or her family had carefully excised any detail that would give away the Morelands' position in society. Her original intention had been to put him more at ease, but the longer it went on, the more deceptive it seemed.

But she continued to put off telling him, fearing that the revelation might ruin everything. What if it changed how he acted around her? How he felt about her? Would he still see her as she was, the Thisbe who walked with him? Or would everything suddenly be awkward between them? Would he decide Thisbe wasn't really a scientist, just an aristocratic woman, like Lady Burdett-Coutts, who liked to dabble in science? Desmond was one of the few men she had met who spoke to her as an equal. She couldn't bear it if her social status changed that. But, no, surely not. After all, Desmond had come to know her. Surely, he wouldn't view her through a different lens just because she had a title in front of her name. The problem was that the risk if she was wrong was too devastating.

With each passing day, she felt guiltier keeping silent. She had to tell him. She promised herself she would do so the day of the final Christmas lecture. If she did not, she wouldn't see him again until the next Covington meeting, and that was over a fortnight away. Yet as they strolled through the park after the last Christmas lecture, ignoring the flakes of snow drifting down around them, she could not bring herself to say the words.

They reached an empty spot, sheltered from the sight of others, and Desmond took her in his arms and kissed her. It was a most satisfactory kiss, and when he raised his head, both of them were breathing a little shakily. Desmond said, "I want to see you again."

"Yes. So do I." Now was the time to confess the truth. "Perhaps you could, um…" She looked into his eyes. The nerves in her stomach danced, and all she could think of was his face changing, turning uncertain, his drawing back from her. "Perhaps we could meet at the British Museum Reading Room. They allow women. It's not mandatory that we stay in the ladies' 'magazine reading' room."

"When?"

"Um, let's see." Tomorrow would seem too eager, surely. "Perhaps Sunday afternoon?"

He smiled. "I'll be there." He bent to kiss her again.

It was a most satisfactory ending to their day, but Thisbe berated herself all the way home for not telling him the truth. It was silly to think that he might withdraw from her. Most people would consider it grand that her father was a duke. Just because Desmond had made a few slighting remarks about "wealthy dilettantes" when they were discussing scientific patrons didn't mean that he would think of her that way. He knew who she was.

She was underestimating Desmond, thinking he would react like other people. He would look past the grandiose home and see the true picture of her family. Indeed, if a man could not do that, she wouldn't want to be with him, no matter how much it might hurt to give him up. She would tell him when they met on Sunday. She would write it down and show it to him if her mouth shut down on her again.

But when she walked into Broughton House and saw the bags and trunks cluttering the entryway, her heart sank. There was something far worse to show Desmond than her home. Her grandmother had arrived.

CHAPTER SIX

It seemed impossible that one woman could need so much baggage for a visit. It raised the fear that her grandmother intended to reside with them for the rest of her days. But the dowager duchess always carried an inordinate amount of clothes when she traveled. And she rarely budged without her chest of "treasures."

"Thisbe!" Her mother turned to her, relief on her face. "Your grandmother is here."

"Yes, I see. Hello, Grandmother." Thisbe went forward to kiss her grandmother's cheek.

The dowager duchess was not especially large, yet somehow she managed to appear so. Her hair was almost entirely silver, her eyes gray, and her face still held the remnants of her onetime beauty. She would have looked the picture of a sweet and doting grandmother had it not been for the ice in her eyes and the determined set of her jaw.

She wore her usual fashionable dress and the jewelry that so fascinated the twins. A gold necklace circled her throat, with a matching bracelet on one arm and a mourning bracelet set with obsidian on the other. Large rings decorated three of her fingers, and around her waist was a chatelaine. From the chatelaine hung her gold-framed pince-nez and other "necessities"—smelling salts, a mirror, digestive tablets, a small sewing kit and miniature scissors, each of them encased in ornate gold containers. The back of the mirror was monogrammed in diamond chips.

"Your mother tells me that Theo is not here," the dowager duchess said, shooting an accusing look at Emmeline.

"Had we known what day you would arrive, I am sure Theo would have made a point to be here to greet you," Emmeline responded pointedly.

"I hope your trip wasn't stressful," Thisbe said.

"Of course it was. Dreadful rackety train—makes one quite ill. I would have preferred to come in the carriage, but I left that for Hermione."

"Lady Rochester was in Bath?" Thisbe asked, exchanging a look with her mother. That explained her grandmother's sudden decision to visit them.

"Yes. She's thinks the waters will help her gout. I told her that not eating a plate of roast beef every night would improve her gout more. Of course, she doesn't listen to me. I felt I had to leave her the coach, given her infirmity, so I traveled by train. I am not one to complain," the dowager duchess said and proceeded to do exactly that about the people on the train, the incompetence of the porters and the presence of ragtag urchins darting about the station.

"I was just telling the duchess that she should go upstairs to rest after such an ordeal," Emmeline said. It amused Thisbe that her mother and grandmother went out of their way to avoid using the other's given name.

"Nonsense. I'm not of an age yet where I must take a nap in the afternoon. Too much sleep dulls the brain, you know." The dowager duchess turned and marched into the formal drawing room, which was rarely used by the duke and his family.

Emmeline sighed as she turned to her daughter. "I am

glad you arrived. Everyone else is out. Well, Bellard is here, but he bolted up the backstairs the moment he heard Cornelia's voice. And I have my suspicions that Smeggars was lying when he told us Henry had gone to his club."

They followed the dowager duchess into the drawing room. She was sitting in a chair beside the massive fireplace. "It's freezing in here."

"We don't usually keep a fire in this room, as we rarely use it," Emmeline replied. "But Smeggars had them set it when you arrived. It should be much warmer soon."

"But where do you receive guests? Don't tell me you still insist on that hideous red monstrosity."

"I prefer the sultan room, yes."

Cornelia sniffed her disapproval and surveyed the room. "This is such a stately reception room. I have always been quite fond of it. You could not find such workmanship as this today." She gestured toward the ornately carved walnut mantel and paneling that framed the fireplace. "I used to come here to speak to Henry's ancestor." She smiled fondly at the portrait of a dour-looking man in seventeenth-century clothing.

"Old Eldric?" Thisbe's voice rose in disbelief. "But he's been dead two hundred years."

"Really, Thisbe, mind your manners," her grandmother scolded. "You shouldn't speak of your ancestors in such an impertinent way. Eldric was the first Duke of Broughton, after all."

"I'm sorry, Grandmother. I was just, um, surprised that you talked to him." Thisbe didn't know why her grandmother's peculiar beliefs still astonished her. "I thought it was only those close to you who…communicated with you."

"Of course, I speak most to my dear Alastair. And my mother visits me often. But they are not the only ones.

The shades reach out to me in many places. They know when one has the Gift as I do. Olivia, as well." She tilted her head, studying Thisbe. "They tell me you may have the Gift as well, at least a bit of it."

This was a new one. Thisbe had heard her grandmother boast about her "gift" for Thisbe's entire life. It had given her goose bumps and even nightmares when she was young. Especially that eerie time when Cornelia said she saw their puppy's death, a month before he strayed onto the road and was killed by a passing wagon. The dowager duchess's pronouncements no longer gave Thisbe the shivers, but her announcement that Thisbe possessed the same talent was vaguely disturbing. "You always said Olivia had it, not me."

"I didn't think so, either." The dowager duchess shrugged. "But Mother assures me that it's there—all the women of our line possess it. Although I find it hard to believe that it exists in Kyria. She takes after you, no doubt." Cornelia looked at Emmeline.

"No doubt." The duchess smiled serenely.

Perhaps it wouldn't be so bad for Desmond to meet the dowager duchess, after all. He was used to his mentor, who believed in ghosts. He might even want to study the duchess. Thisbe suppressed a smile at the thought.

"Where *is* Kyria?" Cornelia looked around the room as if she might be hiding somewhere. "We need to talk about her debut."

"Reed took the other girls to the museum. He's been promising Olivia to do so for some time."

"Kyria went to the British Museum?" Thisbe's eyebrows lifted. "But she dislikes the museum—she says it makes her feel smothered."

"Only the Egyptian and Fertile Crescent sections. It's the mummies, I think. Reed assured her that she wouldn't have to go into that part of it. She wanted to see the ancient jewelry. Also, she suspected Kenneth Duncan was going to call on her today."

"Kyria does have an eye for jewelry," Thisbe's grandmother acknowledged. "She's like me that way. I have always been known for my taste in accessories. When I was a young girl, they didn't wear much adornment, you know, just a cameo or maybe a strand of pearls. Thank heavens that period passed. Well, it doesn't matter. It's Thisbe I'm really concerned about."

"Me? Grandmother, I assure you, I am perfectly fine. You needn't worry about me."

"But I do. You need to take a Season."

"I don't need a Season." This was an old discussion; Thisbe thought her grandmother had finally dropped the notion. "I don't want one."

"Nonsense. Every girl needs a Season. How else are you to find a husband?"

"Perhaps I'll meet him at a lecture," Thisbe said with a smile.

"A scholar?" Cornelia asked in horror. "No, no, I mean someone suitable. Someone of your own station. A Moreland must be careful about marrying properly." She directed a significant look at Emmeline.

Thisbe jumped in quickly. "Anyway, I'm far too old to come out. I'm twenty-three."

"That is precisely what I mean," Cornelia said triumphantly. "You are reaching a desperate age. Soon you'll be regarded as a spinster."

Emmeline rose. "Why don't we all have a glass of sherry?"

Fortunately the subject was dropped after that, and it was not long before the rest of the family began to trickle in, allowing Thisbe to drop the burden of conversation with her grandmother. She moved to give her father her spot beside his mother, ignoring the wounded look he sent her, and soon she was able to slip quietly out the door.

There was no escaping supper and family conversation afterward. Even Uncle Bellard made an appearance, greeting the dowager duchess before scurrying to take a chair at the farthest end of the table, his sense of duty satisfied. Though they normally did not follow the standard practice of the men of the family sharing a postdinner glass of brandy, the duke happily reinstated the custom whenever his mother visited. They could only linger so long, though, before they, too, had to join the women in the grim formal drawing room.

Thisbe's mind drifted as the conversation flowed around her. She looked up at the portrait of the first duke. When Thisbe was younger, she assumed that the dowager duchess told her tales of communicating with the dead simply to draw attention to herself. The practice was also handy for couching her advice as coming from someone else. But when Thisbe was fourteen, she had walked past her grandmother's room one afternoon and seen the woman conversing with the air.

The memory of it made her shiver even now. It had been both shocking and eerie, and Thisbe realized that the dowager duchess really believed she could speak with the dead. Perhaps she needn't worry about scaring off Desmond with her father's title. More likely, he would flee because of her peculiar family.

Later, as she lay in bed, trying to sleep, her mind went back to that scene years ago with her grandmother. She recalled the woman's attentive, even smiling, face. That smile was what had been most chilling. Thisbe had locked her door that night…though she had no idea why she thought a locked door would protect her from ghosts.

In all other ways, Cornelia was normal. Dictatorial and critical, but still much like many others. It made the bizarre statements she dropped into conversation now and then all the more eerie. She treated it so casually, as if conversing with spirits was a common thing. Maybe her grandmother really was mad…

SHE WAS HOT, so very hot. The heat enclosed her, pressing on her like a weight. Why was she here? What was happening? She heard the crackle of fire all around her. Heavy dark smoke billowed up, choking her.

She must get out. She must find him, save him.

In the distance she heard screams, horrible sounds of unending agony. That time would come for her as well, she knew. Closer, there were shouts and jeers, the rumble of conversation in the crowd. She could feel their hatred, sense their excitement. They wanted the spectacle of her death.

"Help me. My child. Help me. Please."

The crackle grew louder, the air so hot it seared her lungs. The kindling was blazing now, the fire catching the larger, heavier logs. She tried to pull away from the flames, but she could not move. Frantically, she twisted and turned to no avail.

Something was lashed around her waist, tying her firmly to the hard post behind her. Sobbing, she tore at the heavy rope, clawing and pulling in desperation. Her wrists were bound as well, making it more difficult to gain any purchase on the thick, rough fiber.

Raising her face to the heavens, she screamed, "Release me…!"

THISBE JOLTED AWAKE. Her heart was racing, her stomach knotted in terror. She was soaked in sweat. The memory of smoke and fire was so vivid, so frightening, that she slipped out of bed and eased open the door into the hallway to look for signs of fire. Nothing glowed anywhere. There was no smell of smoke. It was only a nightmare.

A most peculiar nightmare. There had been none of the running or falling or the frantic sense of being late that occupied most of her nightmares. It had been all fire and fear. Why had she dreamed of fire? There was no fire in the house, no smell of smoke. The room was chilly. Thisbe had a healthy fear of fire, but not an abnormally strong one. And nothing that happened today had anything to do with a fire.

More specifically, why had she dreamed of being burned at the stake, for surely that was what she had envisioned—bound to a post, fire all around her? The danger in her dreams was usually nebulous, even unknown. But this had been vivid and detailed to an unusual extent.

It was easy to see why she had pleaded for help. But why had she said, "My child?" Thisbe didn't have a child and nor did anyone close to her. Even more disturbing, the voice she'd heard had not been her own.

It was almost as if she'd been dreaming someone else's nightmare.

That thought sent a little shiver through her. Thisbe realized how cold she was, standing here in only her cotton nightgown. She hurried back to get into bed, rubbing her arms. She flinched at the little dart of pain in her fingertips. Frowning, she lit the candle at her bedside and looked down at her hands. Her nails were ragged, one of them torn, and the ends of her fingers were red and raw.

Just as if she had been clawing at a rough rope.

DESMOND PEERED INTO one of the eyepieces of the contraption in front of him. Well, that idea hadn't worked. He raised his head and considered the problem, idly making designs on the paper before him. He was amazingly lacking in disappointment, considering that his most recent attempt to build a spectrographic instrument had failed. But it was hard to feel anything but good; he would see Thisbe on Sunday. He smiled to himself.

Meeting her at the reading room was less than ideal. Of course, they could take a stroll together afterward and talk, but he would miss that hour of sitting beside her, keenly aware of her presence. It also felt somehow furtive, as if they were setting up a tryst, which he supposed they were, with the difference that they would be in public view, instead of hiding in private.

He wished like the devil that he could meet her in private. It was wonderful to walk with her and talk and laugh—he thought he'd never laughed, or even smiled, as much in his life as he had with her. But he wanted quite desperately to touch her arm or hold her hand, even if it was encased in her glove. He wanted most of all to hold her. To feel her body in his arms, to drink in the scent of her. To kiss her.

Desmond shifted on his stool. It was foolish to think about that. He knew nothing would come of this romance in the end; he should enjoy the moment, take what he had and not think about what he wanted and the obstacles that lay between him and that future. In truth, it boiled down to one obstacle: he was a man with no prospects.

He sighed and tossed aside the pencil, the thought that had been nagging at him all day returning: Why had Thisbe wanted to meet him at the museum? Why had she not suggested he call on her? Why had she never allowed him to escort her all the way to her home?

Her reasons had been logical—he needed to go to work, it was cold and he wasn't wearing a coat, and so on. But he couldn't help but think that she didn't want him to know where she lived.

Desmond could think of several reasons why that was so, none of them in his favor. The most lowering one was that she was ashamed of him. The most gut piercing was the idea that she was married. In between lay strict fathers who didn't allow her to have men call on her or embarrassment about where she lived or of someone in her family. Unfortunately, the ones in the middle were the least likely. A strict father would not let his daughter go off to lectures on her own, much less spend the entire afternoon there. She obviously loved her family and talked about them with affection. And she dressed too well to be living in a hovel.

The obvious reason was that she didn't want her family to see Desmond. Even the laxest of fathers wouldn't be pleased to have his daughter courted by a man with no prospects, and as a scholar he would be singularly unimpressed by a man who hadn't attended Oxford, as he and her brothers had. Even worse, Desmond had not managed to stay the course at any university.

There was a polished quality about Thisbe—and presumably her entire family—that Desmond knew he did not have. However good his grammar, however little of his Dorset accent remained, his speech did not have that certain tone that bespoke refinement. His clothes were cheaply made, his hair shaggy. His background was… Well, there was nothing there to be proud about, really, other than that he had managed to leave it behind.

He was the sort of man who lost his gloves, who forgot his coat even though the temperature was freezing, who never noticed the time and was often late, who could talk for hours on a subject that put everyone else to sleep. He would never make enough money to support a family, and what money he had he was apt to spend on his research or a book. In short, he was not a man one wanted to introduce to one's parents.

Well. He'd certainly managed to punch a hole in the balloon of his happiness. Desmond turned back to his nonfunctioning instrument. He would probably have to take the whole thing apart.

At that moment, the door to the laboratory was flung open, letting in a blast of winter air, and Carson came in, a grin on his face. "I have news. You'll like this, Professor Gordon."

"I will?" Gordon stood up from his table, pushing up his spectacles. "Have you discovered something?"

"I have indeed." Now that he had their attention, Carson sauntered over to his table and set down his hat, a cat-that-ate-the-canary look on his face. "I have learned that the Dowager Duchess of Broughton is in town."

CHAPTER SEVEN

DESMOND'S JAW DROPPED, and Gordon surged toward the man. Everyone began to throw out questions.

"Are you certain?"

"When?"

"How do you know?"

"Have you seen her? Have you seen it?"

"Have you talked to her?"

Carson threw up his hands in mock surrender. "Wait. Wait. One at a time."

"Quiet." Professor Gordon cast a stern look around at the young men. "Let the man speak." He turned back to Carson. "Tell us."

"To answer your questions—she arrived just yesterday. Apparently she's the sort whose movements attract immediate attention. And, no, I haven't seen her. I hardly move in the same circles as duchesses. I heard my mother and her friends gossiping about it this afternoon, so I eavesdropped. Apparently she's something of a harridan. One of the women said the duchess is mad as a hatter—the whole family is." He paused, then added significantly, "And another woman remarked, 'They say she claims to *speak to her dead husband.*'"

"Are you serious?" Desmond leaned forward.

"I thought that would get everyone's attention."

"You think she knows what the Eye is? That she actually uses it?" Gordon asked in astonishment.

"I've no idea, sir. But it sounded suspiciously like that."

"It's a stroke of luck that she's in town," Desmond said. "You can call on her, sir, ask her directly."

The older man shook his head. "No. She won't see me, I'm sure." He plopped down on his high stool, his expression falling into dejection. He reached into his pocket and pulled out a folded sheet of paper. "I had a reply to my letter. From her man of business. She didn't even deign to write me herself. He says, and I quote, 'The Duchess is not interested in selling or lending any of her possessions. I must request that you not write her on this subject again.'" Gordon stuck the letter back in his pocket, his face stony. "The bloody arrogant woman. The advancement of knowledge means nothing to her."

"That's the toffs for you," Benjamin commented. "The aristocracy cares for nothing but themselves."

"Seems to me it's time for my suggestion," Carson asserted.

"To steal it?" Desmond asked derisively.

"It's not stealing. We established that it was almost certainly stolen from Anne Ballew. If it belongs to anyone, it would be her descendants."

"And no one knows who those are," Gordon said. "So, really, it should belong to the world at large, to science and history. We could *use* it, unlike her, who wants to keep it hidden away."

"That excuse could be used by any thief—I need that money and he's rich," Desmond protested. "Besides, if Carson's gossip is accurate, she apparently does use it."

"But it has no real monetary value," another of the students reasoned. "Annie Blue wasn't wealthy. I doubt it was made of anything expensive."

"Yes," Gordon agreed, sounding more interested by

the moment. "Its value is incalculable to us, but in material terms, it's worthless."

Desmond looked around at the others. Their faces were filled with excitement. "I cannot believe you're actually considering this. Any of you."

"Don't be such a puritan, Dez," Carson told him.

"I don't think considering theft wrong qualifies one as a puritan," Desmond declared.

"This is more important than legalities," Gordon said. "It's for the advancement of human knowledge. If this woman sees spirits, that proves that Annie Blue's Eye works. It makes it even more imperative to investigate it. One stubborn old woman should not be allowed to stand in the way of progress."

"All of you are talking as if it's a surety that you would be able to steal it and get away. That's faulty reasoning. The odds of you stealing it are at best fifty-fifty. First, none of you are thieves so you're apt to bungle it. Second, you don't even know what it looks like."

"I'd know it the instant I saw it," Gordon assured him.

Desmond refrained from rolling his eyes. "Begging your pardon, sir, but you merely *think* you'll instinctively recognize it. Those aren't the only obstacles. This woman is a duchess—she's bound to live in a large house with any number of rooms. How will you know where to look?"

"It'll be near her, I'd warrant. She'd keep it close," Carson countered.

"Marvelous. All you need do is enter a room where someone is sleeping and creep about in the dark, trying to find an object of unknown appearance."

"Go in when she's not likely to be in her bedchamber."

"During the day, in broad daylight, with who knows how many servants walking around?"

"Evening," Carson said. "It's dark, but they won't be in bed. The duchess and her family will either be out at a party or downstairs eating a long and lavish dinner. The servants will be busy downstairs serving or they'll be in the servants' hall, enjoying their master's absence."

"I must say, you've given this a great deal of thought."

"I'm a quick thinker. And I know the schedule of people like that." Carson grinned and tapped his temple, his bright blue eyes dancing.

"This just a game for you," Desmond said in exasperation. "A debate, an intellectual exercise. You have no realization of what the consequences are. To you jail is just an idea, some vague place where common people go. But it's not. This is serious, Carson." Desmond's voice rose. "If you are caught stealing, you'll be tossed in jail—for many years. Don't count on them letting you go because you're the 'right sort of people.' The duchess will have all the influence here. You won't have silk waistcoats and soft beds and good meals. It's gruel and water and inadequate sanitation." Desmond caught himself before he blurted out that he knew jails because he'd visited his father there.

Across from him, Carson dropped his amused expression. "I'm sorry, Dez. I shouldn't tease you. You take everything so seriously. I don't actually intend to break into the duchess's sleeping quarters and steal the Eye. I am much too fond of my silk waistcoats for that." The corner of his mouth quirked.

"Yes, obviously this is hypothetical," Gordon said heavily. "Mere supposition."

"What a waste," Benjamin sighed and shook his head.

One by one they returned to their tasks, but no one seemed able to concentrate. It wasn't long before the others left. Desmond remained; he wanted to make sure

Gordon had given up the mad idea of stealing the Eye. The man had said he accepted it, but the expression on his face was so avid, his bitterness at the duchess's refusal so apparent, that Desmond feared he might give in to his desire to have the Eye.

Apparently, Gordon was of a similar mind, for after the last student closed the door behind him, he said, "Desmond, I want to talk to you."

"Good." He walked over to the other man. "I meant no disrespect earlier."

"No, no, I understand. You're the most practical of them all, the steadiest. That's why I want to ask you—"

"Ask me what? You know I'll do whatever I can for you."

"Recover the Eye of Annie Blue."

"Sir?" Desmond gaped at him. "You said you understood."

"I do. But I didn't say I agreed with you."

"Professor Gordon..." Desmond shook his head, at a loss for words. He had never seen his mentor so blindly stubborn. Yes, the man believed some things that Desmond deemed unlikely, but he had never before been so immune to reason.

"I'd do it myself, but clearly if she discovered the theft, I would be the most likely suspect since I have just written her asking for it."

Desmond's mind boggled at the thought of the portly, dignified gentleman climbing through a downstairs window. "Sir...you cannot."

"They would know nothing of you, however. I could be in public somewhere, have an established alibi while you slip in unbeknownst and take it. Think, Desmond. That woman doesn't deserve to have the Eye. You're from

Dorset, close to Anne Ballew's own village. You have more right to it than some aristocrat."

Could Gordon know his aunt's wild assertions? "I have no connection with Anne Ballew. I have no more claim to it than anyone."

"Dorset does. It would have gone to someone in Dorset if Anne Ballew had had a say in the matter."

"Perhaps so, but that doesn't make it right to commit robbery. It's not as if I think the duchess *should* have it. However she acquired it, it was originally stolen. I really don't care whether some aristocrat loses a bit of property. But it's illegal."

"There's a larger good here than the law. Don't you see it? We have the opportunity to make history. Don't you want to see it? To touch it? To see how it works?"

"Of course I do. I want to examine the thing as much as anyone. I agree that there's a greater good here and that one stubborn old woman shouldn't keep it from the rest of the world. It's disappointing, frustrating...*wrong* that we cannot study it. I want to see it. But not enough to risk jail."

"You won't get caught. You're clever. You don't panic. And I've seen you run."

"The same can be said about many men in Newgate. Besides, it's an impossible task. I don't know what room it's in. I don't know what it looks like. I don't even know where this woman lives, let alone the floor plan of the place."

"I know where Broughton House is, and bedchambers are always upstairs," Gordon said, as if this resolved the matter.

Desmond swung away, throwing out his arms in frustration. "Why me? Why not ask one of the others? Carson seemed especially keen on it."

"Oh, Carson…" Gordon waved away that idea. "He's too impulsive, not responsible."

"Which is why he would be willing to steal it." Desmond stopped, his eyes narrowing. "Is it because he's a gentleman's son? It would be more of a scandal if Carson was caught. Whereas I am disposable."

"No!" Gordon's eyes widened. "No, of course not. Truthfully, it would be far easier to lose Carson than you. You're the brightest of the lot. The best. I can't trust any of the others to accomplish it. I regard you like a son. I remember when you first came to the city." He smiled reminiscently. "How eager you were, how bright. I didn't care that you couldn't pay. I wanted the opportunity to pass my knowledge on to someone who would be able to understand it. To use it."

Desmond felt himself softening. He could not have asked for a better, more generous man to mentor him than Professor Gordon. He owed him so much, and guilt twisted through Desmond at the thought of turning him down. "Sir…I know that I can never repay what you have done for me. And if I have been like a son to you, I assure you that you have been a much better father than the one I had. I would do almost anything for you, but this…" He trailed off.

"Of course." Gordon nodded. "Well, if you cannot, you cannot. I will have to do it myself."

"Professor! No!" He would certainly get caught. Professor Gordon hadn't the first idea what to do, and he was anything but agile. "You mustn't. It would destroy your career."

"No. It will save it. Don't you see? I must have the Eye. Mr. Wallace is growing impatient with our lack of results. I've no idea how long he will continue funding our research. I shan't have enough for this laboratory.

The equipment." He waved his hand around, indicating the contents of the room.

"We'll find another patron," Desmond said, though he was not sure there was another wealthy man out there intent on spirit research. Wallace had been something of a godsend.

"No. And it's not just that. It's… I have become an object of scorn to my fellow scientists. A jest. They overlook everything I've done before, the articles I've written, because I've chosen to focus on the spirits."

"I know. It's very unfair. Your paper on the diffusion of—"

"This is science." Gordon slammed down his fist on the table. "This is more important than the properties of a chemical or what gases exist on the sun. This concerns the very essence of life—the beginning, the spark, the thing that raises us above the beasts."

"Of course it's more important." Desmond had heard these arguments many times before, especially when the professor had downed a tankard of ale. "You mustn't distress yourself over it."

"I was respected. I was admired. I remember Faraday himself once told me I had a bright future ahead of me." He gazed off into the distance, smiling a bit at the memory, then swung back to Desmond. "I have to get that back. With the Eye, I can prove how wrong they were. I can prove that I'm not a doddering old fool."

Desmond's chest ached at the sight of tears glimmering in his mentor's eyes. Gordon was driving himself mad over this. It was cruel that they ridiculed him, unfair that they cast doubt on his earlier work because he was "playing with ghosts." As much as Desmond himself would like to see whether the Eye worked, he wanted it even more for his teacher.

Was it really so terrible a sin to take the Eye? Gordon was right; the Eye was at best a plaything for a spoiled aristocrat. In Gordon's hands, it could be groundbreaking. It could give something to the world. Advance man's knowledge. Would it be so terrible to take one trinket from a duchess's coffers? Would it be as difficult as he had described?

He was young and fast and reasonably agile. If he awakened anyone, surely he could make it out of the house before they could grab him. He had a better chance of success than any of the others. He hadn't served as an apprentice to his father's illegal trade, but he had absorbed a fair amount of information on the art of breaking into a house. At least he knew how to pick a lock.

The odds for him were not as bad as he'd said. He could get into the house and take a look around. Of course, the endeavor was doomed to failure—finding what he didn't know to look for was a fool's errand.

But perhaps that would be enough for the professor. He could find an unlocked window or pick a lock and slip inside, look around the house a bit, find nothing and leave. He could go back to Gordon and tell him that he had been unable to find it. Perhaps his making the effort would be enough to ease the older man's distress. Perhaps it would enable Gordon to accept that he could not steal the thing.

And if by chance Desmond could find the Eye…

"I'll do it."

IT HAD NOT been his brightest decision, Desmond reflected as he walked toward the address Professor Gordon had given him. Gordon had maneuvered him into acceding to his pleas. Desmond had been aware of it at the time, but even so, he saw little way out of it.

He *did* owe Gordon a great deal. The man had helped him in many ways—not only tutoring him without charging him, but also recommending him for the job that he could not have gotten on his own, steering him through university and providing him the opportunity to work on a well-funded research project. How could he refuse? How could he let the man proceed on his own and wind up imprisoned? It would be the deathblow to his reputation as a scientist.

Desmond was honest enough to admit that he was also seduced by the lure of finding the Eye, the possibilities it might open, the chance for them—for him—to find success. However unlikely it was that he could obtain the instrument or that the legends surrounding it were true, the prize that dangled before him was hard to resist.

Desmond didn't expect fame or fortune, but the opportunity to discover, to *know*, to make some mark in the scientific community, lured him. Which brought the lowering thought that perhaps the difference between him and his father was only in the kind of reward a criminal act might bring.

Well, no matter how foolish, he was in it now. He'd promised Gordon, and he would at least make a try to find the thing. He was also going to do his damnedest not to get caught.

He didn't intend to break into the house tonight, though that was probably what Gordon hoped for. Carson's thievery reasoning had been persuasive. The best time to break into the house was probably in the evening, when the inhabitants were downstairs and the servants were busy in the kitchen. But that opportunity had passed now. It would be bedtime, at least for an aged woman, and everyone was more likely to be on the bedroom floor.

The wise thing was to make a plan, to locate the

windows and doors and hopefully get some idea of the layout of the house. It would scarcely do to climb in the dining room window in the middle of the meal. He needed to find the most secluded door or unused room. Or there might be a viable way to get in on the second floor—a tree, say, or a conveniently placed drainpipe.

It was a long walk to Broughton House from the nearest omnibus stop. He wondered if he could spare enough money for a hack the night of the theft—but, no, then there would a witness who knew he was in the area at the time of the theft. He must think more like a criminal.

The houses grew larger and obviously more expensive as he neared his destination. He'd expected that. What he hadn't expected was that when he reached Broughton House, he would find that it took up the entire block. His jaw dropped as he stared at the huge stone building, looming up before him like a more stylish government building, reducing even the grand domiciles across the street to insignificance.

It was hopeless. How could he expect to find one object in this enormous house? He let out a sigh. He had to at least make an effort. Desmond studied the house. A long walkway ran down the side to a far less magnificent door. That was doubtless the trade entrance, where servants and sellers brought food and supplies. Beyond that door, a high wall jutted out from the side of the house.

Walking past the house, he found another walkway leading to a door at the rear of the house. Light shone from the windows near the door, and he concluded that the room must be the kitchen, where the servants were still cleaning the dinner dishes. That would mean that this door was the trade entrance, but if so, where had that first path led? He decided that it deserved a second, closer look. There was a gate in the property wall beyond the door, but the kitchen windows spilled too much light on it for him to examine it. He continued following the wall, turning at the side street. At the very back, where the wall turned the corner, stood another building. There were windows along the upper floor, but the ground floor had none, only two very wide wooden doors—this, then, was the mews where the horses and carriage were kept.

Marveling at the stables that would have dwarfed the cottage where he'd been raised, he walked on. The wall offered no handy tree to climb up and over it, though he did notice that a large tree on the other side hugged the wall. Perhaps, if he took a running jump, he could grab the top of the stone barrier and pull himself up. The tree would provide a handy way to climb down, as well as a quick exit.

He completed the tour and wound up at the side of the house, having found no other gates or breaks in the solid wall. Shivering, he tucked his hands in his pockets for warmth—bloody stupid gloves—as he studied the house from this angle. What sort of people, he wondered, would live in a house this size? How many of them were there? What in the world did they put in all the rooms? He couldn't imagine what one would do with all that space. Or how many servants it must take to clean it.

The gas streetlamp a few feet behind him gave him enough light to see, and he moved closer. Light shone from several of the windows on the floor above, but they were all curtained. It would be safe to explore the area.

He was only a few feet from the small side door when it swung open, and a figure rushed out. Desmond stood, rooted to the ground, staring at the woman hurrying toward him.

"Thisbe!"

CHAPTER EIGHT

DESMOND COULDN'T MOVE, couldn't think, as Thisbe ran to him. She threw herself against him, and then he was kissing her, reason dismissed, lost in the feel of her body in his arms, her mouth on his. Emotions swirled through him—astonishment, confusion, elation—and all were overlaid with a shimmering passion.

His world had just exploded in front of him and he was utterly lost, but this heat was real, this hunger and urgency. Her lithe body pressed into him, her mouth hot and seeking, opening beneath his—all this was real. And right now nothing else mattered.

One hand moved up, tangling in the mass of her hair. Good God, her hair was down, spilling over his hand, sliding between his fingers, silken and rich. His other hand moved lower, curving over her buttocks and pressing her more tightly to him. His desire was evident and he wanted her to feel that, wanted to feel her against him.

His lips left hers and traveled down her neck, and he buried his face in the fall of hair. Her hair smelled of lavender, the scent intoxicating. She turned her face toward his, murmuring her name, and the touch of her breath on his skin sent a shiver through him.

"You're cold," she whispered, pulling away. "Come inside." She took his hand, pulling him toward the open door, and he followed, trying to rein in his surging feelings, trying to *think*. What the devil was going on? How could Thisbe just appear, like a genie from a lamp?

"Do you *live* here?" he blurted.

She gave a little laugh and pulled him into a short, empty hallway. "Of course I do, silly. Why else did you come here to see me?"

Why, indeed. "Um, yes, of course, it's just I thought perhaps you were visiting," he said, relieved that he was able to pull a reasonable excuse out of his stunned mind. "Or—or…you worked here." Now that was stupid; clearly she couldn't be a maid. "Your experiments, I mean." Another daft idea—why would she come to this grand home to mix chemicals?—but she didn't seem to care, and still smiled at him in that wonderful way.

"I do conduct my experiments here. But I live here, as well." She squeezed his hand.

He couldn't stop looking at her. "You are so beautiful."

She was obviously dressed for bed, her hair down and a brocade dressing gown wrapped around her, a delicate bit of a white cotton nightgown peeking out at the top. Her cheeks were red from the cold, and her lips were soft and dark from their kisses. Desire clenched like a fist in his gut.

Thisbe glanced away, looking embarrassed and gratified at the same time. "How did you find me? Did you follow me home yesterday?"

"Yes," he blurted. He was beginning to calm down, his mind starting to work again. Thank God he hadn't entered the place; he didn't know what he would have done if she had found him creeping through her house in the dark. "Yes," he repeated. "Of course. Yesterday."

"I never saw you. You must be awfully good."

He shrugged. "I…hailed a hack after you boarded the omnibus."

"Oh. Then you saw me get into the carriage."

"Yes." He didn't know what she was talking about, but it seemed the safest answer. "I'm sorry. I know I shouldn't have. It was just… I was curious. I wondered why you never let me walk you home."

"I'm glad you did," she admitted and went up on tiptoe to plant a light kiss on this lips. "I was afraid to tell you who I was, but when I saw you from my window, I was so very happy."

"So you are related to, um, the duke?" he asked tentatively.

"I'm his daughter."

It had been obvious from the moment he saw her, but still Desmond felt the blood drain out of his face. "Why, I don't understand… Why didn't you tell me?"

"Here. Sit down." She led him over to the well-worn wooden staircase and sat down on a step, tugging him down with her. "I'll tell you everything."

THISBE COULD HARDLY describe the feelings churning around inside her; the fact was she could hardly even sort them out. She'd been caught in her lie, which should displease her, but it didn't at all. When she saw Desmond loitering outside, looking up at her window, all she felt was a rush of joy. He'd tracked her down, which was really *not* what one wanted a man to do normally, but somehow she found it very satisfying that he liked her so much he'd gone to the trouble of following her. And how sneaky he had been! She had to admire his skill… which was also not what she would usually say.

But mingling with that joy, with the wild pleasure of his kiss, was nervousness. She was now afraid that all the things she had feared would come true or that he'd be angry at her for deceiving him. He had every right to think her deceptive and secretive. She was stabbed with guilt. That faintly wounded look that had flashed in his eyes when he asked her why she had done it made her want to cry.

"I'm sorry, Desmond." She turned to him, their knees touching, and took his hands between hers. "I know I was wrong, and you probably think I'm a liar, but I didn't lie to you."

"You said your name was Moreland."

"It is! That is my last name. Broughton is just Papa's title. I'm Thisbe Moreland. All the things I told you were true. I am a chemist. My family is exactly as I described. My father is a scholar and my mother champions causes. My brothers and sisters are what I told you they were. Come to call on me, and I'll introduce you to all of them, and you'll see."

"Call on you?" His voice vaulted upward. "Me? But I'm not… I can't just call at a duke's house."

"Yes, you can."

"Your butler wouldn't let me in the door. Thisbe…" He leaned back against the wall, despair blossoming on his face. "You and I… You're a duke's daughter."

"I'm also myself!" Thisbe proclaimed and jumped to her feet. "This is exactly why I didn't tell you I was Lady Thisbe Moreland. I was afraid you would pull away from me, as you just did. That you would no longer think of me as the person I am, and see only the title. If I had told you, you wouldn't have asked me to walk in the park or invited me to your shop. You wouldn't have kissed me!" When he didn't answer, she demanded, "Would you?"

"No, I suppose not," he said miserably. "But, Thisbe… how could we ever be anything to each other? I wouldn't fit in your world."

"Stop it! Just stop it. Your world, my world. It's nonsense. We live in the same world. It's just that some people like to put others in tidy boxes and tell you how you must be because you happened to be born to this family instead of the other."

"Thisbe, I don't—"

"You—" She jabbed her forefinger at him, her eyes snapping. "You call yourself an egalitarian. I have heard you talk about equality and the rights of man and all that." She waved her hand in a circle. "Yet there you sit, judging me by my birth. Condemning me to a lifetime of boredom and good manners."

"I'm not judging you," he protested, rising to his feet.

"Yes, you are," Thisbe retorted, her whole jumble of emotions tumbling out in anger. "You're saying I have to be a certain way, consort with certain people, do certain things because my father has a title. In other words, you're saying that I have no freedom at all. And—" as he opened his mouth to speak, she plowed right over his words "—and you're insulting me. You're insulting me and my entire family. You're saying everything I've told you is a lie. You're saying we Morelands are deceiving people about what we're really like. According to you, we're actually terrible snobs underneath our nice words. According to you, I'm an entirely different person than I appear to be. But I'm not. I am the same woman I was the other day in the park, the same person who went to those lectures and discussed all kinds of things with you, the same person who told you about her hopes and dreams. I am the same girl, and I have the same thoughts and feelings that I did yesterday when you didn't know my father has a title!"

"Thisbe, please." Desmond held his hands out toward her. "I think you're—you're the most wonderful girl, and I'm not—"

"Don't you dare say you're not good enough for me, or I swear I shall hit you!" Thisbe stomped up the stairs. "Good night, Desmond. I am going to bed." She turned around, fixing him with a fierce stare. "If you want to—" her voice caught, but she went on "—to be with me, if you care for me at all, then you may call on me tomorrow at my house instead of meeting me in secret at the museum. And if not, then... Well, then, goodbye." She whirled around to hide the glimmer of tears in her eyes and ran up the staircase.

BY THE TIME Thisbe reached the top of the stairs, she regretted her ultimatum and swung around to go back down to Desmond, but she heard the sound of the door closing. Well, he'd certainly seized the opportunity to leave. She ran to her room and peered out between the draperies. He was walking away, hands in pockets, head down. She watched as his long slender form passed the streetlamp and was swallowed by shadows.

She sat down in the chair, a welter of emotions boiling inside her. So much had just happened, so many emotions, so many thoughts struggling to be heard, that she couldn't sort any of it out. She had been so happy to see Desmond, and then that kiss... Just the memory of it sent heat surging up in her again. But when she told him about herself and he started to pull away, it pierced her heart. She pictured herself losing him, and suddenly her fear turned to anger.

It wasn't just that her earlier fears had proved correct. It was that Desmond didn't really understand her, didn't really know her. After all their conversations, their closeness, those dizzying kisses, he immediately looked at her differently. She was no longer Thisbe to him, but the daughter of a duke. If her name could so easily put him off, then she hadn't really known him, either. If he cared more for his archaic notions of class distinctions and what was "proper," she didn't want to be around him anymore.

Except, of course, she did.

Thisbe wiped the tears from her cheeks. It wasn't like her to be so emotional. If there was one thing she was, it was reasonable. She liked to deal with facts. What she needed to do what sort this out and look at it logically. What did she know? What were the provable facts of the situation?

First, she was at fault by not telling him the truth from the beginning. Second, the news had exploded on him, with no preparation at all. Desmond was shocked by her revelation, which was only rational and to be expected. He was dismayed at the prospect of calling at a duke's house. Most people would be. He barely had time to absorb the news, let alone examine the idea and adjust his thoughts. Wasn't it unfair of her to expect him to immediately accept the things she'd told him?

None of that should have angered her so. It was the way he leaned away from her, the look of sorrow in his eyes. He looked at her as if he'd already lost her. *That* was what hurt, not his mouthing antiquated notions of class distinctions. He was already giving her up.

Thisbe sighed and climbed into bed. Perhaps she should just accept it. If she wasn't worth knocking down the barriers for, then perhaps she should let him go, too.

CHAPTER NINE

THISBE SPENT THE next day in suspense. She told Smeggars that he was to let in *anyone* who asked for her, no matter his misgivings. But would Desmond call on her? Was this the right dress to wear? Was her hair too plain? Too intricate?

She joined Kyria and their mother in the drawing room, which earned her a surprised look from both of them. Thisbe usually disappeared to her lab in the afternoon and didn't appear again until the evening meal, lest she get dragooned into chaperoning Kyria.

The duchess made an effort to sit through the calls of Kyria's visitors, even though it went against her opinion of chaperonage, which she considered prison guards for young girls. Kyria enjoyed the social whirl, and for her sake, Emmeline adhered to the rules. She was perhaps not the best of chaperones, as she often left the room, but for the most part, she endured the insipidity of the afternoon visits. When Reed was home, he sometimes relieved his mother of the duties, but at other times, it was Olivia who was called upon to sit in the drawing room, and now and then even Thisbe had to play the part.

Thisbe found this afternoon as stultifying as ever, made even worse by her anxiety over Desmond. One of her mother's friends called on them, which fortunately cut short a visit by a society matron and her daughter, and young men came and went all afternoon. Kyria kept shooting speculative glances at her sister, but the constant presence of her beaux kept her from questioning Thisbe.

Two of Kyria's most tiresome admirers were there and Thisbe was considering giving up for the afternoon when Smeggars came in, looking faintly pained, and announced, "Mr. Desmond Harrison, ma'am."

Desmond, who was approximately the color of Thisbe's sheets, stood just behind their butler. Thisbe shot to her feet before Smeggars got out Desmond's full name, and she crossed the room to him, face glowing. "Desmond. You came."

A smile twitched at the corner of his mouth. "I had my orders."

She took his arm and propelled him across the room to introduce him to her mother and Kyria, then seated him in the chair closest to her mother. She sat down on the other side, neatly buffering him from the other young men, who were eying Desmond as if trying to place him.

Kyria stood up. "I am so tired of sitting. I believe I'll take a stroll down the hall. Mr. Jennings? Mr. Ashworth? Have I shown you the gallery?" Thisbe silently blessed her sister as the men jumped to offer their arms to Kyria. Kyria threw her a smile over her shoulder as they left the room.

Desmond looked scarcely any more comfortable at their absence. Thisbe spoke across him to the duchess. "Mr. Harrison works in an optical instruments shop."

Desmond's eyes widened in panic at this introduction, but Emmeline sat forward, looking far more interested. "Do you? Excellent. Tell me, Mr. Harrison, what sort of hours do you work? Are the conditions there adequate?"

Desmond blinked. "Why, yes, they're, ah… It's a nice place. The owner is a good man."

"What a refreshing thing to hear." The duchess continued to interrogate him about the shop, his work and his opinion on child labor laws. Desmond gradually relaxed, and by the time Kyria and her swains strolled back into the room, the two of them were deep in a discussion of sanitation, or rather the lack of it, in the slums of London.

Kyria glanced at them, then cast a conspiratorial grin at Thisbe. As bits and pieces of their talk drifted over, Kyria's gentlemen callers looked appalled. Thisbe had to admit that dead animals lying in the streets was not a particularly pleasant conversational topic.

"Mama!" The twins trotted into the room—it was rare to see them move any slower. They ran to the duchess, who bent to kiss them and pulled them up into the chair with her.

"What have you been doing?" she asked, and there followed a long and complicated rendition of their activities. The suitors—Thisbe had come to think of them as a single entity—seemed even more dismayed than they had been at the duchess's earlier conversation.

Con, eying Desmond curiously, slipped down from the chair and went to him. "You're tall."

"Yes, I am."

"Not as tall as Theo," Con told him loyally.

"No, probably not," Desmond agreed amicably, smiling at the boy.

Alex broke off his tale and went to stand by his brother. "Who're you?"

"I'm Desmond Harrison."

"Desmond is a friend of mine," Thisbe added.

"Oh." Alex continued to study Desmond in his thoughtful, unswerving way, a practice some people found uncomfortable.

"He's tall," Con informed his brother. "But not as tall as Theo."

"Not as tall as Reed," Alex added.

Desmond grinned. "I seem to be growing shorter by the moment."

"I'm Con."

"I'm Alex."

"I'm very pleased to meet you. Con. Alex." Desmond shook each boy's hand as he greeted them, which obviously delighted the twins, and they shook his hand with gusto.

"Boys..." the duchess said, frowning a bit. "Where is your nanny?"

"Yes." Thisbe looked toward the hall. "Usually when you slip your leash, Nanny follows you."

"She left," Con said casually.

"Left? What do you mean, left?"

"Granna yelled at her," Alex said by way of explanation. "And bam! Bam!" He imitated banging a cane on the floor.

Con laughed and joined his brother in slamming a pretend staff against the carpet. "Bam! Bam!"

"Yes, dear, we understand," the duchess interjected. "What happened then? Your grandmother didn't strike her, did she?"

This question startled the men in the room, though the duchess's children took it in stride.

Con shook his head. "No. But Nanny cried."

"She said, 'I cannot live here,'" Alex added in the twins' back-and-forth style of storytelling.

"'This place is a madhouse,'" Con went on.

"And she ran upstairs."

"What did your grandmother do?" Emmeline asked.

"She slammed the door." The boys let out another chorus of *bam*s as they mimicked their grandmother.

"They both just left you alone?" The duchess rose

to her feet, her eyes shooting sparks. "Really! Has the woman no sense?" She swept out of the room.

"Do you suppose she was talking about the nanny or Grandmother?" Thisbe asked drily.

"Probably both," Kyria responded.

Alex and Con gazed at each other for a long moment, then turned their eyes toward Thisbe and Desmond, then to Kyria and her swains.

"Alex? Con?" Thisbe's suspicions were aroused.

Con gave Alex a nudge, and Alex reached into his pocket. He held out his hand to Desmond. In the center of his palm was an exquisitely detailed, tiny enameled bird sitting on a short round staff.

"Oh, my." Desmond sucked in an appreciative breath and pick up the tiny bird to study it. "This is lovely."

"Is this why Grandmother was angry?" Thisbe asked.

Alex nodded, tears beginning to well. Con stepped closer to his twin so that they were shoulder to shoulder, tears glimmering in his eyes, too.

"Did you find this?" Desmond asked gently, and they shook their heads.

Alex reached into his other pocket and drew out a very small box. It was made of lapis lazuli, with gold trim all around it and golden hinges on the lid. Desmond opened the box. Inside was a sheet of chased gold, and in the center sat an oval indentation, covered in a tangle of golden wires so that it resembled a nest. In the center of the nest was a small hole.

"I broke it," Alex said sadly.

"The bird tweeted," Con explained, humming a bit of a tune.

"It's a music box," Desmond said. "It looks like the spindle came off. Wait a bit." He set the bird back in Alex's palm and reached inside his jacket to pull out a slender leather case. Taking a miniature screwdriver from the case, he carefully unfastened the tiny screws holding the golden plate in place.

"I say," said one of the men authoritatively. "You shouldn't be fooling about with that. Bad enough the boys broke it, but—"

"Hush," Kyria snapped, frowning at him. "If you can't say anything helpful, perhaps you should leave."

The man looked affronted, but closed his mouth. Desmond handed the metal plate to Con to hold and set the tiny screws on the table beside him. He studied the mechanism for a moment. "Aha, here—see, this became disconnected."

He showed the twins, pointing with the end of the screwdriver, and they peered down into the box, their former unhappiness gone. Desmond pulled a set of long tweezers from the same slim case, and delicately poked about inside the machine. Fascinated, the twins watched him pick up the spindle and put it back where it belonged. Carefully, he replaced the plate and set the short hollow stem on which the bird sat back onto the spindle.

"There. Now, you have to be careful with it," he admonished the boys, and they nodded their heads emphatically. "It's not on there as securely as it was—it needs to be soldered, but it'll do."

He closed the lid, then wound the key and opened the box again. The bright little bird popped up and a tinkling tune played. The twins gazed at him in awe, then began to laugh and jump about wildly.

Thisbe's heart swelled within her chest as she looked at Desmond, who was watching the twins indulgently and chuckling. Kyria's callers, on the other hand, stiffly took their leave. Thisbe looked at Kyria. "Sorry. I'm afraid we ran your guests off."

Kyria gave a lazy flap of her hand. "Pfft. They're deadly dull, anyway."

Somewhere in the distance there was the sound of sharp voices raised. "Uh-oh. That sounds like Grandmother."

Kyria nodded and stood up. "Alex, Con, I'm afraid it's time to face the reckoning. You know you shouldn't explore in your grandmother's room." They nodded, coming down from their high spirits. "You need to explain what happened and give her back the box and tell her you're sorry." Kyria took the box from Desmond, and reluctantly the twins fell in with her. She turned back to Thisbe. "I think they may be coming downstairs. If I were you, I'd take this chance to escape."

Thisbe nodded and jumped to her feet. "Desmond, I think it's time you had a tour of the garden."

BUNDLED UP IN their coats, they went out the rear door. Here, in the middle of the city, lay a small park. There was a formal garden just beyond the house, and beyond that trees and grass all the way to the far wall. No doubt, in summer, when everything was green, it was a beautiful sight. Desmond drew in a sharp breath. It was a trifle hard to believe they were still in the city.

Thisbe tucked her hand in his arm, and they started down the central path. Desmond knew it would be hard for him to feel any more perfect than he did right now. Beside him, Thisbe said, "You were very good with the twins."

He laughed. "They're dynamos. Sharp as tacks, too. Did you see how they followed what I was doing to the music box?"

"Yes. There are those who say they're troublemakers, but they aren't, really. They're just lively and curious."

"And quick," Desmond added. "You think they'll be scientists or scholars?"

Thisbe laughed. "Neither would be exciting enough for them, I'm afraid."

They walked along in silence for a few moments. Thisbe's hand slid down his arm to take his hand. Desmond glanced at her, smiling, and laced his fingers through hers. "Desmond…thank you for coming to call this afternoon."

His hand tightened around hers. "I couldn't have stayed away if I'd wanted to. It was so startling last night that I could hardly think. I can't help but see the barriers between us, but that doesn't change how I feel about you." He gazed down at her, his voice serious. "Thisbe, I don't see you any differently because I know who you are. You are just as you have been—beautiful and intelligent and strong. But others…"

"They'll talk, perhaps." Thisbe shrugged. "But everyone already talks about us. They call us the Mad Morelands."

"Mad? But why?"

"Because we are different. We do odd things. Think odd things. Worse, we say what we think. But, you see, we are so very odd that we don't care what others think. Mother offends a great number of people. They say I'm peculiar because I mess about with chemicals. They say I blow things up—but it isn't as if I do that regularly. There was that explosion I told you about."

"And the one that set fire to your draperies," he reminded her.

"But that's only two."

Desmond laughed. "Such a trifling number."

"What I'm saying is that I don't care what society says about me."

"But what about your family. What they would say?"

"You can't be serious. You've met my mother."

"Yes," he agreed. "The duchess was very kind. Tactful."

Thisbe snorted. "*Tactful* is the last word anyone would use to describe my mother. She was herself, Desmond. That's all. She liked you. If she had not, she would have been the same with you as she was with Kyria's callers. Polite, not saying much. Besides, you saved the Greats from Grandmother's wrath. Mother would like you for that alone."

Her grandmother. The dowager duchess. Desmond's mind skittered away from that subject. "Then you think… it will be all right if I call on you again?"

"Yes, of course. It's far better than the British Museum." She turned down another path, taking them away from sight of the house. "I must apologize, too, for not telling you about my family. It was wrong—I shouldn't have kept Papa's title hidden. It was just…everyone acts so differently when they know who I am. They become formal and distant or horribly ingratiating. Women suddenly want to befriend me and introduce me to their friends and invite me to everything. Men tend to flee or act as if I'm someone different. Kyria says she cannot tell which men actually like her and which just want her money and connections."

"Thisbe, I would never—"

"I know." She smiled at him. "I never thought that of you. But I was afraid my name would color your perception of me. It's hard enough for me to be accepted as a scientist because I'm a woman. I think it would be impossible if everyone knew I was a duke's daughter. I feared that you might think me just a dilettante like Mrs. Burdett-Coutts."

"No. No. I know you're not just dabbling."

"I realize that now, but I couldn't be sure of that when I met you."

"I understand. You're right. I admit I wouldn't have felt so at ease with you if I had known the truth. One hates to contradict Shakespeare, but I fear there's a great deal in a name."

She stopped and turned to him. "But I should have told you before now. Once I knew you better. But by then, it was awkward. I was afraid you would be angry with me because I'd kept it a secret, which is a very foolish reason, I suppose, for continuing a deception. But I was afraid of losing you."

"Thisbe." He took both her hands, gazing down into her eyes. "You won't lose me. I have no idea what's going to happen, and I fear what *could* happen, but not seeing you again is not an option."

Thisbe smiled and leaned in to kiss his cheek. Desmond turned his head, and his mouth met hers. For a time, all else ceased to exist. He had no worries, no uncertainties, no entangling guilt. There was only the softness of her body in his arms, the touch of her mouth on his. Their kiss turned hungrier, deeper, and he pressed her body into his.

There was an awareness somewhere deep in the back of his brain that he shouldn't be doing this, that it was dangerous, inappropriate, absolutely mad, but he ignored it, too caught up in the pleasure to pay attention to anything else.

When finally he lifted his head, his eyes glazed, his heart pumped, the blood running like fire through his veins. He gazed down into Thisbe's face, as softened and dazed as his own, and realized how close he was to losing all sense. His arms loosened around her, then fell away as he took a step back, drawing in a deep breath as he tried to quiet the rampaging hunger inside him.

"I'm sorry. I shouldn't— We mustn't." For the first time, he glanced around them. They were out of sight of the house, thank heavens, though Lord knew anyone could have walked up on them at any time in the last few minutes. He had been too wrapped up to notice. That would certainly have put an end to his hopes with Thisbe. No parents, no matter how easygoing or egalitarian, would look kindly on a man seducing their daughter in the garden. "I—I should go."

"Very well." Thisbe nodded, looking no more inclined to leave this moment than he was. "When will you come back?"

"Tomorrow," he replied instantly. "No, I suppose that wouldn't be correct, would it?"

"It sounds fine to me," Thisbe replied. "You can meet the rest of my family." She glanced in the direction of the house. "I suspect my grandmother will be downstairs now. I won't subject you to her just yet, or you might not return."

Again he felt a frisson of unease at the mention of her grandmother. Thisbe had been apologizing for not telling him who she was, and all the while he was hiding something worse. But he quailed at the thought of revealing to her that he was a thief—or, at least, a would-be thief. He would feel ashamed before her gaze, small.

And after she'd just said that people always wanted something from her! Even if he were able to convince her that he had not known of her connection to the dowager duchess, Thisbe would surely have doubts about his goals. She would be bound to wonder if he really wanted her, or her grandmother's possession.

So he said nothing when she linked her arm through

his and led him back up the path. Skirting the garden, Thisbe went around to the gate in the wall he had noticed last night and opened it. She turned to him, and he bent to kiss her goodbye, then kissed her again.

This wasn't helping him leave. He pulled back reluctantly and took a step away. The way she was looking at him didn't help, either. "I'll see you tomorrow."

She nodded, and finally, with an effort of will, he whipped around and left the yard. He couldn't resist, however, looking back. She was standing in the open gate watching him, and that sight alone was enough to warm him even in the January chill.

CHAPTER TEN ·

DESMOND WAS IN no hurry as he walked to Professor Gordon's laboratory. Even though he had told the man that he wouldn't break into the house last night, he suspected that Gordon would be hoping he had. The professor would want a report from him—and he would be anything but pleased when Desmond told him the whole thing was off.

Gordon was waiting, clearly eager to talk to him, but fortunately the presence of the other students kept him from running to question Desmond. Desmond sat down at his table and began to work, but between thinking of Thisbe and feeling Gordon's intent stare, it was difficult to concentrate. His tablemate, Carson, glanced over at him curiously once or twice. Desmond endeavored to look as if he were deep in thought.

He could not hold off his mentor all evening, however, and after the others left, Gordon hurried to lock the door, then swung around to Desmond. "What did you find?"

Desmond took a breath. "I'm not doing it."

"What?"

"I can't. The dowager duchess is Thisbe Moreland's grandmother. It's the house where Thisbe lives. I can't break into it and steal something."

Gordon stared at him blankly. "Who in the name of heaven is Thisbe?"

"Aside from being the Duke of Broughton's daughter, she's…a friend of mine."

"A friend?"

"Yes. I met her at a lecture. She's a wonderful person, and her family, what I've seen of it, are nice people. Good people. I cannot steal from them."

"You know the duke? The dowager duchess?" Gordon's eyebrows soared upward. "Desmond…is this a jest?"

"No, I haven't met the duke or the dowager duchess, but I met the duchess and three of Thisbe's siblings."

His mentor continued to stare at him. "I can't believe it."

"I was rather taken aback myself," Desmond said drily. "I was lurking outside the house—which, I must tell you, is unbelievably enormous. No one could ever search all through it. As I stood there, thinking what a hopeless task it was, Thisbe came out the door."

Gordon plopped down on a nearby stool, looking stunned.

"Professor, I know how much this means to you, but—"

His mentor brightened. "But that means…you don't have to steal it, do you? You can simply ask the duchess for it."

"Ask her to give me the Eye? I don't think so."

"Why not? You're a friend of the woman's granddaughter—she won't feel the same as she did about handing it to a stranger. You can talk to her, explain how important it is. Tell her we need to study it."

"The dowager duchess will have no reason to give it to me. She knows nothing about me."

"Then have your friend ask her. The woman wouldn't refuse her own granddaughter now, would she?"

"Professor, I can't. Miss Moreland will think I had ulterior motives, that I cultivated our friendship to get to the Eye, and I won't have her thinking that. I refuse to ask her for anything. I'm sorry. If you want me to leave the study, I understand, but I—"

"I don't want you to leave. I want you to get the bloody Eye. You don't have to ask her. You could simply bring your friend by the laboratory one day. Let her see the work we're doing. I'll talk to her, explain how important it is. You said you met her at a lecture—she must have some respect for science."

"She more than respects it. She *is* a scientist."

"A girl?"

"Yes, she is a woman. That's not the point. Miss Moreland is not likely to be swayed by your argument. She doesn't believe in this sort of thing."

"But we can show her, convince her."

"I doubt you can, but that doesn't matter. If I bring her here, and you start talking about the Eye, she'll suspect that I have been using her to get the Eye. And if I did that, I *would* be using her, using our…friendship. I won't do that."

"Blast it, boy, think!" Gordon's face reddened. "This is bigger than you or some silly friendship. This is important. It's vital I have the Eye. You know what this means to me, to you, to all of us. This is the chance of a lifetime, and you're throwing it away for some girl?"

"She's not just 'some girl,'" Desmond retorted hotly.

"What? You think you love this girl? Are you daft?"

"I may be," Desmond admitted.

Gordon gaped at him. "Do you think there's a chance in this world that you can marry into nobility? Not just nobility, a duke! Why don't you aim for a royal?"

Desmond flushed. "I didn't say I thought I could marry her. I know that's foolish."

"Foolish doesn't even begin to describe it," Gordon went on harshly. "Have some sense, lad. Even if you can convince her for some mad reason to do it, her father would never allow it. If you tried to elope, he'd send men after you in a second, and even if you were lucky enough to escape with your hide still intact, the marriage would be annulled. You have no money. No name. Your father a crim—"

Desmond looked up sharply at him. Gordon knew about his father?

Gordon had the grace to break off his words. He stepped back, crossing his arms. "Are you really this selfish, Desmond? This unreasonable? To deny science the opportunity to study the Eye? To use it? Just because you are suddenly head over heels about some girl!"

Desmond rose to face him. "Yes. I think I am exactly that selfish and unreasonable. Perhaps you're right, and the study of the Eye is more important than my heart. Perhaps I should care more for scientific discovery than I do for Thisbe. But the truth is, I don't. I am not giving up Thisbe."

Grabbing his jacket, he turned and started for the door.

"Wait! Desmond, please." Gordon hurried after him, adopting a wheedling tone. "All right, I accept that you feel you cannot ask for it, that it would break her trust in you. But, surely, while you're there, you could look around for it a bit. Couldn't you?"

"So that you could steal it?"

"No, no," Gordon said hastily. "Not to steal it. You are probably right—it would be impossible. But to just…see it." His eyes took on the glow of a visionary. "Desmond, think…to know that it actually exists, to know what it looks like. You could describe it, draw it. Maybe we'd be able to replicate it. But even if we can't… I have been looking for this my whole life—I want to have proof that I haven't been chasing a fool's dream. Not to show to others, just for me. Even if no one ever acknowledges it, I would know in my heart that I hadn't wasted my life, that I hadn't ruined my reputation for nothing."

Guilt and sorrow twisted Desmond's gut. How could he destroy the man's last hope? All he asked was for Desmond to keep an eye out for the instrument in Thisbe's house. Gordon wasn't suggesting Desmond steal it or ransack the place. Perhaps it was in plain view. Perhaps the dowager duchess even carried it on her person.

Desmond sighed, already regretting his words, but was unable to say anything else. "Very well. I will look for it."

THISBE HAD NOT really considered the problem of her grandmother until after Desmond came to call. Desmond was bound to meet her; she could hardly introduce him to the rest of the family without introducing him to her grandmother, as well. For one thing, the dowager duchess frequently served as chaperone for Kyria's afternoon callers—causing the less brave of them to cease calling. Thisbe feared that the woman would have an even worse effect on Desmond.

She could, however, at least avoid the meeting for as long as possible. For the next few days, whenever she heard her grandmother's voice, Thisbe managed to whisk Desmond out to the garden for a walk or remember that she needed to make a trip to the bookstore—Olivia was always able to provide an excuse for that—and Desmond, of course, accompanied her.

Another time, when she heard the strident tones of the dowager duchess on the stairs, she took Desmond to see her father's collections room. Desmond had been happy to go, of course; though he knew next to nothing at all about Greek and Roman art, he was, as always, eager to learn, and they spent a pleasant hour meandering about, talking about potsherds, designs and the various periods of ancient art and architecture. Indeed, the duke was so impressed by the young man—though he called him Donald—that a few days later he happily hauled off Desmond to inspect his latest shipment.

One afternoon, Thisbe had been delayed at the apothecary shop and arrived home late. A look in the red salon yielded nothing but her grandmother and Kyria. Nor did a quick peek into her father's study or the music room, where Olivia was reading. Finally she tracked down Desmond to the twins' suite of rooms. Desmond sat cross-legged on the floor with the two boys, a toy lying in pieces before them.

"You see, this spring is what you wind up with the key, and—" Desmond looked up and beamed. "Thisbe! I was just showing the Greats how this clockwork toy worked."

"Thisbe! Thisbe!" Con ran over to take her hand and pull her over. "Dezment is taking it apart." Desmond was quickly becoming their favorite visitor.

"So I see." Thisbe looked down at the collection of parts. "I hope this isn't one of Grandmother's toys."

Both the twins' eyes grew large as they shook their heads emphatically. "It's Livvy's," Alex assured her.

Thisbe kneeled down on the floor beside them and said somewhat dubiously, "I presume you can put all this back together?"

"Oh, sure," Desmond told her cheerfully. "I was showing them how the gears work." He released the key and held out the mechanism. "See, boys, how the spring makes this gear turn, and mesh with this one, and it's connected to this other little spring that moves the leg up and down."

The boys watched, enthralled.

"It looks rather gruesome moving that way without part of its leg," Thisbe commented.

Desmond chuckled. "Ah, but that's part of the attraction for little boys."

"Gr-u-uesome," Con repeated, drawing out the word, and Alex was inspired to jump up and imitate the jerky march of the toy. Con joined in, and the two marched across the length of the room.

Desmond began to deftly fit the pieces back together. Thisbe sat down beside him, her shoulder close to his. She liked to watch his long, agile fingers move; it did something strange to her insides that was altogether pleasurable. She had never really paid attention to men's hands before, but she had decided that Desmond's were undoubtedly the nicest.

"How did you wind up here with the twins?" she asked.

"Your mother was downstairs with them when I arrived. Apparently the replacement nanny didn't last but three days."

"Oh, dear."

"Yes. The duchess was less than pleased. She decided to talk to the agency in person."

"Unlucky them."

Desmond snorted. "I'd say. So I said I would stay with the boys. It sounded like Kyria had visitors, so we came up here."

"Wise choice."

"You know…" Desmond hesitated long enough that Thisbe turned her head to look at him. "Perhaps I shouldn't put my oar in. I don't know if she's the sort your mother would want."

"Who? The sort of what?"

"Nanny. For the boys."

"You know someone?"

"It's my landlord's sister. Her husband's dead and she had to come live with her brother, but I know she'd rather have some independence. She told me once the only skills she had were cooking and cleaning, and her brother doesn't want her to hire out as a servant, says it would reflect badly on him. But I thought…a nanny wouldn't be the same as scrubbing floors now, would it? She's good with children—she raised three lads of her own, and I've seen her with her brother's youngest. She likes little ones."

"You think she could hold up to the twins?" Thisbe looked over at the two boys, who were now climbing onto the low schoolroom table and jumping off.

"She's not old. I think she married young. I'm not sure how fast she is, but she's strong. I've seen her shifting furniture about in one of the other flats. She's not educated, of course, but she speaks well enough. But I didn't know. I thought your mother might not want anyone that didn't come from an agency."

"I imagine Mother would value your recommendation more than that of an agency. After all, she trusts you enough she left Alex and Con in your care. There are any number of people whom she would not trust to look after them…probably including my father."

Desmond laughed. "The duke might forget they were there."

"Exactly." She smiled to herself. "I remember following Papa around when I was little. Theo would get bored and slope off. He was more like the Greats, always running everywhere. But I liked to listen to Papa talk. I didn't know half of what he talked about, but I liked the way he talked to me, as if I were grown-up. And his crates and pots and books were more interesting than Mother's meetings."

Alex jumped up from the floor and turned to look toward the doorway, like a pointer-spotting game. Con, standing on the table and about to launch himself after his brother, swiveled around to follow his brother's gaze. Then, almost as one, they cried, "Granna!" Con jumped down and they took off for the door.

"Oh, dear." Thisbe looked toward the door. "Perhaps she won't come in here."

In the hall there were cries of "Granna! Come see! Come see!"

Thisbe grimaced. There was no escape now. She swung around to Desmond. "I don't think we can avoid her. I have to warn you—"

"You think she'll disapprove of me."

"No. Well, I mean, yes, she probably will, but that doesn't matter. Her approval isn't necessary to me. She doesn't approve of my mother, either…or any number of people, for that matter. The problem is one never knows what Grandmother will say or do. It's not only that she's critical and judgmental—she's also peculiar."

"Peculiar?" His mouth quirked up at the corner. "I thought that was something the Morelands took pride in."

"Not to the extent that we claim to talk to ghosts."

"The dowager duchess does?" Desmond asked calmly.

"Yes. Her dead husband. Her mother. She told us the other day that she communes with the first duke's spirit in the drawing room."

"I shan't be bothered. I'm accustomed to people who believe in spirits, after all." He unfolded his long limbs and stood up, reaching down a hand to Thisbe.

"Desmond, please—please don't mention your professor or his study."

"I would think she would have no problem with that, if she believes as he does."

"One never knows with her." Thisbe glanced over her shoulder toward the door. The dowager duchess's cane had begun to thump down the hall again, punctuating the twins' excited chatter. "She might declare it all folderol because he doesn't agree with her. Or, worse, she'll want to throw in her lot with him. No matter what a thorn she is in one's side sometimes, she is my grandmother, and I can't bear to have her taken advantage of."

"He wouldn't—"

"Please."

"Very well. If you wish it, I won't say anything."

"Thank you." Thisbe breathed a sigh of relief. Now all she had to worry about was warding off whatever way her grandmother would choose to insult Desmond.

"Who fixed it? Who is this fellow Damon?" Her grandmother's voice boomed from outside the room.

"He's Thisbe's," Con answered simply.

"Thisbe's? Thisbe's what?" Thisbe's grandmother asked as she stepped in the door, her face turned down to the little boys tugging on her skirts. Thisbe's mother entered the room behind them.

"Dezment!" The twins pointed triumphantly at Desmond.

The dowager duchess raised her head and saw Thisbe and Desmond standing in the middle of the room. She came to a dead stop and stared. "Good God in heaven!"

"Grandmother," Thisbe began, starting toward her.

Her grandmother paid no attention to Thisbe. Her gaze was riveted on Desmond. Flinging out her hand to point at him like Jophiel sending Adam and Eve from the garden, the dowager duchess proclaimed, "For your love, my granddaughter will die."

CHAPTER ELEVEN

A SHIVER RAN down Thisbe's spine. "Grandmother!"

"Duchess! Really!" Emmeline said, eyes flashing. "That is the outside of enough. I do my best to pay you the proper respect, but I will not countenance you insulting visitors in my home."

Thisbe turned to Desmond. The blood had run out of his face, and he was staring at the dowager duchess in a horror equal to that lady's own. Even the twins had been silenced by their grandmother's words and they stood staring up at her with jaws dropped. The boys turned toward Emmeline, eyes wide, and moved closer together. "Mama?"

"Come here." The duchess smiled at them, reaching her hands out toward the boys. "It's all right. Nobody is going to hurt Thisbe. Your grandmother was only playing a little joke." She directed her blazing gaze at the dowager duchess.

Cornelia sent her a haughty look in return. "What I see is not in my power to control, Emmeline. The man has the cloud of death all over him."

Emmeline, eyes still glittering, said tightly, "Thisbe, why don't you and Mr. Harrison take the twins outside? The duchess and I must talk. In private."

Thisbe jumped to obey, grabbing Desmond's arm and pulling him past her grandmother and out the door. The twins scurried after them. Thisbe didn't like the look on

Desmond's face. "Here." She scooped up Alex and thrust him at Desmond. "You take Alex. I've got Con."

She lifted the boy to her hip and started grimly toward the stairs, but behind her she could hear the dowager duchess as she said, "If you don't care for your daughter's safety, Emmeline, I do." After that, the door shut firmly behind them.

Thisbe went down the stairs and out the back door, moving so quickly she forgot their coats. The twins, rarely deterred by the cold, wriggled down and took off. A moment later, a footman ran out, carrying coats. Then there was a lively game of chase, with the footman, Thisbe and Desmond chasing Alex and Con around the yard.

By the time they caught the pair and fastened them into their coats, Thisbe and Desmond had recovered from the shock of the dowager duchess's words. The exhausted footman retreated to the house, and Thisbe turned to Desmond. "I am so sorry."

Desmond smiled faintly as he draped her cloak around her shoulders. "Well, you warned me…"

"Yes, but that was outrageous even for Grandmother."

"I did feel as if someone walked over my grave." Desmond's tone was light, but he looked away from her as he pulled on his own coat, and Thisbe suspected that his shiver was not entirely due to the cold.

"It gave me a bit of start, too, but, of course, it's all nonsense."

"Of course."

"None of the things Grandmother says about her 'ability' have any validity."

"Has she ever predicted someone's death before?"

"No." Thisbe decided not to mention the puppy whose demise her grandmother had foreseen; after all, it was weeks later that the poor little thing ran out into the road and was struck by a wagon. "It's sheer nonsense." She took his arm and said earnestly, "I hope this will not make you avoid this house."

"I can brave your grandmother. Hopefully she won't bar the door to me."

"I guarantee that won't happen. I think she and Mother are about to have a rather titanic clash."

"Formidable as the dowager duchess is, my money would be on your mother."

He took her hand, and they strolled through the garden, keeping a watchful eye on Con and Alex. It would be all right. Wouldn't it? Thisbe stole a glance up at Desmond. He seemed to be taking her grandmother's prediction in stride, as he had everything else to do with her family. Still, she couldn't help remembering how white his face had gone or the stricken look in his eyes. Nor could she rid her mind completely of that puppy. It had scared her at the time, but she reasoned that away. It was just…she wished the dowager duchess's vision hadn't included that open gate.

HE DIDN'T BELIEVE IT, Desmond told himself as he strode toward the laboratory. It was all superstitious nonsense. He was willing, if it could be proved, to accept that spirits still hovered in this plane of existence, but the idea that people could foresee future events was going too far. It was akin to believing in fairies and elves, or walking around a ladder, or not taking a path because a black cat had crossed it.

It didn't matter what the dowager duchess had predicted or what his aunt had told him. Predictions, ill omens and curses did not belong in the realm of science.

It was ludicrous to think that he could harm Thisbe, and how could love kill anyone, anyway?

The dowager duchess simply did not want him around Thisbe and, given her peculiarities, this was the way she chose to frighten him away. She couldn't know about him; she couldn't know his aunt's fears. Besides, it wasn't as if *everyone* he loved had died. Was it? There was the vicar, after all, of whom he was quite fond, and he was still hale and hearty. So was Professor Gordon. Perhaps it was only women.

No. He refused to enter that quagmire of ignorance and fear. The dowager duchess simply wanted him gone. He could scarcely blame her. He wasn't a suitable marriage prospect for a lady. He was glad there would be a new lecture this week at the Covington, where he could meet Thisbe instead of calling on her.

When he walked into the laboratory, he saw that Professor Gordon was watching him intently from the other side of the room, waiting, as always, for Desmond to bring him news of the Eye. It was no surprise when Gordon asked him to stay after the others. That made the third time in a week; it was little wonder that the others glanced back at him curiously as they left.

"Have you made any progress?" Gordon was at his table as soon as the door closed.

"No, sir. I'm not at all sure it's possible."

Gordon's face fell, which caused Desmond a twinge of guilt. His excuses were valid, but the truth was Desmond hadn't wanted to search for it. "The duchess is hardly likely to use the thing in plain sight of a stranger. How am I to go about looking for it? There's always someone with me—I cannot simply go wandering about the house alone. The place is enormous. I haven't even seen all the rooms on the ground floor, let alone the upstairs."

"You must try," the other man said urgently. "Desmond, don't you realize how important this is?"

"Yes, sir, I know how eager you are for me to find out something about it. But it's difficult. I didn't even meet the dowager duchess until today."

"What is she like? Would she be open to reason on the matter?"

"I doubt it. She's… Well, she's odd." He couldn't bring himself to tell his mentor what the woman had said to him today. "She's antagonistic, even hostile. I gather from what the others say about her that everyone has difficulty dealing with her."

"What am I going to tell Mr. Wallace?" Gordon moaned, shoving his hands back into his hair and beginning to pace.

The man looked so woebegone that Desmond offered what little bit of information he had gleaned. "She wears a belt, a chatelaine, around her waist with all sorts of things hanging from it. One of the things on a chain is a set of spectacles. I thought— I wondered if that could be the Eye. If perhaps the spectacles had some sort of unique lens." Desmond tried to recall whether Thisbe's grandmother had held the spectacles to her eyes when she made her prediction this afternoon. Could it be that she had used the Eye to view death hovering over him?

Gordon swung back around, looking hopeful again. "That could be it. You must get a look at those spectacles. Is it hung with a ribbon? You could snip it off."

Desmond sighed. "I'm unlikely to be that close to the woman. But I will try to get a closer look. Sir, surely Mr. Wallace will not be unreasonable. He must realize what a difficult task this is. He tried to deal with the woman himself—he knows what she's like. He is aware how little knowledge we have about the Eye. He can't expect us to be able to find it."

Gordon snorted. "Wealthy men don't bother with the reasons—they want results. The dowager duchess has been here for over a week. He wants to know why we haven't located it. I can only put him off with promises for so long."

"You promised him you would get it?" Desmond's eyebrows soared upward.

"He was demanding answers. I had to tell him something. Desmond, you must talk to her. Explain."

"I cannot," Desmond said flatly. "Sir, please don't ask this of me."

Gordon drew back, looking hurt. "I was certain you would help me. That you cared about…all this." He swept his hand around the room.

"I do care. I've devoted a great deal of time to it, tried countless arrangements of lenses and mirrors, different crystals. I work on it every day. But this isn't a matter of hard work."

"No, it's a matter of disloyalty," Gordon snapped.

Desmond drew back as if he'd slapped him. "Sir. I have never been disloyal to you. I have always done my best to repay what you've done for me, to work the hardest and the longest, to be the most thorough."

"What else would I call it when you refuse to do the one thing I desperately need? Wallace will leave me, take away all his funds. I'll never be able to prove my theories. Without the Eye, I'm doomed."

"Sir, I'm sure it's not so dire a situation." Desmond had never seen the man like this. "You'll see."

"No, I won't see." Gordon's voice was stained with bitterness. He sighed and walked away, taking out his handkerchief to clean his spectacles.

Desmond watched him. What a tangle this all was. It was sheer happenstance, cosmic bad luck, that had landed the problem of the Eye in his lap at just the same moment he had met Thisbe. Perhaps his aunt was right, and he had been cursed from birth.

He had only made everything worse by not telling the whole story to Thisbe as soon as he realized who she was. Maybe she would have believed him if he told her that he had no idea of her identity. After all, she had concealed that from him—how was he to know?

But he had been so frantic to keep Thisbe from suspecting that he had deceived her that he had created even more deception. If she was to find out about the Eye now, after all this time had gone by without Desmond telling her, her reaction would be even worse. He had been in her home, met her family; he had kissed her, held her—all the while keeping this secret. What else could she think but that he had also been deceiving her from the first?

When she told him today about her fears that her grandmother would be taken advantage of, it had been like a knife to his ribs. She would despise him if he told her the truth now. He would lose her forever, and that was not a risk Desmond was willing to take.

As SOON AS Desmond left, Thisbe herded the twins back inside despite their protests. In the twins' rooms, she found one of the upstairs maids, looking glum. Clearly, she had been assigned the task of looking after the boys. Thisbe handed them over and went to her grandmother's bedchamber. It wasn't surprising to find the dowager issuing contradictory orders to her hapless maid as the unfortunate woman emptied the drawers and cabinets.

"Grandmother, what are you doing?" Thisbe was sure she knew the answer.

The duchess drew herself up to her fullest height, tilting her chin up, and proclaimed, "I am leaving this house, my home, as *she* wishes."

It was never a good sign when Emmeline became *"she."*

"I am sure Mother didn't tell you to leave Broughton House."

"I know when I am not welcome," Cornelia replied darkly.

Thisbe turned to the duchess's personal maid. "I'd like to talk to my grandmother alone, please."

"Yes'm." The woman bobbed a grateful curtsy and hurried out of the room before the dowager duchess could issue a countercommand.

"Really, Thisbe, you have no right to be ordering Goodwin about."

"Yes, I know. But would you rather have the servants privy to our family disagreements?"

Cornelia gave a little moue of distaste. "Well, what do you have to say? More of *her* babble about equality?"

"No. I have no interest in interfering in your long-standing disagreement with Mother. But I am asking you not to leave the house in high dudgeon over it."

Thisbe was certain that her grandmother had no intention of departing; she hadn't even had her trunks brought down from the attic. A threatened departure happened at least once every visit. Cornelia enjoyed creating a disturbance, blaming Emmeline and being pleaded with to stay. That task had once fallen to Thisbe's father, but in recent years, Thisbe had taken it off the duke's shoulders. If her pleas didn't work, she would send in Theo to cajole their grandmother.

"I am sure my mother had no intention of tossing you

out of the house. You know how it will distress Papa. He so dislikes for you and Mother to disagree."

"Of course he does. He's a good son. But he is under *her* control."

"Mother does not control Papa. But he loves her very much, just as he loves you, and if you leave, it will make him terribly unhappy."

"I will not have that woman giving me orders."

"What did Mother say?" Thisbe knew her mother did her best to be pleasant to the dowager duchess, but sometimes her temper got the best of her. "Did she tell you to leave?"

"She told me she would not allow your guests to be insulted in that way," Cornelia said, indignation rising as she remembered the conversation. "She said she expected me to be polite and not say wicked things to innocent young men."

"I'm sure what she meant was that she was shocked you said something so untoward, given that she knows you are a very proper woman. One who is always appropriate and courteous."

"Ha! As if a country squire's daughter knows more about proper behavior than I. My father—"

"Yes, Grandmother, I know." Thisbe found her own patience wearing thin. "Your father was a count, and he was a very important man. Your mother's line was equally highborn. But do you think your mother and father would have approved of your rudeness?"

"I wasn't rude! I was truthful."

"Sometimes one cannot be both truthful and polite. As I remember, *you* told me that when I asked Lady Montgomery why she had killed squirrels to wear on her arms."

Cornelia chuckled at the memory. "It was a mink, I

believe, but that stole was a ghastly mistake. Poor Dorothy had no taste whatsoever, I'm afraid."

"But she was your friend, and I shouldn't have spoken so."

"Yes, you're right." Cornelia narrowed her eyes at Thisbe. "But don't try to cozen me, young lady. It's not the same thing at all. I am concerned for your safety. There's no room for manners when my granddaughter is threatened."

"Grandmother..." Thisbe kneeled by the duchess's chair, gazing up at her with her most pleading expression. "Mr. Harrison is not a threat to me. He's a kind, wonderful man, and I'm certain he would never hurt anyone. You should have seen how good he was with the Greats."

"Those monkeys." Cornelia's eyes twinkled and her mouth curved up, belying her words of disapproval.

"Yes, and he had them quiet and interested. He's very intelligent and educated and—"

"Pshaw!" The duchess waved off Thisbe's words. "I'm not talking about that. I'm talking about lineage. He's not one of us, Thisbe. I could see it at once."

Thisbe gritted her teeth. "That doesn't make him a bad man. It doesn't mean he's going to *kill* me."

"Mmm." Her grandmother tilted her head to one side, considering. "I didn't say he would kill you—I didn't see that. But I saw that you would die because of him. It's an entirely different thing, but the outcome is the same. You must stay away from this young man."

"Grandmother...there's no way you could know that."

"I know you scoff at my abilities, just like the others. You shouldn't. Nor should Olivia. Sadly, I don't believe Kyria has the talent. Most likely it's that red hair."

"Red hair! Of all the nonsensical—" Thisbe caught

herself. Why was she arguing about the mechanics of something she didn't believe in?

"You know that I have the power. You've witnessed it. Remember the puppy?"

"Yes, I remember the puppy. You said Rajah would die."

"You see?" Her grandmother leaned back with a self-satisfied smile. "I saw death on him. I saw that gate."

"But it was a month after you predicted it. And it wasn't even the same gate. You saw the garden gate and it was the one to the road."

"Those are minor details. It was an open gate, and I saw the mark of death upon him. I asked my mother about it that night, and she said I was right."

Thisbe refrained from pointing out that the opinion of a ghost was not the most accurate proof of a vision. "What exactly did you see when you looked at Desmond?"

"There was a dark aura clinging to him, a veritable black cloud of death. And it was linked to you. It was oozing across the space between you and touching your arm. Clearly, in the future, it would overwhelm you."

"But you didn't see me die, did you? There was no knife or gun or any vision of the act."

"I cannot command these things, Thisbe. They simply come to me—they're drawn by my unique power. Sometimes I catch only glimpses, things too vague to even mention. I saw Charles Berkwyler on a horse, but I didn't know what that meant. I thought it was quite frivolous, as they sometimes are. But less than a year later he died in a hunting accident." She gave Thisbe a meaningful look.

"But he was shot!"

"That's what I'm trying to explain. One has to interpret the meaning. Clearly, riding a horse had to do with hunting—Berkie was wild about the fox hunt. It meant that he died while hunting."

"Then couldn't the vision you had mean something else, too?" Thisbe argued. "Perhaps it doesn't mean death—it's sadness or loneliness or…something."

"It's death," Cornelia said flatly. "Why do you think black is the color of mourning? Even if it had been red or purple or pink, I would have known it meant death. It simply permeated the air."

"But you don't know that it means that I am going to die. Desmond told me that his mother died giving birth to him, so perhaps it means that he…*comes* from death. Or perhaps it was that I was fated to die early but Desmond has pulled it away from me. Or that I should be with him, that he is the person who can protect me."

Her grandmother shook her head sadly. "I can see that you are going to ignore my warning. You are bound and determined to let this fellow hang about, no matter what the consequences." She used her cane to push to her feet. "Clearly, your mother refuses to do anything to protect you. The two of you are so headstrong that you will insist on allowing him and his deadly aura to invade this house." The dowager duchess paused, tilting her head in the disconcerting way she had, then nodded. "Yes, I can see that."

"See what, Grandmother?" Thisbe rose to face her.

"The first duke has reminded me that I have a duty. It's very unusual for him to stray so far from the drawing room, you know, so it is of the utmost importance. I am the only one who realizes the danger. I cannot leave, no matter how poorly your mother treated me. I must remain to protect you."

"I'm glad." It was one of her grandmother's more innovative reasons to back down from one of her decisions. "But, please, promise me you will not be unkind to Desmond."

"I am never unkind. But I agree—I don't think it is the poor chap's fault. I won't shun him. After all, I must be with you to keep you from harm."

Thisbe nearly groaned at her grandmother's words. Perhaps she shouldn't have tried to mend the breach between the two duchesses. Well, she would just have to find a way to get around her grandmother.

Thisbe went to her laboratory; work usually soothed her. But today she had trouble keeping her mind on what she was doing. She was not disturbed by her grandmother's prediction. Thisbe didn't believe in portents or omens. However, the way her grandmother dwelled so much on death *was* disturbing. Not just the belief that she could converse with ghosts or her "visions" of impending death, but also her conversations with her friends. They were marbled with death—who had died unexpectedly, who was about to die, who ought to die but was stubbornly hanging on.

It hadn't struck her as odd before. After all, the dowager duchess was aging; she was bound to know many people who had died. That was something old women did, wasn't it? Sit about gossiping about their friends' illnesses and deaths?

But, really, when Thisbe thought about it, her grandmother wasn't *that* ancient. She and most of her circle were in their sixties. Surely, their peers weren't dropping all around them. And surely, no other woman her age went to *that* many funerals. It was as if the dowager duchess collected experiences with death.

The Moreland family had more than their fair share of peculiarities. But most of the time it was simply that they broke societal rules—like Aunt Penelope going off to France to be an opera singer, or Thisbe herself becoming a scientist, or Uncle Bellard's collection of tin soldiers. Such things were unusual, not insane. Talking to people who weren't there was a step beyond that.

The most disturbing thing was that incident with the dog. She would never forget the way the dowager duchess had bent down to pet Rajah a month before he died and said, "Poor dear, you'll be gone soon, won't you? They really should be more careful with that garden gate." Nor could Thisbe forget the icy chill that ran down her spine when she heard how Rajah had died.

It had been as eerie a moment as the time Thisbe caught her grandmother talking to an invisible person. As eerie as her foretelling Thisbe's death today.

It was all nonsense, of course. Her grandmother was prone to conveniently "interpret" her visions to mean whatever she wanted them to, like Mr. Berkwyler's hunting accident. The incident with Rajah had been coincidence. It wasn't uncommon that a dog might die because a gate had been left open.

Her grandmother had said that about Desmond because she thought him "not one of us." She didn't want Thisbe to fall in love with him. It had nothing to do with premonitions. Still, Thisbe couldn't stop thinking about that puppy.

CHAPTER TWELVE

THE FIRE COMPLETELY encircled her now, the air thick with black smoke. Her nose was filled with the acrid scent of it. She struggled to breathe. Only seconds had passed since they'd lit the fire, but already the wall of flames was so close to her that her skin burned even though the fire had not yet touched her. The logs popped and sizzled, sparks leaping out. It would be only moments before one of those sparks landed on her skirts, and then she, too, would go up in flames. Panicked and desperate, she tried to twist away, but she was held too tightly.

Through the smoke, she could see her enemy: his cold smile, the even colder eyes, his face set in satisfaction. He had won. She had failed. Even in her last desperate attempt to thwart him, she had failed. He'd ruined her. He'd sent her to this horrible death. All for power.

She hated him with all her heart. Hated him with as fierce a force as she loved her family. Her own power was diminished now. She could not prevent the agony that lay before her. But perhaps she had enough for vengeance. She dug deep inside, pulling on the dark that dwelled in her, feeding on her pain, her rage.

The sky grew darker, the wind picking up. She felt the dark hunger surge within her, the power rush through her veins. The wind tossed the flames, and they caught the hem of her skirts. In an instant her clothes were on fire. An unbearable pain seized her...

THISBE BOLTED UPRIGHT, pain stabbing through her leg. She reached down, gripping her calf. A cramp. That was all it was. She massaged the knotted muscle and ignored the smell of smoke that was still in her nostrils. She forcibly brought her nerves back into order, choked down the terror in her chest. Nothing had happened. It was just that blasted dream again.

It had been bad enough the first time; this one was even worse. Fire and pain in fuller measure. Had the cramp in her leg been the cause? But the cramp, painful as it was, didn't compare to the agony of her dream. Nor did it account for the sweat that covered her body or the throbbing in her feet.

Why was she having these terrible dreams of being burned at the stake? It was beyond bizarre. And who was that man? There had been such evil in his eyes. Thisbe shivered at the memory.

The cramp had eased a bit, and she slid out of bed to walk out the rest of it. But when her feet touched the ground, she let out a little grunt of pain. The bottoms of her feet were obviously sore. Lighting the candle, she sat down and lifted a foot to examine it.

Her jaw dropped and she stared in astonishment. There were three blisters on the sole of her foot.

THE NEXT DAY, there was a carriage in front of the laboratory when Desmond left work. As Desmond walked away, the door of the carriage opened behind him, and a voice called, "Harrison."

Desmond turned. A gentleman leaned out of the door of the carriage. He held a gold-knobbed cane in one hand, and he used it to gesture at Desmond to come closer. With an inward sigh, Desmond started toward the man. "Mr. Wallace."

"Please, get in," Wallace said politely. "Too cold to stand about outside."

"Yes, sir." What else could he say to the man who controlled the purse strings their project needed? Desmond climbed in and sat down facing the professor's patron.

Zachary Wallace was a thickset man with a square face and pugnacious jaw. Desmond had heard that the man had made his fortune in coal mining, though his build was more one of a miner than an owner. No aristocrat, he was nevertheless swimming in money. His suit was finely tailored, and a gold watch chain stretched across his waistcoat. He had a gold ring on one hand, and on the other an onyx signet ring. Rubies flashed in his stickpin and cuff links. Against the cold, he wore a heavy coat with dark fur decorating the collar, and kid leather gloves. A hot brick wrapped in cloth sat on the floor, warming his feet.

Desmond had been in his presence a few times when Wallace had come to the laboratory, but he had never spoken to the man. Now, as Wallace began to talk, beneath the patina of upper-class tones Desmond heard a hint of an underlying Yorkshire accent.

"I understand you have access to the Moreland household," Wallace began.

"I have become friends with them to some extent," Desmond replied carefully.

"Gordon tells me you have influence with the duchess's granddaughter. It's time you used that influence to acquire the Eye."

"Sir… I cannot trade on my friendship with her."

"Indeed?" Wallace quirked an eyebrow. "You could, I imagine, find it within you to do so if the reward was enough." Desmond shook his head, but the other man went on, "Gordon tells me that your affection for your mentor is not enough to sway you, nor is the duty that you owe him."

"I have great regard for Professor Gordon, and I am fully aware of all that he has done for me, but—"

"But it isn't as persuasive as gold," Wallace interrupted.

"That's not what I was going to say."

"Nevertheless, that is what is important. I am prepared to reward you for bringing me Annie Blue's Eye." He reached inside his jacket and pulled out a thin leather wallet, then began to extract bills from it. He fanned them out and held them toward Desmond.

Desmond couldn't deny a spurt of longing at the sight of the money Wallace offered. It would pay his rent for a year. But he shook his head.

"No? Perhaps you require more?" Wallace added another note, then another. "You could leave your job, devote yourself full-time to your research." He added another bill. "I might even consider funding some project of yours. I am, after all, devoted to expanding the horizons of knowledge."

"That is a very generous offer, sir, and I appreciate it. But I cannot. Truly, I cannot." Losing Thisbe's regard was not worth any amount of money. "I'm sorry."

Desmond reached for the handle, but Wallace blocked it with his cane. "You don't have to answer now. Think about it. Consider the advantages. We'll talk again."

Desmond nodded and bolted from the carriage. Head down, he hurried toward the omnibus stop, his chest tight. It wasn't easy to quell the pang of regret at refusing Wallace's offer. The thought of not having to worry about money, of being able to devote himself to science, was a wish answered, a dream come true. But Desmond would not use Thisbe.

When he reached the omnibus stop, he found that he had missed the vehicle. They ran infrequently this late at night, so he settled in for a long, cold wait. As he stood there, he felt a tingle run up the back of his neck, the sort of feeling he got when someone was watching him. He turned to look back down the dark street from which he'd just come, wondering if Wallace had followed him.

There was no sign of a carriage. And why would Wallace have come after him, anyway? Nor was there a sign of anyone on foot. Still, he looked up and down the street, as well as along the cross streets. He was the only person about except for a man hurrying in the opposite direction, huddled to himself in the chill.

Desmond was tired; no doubt that accounted for the odd feeling. He had been getting up at four every morning to work so that he could leave in time to call on Thisbe in the afternoon, and afterward he'd spend the evenings at the laboratory. It was beginning to wear on him.

The omnibus arrived, and he boarded. But later, after he stepped down from the vehicle and started toward his home, the peculiar sensation stirred in him again. He whipped around. There was no one there. Had he seen a flicker of movement out of the corner of his eye? Were the shadows slightly deeper in one of the doorways?

No. He was being absurd. But he picked up his pace, listening intently for the sound of footsteps besides his own. When he reached the outside stairs to his flat, he glanced back. There. He was certain there had been movement in that narrow alleyway between the buildings. He waited, alert. An instant later, a rat scurried out of the mouth of the alley, followed by another. Desmond relaxed. Just rats. No one was following him. There was no reason for anyone to follow him. He was starting at shadows. Next thing he knew, he'd be seeing the dead, like the dowager duchess. He would not consider what might have startled the rats out of the alley.

WHEN SHE FIRST saw the blisters on her feet, Thisbe turned cold inside, her brain incapable of formulating any thought other than that burns caused blisters. But as she applied ointment and wrapped strips of bandages around her feet, she remembered that only a day ago, she had worn a pair of new shoes. They must have rubbed against her skin in those places, creating blisters. She just hadn't noticed that they hurt until she'd jumped out of bed, hitting the floor with her bare feet.

It was a relief to have a rational explanation, and she had to smile at her own foolish, primitive fear in tying them to her nightmare. By the next morning, the sores were much improved, and she hardly noticed them. She was far too busy being annoyed with her grandmother.

The dowager duchess followed through on her promise to protect Thisbe, and she spent the next afternoon in the red sitting room with Thisbe, not even going upstairs for her usual "not a nap." All through Desmond's visit, Cornelia kept her basilisk stare on him. It was a distinct relief the next day for Thisbe to meet Desmond at the Covington Institute lecture, free from any prying eyes.

They both arrived early and were deep in conversation when a man stopped beside them. "Desmond. I wondered if you'd be attending this."

Thisbe looked over with interest at the speaker. He was a young man, fashionably dressed, with dark blond hair and blue eyes. He was smiling faintly, his eyes alight with a curiosity to match Thisbe's own. Was this one of Desmond's friends? A coworker? It occurred to her that Desmond had never introduced her to anyone.

Her gaze returned to Desmond, who was staring at the other man with a shocked expression. "Carson. I— What are you doing here?"

Carson lifted his eyebrows faintly at Desmond's abrupt tone, but he said mildly, "You recommended the last lecture so highly, I thought I would try this month's offering."

"I see. Well, I hope you enjoy it."

"I'm sure I shall. It's already quite entertaining." Carson sat down beside Desmond. "Hope you don't mind if I sit with you. It's always more enjoyable when one is with friends." Carson's bright blue eyes were sparkling with amusement as his gaze went from Desmond to Thisbe and back.

Finally Desmond said, "Miss Moreland, I'd like to introduce Carson Dunbridge. Carson, this is Miss Moreland."

"Miss Moreland." Carson's gaze sharpened. "What a pleasure to meet you." Thisbe offered her hand, and he leaned across Desmond to shake it. As he sat back in his seat, Carson cut his eyes toward Desmond and murmured, "Aren't you the sly one?"

Desmond tensed beside her. Obviously there was something going on here, though Thisbe wasn't sure what it was. Carson seemed pleasant, but Desmond had been noticeably reluctant to introduce them, and he still seemed none too pleased, remaining largely silent. Carson, on the other hand, seemed perfectly at ease, even amused. And what had he meant with that remark to Desmond that he was a sly one?

As they talked, it became clear that Carson, too, worked at Professor Gordon's laboratory. Thisbe had a growing suspicion that Desmond had not told any of his acquaintances about her. Perhaps that private amusement of Carson's was at finding out that Desmond had a secret female friend. As best Thisbe could tell from listening to her brothers and their friends, men got a strange enjoyment out of teasing one another about romantic conquests.

The teasing might explain Desmond's continued stiffness and silence, but she couldn't understand why he kept glancing at her uneasily or why his eyes turned stony when he looked at Carson. It occurred to her that she had seen similar behavior from time to time among Kyria's suitors. Could it be that Desmond was jealous?

It was silly, of course, and she should be annoyed that Desmond would have so little faith in her that he feared she would prefer some stranger over him. Still, it also gave her a certain odd sense of satisfaction.

When the lecture ended, Desmond jumped to his feet and announced, "I fear Carson and I have work that needs to be done back at the laboratory."

Thisbe tried to hide her disappointment. They usually lingered after a lecture and took a long walk, as well. She suspected that Desmond's reluctance had something to do with Carson, and she felt a flash of resentment at the man.

Carson, with a sardonic glance in Desmond's direction, agreed. "Yes, I fear we do. It was a pleasure to meet you, Miss Moreland." He directed a bow toward Thisbe and stepped back, looking toward Desmond expectantly. "I'll walk with you."

Desmond's jaw tightened, and the stony gaze turned more heated, but before he could speak, Thisbe said quickly, "You must allow me to drive you gentlemen to your laboratory."

"That's not necess—" Desmond began.

"Thank you—that's very kind," Carson said at the same moment. "We shall enjoy having the pleasure of your company for a few moments longer."

· Thisbe chose to ignore Desmond's response. Really, this was getting a bit irritating. She led the two men out to the Moreland carriage, and they climbed in, sitting down across from Thisbe. She couldn't help but wish Carson somewhere else. It would have been wonderful to be alone in the vehicle with Desmond. They could have held each other and shared a few kisses. As it was, they could only carry on a general conversation.

When they came to a stop, Thisbe looked out the window at the narrow, unprepossessing brown brick building. "This is your laboratory?"

"Yes, down those stairs," Desmond said.

Thisbe waited for an invitation, but Desmond said nothing more. Not being one to sit back and let others direct her course, Thisbe said, "Perhaps I could come in and see your laboratory."

"No." This time Desmond was swifter than Carson. "That is, um, Professor Gordon doesn't allow visitors."

Thisbe didn't miss the odd look Carson sent Desmond, but Carson agreed. "He's quite adamant about it. Thank you, Miss Moreland. It was a pleasure to meet you."

Carson climbed down and walked away from the carriage. Thisbe turned to Desmond to ask the reason for his strange behavior, but Desmond seized the opportunity to lean forward and kiss her, and Thisbe forgot all about taking him to task.

DESMOND LEFT THE carriage in a black mood, which the sweetness of Thisbe's kiss only partially erased. Perhaps his aunt was right; he *was* cursed. He had handled the whole matter terribly. He'd been tongue-tied, abrupt, even rude, and doubtlessly all it had accomplished was to raise questions in both Thisbe's and Carson's minds. Worse, he had barred Thisbe from coming into the laboratory.

She was bound to be insulted. What was he to say if she asked him to explain his behavior?

Carson waited for him at the bottom of the steps, leaning against the door frame, arms folded and one eyebrow quirked. He straightened from his lazy position and said, "What are you playing at, Dez?"

"I'm not playing at anything," Desmond replied sharply. "Why the devil did you come to that lecture today? Have you been following me?"

Now both of Carson's eyebrows shot up. "Following you! My dear chap, you have an inordinately high opinion of my interest in your whereabouts. I told you why I came. You seemed to have enjoyed it a great deal last time." He grinned. "Now I understand why."

Desmond grimaced and walked past Carson into the laboratory. The move did nothing to end the conversation, for the place was empty. Desmond sighed and sank down onto his stool, resigning himself to a conversation about Thisbe.

He must tell Carson something to satisfy his curiosity; it was the worst luck that out of all of Gordon's band of scientists, Carson had been the one to catch him with Thisbe. None of the others were likely to ever see Thisbe, let alone talk to her, but Carson belonged to her world. He might meet Thisbe at some party; no one would think it odd if Carson called on her.

"I assume you know who Miss Moreland is," Desmond began.

"If you mean, do I know that the Duke of Broughton's family is named Moreland, the answer is yes, I can guess her identity. I don't remember the girls' names, but I know there are a few." He strolled over to sit down facing Desmond. "Does Gordon know you have an entrée into the Mad Morelands?"

"Don't call them that," Desmond snapped. "They're not mad at all. They're more intelligent than most of the people in the world—they're just…different."

"Well." Carson pulled back, a speculative expression on his face. "You're very…*impassioned* about the Moreland family. Is there something more there than getting Annie Blue's Eye?"

"I'm not trying to get the Eye. I didn't seek Thisbe out because she was a Moreland. I'm not using her to get inside their home."

"I don't understand."

"I met her by chance. I didn't know who she was." Desmond looked at Carson. He wasn't sure he could trust him. However, Carson was probably as close to a friend as he had. And, in any case, what choice did he have?

With a sigh, Desmond poured out the whole story, beginning with the first lecture, though he carefully excised any mention of the kisses they had shared. Carson listened to the end without speaking. Then he let out an explosive breath and said again, "Well." He rose and began to pace. "This is certainly…unexpected."

"I realize it sounds like the stuff of melodrama."

"Oh, it's far more implausible than melodrama." Carson's lips quirked. "If it were anyone but you telling me this, I would be certain you were playing a prank." He returned to Desmond. "I must say, you're a more honorable man than I. I would have used her to get the Eye."

"*You* aren't in love with her."

"Clearly you are."

Desmond shrugged helplessly. "I know it's impossible—there's no hope for me. But I can't change how I feel."

"Gordon must be furious."

"Disappointed is more like it. *Deeply* disappointed. I

feel like a worm for ruining his hopes. But I simply cannot steal from her family."

"But if you explained to her how it happened…"

"Really? If you were she and I gave you such an unlikely story—'I'm not a fortune hunter and I met you entirely by chance, but, by the way, I would really like to have a valuable object in your grandmother's possession'—would you believe it?"

"When you put it that way…"

"Especially now, after I've known who she was for over a fortnight, and I still haven't told her about it. I *have* been hiding it from her."

"But you haven't tried to find the Eye during that time—surely that's proof of something."

"I told the professor I would look for it."

"And have you?"

"Not to any great extent. It's not easy to rifle through anyone's possessions when you have someone with you all the time. I could… It might be possible to learn about it through her little brothers. They're into everything. If anyone has seen it, they have. And they wouldn't have any idea it would be wrong to tell me. But I can't abuse the trust of two children. I feel guilty even thinking about it."

"You know your problem, Desmond? You feel too bloody guilty. A little dose of self-interest would do you some good. Perhaps I could lend you some—I've plenty to spare."

Carson's quip brought a ghost of a smile from Desmond. "It's kind of you to offer, but I doubt it would help." He studied his hands for a moment. "Carson, will you…? Could you not tell her about all this?"

"Miss Moreland?"

"Yes. Or anyone, really."

"I doubt I'll ever see the woman again," Carson said.

"You could make it a point to."

"You mean, if I wanted to get the Eye for myself?"

Desmond nodded. "If you ask her for it for the laboratory, she will know that I knew it, too."

Carson eyed him for a moment. "I think it'd be safest for you to tell her the truth. But, no, I won't seek her out. I won't ask her about the Eye. And I won't tell the others about her."

"Thank you." Desmond was flooded with relief.

"I hope you know that Gordon and Wallace won't stop," Carson warned.

"Good luck to them trying to locate it in that house." Desmond turned to his work with an easier mind. He wasn't always sure of Carson; the man was only half joking about acting in his self-interest. But this time he believed him. Even before he'd learned the story, Carson hadn't said anything to expose Desmond's deception to Thisbe, though he'd had ample opportunity.

Professor Gordon didn't come in all evening, and the other two students were late, so he and Carson had worked in uninterrupted silence. Carson left before him, and Desmond soon followed. He was desperate for sleep, and he dozed off riding the omnibus, waking up only because the conductor woke him at his usual stop.

Still bleary-eyed, Desmond trudged toward his flat, paying little attention to either side of him. As he passed a narrow dark alley, a place where he normally kept a careful eye out for a footpad, a hand lashed out, grabbing him by the arm and jerking him into the mouth of the alley.

His attacker slammed Desmond against the wall, then braced his arm across his chest, leaning his weight against Desmond and putting the tip of a knife to his throat. For an instant Desmond couldn't breathe, but he recovered and said, "If you're wanting money, you've picked the wrong man."

"I don't want your money," the other man growled, sticking his face close to Desmond's. "It's the Eye I'm after."

CHAPTER THIRTEEN

"THE EYE! GOOD GOD, you, too?" Desmond was now more annoyed than afraid. Clearly the man wasn't about to slice his throat if he wanted Desmond to find the Eye for him.

"Not me. I don't know what the bleedin' hell it is. But I know someone who wants it bad."

"I don't know what it is, either," Desmond responded, straightening from the wall and giving the man a push back. "I've never seen it. I don't know anyone who has. I think the Eye is probably a figment of Mr. Wallace's imagination. That is who you work for, correct?"

"None of your business who I work for." The man stepped back. He still held the knife in one hand, but carelessly. "All you need to worry about is getting me that Eye."

"I won't. You're wasting your time. More important, you're wasting mine." Desmond started around the ruffian, but the man held out an arm to block him.

"Now, wait. He's willing to pay you. More'n he's ever paid me, I'll tell you."

"Then perhaps you should get it for him."

The man snorted. "I'm no bleedin' housebreaker. Anyway, it's you he wants."

"Look. I told Gordon, and I told Mr. Wallace, and now I'll tell you the same—I will not steal the Eye."

"I wouldn't be so sure about that." The man made a fist and began to ostentatiously crack his knuckles.

"People will do almost anything if they have reason enough."

"You intend to beat me into finding it? Don't you think it would make the Morelands a bit wary of me if I came in all black-and-blue?"

"Maybe you won't be the one who's black-and-blue. Have you thought of that?" The man's eyes glittered even in the dim light from the street. "Maybe it'll be someone else. Someone you'd hate to see hurt. Maybe that girl."

"Thisbe?" Rage shot through Desmond. He grabbed the lapels of the man's coat and shoved him against the opposite wall. "Don't you dare threaten her. You touch her, and I'll kill you."

A mocking smile curved the other man's lips. "That important to you, is she?"

Desmond realized he'd made a terrible mistake, letting the man know how powerful a weapon Thisbe was. "I'm not doing it." Desmond kept his voice flat and hard. "You think you can attack a duke's daughter and get away unscathed? You'll be in irons before you have time to turn around." He let go of the man's jacket and walked past him, then swung back and added, "Mr. Wallace should remember that I could go to the police and tell them everything."

Desmond walked away, and the thug didn't follow. Would that threat be enough to stop Wallace? Desmond had no idea. He wouldn't have suspected Wallace would go so far as to steal the thing, let alone try to coerce him into doing it. It was a bluff; surely, it was a bluff. If the man killed Thisbe, he would have lost his bargaining chip with Desmond. But he wouldn't have to kill her; he might injure her to convince Desmond.

A chill ran through Desmond, and he came to a halt, his heart pounding. This, he thought, was what the dowager duchess had meant: Desmond's love would cause Thisbe's death.

She knew. The duchess had seen into the depths of him and found what his aunt had always known. Those whom Desmond loved died.

Desmond remembered sitting at the hearth in their cottage, the heat of the fire at his back. Its flames flickered red and gold across Aunt Tildy's face, a sight as mesmerizing as her low voice as his aunt repeated the tale of Annie Blue. "You're her heir. You bear her mark—it's the bargain she made with the devil. She was seduced by his promises of knowledge and power, and when she agreed to his wicked offer, the devil touched her. Right there."

His aunt tapped his back, where the red sickle-shaped mark lay beneath his shirt. "Annie gave him herself and her offspring, whichever ones he chooses. It don't happen to all. I have no gift nor curse. Nor did your mam. But our grandma did. Aye, and she was blighted. Only one of her children lived. The Wicked One would come in the night and take away their breath. 'Twas she who told me about the curse."

His father had known it, too. He didn't say it in the light of day, but at night, when he was deep in his cups, his words were always the same: "You killed her. I cannot look at you without seeing her lying there, pale as a corpse and holding you, making me promise to take care of you. Well, I did—I have. But I can't love you."

Desmond had denied it all these years, shrugged it off as one of his aunt's ludicrous tales, merely the expression of his father's bitterness. He told himself that the birthmark on his back was only a birthmark, not some harbinger of doom. He reminded himself that women often died in childbirth.

But he could not escape the memory of standing at the

foot of his sister's bed as she breathed her last, her husband on his knees beside her, grieving. Aunt Tildy had looked across at Desmond and nodded. She knew it, and deep in his soul Desmond felt the awful canker of truth, the truth that twisted through him now.

Whoever he loved died.

THISBE GLANCED OVER at Desmond. He was craning his head, looking behind them. She had managed to escape her grandmother's presence on the pretext of visiting the apothecary. Instead, she had met Desmond as they'd prearranged, but the pleasant time she had envisioned had been marred by Desmond's strange behavior.

He had been behaving oddly for days now. There was the day of the lecture, when he had been so stiff and silent and reluctant for her to see his laboratory. She had managed to dismiss that as jealousy of Mr. Dunbridge, and perhaps Gordon really had issued an edict against visitors. He wouldn't be the first to guard his experiments closely.

But Desmond had not been his usual self. He was quieter than usual—though that could be explained by the dampening presence of her grandmother—and Thisbe caught him gazing at her with a peculiar, almost wistful expression. Yesterday, when she walked him to the door, their only moment alone, and whispered her plan to meet him at the apothecary, he looked as alarmed as he did pleased, and he made her swear to take the carriage to the shop even though it was only blocks away.

Today he was distracted, continually glancing around, his arm beneath her hand hard with tension. He was assiduous about walking between her and the street in a way that seemed far beyond the demands of courtesy.

"Desmond, is there something wrong?" she asked at last.

He glanced at her, startled. "No. No."

"You've been acting…differently."

"Oh. Beg pardon. I've, uh… I was thinking about some changes I could make in order to produce a spectrogram." He launched into a discussion of prisms and angles and mirrors that left even Thisbe confused.

"I don't understand. You're trying to see in a different dimension? How is that possible?"

"Well, there's the problem," he admitted. "We are so limited in what we can perceive. What we can see or touch or hear or smell. But there's so much else in the world besides that. Think of the discovery of chemicals in the sun. They were unseen, but one could figure them out through computation. So if I could figure out the right computation—"

Desmond was so caught up in his argument that he scarcely noticed as Thisbe crossed over to a vendor's cart to buy roasted chestnuts. The sidewalk was crowded, and Thisbe was edged toward the curb. Suddenly something hit her in the back, knocking her out into the street.

"Thisbe!" Desmond jumped to grab her, but a man behind her caught her before she landed on the cobblestones.

The stranger lifted her up and said, "Blasted street urchin."

She looked up at the man. "Thank you."

Desmond clamped his hand around her other arm, staring at the man.

"Something should be done about those little ruffians," her rescuer went on and turned to look at Desmond. "The lady could have been thrown into the street right in front of a carriage." With a smile, he doffed his hat and walked away.

Thisbe turned to Desmond. He was gazing after the

man, a stricken expression on his face. "I'm all right. You needn't worry. Desmond…you're hurting my arm."

"What? Oh." He relaxed his hold. "I'm sorry. I didn't realize. Oh, God, Thisbe." He pulled her into his arms, heedless of the people all around them. "I'm so sorry. Forgive me."

"I'm fine." Thisbe smiled up at him. "It's not your fault. It was a child running by. Nothing was hurt but my dignity."

Desmond became aware of the interested stares all around them, and he released her. "Sorry. I thought I could protect you, but clearly not." He glanced around. "Where is your driver? He should take you home."

"Don't be silly. I'm not made of glass. I shan't shatter. Come, I want that walk in the park you promised me."

With an almost agonized look, Desmond agreed. He was quiet all the way to Hyde Park. It had begun to snow, white flakes drifting lazily down and settling on them. Thisbe was glad, for it meant fewer people in the park. There was no one in sight right now, and she was bold enough to take Desmond's hand. Her even bolder thought was that she would very much like to kiss him. It had felt so good to be in his embrace for those few moments after she'd fallen.

She steered a path toward a large fir tree that offered shelter beneath its branches. Desmond was in a brown study, hardly noticing where they walked. He hadn't told her the truth before; she was sure of it. There was something wrong with him today. Thisbe leaned against him, wishing he would share his burden with her.

He stopped and pulled her into his arms, his embrace hard and tight. He kissed her, his mouth demanding, almost desperate. Thisbe returned his kiss full measure, wrapping her arms around his neck and pressing her body into his. Desire, thick and hot, poured through her, and she wished that she could feel his body more closely against hers, without the padding of their coats. She wished, shockingly, that she could feel his skin against hers. A shiver shook her at the thought.

Desmond lifted his head and gazed down into her face. Color flared along his cheekbones, and his chest rose and fell in rapid pants, but the look on his face was not desire. It was…despair. "Desmond? What is it?"

"I love you," he said, the words seeming torn from him. "Oh, God, Thisbe, I love you more than anything." His hand caressed her cheek.

A different sort of warmth spread through Thisbe, a mixture of surprise and joy, and she began, "I lo—"

"No." Desmond raised a finger to her lips, stopping her. "Don't say it, or I will never get through this."

"Get through what?" She frowned, puzzled, as his arms fell away from her and he took a step back. Was he about to ask for her hand in marriage? Her nerves began to dance; it was too soon, surely, too sudden, and yet… she knew she would say yes.

"We cannot see each other anymore."

His words were so far from anything she had expected that Thisbe could only stare.

"I thought it would be all right. I thought I could keep you safe. But I see now—I can't keep you from danger. I *am* the danger."

CHAPTER FOURTEEN

"Danger!" Thisbe gaped at him. "What are you talking about? How can you be a danger?"

Desmond felt as if he were being ripped in two. But he had known what he had to do the moment he saw Wallace's thug grab Thisbe's arm. He had to protect Thisbe, no matter how painful it was. "Your grandmother was right. I will be the death of you, Thisbe. You cannot love me—I cannot love you."

"You're talking about my grandmother's prediction?" Thisbe's voice rose in astonishment. "That's mad. She can't see into the future."

"Maybe not. But she can see me." Desmond thumped his chest on the last word. "She looked into me somehow and saw it. I told myself it was nonsense. That I would protect you. But now, after what happened, I—"

"Because I fell down?" Thisbe stared. "Because of that one silly accident, you think I'm going to die if I'm with you?"

"It's not just that." He swung away, jamming his fingers back through his hair. How could he convince her? "Everyone who loves me dies."

"Everyone dies, Desmond."

"Not long before their time. My birth killed my mother. My sister, whom I loved more than anyone in the world, died at twenty in the same way. My aunt is dead. God only knows what has happened to my father."

"Desmond, women die in childbirth. It's awful that both your mother and sister died, but it's not unique to you. Your aunt and your father are older. It's not that odd—"

"No? Is your father dead? Your mother? Your aunts and uncles?"

"Well, no, but—"

"But what? Even your grandmother and great-uncle are still alive. Do you think it's really a coincidence that none of my relatives are?"

"I don't know. Such things happen, surely. It's certainly not because of you."

"That is what I've always told myself."

"Yes, because it's true. It's reasonable. My grandmother's prophecies are not."

"How do you know?" he asked. "How can you be so certain that she isn't aware of the spirits of those who have died? That she can't sense that death is drawn to me? My aunt sensed it, too. She saw it in me, just as your grandmother did. Thisbe, I *saw* my sister."

"Saw her? I don't understand."

"After she died, one night she came and stood by my bed. I saw her as plain as day. Whatever my logical mind tells me, I cannot dismiss what I saw."

"It was a dream," Thisbe countered.

"No. It wasn't. I saw her." He sighed. "Thisbe, I bear a mark—Aunt Tildy called it the mark of death."

"A mark? You mean a birthmark? That's nonsense— it's just happenstance. A random occurrence."

"I know all this sounds foolish to you." He should tell her the whole story—reveal everything he knew about the Eye and the men who wanted it, explain why she was in danger. She would be sure to stay away from him then; she would hate him for deceiving him. But his throat

closed when he thought of it. He could not bring himself
to admit what he had done. He could not bear to see the
disgust on her face. It was hard enough to give her up
without making himself a thorough villain in her eyes.

"Yes, because it *is* foolish," Thisbe replied. "How can
you claim to love me and then toss me aside?"

"Don't you see? It's *because* I love you. I cannot let
anything hurt you."

"You mean, anything other than you?" Thisbe's eyes
glittered.

Her words pierced him. "Thisbe, no…"

"I don't care about your superstitions. I'll brave it."

"I know. You would brave anything. But the consequences are too great. I cannot gamble with your life."

"I see." Thisbe drew herself up to her fullest height.
Her eyes were the brightest green he had ever seen, her
lustrous black hair dotted with snowflakes, her cheeks
high with color. She was breathtakingly beautiful, and he
drank in the sight of her, storing it away for the future.
"Well. Then…I shall go home."

Desmond started forward, but she stopped him with
a flash of her emerald eyes. "No. I don't need an escort.
I'm sure the coach is right outside the park. I am perfectly fine alone."

There was nothing he could do but watch miserably
as she walked away and trail along after her to make
sure she reached her carriage safely. Thisbe climbed into
the waiting vehicle without a backward glance, and it
drove away. She was gone. He stood there a moment,
staring bleakly into the rapidly increasing snow. Finally,
he turned and made his way to the laboratory.

Only Professor Gordon was there. He raised his head
as Desmond approached.

"I have a message for Mr. Wallace," Desmond told him.

Professor Gordon's eyebrows rose. "Mr. Wallace?"

"Yes. I'm not sure whether you know about the ultimatum his man delivered to me."

Gordon shook his head. "I don't know what you're talking about."

"I'm glad to hear it. But if you will, please give him my answer. His threats are useless now. I won't be seeing Miss Moreland again, and I am no longer welcome at Broughton House."

"What?" Gordon stared. "You mean—"

Desmond nodded. "I'm not risking jail for Wallace or anyone else. I have broken it off with Miss Moreland. There's no longer any possibility that she will help me. Her grandmother already hates me and will do so even more now. She wouldn't give me the time of day, much less the Eye."

Desmond turned and walked back to his desk, maintaining his air of unconcern, though his insides were in a turmoil. He had done what was right, he told himself. What he'd had to do. He would simply have to get accustomed to this hole in his chest.

THISBE SHIVERED DESPITE the fur-lined lap rug she had thrown over her legs. It was, she knew, because the ice in her chest came from the inside, not the chill in the carriage. She wished she was home; the coach ride seemed endless. Whether news was good or ill, it was better in the encircling warmth of her family.

She ran into the house and up the stairs. Kyria, starting down the stairs, turned immediately and followed her. "Thisbe! What's wrong? What happened?"

"Oh, Kyria..." Thisbe swung around. "He doesn't want to see me anymore." Then, to the astonishment of both women, Thisbe burst into tears.

Kyria put her arms around her sister. "What? Who? Surely you're not talking about Desmond!"

"I am. I am."

"No. You must be mistaken. The man's mad for you."

"He's not." Through her sobs, Thisbe poured out the story of their conversation.

Down the hall doorways opened and closed, and before long Olivia joined them, then the duchess and even the dowager duchess herself. Emmeline took charge, pulling Thisbe into a hug and rubbing her back soothingly, and said, "There, there, sweet girl."

Thisbe leaned her head against the duchess's shoulder as if she were a child again. Except this was no scraped knee or wounded feeling that could be banished by the awesome power of her mother. After a time, Thisbe quieted. She lifted her head and brushed away her tears. "I'm sorry. I never cry."

"Everyone cries sometimes. Come, let's sit down and straighten this out." The duchess put her arm around Thisbe's shoulders and steered her over to a bench against the wall. Pulling out a handkerchief, she handed it to Thisbe. "Now. What has happened?"

"Desmond jilted her," Kyria said.

"Kyria!" Olivia glared at her older sister. "Don't say that. He did not. They aren't even engaged. He just—"

"He just said that he wouldn't see me anymore," Thisbe revealed.

"But why? He seemed such a nice young man—that nanny he recommended has been a godsend," Emmeline said. "Why would he break it off with you like that?"

"Because of Grandmother." Thisbe sent a baleful glance at the dowager duchess.

Emmeline swung toward Cornelia. "What did you do?"

"No, she didn't do anything," Thisbe quickly explained. "It wasn't anything new. It's just… Desmond believes what Grandmother told us."

"Well." Cornelia rapped her cane sharply against the floor. "Good. The boy has more sense than I thought."

"He believes in Grandmother's ghosts and goblins?" Kyria asked in astonishment.

"Don't be impertinent, young lady," the dowager duchess snapped. "I don't believe in goblins. The spirits of the dead, however, are very real. The fact that you haven't the ability to see them does not alter that fact." Cornelia nodded toward Olivia. "Olivia would understand if she would only stop hiding from it."

Thisbe sighed. "He says he can't dismiss your warning. Apparently his aunt filled his head with nonsense about a birthmark on his back that she says is the mark of death."

"I knew it!" their grandmother said triumphantly. "I saw death clinging to him."

"And he thinks he saw his sister's spirit after he died."

"Really?" Olivia's eyes widened.

"I'm certain it was only a dream," Thisbe said. "I'm not sure he fully believes Grandmother's prophecy himself. But he says that if there's any possibility of danger to me, he must avoid it."

"Quite right." Her grandmother came over to pat Thisbe on the shoulder. "It will be all right, child. You'll see. The man did exactly as he should. I am rather impressed by him."

"I'm not," Emmeline said. "I don't know when I've been more mistaken about a person's character. I'd like to give him a piece of my mind." She paused. "Thank goodness Theo went to Bristol yesterday."

"Yes," Thisbe said with conviction. If Theo had been

here, he would probably have gone storming off to thrash Desmond.

"The point is—" the dowager duchess retook the conversational reins "—Thisbe is young, and this was only a brief infatuation. You'll forget about this Harson fellow."

"Harrison," Thisbe corrected, unsure why she bothered.

Cornelia ignored Thisbe's interjection. "There are any number of young men in the world who are much more suitable partners for you. This is all the more reason for you to have a Season."

"Grandmother...I don't want a Season."

"Not the whole Season," Kyria agreed, sitting down on the other side of Thisbe. "That would drive you mad. But you should attend a party or two. It would do you good to get out—the worst thing one can do is sit around moping over a boy. There's a ball next week at the Throckmorton house—you should come with us."

"Indeed." The dowager duchess nodded. "An excellent idea, Kyria. Thank goodness you have some social sense."

"They have a point," Emmeline said.

"Not you, too." Thisbe sent her mother a horrified look.

Her mother patted Thisbe's knee. "In general, I think balls and such are a waste of time, but Kyria is right. A party might be exactly the thing to help you forget your troubles for a while."

"Going to a ball and partaking in insipid conversation will not make me forget Desmond."

"No, but your irritation at the insipid conversation might take your mind off him," Kyria quipped, and Thisbe had to laugh despite the pain in her chest.

"Come." Kyria took Thisbe's hand and tugged. "We'll

ask Cook to make us some hot chocolate, and we'll gossip and try on frocks."

"I don't want to try on frocks," Thisbe protested, but she let her sister pull her up and lead her toward her bedroom.

"Then we'll just spend the afternoon vilifying Desmond Harrison."

"I don't want to even think about the man."

Unfortunately, Thisbe found that it was impossible not to think about him. Even burying herself in her work didn't help. Reading a paper about the use of the spectroscope in the discovery of rubidium made her think of Desmond. In the midst of an experiment, her mind drifted off to memories of their time together. She wondered what he was doing, if he missed her or regretted his decision. She remembered his kiss, his touch, the feel of his arms around her, and every thought brought that now-familiar ache to her chest.

More than once, she decided that she would go talk to him, but her nerve failed her. Surely she had more pride than to chase after a man who didn't want her, which was, she was convinced, the real reason he parted from her. Desmond couldn't actually believe that being with him would kill her. It was too absurd, too superstitious. Why, he had told her how little he believed in superstition. He was a scientist, and even if he was engaged in Gordon's spiritual research, he did it out of scientific interest. It didn't mean he believed in dark omens or deadly birthmarks.

No. Desmond simply was not interested in her. It had been an infatuation, and it had ended. Thisbe could only hope that her grandmother was right, and it had been an infatuation for her, as well. In a few days she would stop thinking about him, stop missing him, stop aching to feel his lips on hers.

She was sitting in the laboratory, idly spinning a glass stirrer on her table, going over what Desmond has said for the hundredth time, when Olivia burst into her room, breathless and braids flying.

"Thisbe! Theo came home."

That lifted Thisbe's spirits. She popped to her feet. "Good. Where is he? His room? The sultan room?"

"No. That's the thing—Grandmother told him about Desmond, and Theo went charging off to find him."

"Blast it! Why did she have to do that?"

"She wanted to tell Theo about her moment of triumph, I imagine. But that's not the problem. Theo will flatten him—you know he will. He took honors in boxing at Eton."

"He doesn't know where to find Desmond. Theo will charge about for a while, and that will calm him down. He'll return and—"

"He was going to talk to John the coachman," Olivia replied in a voice of doom.

"Thompkins? My God." Thisbe ran for the front door. Grabbing her coat from the rack by the door, she darted out, not pausing to put on a hat.

Theo had taken the carriage, she assumed, so she had to find a hack. Lifting her skirts more than was maidenly proper, she ran for a busier street. Where would Theo find Desmond? In the past, this was about the time he would come to call on her. Since he was no longer engaged in that occupation, he probably went to work at a normal time. He would still be at the optical shop.

She stopped a hack by running in front of it. It was only after she got in that she remembered she had also run out without taking any money. Oh, well, she'd make Theo pay him; he deserved it.

When they reached the shop, Thisbe sprang out and ran for the door, which was standing open. That wasn't a good sign. She had been counting on Thompkins not knowing the shop's address, since he'd never taken her there. Behind her, the driver of the hack let out a roar, but she paid him no attention. Her heart was racing, her stomach sick with dread.

The front of the shop was empty and the curtain to the back was half-ripped-off and dangling. She ran through the opening. A large group of men was clustered at the other end of the room, mouths open, watching the scene before them. They blocked her view, so she could see only Theo's head rising above everyone else. Oh, God, where was Desmond?

"Damnation!" Theo's voice rang out as Thisbe rushed toward them. "Fight back, would you!"

"No." It was Desmond's voice. "You're right. I am to blame." His head rose above the others, too, now; he had obviously gotten to his feet. Blood streamed down one side of his face.

Thisbe let out a cry of distress at the sight of him. "No! Theo! Stop this!" She started to push her way through the men. One or two fell back, startled, but she had to hit another with her fist to get him to move. She emerged behind Theo.

Her brother was already turning around at the sound of her voice. "What the devil are you doing here? Stay out of this."

"Thisbe!" Desmond's voice was only a whisper, but she felt it all through her.

She didn't look at him as she grabbed Theo's arm. "Don't. Stop this right now."

Her twin glared at her mulishly, jaw set and eyes lit with a green fire. "Go away. It's nothing to do with you."

"Ha!" She stepped between him and Desmond, setting one fist on her hip and pointing the other at Theo. "It's precisely to do with me." She poked her twin in the chest. "You cannot run about hitting people just because they've done something you don't like."

"For pity's sake, Thiz…" Theo grimaced, but his fists were no longer clenched, and she knew she had won.

Still, she gave him another poke just to emphasize her words. "I can fight my own battles, thank you. I'm not a child you must protect. I am a grown woman, and I have to face the consequences of my own mistakes."

"I know, I know. Stop doing that, would you?" Theo raised a hand to deflect another thrust of her forefinger.

"Good. Then we are agreed." Thisbe went back to his side, linking her arm through his, and finally let herself look at Desmond.

He was still standing in the same spot watching her, his eyes avid on her face—or, at least, one eye, for the other was rapidly swelling shut. The skin around that eye was red, and there was another spot like it near his mouth; they would both soon be black-and-blue. His lip was split and trickling blood, but it was the cut by his eyebrow that had streamed blood down the side of his face.

Thisbe's stomach clenched, and she had to fight back tears at the sight of the damage Theo had done to Desmond. She wanted to tend to him, to wash away the blood and fuss over him. At the same time, she was stabbed by a longing so fierce she could hardly bear it. His tousled dark hair, his long lean frame, his face, so familiar and yet so lost to her. And the longing in his eyes as he looked at her… How could he have cut himself off from her?

She willed him to come forward, to reach for her, even

to take one step toward her. She waited for one long, aching moment, then said hoarsely, "I'm sorry, Desmond. I apologize for my brother."

He shook his head. "I understand."

"Come on, let's go." Theo turned away, pulling Thisbe along with him, and she didn't resist.

The crowd melted back as they walked up the aisle between the tables.

"The bloody bastard wouldn't even fight back," Theo grumbled.

"Perhaps he has more sense than you."

"I doubt that, or he wouldn't have given you up."

Thisbe smiled and gave his arm a little bump with her shoulder. "Thank you for that." She gestured toward the partially hanging curtain between the shop and the back. "I take it you're to blame for that."

"I was in a hurry."

A man stood blocking the front door, arms crossed and a long carriage whip resting inside his elbow. "I want me money, missy. First ye run out in front of me and scare my team half to death, and then ye bolt without paying."

Theo raised a sardonic eyebrow at Thisbe, and she echoed, "I was in a hurry."

Theo looked coolly at the man, who began to fidget under his gaze. "I trust you were not planning to use that whip on a young lady."

"What? No. I just… I mean…" He began to stammer.

"Never mind." He waved the man out the door. "Take us home, and I promise I'll make up for your troubles."

The driver doffed his hat to him and hustled back to his coach. Theo climbed into the hack after Thisbe and settled down beside her. "Where's the carriage? Did you send it home?"

"No. Thompkins wanted to take me, but it would have

taken too long, so I got the address from him and took a hack."

"How did he know this address?"

Theo shrugged. "He sent me to the laboratory, and they told me where Harrison was." He paused. "They're an odd bunch, aren't they?"

"You think all scientists are odd."

They rode in silence for a moment, then Theo sighed. "I'm sorry. I shouldn't have done that. It just creates more of a stir."

"I wish you hadn't," Thisbe agreed. "But I don't blame you. I'd feel like hitting any girl who hurt you. The person I blame is Grandmother. She should have waited and let me tell you."

"Is all that true? Did she scare him off with her stupid prophecy?"

"I don't know. He said he was doing it to protect me. But it doesn't seem very likely, does it? That he'd believe the dowager duchess can see death? Or that he's cursed?"

"Well, she can be pretty convincing—she could have made a living on the stage if she hadn't married our grandfather. Even a rational man can believe in something he fears."

"So you're saying it's just that he's a coward?"

"I don't know. He wouldn't fight me, but he didn't try to run, either. He didn't seem afraid. He seemed... I don't know, resigned, I suppose. And sad."

"I'd be sad, too, if you were pounding on me."

"No, I mean before I hit him. When he saw me come into the workroom. There was a back door, but he didn't bolt for it. He just stood there, waiting for me. I think we're all cowards when it comes to someone you love getting hurt. I remember once when Reed and I were going to...well, someplace we shouldn't have been, we she turned away, glass in hand, she was startled by the sound of her own name. "Miss Moreland."

She turned to see the young man she had met at the last lecture with Desmond. What was his name? "Good evening."

He crossed the floor to her. "I'm sorry. I should have said Lady—"

"Please do not, Mr. Dunbridge." The name came to her in a flash. "I prefer Miss Moreland."

"I wasn't sure. It's such a different setting." He gestured toward the nearest empty chairs. "Would you like to sit?"

"Yes, that would be nice." She smiled. "I'm glad to see you."

"You are?" His eyebrows rose a little.

He must expect her to resent a friend of Desmond's. In fact, there was a flickering hope inside her that he would let drop some news about Desmond. "Yes, it's good to meet someone who can talk about more interesting things than his club or his horse."

Carson chuckled, and lines of laughter crinkled at the ners of his bright blue eyes. He was a handsome man fashionable, aristocratic way. Thisbe wished that he led to her, that she didn't prefer a dark mop of hair mpled suit.

sat and talked for a while. It was, as she had e entertaining to discuss theories and experi- social chitchat, but, disappointingly, he didn't bject of Desmond. Finally, she was reduced ut him. "How is Mr. Harrison?

a few bruises, he see said, mouth curving up men seemed to find in

ran across a footpad. He pointed a gun at Reed, and I handed over my money without a thought of challenging him. If I'd been alone, I probably would have—"

"Done something stupid and gotten shot," Thisbe said, finishing for him.

He flashed a grin at her. "You don't have much faith in my abilities."

"You sound almost as if you believe Desmond." When Theo shrugged, she went on, "And yet you attacked him."

"Whatever his reason, he still hurt you," Theo said simply. "He shouldn't have started if he couldn't finish."

Thisbe leaned her head back against the seat. Could it be as Theo suggested? She thought of Desmond's expression when he looked at her. Did he love her, as he'd said? Not that it made any difference now. She would never see Desmond again. Her throat was tight with tears.

Theo studied her. "Would you like me to stay? I could put off my trip."

Thisbe blinked away the tears forming in her eyes and forced a smile. "And miss exploring the Amazon because I am being weepy? I think not. I'll be fine, Theo. Really. I refuse to spend the rest of my life mooning over a man." She lifted her chin. "It may take a little while, but I will forget about Desmond."

Someday.

CHAPTER FIFTEEN

THISBE LOOKED ACROSS the ballroom at the throng of guests, and her heart sank. "Why did I let you talk me into this?"

"Because you realized how very wise I am." Kyria flashed her a grin.

"You didn't tell me it was going to be such a crush."

Kyria took her sister's hand and gave it an encouraging squeeze. "It won't be so bad. You'll see. Dancing is the surest way to mend a broken heart."

"Do stop talking nonsense, Kyria," their grandmother said from Thisbe's other side. They had, Thisbe noticed, flanked her so that she couldn't escape. "Stiffen up, Thisbe. You're a Moreland—we are never intimidated."

"I'm not intimidated. I'm envisioning a boring evening packed in with a swarm of people I either don't know or don't like. Now I wish I'd taken Theo up on his offer." Theo, with the face of a martyr, had said he would squire the ladies to the party, but Thisbe had kindly let him escape.

"It's better that Theo's not here," Kyria assured her. "You would have spent the entire evening talking to him."

"That's what I mean."

"Theo is a disaster at parties," Cornelia pronounced. "He's immediately surrounded by marriageable young ladies and their mamas, and he is remarkably unskilled at fending them off. I cannot imagine why he was never

taught better, but…" She gave an eloquent shrug that spoke of the poor influence of an untitled mother.

"Reed is perfectly adept at parties," Kyria pointed out. "It's not their upbringing—it's Theo's nature. The man has no problem facing snakes and sand and tribes of Bedouin, but show him a gala, and he flees."

"Yes, it's too bad Reed wouldn't come," their grandmother said.

"Reed had a prior engagement." Thisbe took up the defense this time.

"Easily broken. They were just men." With that parting shot, Cornelia marched off to sit with the other dowagers against the wall.

"I can't see how she's considered a chaperone," Thisbe commented. "She'll spend the whole evening there gossiping with her friends."

"For which I am enormously grateful," Kyria re[plied]. "Come along—just stay with me."

Kyria unfurled her fan and started forwa[rd] had little choice but to trail after her. Wit[h] one of Kyria's admirers popped up, br[inging them to a] halt, and soon the men had formed a[ ] circle around them.

Thisbe was as bored as s[he] men all talked nonsense, a[nd] dance floor. Some of the[ ] Thisbe to dance, b[ut] dancer, and she [ ] proximity to a s[ ]

After a struggle[ ] [re]ad only reached he[r] [sh]e as poor as her own, [ ] [ ]d her sister and head[ed] other about. "He won't speak of how he got his bruises, which leads one to believe perhaps a lady was involved." Carson paused invitingly. When Thisbe offered no response, he went on, "Desmond is devoted to his work. He does little else."

It was perfectly useless information, but she could hardly ask the things she wanted to know: *Is he sad? Does he miss me? Or is he in fine spirits and glad to be free?*

"Well." He rose to his feet. "Regrettably, I should take my leave. I have already occupied more of your time than is proper, I fear."

"Oh." Thisbe glanced around. Two of the nearby women were watching them with great interest. "Yes, of course." She stood up.

"Perhaps, if it were welcome, I could ca—"

"Dunbridge, my boy." A blocky gentleman strode toward them, his face wreathed in a smile.

Carson's lips twitched with annoyance, but he quickly smoothed out his face and turned to the other man with a deferential smile. "Mr. Wallace. I didn't realize you were here."

"Oh, yes. Never miss one of Roddy's revelries." He looked pointedly in Thisbe's direction.

"Miss Moreland, allow me to introduce you to Mr. Zachary Wallace. Professor Gordon is fortunate to have Mr. Wallace's interest in our research. Mr. Wallace, Miss Thisbe Moreland."

"Ah, Miss Moreland. Pleasure to meet you." He beamed at Thisbe.

"How do you do?" She nodded in greeting. So this was the patron of Desmond's project. He was expensively dressed; even as immune to fashion as she was, Thisbe could see that. He was ostentatious, with rubies flashing hcre and there, and his fashionable affectation of a cane boasted an ornate golden lion's head. He didn't really appear the sort of man who would be interested in spiritual matters—or scientific ones, either—but she supposed she shouldn't judge one on appearances.

"Yes, yes," Wallace went on, though no one had asked a question. "Such a pleasure. I've heard so much about you."

"You have?" *Why?*

He said chuckled in an indulgent way. "A female scientist—can't expect to go unnoticed now, can you?"

"I see." It was hardly the sort of recognition she wanted. Nor had she realized her attempts to publish had caused even a ripple among the male-dominated Royal Institution and its members.

"I had hoped young Harrison would have introduced us."

Thisbe simply looked at him, having no response to that. Desmond had talked about her to his patron? Was her relationship with him gossiped about throughout the scientific community? It was an embarrassing thought.

"Our Desmond has an uncommon attachment to scruples," Carson murmured.

"Be that as it may, it is a delight to meet you now," Wallace continued. "We must have a chat soon."

"Indeed," Thisbe replied vaguely. "If you gentlemen will excuse me, I must find my sister."

"Carson must bring you to my gala next week," Wallace said quickly. "A small thing, of course, compared to this, but, I hope, enjoyable. It will give us a chance to talk again."

"Of course, sir," Carson agreed. Thisbe smiled politely.

"I'll send you an invitation," Wallace said to her. "The duke and duchess, too."

"I'm afraid my parents don't socialize much," Thisbe disclosed.

"And the dowager duchess, of course. Is she here tonight? I would love to meet her, as well."

"Um, yes, she's here somewhere." Thisbe made a show of glancing about the room. "I don't see her right now." Thisbe could imagine all too well how her grandmother would react to this too-friendly man. "Now, if you will excuse me."

"Of course. Excuse me, sir, I must escort Miss Moreland." Carson bowed and offered her his arm.

As they walked away, Thisbe said drily, "I didn't really need an escort to cross the ballroom."

"I know." Carson grinned. "But it was the best I could come up with on the spur of the moment. I apologize for our patron. He can be…very enthusiastic."

"Mmm."

"But I do hope you will allow to me escort you to his party. They are rather extravagant affairs—he invites all of us."

It was, she suspected, a not-so-subtle hint that Desmond would be there. It wasn't Desmond's idea of fun any more than it was hers, but if the man who paid the laboratory's bill asked, he would attend. Desmond's presence was a very good reason not to go. She said, "Yes, I should like to, thank you."

The party turned out not to be endless, despite Thisbe's grim conviction to the contrary halfway through it. After they got back to the house, she went straight to her room, grateful to rid herself of the elegant ball gown and all the accoutrements Kyria and her grandmother deemed necessary to attend a dance—bracelet, pendant, hair ornaments, elbow-length gloves, fan, even a minuscule card and pencil.

Later, hair down and her headache easing, clad in her nightgown and heavy robe, she sank into her chair with a sigh and began to brush out her hair. It was warm and comforting here in front of the low fire, and the smooth sweep of the brush through her hair was soothing.

That was the last time she would follow Kyria's advice on recovering from a broken heart—as if Kyria had ever suffered from that malady herself. It hadn't helped a whit; the only difference was that now her feet hurt as well as her heart.

Thisbe rose and went to the mantel, where she had placed the kaleidoscope Desmond had given her. She had thought of putting it away in a drawer, where it wouldn't tug at her heart each time she glanced at the fire, but that would have made it too easy for the twins, who were fascinated by the instrument. More than that, though, she knew she kept it there because it was all she had of Desmond.

She picked up the instrument, then looked into the light of the fire, turning the front of it so that the flames tumbled into a myriad of designs. She thought of the moment Desmond gave it to her. The look in his deep, dark eyes. The kiss that followed.

She shouldn't have agreed to go to Mr. Wallace's party. It had been a relief when Wallace joined them, for she was almost certain Carson was about to ask permission to call on her. But then she had committed herself to his party and in doing so gave Carson permission to call on her, anyway.

It wasn't that Mr. Wallace was a terrible person. He just…made her uncomfortable. He'd been too eager to have her attend his party, too desirous of meeting her parents and grandmother. She couldn't help but feel that he wanted something from her—in all likelihood, the entrée into the upper echelon of aristocratic society that friendship with the dowager duchess could provide.

She didn't want to have to fend off Wallace's attempts to ingratiate himself. And she didn't like parties, anyway. She would be as bored and out of place as she had been this evening. There would be a crush of people, and she would know no one there but Carson. And Desmond.

Of course, that was the sole reason she had agreed. She wanted to see Desmond, even if it was across the room. That was another foolish thing. Seeing him wouldn't fill the emptiness within her, wouldn't vanquish the longing for his touch. It was bound to make it all worse. Yet somehow she could not quell the desire to see him.

Kyria, of course, was elated that Thisbe was being squired to another party. Kyria was certain that her plan had worked, and Thisbe didn't want to burst her bubble. It was irritating, though, that her grandmother was also pleased with the idea: "Dunbridge has little name to speak of, but his family is old and there's never been a scandal. You'll find better, but at least you're on the right path."

It didn't help Thisbe's mood that she continued to have that strange dream. It was always the same—the fire, the helplessness, the woman with her insistent appeal for help. It always jarred Thisbe awake, sweating and scared, and even though she was now familiar with the dream, it took a long time to go back to sleep.

Lack of sleep left Thisbe with eyes that were shadowed enough that even her father noticed. Coming upon her in the library one evening, he paused in the midst of searching for the book he wanted and asked, "Thisbe, dear. Are you all right?"

"Of course, Papa." Thisbe smiled and set aside the tome—she'd read the same page three times now, anyway. Rising, she went over to kiss him on the cheek. "You needn't worry about me. I just haven't been sleeping well, that's all."

"That boy—what is his name?"

"Desmond," she said evenly. "But it's nothing to do with him. I keep having a nightmare."

The duke's mild face wrinkled in concern, and he put his arm around her, steering her toward the sofa to sit. "Tell me all about it, as you used to."

"I'd forgotten that." Thisbe smiled faintly at the memory of her father sitting down on her bed and holding her after a nightmare. It had felt so safe and warm in his arms. "I would tell you about my scary dream, and you'd chase it away with a tale of Greek heroes."

"Ah, yes. Heroes' tales always have to do with fear."

"This one wasn't about monsters or being lost or any of the usual things." She related her dream in detail, and added, "It doesn't seem very big in the telling, does it?"

"It doesn't matter how long or how threatening dreams are—it's the emotion they bring up in one that makes them frightening. Let's see…" He adjusted his glasses, gazing thoughtfully down at the carpet. "Fire. I would imagine that's common—everyone is scared of fire."

"It's not really the fire that frightens me. I feel so helpless. I can't move. It's as if I'm paralyzed or bound. And her panic washes through me, but I haven't the least idea what it is she wants. I can't do anything."

"Hmm…" the duke mused. "She doesn't give you much to go on, does she?"

"I doubt it means anything. I'm not like Grandmother— I don't see the future."

"Egad, I should hope not," he said in alarm. "But I wasn't saying that your dreams are omens of the future.

I find that my dreams have something to do with what I'm feeling."

"But I'm not frightened of anything."

"I remember when I was courting your mother." The duke leaned back, his whole face brightening as it always did when he talked about Emmeline. "I had the most dreadful dreams."

"Really? I would have guessed you'd have happy dreams after falling in love."

"One would think. But mine were about running, trying to find something and not getting anywhere, or being lost in the fog and unable to find my way. Sometimes I dreamed that your mother was in danger, and I couldn't get to her. Horrid things." He gave an exaggerated shudder. "After I married her, they went away. So, you see…" He gave her a significant look. The duke had a habit of not concluding his arguments, thinking that everyone else followed his reasoning.

"The nightmares were no match for Mother?" Thisbe ventured.

He chuckled. "Nothing is. But the thing is…I realized they were because I was scared I wouldn't win her. What if she didn't love me? What if something happened to her? What if my mother scared her off? I was so happy during the day, being around Emmeline, thinking about her, I didn't notice it. But at night, the dread crawled out and overwhelmed me."

"Then why don't I have sad dreams?"

He looked at her with sympathy. "I don't know. Perhaps you admit the sorrow, but there's something more beneath it."

"The helplessness? Because I have no control over it?" Thisbe sighed. "Oh, Papa…" Tears welled in her eyes and she leaned her head against his shoulder.

"You wouldn't like giving up without a fight."

"How can I fight the fact that he doesn't love me?"

"Are you certain? Because I saw that boy's face when he gazed at you, and that was the way I looked at Emmeline."

"You still do."

"Yes. I always will."

"That is what I want—the kind of love you and Mother have," Thisbe told him. "If Desmond loves me, he doesn't love me enough. He's not willing to risk everything, not willing to fight for me. I wouldn't give *him* up because of some silly prophecy. I'd make sure nothing harmed him."

Henry chuckled. "No doubt you would. You're so like Emmeline."

"Me?" Thisbe asked in surprise. "I'm not like Mother. Kyria is the one like Mother."

"Kyria looks like Emmeline more than you do, that's true. But here." He tapped his chest. "And here." He tapped his forehead. "Inside, you're very much like Emmeline. Thisbe…" He leaned forward earnestly. "Beautiful as your mother is, that wasn't what made me fall in love with her. It was the strength and spirit that fairly shone from her. Her determination, her fierce conviction in herself and her beliefs. She never let anything stand in her way." The corner of his mouth quirked up. "Not even my mother."

"But I'm not like that. I've never fought to right wrongs or make the world better. I've never stormed the barricades."

"Your interests are not the same, of course. That's only natural. But you have the same qualities. Look at what you've done—you plagued that poor German chap until he let you study with him. You've fought to be recognized as a scientist. You've written papers."

"Which they wouldn't publish," Thisbe interjected.

"But that didn't stop you. You continue to write, to study, to experiment. I've never known you to give up on anything. I can't imagine that you will surrender here, either."

"But how can I fight this? I can't make him ignore Grandmother's warning. I can't make him love me."

"Maybe not, but you can change his thinking. You can make him understand what you feel. I don't know his mind, but it sounds to me as though he's a lad who is nobly sacrificing his feelings on the altar of your safety. He's naive, perhaps—certainly wrongheaded. He sees his own hurt, but does he know yours? Have you told him what you feel for him? Have you explained your pain and sorrow? Your will to fight?"

"Yes, I—" She hesitated. "I'm not sure."

"That part is still in your hands, and I know you too well to think you'll let someone else decide your future. If you truly want Desmond, you'll find a way to bring him back into your life."

CHAPTER SIXTEEN

DESMOND APPROACHED THE party sunken in gloom. This was the last place he wanted to be. Neither food nor drink appealed to him. Sleep did. One would think he would sleep more now that he no longer rose early to go to the shop so he could spend time with Thisbe. Instead, it had been a struggle to fall asleep, and once he did, his rest was fitful. He was plagued with nightmares, many of them involving Thisbe in imminent danger and himself unable to reach her. In one particularly horrid dream, it had been he who had plunged the knife into her, thinking she was an attacker.

His was not a state in which to think clearly. He'd made a mistake on a telescope that required him to take the thing apart in order to correct it. His mind was blank and dull at the laboratory; he hadn't the least desire to develop a spectroscope that would reveal a hidden world of spirits. Indeed, he had lost nearly all interest in that hidden world.

A gala given by Mr. Wallace had even less appeal. Wallace included Gordon and his workers, as well as other scientists, in one of his parties now and then. Desmond supposed the man sought to prove he was a true man of science, not just a dabbler—though it seemed unlikely to Desmond that such a status would impress any of Wallace's peers. More likely, Wallace sought to impress the scientists with his importance. Not that there was any need to do that, either; Wallace's checkbook had already done that.

Whatever the reason, Desmond could not understand why Professor Gordon had insisted on Desmond going to the bloody thing. Wallace wouldn't want him there. Frankly, Desmond was surprised the man hadn't cut him from the group. The drubbing from Thisbe's twin must have convinced them that Desmond was no longer useful to them in the quest for the Eye.

Reflexively, Desmond touched his cheek. The bruises had largely faded, except for a faint blue-and-yellow spot beside his eye, but it was still a trifle sore. Lord, but that man had a punch—though it was not as strong a blow as seeing Thisbe rush in to save him. No, not to save him— to keep her brother from creating an even worse scene.

The sudden sight of her had rocked Desmond. She'd been so beautiful—green eyes flashing, cheeks high with color. She'd been…just so much herself. He'd almost gone to her. Almost pleaded with her to forgive him, to let him into her life again. He wanted to tell her he'd been miserable without her, wanted her arms around him. Wanted all sort of impossible things.

Fortunately, one of the things he'd learned growing up was not getting the things he wanted. He'd said none of it, just watched her walk away, arm in arm with her brother. He had done what he had to do, and she was safe from Wallace's ruffian. Safe from Desmond himself.

Wallace's house was grand and luxurious, but, having been inside Broughton House, Desmond was no longer awed by it. Wallace stood at the entrance to the ballroom, greeting guests. A familiar burst of fury rose inside Desmond at the sight of him, but he pushed it down. He would pay the requisite fealty to the man, find Gordon to prove that he had attended and then slip out.

Wallace greeted him coolly, and Desmond managed a polite, equally meaningless reply. Having passed that gauntlet, he headed into the ballroom, looking for Gordon. He caught sight of him standing amidst a cluster of scientists and students, but as Desmond started toward him, a voice to his right brought him to an abrupt halt. "—that's a ridiculous notion, and I find it hard to believe that a man of learning doesn't realize that."

Thisbe. A ripple of nerves ran up his spine. No, it couldn't be. It was. His eyes found her immediately, tall and slim and cool in a shimmering dress the color of amber. She was talking to a shocked-looking older man, and beside her, smothering a laugh, stood Carson Dunbridge.

Rage shot through Desmond and he strode over to them, grabbing Carson's arm and yanking him aside. "What the devil is wrong with you! How could you bring her here?"

Carson said nothing, merely lifted his eyebrows in that supercilious expression that never failed to raise Desmond's hackles. Thisbe, of course, strode over to them, leaving the other man staring after her in shock and indignation before he turned and hurried off.

"Desmond, just what do you think you're doing?" Thisbe was devastating up close. The neckline of the golden ball gown swooped across the top of her breasts, setting up any number of unwelcome sensations in Desmond's gut. He caught the barest scent of her perfume.

For a moment his tongue cleaved to the roof of his mouth before he managed to speak. "You should leave."

"I beg your pardon." Thisbe's eyes, already stormy, took on a flash of fire. "Why should I leave? You leave."

"I intend to, trust me." Desmond thought he might explode from the conflicting emotions storming around inside him. He turned to Carson. "How could you do this? Bring her right into—"

"Mr. Dunbridge did not *bring* me anywhere." Thisbe brought Desmond's attention back to her with an ungentle rap of her fan on his arm. "I came here at the host's invitation."

"Wallace? You met Wallace? How? Why? Damn it, Carson, if you—" Desmond's eyes narrowed. "What game are you playing? Do you plan to pursue her now? I swear—"

"Jealous, are we?" Carson's lazy tone was insufferably amused.

"Desmond! Stop it! Stop it right now." Thisbe stepped between the two men, scowling at Desmond. "I am growing tired of mediating your brawls."

"I never asked you to." Desmond didn't need Carson's poorly concealed laughter to know that he sounded childishly sullen. He wanted to kiss Thisbe. He wanted to shake her. He wanted to drag her from the room. Carry her to safety. To his bed.

Thisbe turned to the other man. "Carson." *So now it was Carson, not Mr. Dunbridge.* "Would you excuse us, please? I need to talk to Desmond."

"Are you certain?" Carson asked, slanting a sardonic look Desmond's way. "He seems rather…unstable."

"I'm certain," Thisbe said firmly, and Carson sketched a bow and left. Thisbe turned back to Desmond.

"Thisbe, I swear to you—"

"We must talk." She glanced around. "It's too cold to go out to the garden. There's bound to be an empty room around."

"Thisbe, no, we can't slip off together. It'll be—"

"A scene?" She quirked an eyebrow. "Thank you, but

I think you have already created one of those. I'm trying to keep it from growing."

Desmond looked around to find several gazes discreetly, and not so discreetly, focused on them. He nodded and followed her out of the room. She walked quickly down the corridor, glancing in one room after another.

"Ah, the library. Perfect. No one will come in here." The room was lit, though dimly, by gas sconces on the wall, leaving much of it shadowy.

She took his hand to lead him into the room and closed the door behind them. He should have objected to both, but he didn't. It felt too good to have her hand in his once more.

Thisbe turned to face him, letting go of his hand. Desmond's heart raced. He struggled to push aside the warring sensations within him. "Please, you have to understand. This is dangerous for you. You can't—"

"Be with you?" She cut him off, then rendered him utterly speechless by stepping forward, taking his face in her hands and looking into his eyes. "Desmond…do you want me?"

Desmond let out a strangled noise.

"Do you want to be with me?" She stretched up to place a soft kiss on his lips. "To kiss me?"

His head whirled, her perfume filling his nostrils, her lips as soft, as delectable, as he remembered. He put his hands on her waist. To hold her away, he thought. "Of course," he said. "That's not the point."

"I think it is." She moved closer, so that her body was now only a centimeter away from his, almost touching him all the way up and down.

"Thisbe…" He spread out his fingers against her sides, his thumbs brushing tantalizingly close to the swell of her breasts. "You can't."

"I can." She brushed her mouth against his again, her fingers sliding back into his hair, and a tremor ran through him. "I want to be with you." Her voice was only a whisper; her breath caressed his cheek. "I miss you. I think about you until I think it will drive me mad."

"Thisbe." He closed his eyes. "I do, too."

"Then it's silly to be apart, isn't it?"

He kissed her cheek; her skin was soft as velvet, and the little intake of her breath made his own catch in his throat. He bent to kiss her neck, then the white shoulder so temptingly close. His fingers pressed into her waist, carrying that last little sliver closer so that her body was flush with his. His mind was a blank; he seemed incapable of saying anything except her name.

Slowly, his fingers slid up, his thumbs finding the curve of her breasts and following it. Thisbe made an odd soft sound, and he felt her body turn hotter beneath his hands. He lost all sanity then and kissed her. His mouth was hard and hungry, and his arms wrapped around her, crushing her into him.

He wanted to brush everything from the library table and lay her down on it, wanted to cover her body with his, feel her soft and welcoming beneath him. One arm still tightly around her, his other hand came up to cup her breast. He moved higher, his fingertips touching the lace trim of her neckline and then the amazingly soft skin of her breast. His thumb teased at the edge of the material, then slid beneath, moved under the cotton of her chemise. And there it was, the bud of her nipple, prickling beneath his touch. His mouth trailed down her neck and onto the expanse of her chest, her collarbone hard beneath her skin, moving downward. He barely suppressed a moan.

The door opened behind them, and Desmond jerked. He whipped around, pressing Thisbe against the wall, covering her from sight with his body. A slice of brighter light fell on the floor, and a disappointed voice said, "Just the library." The door closed again.

Desmond let out a curse and swung away. "God." He heaved in a breath, thrusting his hand back through his already disordered hair. What was he doing? "I'm sorry, Thisbe."

"I'm not." Thisbe's voice was unsteady, but it throbbed with intensity. He could feel it all through him.

"You don't understand. We cannot—"

"Why not?" There was a lash of anger in her voice now. "I don't care about the danger. I don't even believe in it."

"You should." He turned around to face her, hoping this four or five feet was a safe enough distance away. Clearly, his control when it came to Thisbe was almost nonexistent. His voice rasped, and he cleared his throat, struggling to pull himself into order.

"I don't believe in curses, Desmond. Neither should you. It's foolish, archaic."

"It's not just that." He searched desperately for a way to convince her that wouldn't make her despise him.

"Then what else is it?" she demanded, fists planted on her hips.

"You cannot trust Carson."

"I thought he was your friend."

"He is. He was. But where you're concerned, it's different. You cannot trust Wallace, either."

Thisbe gaped at him. "You realize, don't you, that you sound a little mad?"

"Think. Why would he invite you to this party?"

"He had to have an ulterior motive?" Thisbe's eyes flashed. "He couldn't have thought I deserved an invitation just as male scientists did? I noticed there were a number of them here tonight, including you."

"It's not that! You know I respect you as a scientist as well as a person. It's just—" He clenched his jaw.

"Go on. It's just what?" Thisbe demanded. When he said nothing, staring at her in frustration, she let out a noise that was somewhere between a sigh and a growl, then swung around, heading for the door.

"Wait! Thisbe! Oh, the devil. They want the bloody Eye!"

CHAPTER SEVENTEEN

THISBE STOPPED AND turned around, her anger vanishing in the face of real concern about Desmond's mental state. He looked like a man teetering on the edge of sanity—his hands clenched in his hair as if he would pull it out by the roots, his eyes wild, his entire body rigid with tension. Carefully, she said, "They want a bloody eye?"

"Noooo." He elongated the word, almost a moan, but at least he relaxed, his hands dropping to his side. He still looked comical, with his hair sticking out in every direction from his treatment of it, but Thisbe had no inclination to laugh. Despair was written all over his face. "Not a bloody eye. *The* Eye. The Eye of Annie Blue."

"Desmond…you aren't making sense. Who is Annie Blue? And why would any of these people want her eye?"

"Because they think your grandmother uses it to see the dead." Thisbe's jaw dropped, but he went on in a leaden voice, "Wallace has a letter… Arbuthnot something had the Eye in his possession."

"Arbuthnot Gray? My great-great-whatever-grandfather Arbuthnot? Desmond, is this a jest?"

"No! No, I swear to you. Anne Ballew was an alchemist. My aunt Tildy believed I am descended from her, which, of course, is nonsense."

"I think I'd better sit down." Thisbe took a seat in one of the chairs by the library table, her mind whirling.

Desmond didn't sit, though he clutched the top of a

chair as if it would keep him in place. "People nicknamed her Annie Blue. She was very famous—she was burned as a witch. She claimed—people believed, anyway—that she could see the dead. Communicate with spirits. And she had this instrument."

"Called the Eye." Thisbe relaxed in relief. Desmond wasn't out of his mind. He was talking nonsense, but at least it wasn't gibberish.

"Yes."

"And Mr. Wallace believes my grandmother inherited this thing?"

"Yes. You know the subject of Professor Gordon's project. An instrument that—"

"An instrument that could reveal ghosts to humans." Thisbe rose slowly to her feet as all the warmth drained out of her. "Some optical instrument, say, something along the lines of a *kaleidoscope*. That's it, isn't it? That is why you—you—"

"No! Thisbe, no, that's not why— I didn't *know* you."

"But you made sure you got to know me, didn't you?" Thisbe felt sick at her stomach, but her mind raced on. "That's why you came to that lecture, isn't it? That's why you chose *that* seat. You thought you could get to Grandmother through me. That I could persuade her to give it to you."

"No. I swear to you."

"I have a little trouble believing anything you swear," Thisbe retorted hotly.

"I didn't know who you were when I met you. I didn't know the Duchess of Broughton was your grandmother. I didn't know that was where you lived until you came out the door."

Thisbe drew in a sharp breath. A shard of ice speared

her chest. "You didn't come to see me that night. You were there to—to what? Steal it?"

"No. I mean... I wasn't going to take it."

"Then what? You came merely to locate it? Get the lay of the land so someone else could steal it?"

He looked at her helplessly. "Thisbe, please... Professor Gordon was desperate. I owe him so much."

"Whereas you owe me nothing. I understand."

"It's not a matter of owing. I love you."

"Don't. Don't you dare." A saving rush of anger expelled the chill. "Why in the world didn't you just ask me?"

"Because I didn't want you to think exactly what you're thinking," Desmond snapped back. "Blast it! I didn't try to steal it. I didn't want to use you."

"Stop." She made a sharp gesture. "Come with me." She turned and strode from the room, her steps sharp and fast against the tile of the corridor.

"Where? Thisbe, what are you going to do?"

"We're going to visit my grandmother."

With a sigh of resignation, he followed her. Desmond didn't try to speak as she marched down the stairs, though as they waited for their coats from the butler, he said tentatively, "Um, shouldn't we tell Carson you're leaving?"

"I'm sure he will figure it out." Thisbe wasn't pleased with Carson, either, though it was nothing compared to the roiling feelings she held for Desmond at the moment.

It was an inconvenience that her carriage was not there since she had come with Carson, but it wasn't far from Wallace's house to her own. And a brisk walk in the cold night air made awkward conversation less likely. Desmond didn't try to talk to her, and she was glad, though her own mind was occupied with all the things she would say to him if he should once more try to persuade her that he had done nothing wrong.

He didn't know. He didn't mean. He didn't intend. Well, what he *had* done was lie to her. Deceive her. Pretend feelings he didn't have. Once he met the dowager duchess, he must have realized that using Thisbe to get to her was a lost cause. But at least the dowager duchess's premonition had given him a handy excuse to remove himself from Thisbe's life after that.

It gave Thisbe some small sense of satisfaction to see the expression of uneasiness on Desmond's face when they reached the house. The dowager duchess, they were told, had already retired, but Thisbe didn't hesitate to head up the stairs to her grandmother's rooms.

She knocked on the door. "Grandmother, I need to talk to you. It's important."

A moment later, the duchess's maid opened the door and curtsied to Thisbe before slipping out the door. Her grandmother stalked into her sitting room. She had taken off her usual load of jewelry and changed her clothes, but she was no less formidable in her heavy brocade dressing gown and the turban she often wore as a nightcap.

"What is it, Thisbe?" The duchess narrowed her eyes at Desmond. "What is *he* doing here? This is scarcely the time for visitors."

"Desmond has come to ask you something. Rather, I have come to ask you something for him. He felt it too forward to do it himself." Thisbe caught the surprised look on Desmond's face at her words. No doubt he had expected her to lay out all his sins for the dowager duchess. It was probably the sort of thing *he* would do. "As you know, he is a scientist, and he is conducting an experiment that I think would interest you."

"I find that unlikely."

"He and his colleagues are trying to prove the existence of spirits in the world around us."

"Well, of course they exist. Sounds like a waste of time to me."

"I agree, but they think the matter worth studying. His professor believes that you are in possession of an artifact that would help them in this study. It's called 'Annie Blue's Eye,' I believe."

"The Eye. Of course!" Cornelia turned to Desmond, her voice dropping into the low, dramatic voice that usually accompanied her mystical ramblings. "I should have known you would want my Eye. With that miasma of death that surrounds you, it's clear you would be drawn to it…and to my granddaughter."

Thisbe ignored her grandmother's theatrics. "The important thing, Grandmother, is that his group would like to study the Eye."

"Nonsense," the duchess scoffed. "One cannot make sense of the Eye—there is no rational explanation. It is of the spirit. Beyond our limited comprehension."

"But wouldn't you want to prove to everyone that you have been right all these years? That you can speak to the dead?"

"Of course I can speak to the dead. I don't need proof— I've done it for years."

"But to make it common knowledge would be important. To show the rest of the world."

"Why would I care what the rest of the world thought?" Cornelia countered unanswerably.

"But, Grandmother—"

"No." The dowager duchess cut her off decisively. "It's no use to try to wheedle me out of it. Anne Ballew's Eye belongs to me. To us. It has been handed down for generations. I have a sacred duty to protect it. I can't lend it to strangers."

"I could oversee the experiment if you wished. I could carry it back and forth to their laboratory. I would be there all the time to make sure no harm came to it."

"Simply being in other people's hands would bring harm to it. It passes down through the maternal line, mother to daughter to granddaughter. She was our ancestor, you see. Anne Ballew was not the commoner most people believe."

Trust her grandmother to have come up with this dramatic notion. Skeptically, Thisbe said, "I have never seen her name on the family tree."

"They wouldn't have made it public!" Cornelia opened her eyes in horror. "She was burned at the stake, dear, not exactly what one wants to tell everyone."

"Then how do you know—"

"I just know," the duchess said with finality.

"Ma'am." Desmond spoke up for the first time. His eyes were bright with that eager curiosity that always rose in him at the opportunity for discovery. The familiarity of it made Thisbe's heart ache. "I wondered… Could we see it? No one even knows what it looks like, exactly. It would be a wonderful thing just to view it."

The duchess scowled, but Thisbe forestalled whatever she was about to say by reaching out to her grandmother. "Please. I should very much like to see it, too."

Cornelia hesitated, glancing from Thisbe to Desmond and back again. Finally, with a sigh, she gave in. "Very well. You will only keep picking away at it until I do."

She started toward the connecting door to her bedroom, then swiveled back and said, "Stay here."

Thisbe and Desmond waited, listening to the dowager duchess rummaging around in the other room. She let out an exclamation, followed by the opening and closing of drawers and doors. Finally, she emerged with a small, beautifully carved box in her hand. She shook the box at them and said, "The twins found it, obviously, and put it back in the wrong place. Those little imps—they're worse than magpies when it comes to shiny objects."

Thisbe's grandmother didn't hand Thisbe the box, but opened it to reveal the contents. Inside, nestled on a bed of dark green velvet, sat a single large lens in a carved wooden frame, attached to a handle of the same wood.

"It's a quizzing glass!" Thisbe reached out to touch it, and the duchess gave her hand a little slap.

"No, you don't. This doesn't leave my hands. It wasn't a quizzing glass originally—the frame was added last century, when quizzing glasses were so popular. It helps to conceal its real purpose." Cornelia lifted the glass from its box and held it up to reveal the other side of the lens, which was covered by several small clear quartz crystals, creating multiple facets. Cornelia held it up against the light of the lamp, and a multitude of dazzling colors shot from it in all directions.

"It's beautiful," Thisbe breathed.

"Fascinating." Desmond, drawn by the glass and its display, took an unconscious step forward.

Cornelia slapped the glass back into its box and closed the lid with a decisive snap. "There. That is the Eye."

"But, Grandmother..." Thisbe protested. "Can't we at least look through it? See if... I mean, *what* it reveals?" She herself itched to touch it; she could only imagine how much Desmond wanted to use it. Not, of course, that Desmond's wishes mattered to her.

"Absolutely not." The duchess held the box behind her back, as if they might try to grab it from her.

"Please, Your Grace." Desmond spoke for the first

time. "It would be invaluable. I swear I'll do nothing to it."

"Hmph." Cornelia sent him a sour look. "I can't depend on your oath. Do you think I don't realize why you took up with my granddaughter?"

Desmond let out an exasperated groan. "It wasn't how you think."

"It's pointless to get into that," Thisbe told him in a voice as final as her grandmother's. "But I don't see why we couldn't try it out, Grandmother."

"Young lady." This tone of address, Thisbe knew, indicated that her grandmother was reaching the end of whatever forbearance she had. "The Eye was entrusted to me. No one else may touch it—ill fortune would befall anyone who did, I'm sure. Besides, *he* would see nothing." She cast a dismissive glance at Desmond. "Only a holder of our line is able to use it—a female of Anne Ballew's own bloodline."

"Well, I am—" Thisbe began, but her grandmother quelled her with a look.

"Its wisdom is open only to a true believer. I suspect it will be Olivia who has the power to see the departed ones. Now…" She gave them a dismissive nod. "I have done what you asked. It's time for you to go." Cornelia turned to Desmond. "I trust I will never see your face here again."

She marched into her bedroom and closed the door, leaving Thisbe and Desmond staring after her.

"Well." The anger that impelled Thisbe had drained out, and she felt suddenly flat. "That's it, then. Go back to your professor and his patron and tell them that the dowager duchess refuses. She will not change her mind."

"No. I can see that." Desmond's eyes were bleak. He followed her out of the room and down the staircase. He was silent all the way, but at the front door, he turned to her. "Thisbe, please believe me."

She ignored his words. "It's no use trying to steal it. It will be under lock—"

"I would never do that!" His voice was rough with anger. "Damn it, how can you think that I—"

He broke off, swung away his gaze, then faced her again. "I realize that I am forever ruined in your eyes. But I beg you to remember that you are still in danger. Don't trust Carson or Wallace or—"

"I have no intention of trusting anyone." Ever.

Desmond opened the door and paused, gazing down at his feet. "I meant everything I told you. None of my feelings, none of my regard for you, was ever false. I want you to believe that. I never pursued you for the Eye, and the only reason I left was because being with me put you in danger." He lifted his head, his eyes searching hers.

Thisbe swallowed hard, pushing down the sobs that threatened to engulf her. Looking back at him with a hard, flat gaze, she kept her voice cold. "Fortunately, that won't be a problem anymore, will it? Goodbye, Desmond."

CHAPTER EIGHTEEN

THISBE WAS STANDING *in a dark, cold corridor, the flames of a torch behind her casting flickering shadows over the walls. Through the iron bars of a gate, she could see into a room that, though not large, contained several women. Some were on their feet, roaming about aimlessly; some sat, leaning against the wall. Still others were lying on the floor, a few on makeshift beds of straw. The walls were stone, darkened by dirt and smoke, with smears of green mold. A single barred window high on the wall offered the only light. It was unshuttered, open to the January air, and the place was bitterly cold. The only fire, a low collection of kindling, produced more smoke than heat.*

One woman stood apart from the others, silent amidst the talk and curses and groans. The clothes she wore had once been elegant, but dirt and rough treatment had obscured the quality of the brocade skirt, and the stiff, doubtlessly embroidered bodice had been taken from her, leaving her clad in only a simple shift in the chilly air. Even the snood had been snatched from her head, so that her thick black hair tumbled over her shoulders and down her back.

But her face was still attractive in a strong-boned way, and her large dark eyes were sharp and intelligent, unlike the dull stares on most of the others. She looked back at Thisbe, her chin tilted up a little, her gaze defiant.

"It's time, then." She swept back her hair, combing

*it with her fingers into some semblance of order, and
stepped out of the cell.*

*Suddenly, Thisbe was somewhere else, an open square
in the midst of the city. There were people all around and
the air was rank with the smell of smoke and roasting
flesh. People talked and shouted and laughed all around
her, but tormented shrieks rose above all the noise. The
sound chilled her blood.*

*She didn't want to turn to see what lay behind her,
but she could not stop herself. Two separate fires blazed,
consuming the piles of logs encircling them, and in the
center of each was a person engulfed in flames. Her
stomach lurched at the sight, but the rabble around her
cheered and laughed.*

*Between the two fires stood another circle of wood.
Smaller sticks of kindling were piled against a row of
thick logs. The kindling would catch fire quickly and
the flames would eat away at the heavier timber until
it, too, roared to life. In the center stood a stout post,
empty. Waiting.*

*Thisbe swallowed the bile that rose in her throat, her
hands curling into fists, her nails biting into her palms.
No. No. Panic rose in her chest. She wanted to run, but
her legs were heavy as stone. She could not lift them,
could not budge from this spot.*

*An excited murmur ran through the crowd, and Thisbe
swung around to see what had caused the stir. A proces-
sion was walking down the street toward them. Behind
them loomed an impressive building, towers on either
side. A black-clad priest, clutching a crucifix, led the
way. Behind him marched two guards wearing armor
breastplates and helmets, long pikes in their hands. A
woman walked between them, slender and delicate beside their bulk. Her hands were bound before her with*

rope. Her long black hair spilled down her back, the ends fluttering in the cold breeze.

It was the woman from the prison cell. She held up her head, pride evident in her carriage, her pale face expressionless. The crowd pointed at her and shouted invectives. "Witch! Heretic! Blasphemous whore!" She ignored them, just as she ignored the pitiful burning creatures lashed to their posts.

She faltered only once, when they turned onto the path to the waiting pyre, but in the next instant, she straightened, her face, though paler, set in the same indomitable lines. The priest stepped aside as the guards led her the last stretch to where the executioner awaited.

Thisbe cried out, but no sound came from her throat. She ran forward, but the crowd thickened in front of her. She pushed her way through the people, but she could not shove them aside quickly enough.

The guards bound the woman to the post, winding the rope tightly around her waist. Thisbe screamed again and again, but her voice remained silent. No matter how she pushed and wove her way through the mob, more and more of them seemed to block her path. Her heart pounded; sweat trickled down her face despite the freezing air.

The executioner took up a torch and walked toward the pile of logs. The woman looked out across the crowd, and her gaze locked on Thisbe's, her dark eyes fierce in their resolve. Save him. *The voice resounded in Thisbe's head.* Save him.

Thisbe leaped forward as the executioner plunged the torch into the kindling...

"No!" THISBE'S EYES flew open. She was still for a moment, letting the world around her settle into reality once again.

There had been no pain this time, but the nightmare had been even more frightening. Her stomach roiled as she remembered the stench, the hatred that filled the air, her own helplessness to stop the horror unfolding before her eyes.

Her throat was raw and dry. She slipped out of bed and poured herself a glass of water from the pitcher. She drank it down thirstily and sank onto the chair, heedless of the chill in the air. Another mad dream.

At least this one was easy to explain. She'd gone to bed in a turmoil, heartsick over Desmond's betrayal, her mind filled with his story of Anne Ballew and her death, burned at the stake as a witch. It was no wonder her nightmare had been of just such a scene. It was reasonable. Awful but understandable. It hadn't been real. Only a nightmare.

Still…that didn't explain why had she dreamed of someone burning at the stake weeks ago, before she'd even heard of Anne Ballew.

Thisbe shivered. No. That was too mad. She could not think about that tonight. She crawled back into bed and pulled the covers up to her head.

THE NEWS OF Desmond's perfidy was all over the house the following morning. Clearly the dowager duchess had wasted no time in spreading the news. Everyone was careful not to mention the matter at breakfast, but Thisbe found the sympathetic looks almost as difficult to bear. Her sisters pulled her into the game room afterward, Kyria cheerily suggesting a game of cards.

"I'm sure you intend to take my mind off last night," Thisbe told them as she followed Kyria and Olivia into the room. "But I am not good company today."

"Then we'll talk. Or we could go to the music room," Kyria suggested.

"Or the bookshop," Olivia said.

"No." Thisbe shook her head. "I'm too furious to do anything."

"Perhaps it's not as bad as it appears," Kyria offered tentatively.

"It is. I thought the way I felt the past week was the worst I could feel. But I have discovered that the boundaries for pain are apparently limitless." Thisbe sighed and dropped down onto a chair. "Now I sound like Grandmother, turning this—this losing a gentleman caller into a grand tragedy."

"Desmond was a good deal more than a gentleman caller, and you know it," Kyria told her. "It feels like a tragedy to you. You're allowed to emote a bit."

"Maybe, but I shouldn't make you endure it."

"Don't be silly. That's what we're here for." Kyria took a chair at the card table, and Olivia sat on Thisbe's other side, their faces so earnest and concerned that Thisbe couldn't help but feel warmed.

"At least earlier I could cling to the idea that Desmond loved me, that it was only his superstition that kept us apart. But now I know that he never loved me at all. Everything he did was a sham."

"Are you certain?" Olivia asked.

"He as good as confessed it."

"I don't understand exactly what happened," Olivia said. "What did he do? What is this thing Grandmother says he wanted to steal?"

"Some old artifact that Grandmother owns. They call it the Eye of Annie Blue."

"Sounds like one of Olivia's stories," Kyria commented.

"It is, rather. It's a strange quizzing glass that they think can enable one to see spirits."

"Ghosts?" Olivia stared.

"Yes." Thisbe described the details of the evening before and Desmond's confession. "Of course, Grandmother refused to lend him the Eye. Desmond left. And that's the end of our 'courtship.' I'll never see him again, and good riddance." Tears welled in her eyes. "I feel so stupid. I thought he loved me. I was blathering on about how I didn't care about the danger—I wanted to be with him. He must think me an utter fool."

"I don't understand why he told you what he'd done." Kyria frowned. "It goes against his own interest."

Thisbe shrugged. "Does it matter? He was warning me away from Wallace and Dunbridge. That was a kindness on his part, I suppose."

"But why did he break it off with you earlier?" Olivia asked. "When he told you he was a danger to you."

"I don't know. I presume he saw he would never get the Eye and was tired of having to pretend an affection for me."

"Or maybe he told you the truth," Olivia suggested. "Maybe he really didn't know who you were in the beginning."

"Olivia! How can you stand up for him?" Kyria turned on her younger sister.

"I'm *not*. I'm just trying to be fair. Thisbe didn't tell him who she was when they met, either."

Kyria let out a dismissive snort, and Thisbe said, "It beggars belief that he 'accidentally' ran into me at the exact time he was also trying to get our grandmother's Eye. Besides, I told him my name was Moreland. Surely that would make him suspect I might be related."

"Maybe he only knew the Duchess of Broughton, not

Moreland," Olivia countered. "Not everyone is conversant with all the titles and names in the peerage."

Thisbe frowned at her. "You still like him."

"I'm furious with him for hurting you," Olivia replied. "And I think he was wrong—and foolish—not to tell you. All I am saying is that it doesn't mean he lied to you about *everything*. Even if it started out a deception, he could have fallen in love with you later."

"You read too many novels."

"Forget Desmond," Kyria told her. "You should—"

"I am *not* attending another one of your parties," Thisbe interrupted.

"I wasn't going to say that. I was going to say that you should see that other man—Mason."

"Carson."

"Whoever. You liked him enough to let him escort you to a party."

"Because I hoped Desmond would be there," Thisbe confessed. "I have no interest in Carson and, anyway, he is after the Eye, too. I intend to avoid all male company from now on."

Olivia spoke up again. "I don't think it's odd that Desmond was afraid you'd hate him if he told you the whole story. I mean, that's what happened, after all." Olivia sighed. "And, yes, I do like him."

"Perhaps *you* should marry him," Thisbe responded.

Olivia rolled her eyes. "Don't be testy. *I'm* not the one in love with him. It's just… He's smart and funny and very nice. He was perfect for you. You were so happy."

"I'm *not* in love with him." When both her sisters looked at her in disbelief, Thisbe amended, "At least, I don't want to love him. I am determined not to love him."

"How do you plan to do that?" Kyria asked.

"I will devote myself to work. I've been lax the last

few days, but I shall simply make myself concentrate. I refuse to let Desmond Harrison mess about with my life."

"Do you think Grandmother's prediction was true?" Olivia mused. "I mean, it seems more likely now that Desmond actually was dangerous."

"Only to my heart," Thisbe retorted. "Do you honestly think the dowager duchess can tell the future?"

"No. Not really."

"Grandmother is making it up, as she always does," Kyria said. "You know how much she loves a dramatic scene. She didn't like Desmond, and it was a grand way to get rid of him and make herself look important and mystical."

Olivia snorted a laugh. "You just don't like Grandmother."

"Because she doesn't like me," Kyria protested. "I don't care that I'm not her favorite, but it does seem one's grandmother ought to at least like her."

"It's because you look like Mother," Thisbe told her.

"I know. Still…"

"You should be glad she isn't always telling you that you have 'the sight' and are like her," Olivia added. "I mean, ghosts are interesting in novels, but I don't think I'd really like to *meet* one."

"Do you think she made up all that about Annie Blue, too?" Kyria asked.

"She couldn't have made it *all* up," Thisbe said. "That's what Desmond called the quizzing glass, too—Annie Blue's Eye. So there must be some sort of legend about the woman."

"The part about her being tried as a witch might be true, too," Kyria offered. "They were doing a lot of that in the 1600s."

"It happened a good deal with the Tudors, as well," Olivia agreed. "Bloody Mary and so on."

"That was heretics. But, then, witches would qualify, I suppose," Kyria mused. "Whatever you call them, it was gruesome."

"Which would also appeal to Grandmother," Olivia pointed out.

"You know whom you should ask," Kyria told Thisbe. "Uncle Bellard. If anyone would know anything about this woman, it would be him."

"I would ask him…if I wanted to waste my time on such nonsense," Thisbe said. "But I intend to spend my time working."

Despite her words, the next morning found Thisbe walking toward the remote set of rooms where her great-uncle lived. Her work had not gone well the afternoon before, and she had slept poorly, bothered again by a dream of the same woman standing in the midst of a fire. This morning would probably prove just as useless, so she might as well spend her time trying to discover something about the Eye. And, yes, she admitted, she was too curious to leave it alone.

"Thisbe?" Bellard opened the door to her with his usual vaguely bemused smile. "How are you? Your grandmother isn't with you, is she?" He cast a look of trepidation down the corridor.

"No. She has no idea I'm here. I'm not sure she even knows where your rooms are."

"Good." He nodded happily and showed her into his sitting room. "Come in. Come in."

As usual, his re-creations of battles were scattered about on tables all over the sitting room. The walls of the room were lined with tall shelves of books, and books were stacked on the floor and chairs and every vacant space on a table.

"Would you like some tea? Doris just brought up a fresh pot."

They had no maid named Doris, but Thisbe didn't point that out. Names were of no interest to her uncle unless they belonged to some person from long ago.

"She brought scones, too." His eyes twinkled at Thisbe. "Dear Emmeline is always worried I may starve up here when Cornelia visits."

"I fear Grandmother will be here for some time."

"Yes, I heard Hermione was staying in Bath. Well, at least *she* won't be joining us. That's a bit of good news." He cleared some books from a chair and poured her a cup. "Are you hiding from Cornelia, too?"

"No, but my question concerns her. Have you ever heard of a woman named Anne Ballew?" As her great-uncle fell into his thinking posture, arms crossed, eyes tilted up toward the upper shelves, Thisbe went on, "I believe she was an alchemist. She was burned as a witch, from what I've been told. Although, really, I'm not completely sure she even existed."

"Anne Ballew. Anne Ballew. It has a certain familiarity. When did she live?"

"I'm not sure. Long enough ago that she was executed for witchcraft."

"That could cover a great number of years. People have always been frightened of things they don't understand. The Middle Ages. The Lancashire witch hunts in the seventeenth century—though the alchemist part seems earlier than that. You know, alchemists were something akin to scientists. Learned men pushing the boundaries of knowledge. John Dee, Elizabeth's adviser, was quite well-known and respected. Odd for a woman to be an alchemist, though. Wait." He held up a finger. "Anne Ballew. Annie Blue. That was what she was called, as I remember. It was John Dee that made me think of it— she was something of a protégée of his."

"So, Elizabethan times?"

"Yes, or I suppose she could have been a bit earlier, during Mary's reign. A lot of executions for heresy at both times." He shrugged. "But I'm afraid that's the extent of my knowledge."

"Do you think it's possible she could have been one of Grandmother's forebears?"

"Anne Ballew?" His voice registered surprise. "I can't see how, dear. Cornelia comes from a long line of proud people. It's hard to imagine finding an alchemist among them. Or a witch. Who suggested that she was?"

"Grandmother."

"Cornelia herself?" His eyebrows shot up.

"Yes. She claims that's where she got her powers."

"Her powers? Oh. That." His face cleared. "Anne Ballew communed with the spirit world, as well?"

"Apparently there is a legend that she could, and she used a certain instrument to do so, a sort of lens that enabled her to see them."

"Interesting. Does Cornelia have this supposed magical lens or is she searching for it?"

"She has a large ornate quizzing glass that she says was called 'the Eye of Annie Blue.'"

"That has quite a ring to it."

Thisbe nodded. "Apparently other people have heard of the legend. Grandmother said that Anne Ballew was actually from a 'good family.' Not a commoner, as apparently others believe."

"Naturally she would say that." Bellard tapped his

upper lip. "Let me think… Cornelia's maiden name was Bellingham, was it not?"

"Yes, but the first mention of its existence was in a letter from her great-grandfather or something like that. His name was Arbuthnot Gray. So we only need to go back from there. That would cut off some research."

"Gray—Gray…" He tapped his finger against his upper lip. "I remember Cornelia talking about her grandmother being a Gray. Not one of those tragic Grays. Poor little Jane—it was never a wise thing to get involved with the Dudleys. She did have a legitimate claim to the throne, you know, though, of course, much further down the line than Mary or Elizabeth."

"Yes, no doubt you are right," Thisbe agreed, drawing him back to the original subject. Once started on history, Bellard could go on for hours. "Do you suppose you might have a family tree of my grandmother's line of Grays?"

"Oh! Yes, yes, quite forgot what I was doing—it's so easy to get distracted when it comes to the Tudors. Let me think. Her Grays were, I believe, from the Cotswolds. Ah! I have it." He jumped up from his seat and went to the shelves.

Thisbe watched as he scanned the bookcases, now and then muttering to himself, and once pushing the ladder along to a different spot. "Yes! Here it is, *The Great Families of the Cotswolds*. Bit pretentious, don't you think?" He pulled out a massive tome. "More like a history of half the families of the Cotswolds."

He laid the book on a table, pushing aside a few tin horses and cannons, and began to leaf through it. "Gray, Gray, Goodwin, Gorton… Yes, Gray, here it is." He glanced about the room and began to search the pockets of his jacket. "Now, where are my glasses?"

"Atop your head," Thisbe told him, joining him at the table.

"Why, so they are." He smiled in pleased surprise and settled the spectacles on his nose. Bending over, he began to read. "Good Lord, they go all the way back before the Norman Conquest." He thumbed forward a page or two. "Yes, here we are. Arbuthnot." He trailed his finger up the page, turning back to do the same on the next.

"Grandmother says that it was handed down, mother to daughter. So it could have been Arbuthnot's wife's family or his mother's and so on. Does that show their trees, as well?"

"Not unless they were from the Cotswolds. It has only the wives' maiden names and dates, and some of them they're not sure of. Goodness, here's one where the wife's name is a blank. Arbuthnot's wife was from Wells—Cecily Hargreaves." He flipped through several more pages and began studying the lines. "Her mother, apparently, was a Penburton. Her father's mother was a Carrington. This is mushrooming a bit, isn't it?"

Thisbe sighed. "It's probably a hopeless chase. It would take hours to trace all the possibilities."

"No, no, dear, don't be discouraged. We shall split up the work. I will continue climbing the family trees, so to speak. I have a good deal of experience in that type of research. You start looking through histories of the Tudors to see if you can find a mention of alchemists and this Anne Ballew. You can try a biography of John Dee, perhaps—that might be helpful. Oh! I just remembered. Alfred Symington sent me a book he wrote—we correspond now and then, though he's rather fonder of folklore than I. Now, what was it called? It was tales of witchcraft, I believe. I fear I never read it. It's not one of my interests. But I'm sure I kept it—I know him, you see, and in any case, one cannot simply toss a book away." He looked appalled.

Thisbe turned to survey row upon row of shelves. "Do you know where it might be?"

"Goodness, no. It could be in history or religion or perhaps… Well, truth is it could be any number of places." He brightened. "We can call up young Livvy— she enjoys digging through books. She's been up here quite a bit lately."

Unsurprisingly, Olivia was happy to leave her Latin grammar book and join them in Uncle Bellard's rooms. While Thisbe took on the task of finding alchemists, Olivia chose to research the subject of witches. Uncle Bellard got diverted now and then by some connection to a historical event and Olivia wandered off into a discussion of spiritualism in the United States; even Thisbe was waylaid once by a biography of Isaac Newton. But they kept at it, working steadily through teatime.

Though they found nothing about Anne Ballew, they doggedly returned to the search the next morning. Bellard followed strand after strand of Cornelia's lineage, but in the end he announced with certitude that there was no Ballew in the dowager duchess's ancestry.

"I did find one of her grandfather's cousins who was hanged, however," he said with a mischievous glint in his eye. "A Jacobite. He would only have been banished to the colonies if he hadn't offended the judge by questioning the judge's understanding of the law."

"That sounds fitting." Thisbe laughed. She turned toward Olivia. "Have you found anything?"

Olivia shook her head. She was sitting on the floor with her back against the wall, a veritable fortress of books stacked up around her. "Did you know that there were two sisters in the States who fooled everyone into thinking they were 'channeling' spirits? They held séances where spirits would make rapping noises and such. Why do you suppose a ghost could rap on something but couldn't speak?"

"Perhaps these sisters didn't have Grandmother's 'gift' of speaking to the dead." Thisbe flashed a grin at her sister.

"Many people believe the sisters manage all the rapping and noises themselves. But their followers are adamant that it's all true. Spiritualism is a sort of religion over there."

"It's reaching England," Thisbe replied. "Desmond's mentor studied spirit photography from some chap from New York City."

"*That* was interesting," Olivia admitted. "My supposition is that they were using plates that had been used before and not cleaned properly." She grimaced. "It seems a really rotten thing to do to someone in the throes of grief."

"It is."

"What did you say? Spiritualism?" Uncle Bellard looked up from his book. "Isn't that what that nice young lad who calls on you does, Thisbe?"

"Desmond isn't a Spiritualist," Thisbe protested. "He agrees that spirit photography is a swindle. Desmond is a scientist conducting an experiment to prove or disprove the existence of—" She stopped abruptly, aware of Olivia's gaze on her. "Not that it matters what Desmond thinks." She frowned at her sister. "Have you learned anything about Anne Ballew?"

"No. I'm still trying to find the book Uncle Bellard's friend wrote."

"He is more a correspondent than a friend," Bellard remarked. "But I am sure I have it. It won't be out here."

He gestured toward the books scattered about the room. "Those are ones I'm using. It will be tucked away on one of the shelves. Have you tried down there?" He nodded toward the opposite wall.

Olivia stood up and started toward the bookcase, but stopped. "Uh-oh, I hear the Greats."

It was, indeed, the pounding of tiny feet that heralded the approach of the young twins.

"I don't think they have a pace slower than a run. Of course, that's good—it gives one warning." Thisbe cast a worried glance at her great-uncle's miniature military figures.

Bellard caught her look. "No need to fret. They're well-behaved with the soldiers…though Alex does have a regrettable tendency to now and then stick one in his pocket. Not that he means any harm, you understand. I think perhaps he's inherited the Moreland fondness for collecting things."

Con hurtled into the room, exclaiming, "I won!"

"Did not," Alex protested automatically. "I helped Miss Katie." He cast an angelic look back at his caretaker.

"Aye, and so you did," the woman said, swooping him up and kissing his cheek with a loud smack. "But you still cannot have the biscuits until teatime."

"I helped, too," Con announced, never one to be left out.

"Aye, I'd be lost in this place without you two," their nurse agreed cheerfully.

At least Desmond had given them Katie, Thisbe thought somewhat sourly. The woman had been a godsend. She was able to take the twins in stride and managed them better than any nurse before her.

The twins and Bellard spent the next few minutes examining the newest additions to his collection, the boys astonishingly quiet. Even Con wasn't rattling away as he usually did. After a few minutes of awe and serious discussion, the boys were off again, running to their sisters for a hug and a kiss, then pelting out the door and down the hall, Katie in their wake.

After that interruption, the room was silent again until Olivia cried, "Ha! I found it!"

"Symington's book?" Bellard asked. "Excellent."

Olivia was looking through it as she walked back to her nest of books. "Middle Ages. Fourteenth century, the Tudors. Oh, my, this is a large section." She scanned through the pages, and suddenly her eyes widened. "She's here! Thisbe, she's here!" She looked up at her sister, beaming. "Anne Ballew."

"What does it say?" Thisbe hurried over to her. They had been searching for so long it seemed as though they had won a prize.

"She was from Dorset." Olivia scanned down the page.

"Dorset. That's where Desmond grew up."

"You think that's significant?" Olivia asked.

Thisbe couldn't help but remember Desmond's words when he first told her about the Eye. His aunt believed he was Anne Ballew's descendant. But the fact that they were both from Dorset didn't prove anything; there were thousands of people from Dorset. She shook her head. "No. I'm sure not. It just seems…odd."

"Go on, Livvy." Bellard joined them.

"Doesn't say anything about her having a husband or children. She was a 'woman of great knowledge for her day, a well-educated and highly respected alchemist.' An associate of John Dee. Moved to London. 'The common mob knew her as Annie Blue and believed that she was a powerful witch, capable of speaking to the dead and

even commanding them. Feared as a necromancer—'"
Olivia looked up. "What does that mean?"

"I believe they're saying she could raise the dead,"
Bellard replied gravely.

Olivia's jaw dropped.

"What else does it say?" Thisbe whisked the book
from Olivia's hand to look at the open page.

There, above the name Anne Ballew, was a drawing
of a woman with a long face and dark, compelling eyes,
her black hair bound up in an Elizabethan head covering. Thisbe went cold all over.

It was the woman of her nightmares.

CHAPTER NINETEEN

"THISBE? ARE YOU all right?" Olivia peered into her face.

Thisbe most definitely was not, but she wasn't about to tell anyone her insane notion. "I, um, was just…surprised, I suppose, to see a picture of her. I hadn't expected there to be one."

"It wasn't all that unusual," Uncle Bellard commented. "People who had money often had their portraits made. I wouldn't be surprised if she had accumulated some wealth, given her fame."

"Certainly her clothes would indicate that," Olivia agreed.

"Do you think this is actually a portrait done at the time? Or a drawing of the way someone imagined her years afterward?" Thisbe asked, unable to look away from the picture.

"It would have to be an engraving of the original portrait, to have a plate for printing," Bellard said. "Although…I'm not sure. Perhaps now they are able to do it with photography. Everything is changing so rapidly these days."

Whether it was Anne Ballew or an imagining of her, it didn't change the fact that the woman in the book looked like the woman Thisbe had seen the last two times in her nightmares. Which was, of course, impossible.

Bellard studied the drawing. "I believe this was drawn at the time she was alive. The style looks very much like other portraits of that time. A little flat, like the earlier paintings of Elizabeth."

"Not as well-done," Thisbe said.

"There were many portrait painters, and I'm sure that many of them lacked the skills of, say, Holbein."

Thisbe nodded. There was nothing to say that this was exactly how Anne Ballew had appeared. Even if it was done at the time, the artist probably flattered her a bit, made her fit the Elizabethan ideal, and he had not necessarily been the most skilled artist. Then an engraver had copied it, which would have changed it again, at least to some extent.

Her mind was playing tricks on her. That was all. Like the victims of the spirit-photography charlatans, who had seen what they wanted to see, Thisbe had seen what was on her mind. There was some resemblance between the two women—the dark hair and eyes, the long face—and her mind had conveniently blended the two. She couldn't have dreamed about a woman she'd never seen any more than her grandmother could gaze into the future.

"What does it say about her?" Thisbe stepped back. She didn't want to look at the drawing.

"Only that she was condemned for her 'vile and heretical' practices and burned at the stake on January 27, 1556. Based, apparently, on the testimony of her neighbors and another alchemist, John Chisholm." Olivia's eyes widened. "This other alchemist fellow swore he saw her in the graveyard, calling up the dead."

"Jealousy," Bellard suggested. "Minor territorial disputes, envy, fear—those were the basic ingredients for accusations of heresy and witchcraft."

"That's all." Olivia shrugged and closed the book. "No mention of the Eye or any magical instrument."

"Ah, but now we know that she died in the Marian persecutions." Their uncle hastened over to a glass-fronted bookcase. "Bloody Mary—you'll remember she was Catherine of Aragon's daughter—executed almost three hundred people during her reign, trying to turn England back to Catholicism."

"Burning people seems an odd way of wooing back disbelievers," Thisbe commented drily.

"Religion can be a frightful thing in the hands of zealots," Bellard responded. "The burnings were all over the country. In London, they were carried out in Smithfield."

"Where the market is?" Olivia asked.

"Yes. In front of St. Bartholomew's Hospital. It was one of the few large open spaces, just outside the old city walls."

Ice trickled down Thisbe's spine. She thought of the wide expanse where the woman in her dream had walked past the spectators to her execution. "Where crowds could gather."

"Yes, the mob was always eager to witness such a spectacle."

"How did they get there? The prisoners, I mean. Did they walk?" Thisbe asked, hoping for an answer that would negate her dream.

But Uncle Bellard nodded. "Yes, it was quite close to Newgate Prison—not the present one, of course. The old one burned down in the Great Fire of 1666, but it stood in the same location. Just a short walk down Giltspur Street to the place of execution."

Thisbe felt queasy. "The old Newgate—did it have a tower on each side?"

"Why, yes." He smiled at her display of knowledge. "Here. Let me see." He looked over the shelves beside him. "Ah, yes. Here it is." He opened a book and flipped through the pages, then held it out to Thisbe. "This is a drawing of Newgate at that time."

It was the building she had seen behind the woman in her nightmare. Thisbe's hands shook as she handed the book back to her uncle. He was already pulling out another old volume, and said happily, "Now, this should tell us something. It's *Foxe's Book of Martyrs*." He shoved aside some papers on a table to lay the book on it.

"What's *Foxe's Book of Martyrs*?" Olivia came over to join them.

"It's a recounting of Christian martyrs starting from the very beginning—an enormous task. John Foxe wrote it early in Elizabeth's reign. It was a very influential book at the time. There were few books, you understand, and this one had great appeal. Even those who couldn't read could look at the drawings of various gruesome tortures and deaths." He flipped through the pages quickly. "It was very thorough and detailed. For our purposes, the important ones are the Marian martyrs. Let's see, yes, here we are, 1555."

He moved through the pages more slowly now, running his finger down the lines and muttering beneath his breath. "Look at all these—several a day sometimes." He shook his head. "January... Ah." He tapped his finger triumphantly on one paragraph. "Ann Bellow. What do you want to bet that is our woman? Spelling was so variable then."

"What does it say?" Thisbe leaned in, as did Olivia on her great-uncle's other side.

"Disappointingly little, I'm afraid. It just lists her as one of six martyrs who were burned on that day. 'Ann Bellow, artificer.'"

"What's an artificer?" Thisbe asked. "A profession?"

"It means someone who creates things. A craftsman

or inventor." He sighed. "They often gave short shrift to women, I'm afraid, even in regard to their martyr-dom. Here's one that says only 'wife of' someone. And, of course, her heresy wasn't really Protestantism. They do point out that it was most unusual to have so many women executed thusly. January 31 has a group of five women." He looked over at Thisbe. "Sorry, my dear. I'm afraid that's it."

"I doubt we'll find much more." Thisbe glanced around the room at the hundreds of volumes. She felt odd, rather remote, as if the world had suddenly changed around her. "At least we know she existed."

"And that she supposedly could speak to the dead, as Grandmother claims," Olivia added. "Do you suppose she used the Eye? What do you think it's like when you look through it?"

"My guess is that it's all prisms and mirrors and such, along the lines of a kaleidoscope, and what you see through it is a shadowy blur, which believers can in-terpret any way they want," Thisbe mused. Obviously her reaction to the drawing of Anne Ballew was proof that even a reasonable mind was suggestible. "I'm sorry, Uncle Bellard. I'm afraid I've wasted your time."

"Dear girl, not a waste at all." He took her hand and patted it. "I enjoyed it, and now that I'm on the hunt, I believe I'll continue following the trail of Cornelia's fam-ily. Who knows what interesting tidbits I could turn up."

"I'm going back to work." Thisbe turned to Olivia. "I wasted your time, too. I think there's no use in look-ing any further."

"I think I'll stay here," Olivia said. "I want to see what else I could find about those séances in the States."

Thisbe walked back to her laboratory, but she knew she wouldn't be able to work. She felt much too unsettled by what she'd learned. Thisbe's nightmare visitor was Anne Ballew; the certainty rested in her chest like lead.

The idea was impossible. It wasn't logical. Yet she could not deny what she had seen; she couldn't dismiss an observation because it made her uncomfortable. After all, science required an open mind. A scientist followed the facts. And the fact was she had recognized Anne Ballew.

But how could she have dreamed of a woman she'd never seen? Or dreamed of fire before she knew the woman was burned? How could she have seen the place of Anne Ballew's execution or the old Newgate Prison that had disappeared two hundred years ago?

And, aside from the inexplicable "hows" of it, there were the equally mysterious "whys." What did the dreams mean? Why was she the one who was seeing them? Her grandmother seemed a far likelier choice, given her supposed ability to commune with the dead. Why had Thisbe felt the sensations that Anne Ballew had, as if she and Anne were the same?

She wanted to talk to someone about this, but who? *Desmond* whispered through her mind, but she thrust it away. Theo? Kyria? But they would have no better understanding of it than she did. And they might very well stare at her as if she had lost her mind. Which, perhaps, she had.

There was her grandmother, who would at least believe her, but she would make far too much of it and interpret the thing in whatever way suited her. She would say it proved her theory that they were descended from Anne Ballew.

The thing was…what if her grandmother was right?

They had found nothing to prove that Anne Ballew was the dowager duchess's ancestor, but neither had they found anything that proved she was not. Absence of proof wasn't really proof. What if Anne Ballew's line had gone down from mother to daughter for multiple generations, ending now with Thisbe and her sisters? The woman was speaking to her descendant, reminding Thisbe that she owed her very existence to her ancestor.

It made as much sense as anything else in this strange situation. Unfortunately, that was none at all. Dreaming about a woman who'd died centuries earlier went so far past the realm of reality that it teetered on the edge of madness. Yet here she was, a heretofore rational woman, attempting to reason out what the nightmare Anne Ballew wanted of her.

The woman had asked for help. "Help me, save me"—something like that. Or maybe it had been "save him." Had she mentioned a child? Thisbe wished now that she had written down the exact words right after the event. It would make sense if, in the throes of her death, Anne's last thought had been of her child. But what could Thisbe do about it? Anne and any child of hers had been in the ground three hundred years.

And now here she was, calling the nightmare figure "Anne," as if she knew her. As if the figure were not a figment of Thisbe's own imagination. As if one's dying wish could travel down through the centuries into a dream.

She tried to put the problem of her dreams out of her mind, but she kept returning to it, like a tongue to a sore tooth. After a night spent tossing and turning—though, thankfully without dreams—Thisbe arose early and went up to her great-uncle's room, carrying a breakfast tray for him.

Knocking softly, Thisbe opened the door a crack—it was always problematic whether Bellard would either hear a knock or answer it—and peeked in. Uncle Bellard was seated at one of the tables with a large book before him, and was scribbling away on a piece of paper.

He looked up and smiled. "Ah, Thisbe. Is it time for breakfast already?" He glanced toward the windows. "I should open the drapes."

"I'll do it." Thisbe set the tray on the table and went over to draw the drapes on the row of windows along the far wall.

When she returned to her uncle, he had plowed through half his food. "I didn't realize how hungry I was."

"You missed dinner last night." Thisbe sat down across from him and poured their tea.

"Really?" He tilted his head, considering the matter. "I believe I did. I've become quite caught up with this search for your ancestor. I followed some of the side paths that I didn't yesterday—still no Ballew, but Cornelia was doubtless right in saying her family would have changed their name."

"Do you really think we're descended from Anne Ballew?"

"I haven't the slightest idea." He beamed. "But it's terrific fun tracking them down. Now, tell me what brought you here so early in the day."

Thisbe took a fortifying sip of tea. "Uncle Bellard, you are the most intelligent person I know."

"Why, thank you, dear." He patted her hand. "But it's rather hard to judge such things. Henry is very bright, and my sister as well, though Hermione has put her brain to no good use."

"I wanted to ask your opinion about something. I've been having this dream. Well, dreams." She told him about her dreams, the portrait of Anne Ballew and her wild suppositions about the connection. After finishing, she asked, "Do you think that any of that is possible? Or is it pure madness?"

"I don't know, dear. I suppose it could be either." Bellard seemed unalarmed by the possibility that she had lost her mind. "Let's consider these dreams. First, you dreamed of being at the stake, then of being *in* the fire, and—"

"Well, actually, I had another strange dream before that," Thisbe said. "It wasn't about fire or Anne Ballew, but it was peculiar and vivid, like the others. It was very vague, but I felt as if something was hunting for me, trying to reach me, and then I— Something grabbed my leg, and I woke up."

She refrained from mentioning the nail marks she had found on her leg afterward, just as she'd omitted the blisters and raw fingertips that had mirrored her other dreams. Those things were entirely too strange to tell anyone, even her open-minded uncle. He popped up from his chair to pull a book from the shelves.

"I see." He contemplated what she had said. "So the first dream is of something searching for you and ultimately latching onto you. Then you experience the binding and the fire as if you are the one at the stake. And lastly you see Anne Ballew in the same situation."

"So if our alchemist's spirit, for want of a better term, had found a way to communicate with you, the first dream could be her search for you. And then she found you. And when you experienced the fire…"

"She was inside me?" Thisbe's voice rose to a squeak. "Controlling me?"

"Not possessing you, no, but perhaps trying to, um, establish her actual identity."

Thisbe stared. "Which she accomplished in the last dream, when I saw her at the execution."

"Exactly."

"But, Uncle Bellard, that's—that's preposterous."

"Oh, yes." He nodded cheerfully. "But it's quite interesting to think about, isn't it?"

"I suppose. But it doesn't make it any less insane."

"I shouldn't worry about that." Bellard reached out and patted her hand. "I will return your compliment by telling you that you are one of the most intelligent people I know. You also have your feet on the ground more solidly than any of us Morelands—though I do believe Reed is very practical, as well. You see things clearly, your thinking is precise and you've never believed in absurdities. No one would say you're given to flights of fancy, let alone insane."

"Thank you." Thisbe smiled back. "But I have trouble believing it myself. It's so absurd."

"Many things have been deemed absurd, only to later be proven correct. The universe is limitless but our understanding of it is small. The fact that we cannot explain how something happened doesn't prove that it did not happen."

"True." Thisbe nodded. It was much the same thought she had had the afternoon before.

"Your young man and I had an interesting conversation along those lines one afternoon. Mr. Gordon's research provokes disdain, but are we being too narrow in our thinking? Shouldn't we explore such things rather than immediately dismiss them? If so, then mustn't we admit that the same principle applies to the things Cornelia has been saying all these years? Just because we cannot see the spirits, does it prove that she cannot?"

Thisbe's heart squeezed in her chest at her uncle's mention of Desmond, but she ignored it and said, "But Grandmother's tales are always so…"

"Grandiose and self-serving?" Bellard ventured. "That is true, and I suspect she embellishes her stories. But, again, the fact that one has lied or exaggerated doesn't mean she isn't telling the truth about other things."

"What should I do? I want to stop having these dreams. If I could figure it out, maybe they would stop."

"I think your answer is to talk to your grandmother," Bellard replied. "I'd examine this Eye thing. Use it and see what one really sees. I trust your judgment—you should, too. You have to explore the possibility before you can reach any conclusion."

"You're right." However galling it would be, she had to talk to her grandmother.

The dowager duchess proved to be as annoyingly delighted as Thisbe had foreseen. "At last you have seen the light. I have waited so long for one of my granddaughters to recognize their gift. I knew it wouldn't be my daughter—Patricia was altogether too flighty. I thought it would be Olivia—I wonder if it's possible that both of you…"

"Grandmother, I don't have any gift. Surely I would have noticed it before now if ghosts were hovering around me."

"It may take time to develop, but it will come," Cornelia said complacently. "Now that you are willing to accept it."

"What I want is to learn more about Anne Ballew. How do you know she is your ancestor if she changed her name?"

"Sadly, Anne herself is someone I've never been fortunate enough to contact. All I know about her is what my grandmother told me. Anne was an alchemist, and she was well-respected, accepted by her peers even though she was a woman. But she had more than brains. She had a gift, more powerful than anyone before her—or since, for that matter."

"This power—I don't really understand it. Are you saying it's magical? That she was a witch?"

"That's the creation of small minds. There was no magic—she didn't brew potions or dabble in witchcraft. She had an ability, like one's ability to think or see or hear. It's just that very few people possess that sense, and most of those who do dismiss it. It's an uncomfortable gift."

"I would think so. What does the Eye do exactly? Have you used it?"

"Yes, from time to time. However, my ability is strong enough that I don't need it, usually. It makes the spirits in the air easier to see. I used it when I was beginning."

"Are you really able to see Old Eldric? My grandfather?"

Cornelia nodded emphatically. "Those who are closest to me are the most visible. All that talk about necromancy is nonsense, of course. One cannot raise the dead with it—and, frankly, I don't know why anyone would wish to do so. Why would anyone want an old moldy corpse walking about?"

"But people believed she could."

"Oh, yes, the legend persists even to this day."

"What about her family? She must have had children if we are descended from her. What happened to them?"

"That is one thing we don't really know. One presumes they moved to the edges of civilization to conceal themselves. Scotland, perhaps."

"But you know that they changed their name. At least one of them."

"They must have. Else why would Ballew not be on the family tree?"

"That's a rather circular argument, don't you think?"

Her grandmother shrugged. "We know we are descended from her because we have the Eye."

"Someone could have stolen it."

"Ah, but then they would have had the instrument but not the ability to use it. We have the ability *and* the Eye."

"That's all you know?"

"Yes. What else would there be?"

"Does it…give you any other ability than seeing the dead?"

"Other abilities? You mean seeing that that young man draws death to him, that you would die because of him?"

"Yes. Or like dreams."

"I saw him without using the Eye. And dreams… I don't know what you're talking about."

"I just thought you might have prophetic dreams, as well."

"No. I'm not an oracle, Thisbe," Cornelia scoffed.

"Of course not. Grandmother, please show me the Eye again. I wasn't paying enough attention the other day—I was angry."

"As well you should be. Imagine that young man trying to worm his way into your affections! It's a good thing I saw him for what he is."

"Yes, well, could you get out the Eye for me? I wanted to look through it."

"I don't know, dear. I couldn't use it until my grandmother died. It's meant only…"

"For the one who carries it. I know. But I was interested in how it worked."

"Well, you most certainly cannot take it apart to see how it works. Don't think I don't remember my cuckoo clock."

"Grandmother, I was six years old then. I won't try to take it apart. I only want to examine it."

"Very well." The duchess went into her bedroom.

Moments later, Thisbe heard a loud wail, and she ran to her grandmother. "What's wrong?"

The dowager whirled to face her. "The Eye! They've taken it."

"The twins again? We'll get it back."

"No, no, you don't understand. I put it in the safe." She pointed to the small square door hanging open halfway up the wall. "Even the Greats couldn't have gotten into that. The Eye is gone!"

CHAPTER TWENTY

"DESMOND…" THE NAME came from Thisbe in little more than a whisper, the now-familiar pain a storm in her chest.

"That blasted man stole the Eye!" The duchess slammed the safe door shut. "I should have known."

"So should I," Thisbe added grimly. Why had it come as a shock that Desmond had betrayed her yet again?

"I shouldn't have shown it to him," Cornelia went on bitterly, turning an accusatory gaze at her granddaughter.

"I know, Grandmother. This is my fault. I was too impulsive. After what I'd learned, I should have realized he couldn't be trusted to even see the thing." A saving anger shot through Thisbe, fury drowning out all pain and regret. "Don't worry. I will get it back."

Thisbe strode down the hall, her mind suddenly clear and hard as glass. The Eye had always been Desmond's goal. It struck her with great clarity that Desmond had been the one who suggested they hire the twins' nanny. Katie, his landlord's sister, presumably Desmond's friend. A woman who wouldn't look out of place anywhere in the house, since the twins went all over.

No wonder he'd given up his pretense of affection for Thisbe. He had insinuated an accomplice into the house, someone better placed than he to search for the Eye. Then Thisbe, like a fool, had revealed the Eye's hiding place to him. He might not know the exact spot, but he was able to narrow down the area Katie would have to search. He could tell her that her charges had found the thing before.

Her fury bubbled even higher at the thought that they might have used Alex and Con to pursue their goal. Well, she'd deal with Katie later. First and foremost, she had to find Desmond and wrest the Eye from him. Katie wouldn't have kept it; she would have given it to Desmond.

Thisbe grabbed her warm cloak and ran out to hail a hansom…though this time she remembered to grab a handful of coins as she left. As the hack carried her toward the optical shop, she brooded, stoking her anger. How could he? How could she have been so mistaken about him? Even when she knew Desmond had wooed her in order to get the Eye, she had hoped deep down that it hadn't been entirely a sham with Desmond, that he had some feeling for her, at least a kindness.

Desmond had played her for a fool once again. Well, he wouldn't anymore. She was done with being gullible and naive. She was contemptuous of trust in anyone but her own family. She was impervious to Desmond's dark eyes and sweet smile.

After paying the driver and telling him to wait, she marched into the optical shop. The middle-aged man behind the counter widened his eyes and stepped quickly around the counter, holding his hands out as if to stop her. "No, miss, please, I beg you, not another fight. My shop—"

"I have no intention of doing anything to your shop. I'm after just one man." She directed a gaze worthy of her grandmother at him. "Step aside."

He moved back with a moan, hands to his head. "Another morning lost."

Thisbe shoved aside the curtain, and her eyes went

straight to Desmond sitting at the back, his dark head bent over his work. Around her, everyone froze for a moment, then scrambled to their feet and turned toward Desmond, ready for another round of entertainment. Desmond's head came up at the clatter, and his eyes went to Thisbe. An expression flashed across his face—in the past Thisbe would have interpreted it as pleasure; now she wouldn't even try to guess at his emotions.

"Thisbe." In the utter silence of the shop, his word was clear. He started toward her, and Thisbe rushed toward him.

"How could you!" Thisbe had intended to be cold, hard and relentless, but she couldn't hold back this hot rush of anger. "I trusted you! Of all the things you've done, the lies, the deception, the—the betrayal, I didn't expect this of you."

Desmond stopped. "What? I don't kno—"

"Don't you dare deny it!" She came to a halt a yard away from him. She had meant to slap him, had contemplated it with eagerness all the way over here, but now, looking into his face, she could not. Nor could she stop the tears that welled in her eyes. "You stole it. You stole the Eye, and I want it back."

His jaw dropped. "What? I... The Eye—it's missing?"

"Did you think I wouldn't know it was you? Did you think I was such a love-struck ninny I'd not go to the police? Well, you're wrong. That's exactly where I'm going if you don't return it this instant."

Desmond grabbed his jacket and took Thisbe's arm, starting for the door. "I think this is better taken up outside, don't you?"

Thisbe said nothing but went with him. Now, with the first spate of rage over, she was aware of all the curious eyes and ears in the room.

"Desmond, where are you going?" the owner of the shop exclaimed as they walked past. "Are you leaving again? Blast it, Desmond, you can't—"

Desmond closed the front door behind him, cutting off his employer's words. He turned to her. "Thisbe, I did *not* take the Eye. I swear to you, I didn't."

"I can't take your word anymore. You lied to me!"

"I did not lie to you."

"Omitting the truth is a lie."

"You did the same thing!" Anger flared in his eyes. "Damn it, Thisbe, I was not solely to blame. You hid your identity from me. How was I supposed to know who you were? Who your grandmother was? I don't know the family tree of every blasted peer in the realm."

"Even if that is true, which I doubt, the fact remains that you didn't tell me after you found out who I was." Thisbe slashed her hand through the air. "This is pointless. I'm not here to argue about who is to blame for what. I am here to get back the Eye. I have no desire to air our family matters to the world, so I would prefer not to have to turn this over to the authorities. I would think you would rather not be investigated by them, as well. Give me back the Eye, and we can go our separate ways."

"I. Don't. Have. The. Eye," Desmond said through clenched teeth. "Why are you so bloody determined to put the worst possible connotation on everything I've done? Stop being bullheaded and think about it for a moment. Why would I take the Eye, knowing I would be the most obvious suspect? Why wouldn't I have taken it before?"

"You didn't know where it was until I stupidly showed you its location."

"Oh, for—" He broke off and glanced around at the

passersby, who were slowing their steps and watching them. "Is that your hack?"

Before she could answer, he took her arm and steered her toward the vehicle. Thisbe jerked her arm from his grasp, sending him a baleful look, and marched off to the carriage.

"Where to, miss?" the driver asked.

"I don't know." She hesitated, glancing back at Desmond.

He spread his arms wide in a manner she found immensely annoying. "Do you want to search my room? Will that satisfy you?"

"Very well." Thisbe climbed into the carriage, leaving Desmond to give the man their destination. It apparently required a good bit of explanation, but Thisbe didn't mind. It gave her a chance to calm down. However satisfying it had been to spew out her rage at Desmond, it would serve no purpose to let her emotions rule her. She must be calm. Logical. Make him see that hers was the correct course. Desmond was, despite all else, a man of reason and intellect.

He climbed in and sat down beside her. The hack was small, with only one seat, and he was uncomfortably close to her. Their arms almost touched. She looked down at his long legs, stretched across the width of the carriage and still looking too cramped. Why did she find that so endearing? And why did she still feel this way when she looked at him? How could she want to smooth back the lock of hair that fell across his face, or place her palm against his cheek? How could she want to kiss him? Thisbe turned quickly away, looking out the window.

"Letting me know the Eye was in your grandmother's room was scarcely giving anything away," Desmond said, taking up the argument again. "I didn't see where she hid it."

"You knew it was in her bedroom."

"Anyone would have guessed that it would be there. I could have searched her rooms before," Desmond said.

"Perhaps you did."

"You know I didn't. You were with me every minute I was in your home."

"Which is exactly why you didn't steal it earlier. That's why you slipped your cohort into our house."

"My cohort? What— Who— Good Lord, do you mean Katie?"

"Yes. Katie. The woman you so conveniently knew, who could so conveniently start immediately, whom we would all trust because we trusted you. Whose presence anywhere in the house would never be noticed as yours would have been."

"Don't." His eyes hardened. "Don't you dare bring Katie into all this. She is entirely blameless—she knows nothing about the Eye. I gave your mother her name because I wanted to help the duchess, and it was a pleasant bonus that I was able to help Katie, as well. That is all. If you let her go because of this, without any proof, it would be heartless."

"*You* want to talk to me about being heartless?" Thisbe said in patent disbelief.

"At the moment, I don't want to talk to you about anything at all."

Unbelievably, foolishly, his words stung, and Thisbe had to glance away to hide the tears that suddenly filled her eyes.

Despite his words, Desmond continued in a low, bitter voice, "I never thought I would see you act like an aristocrat." He knocked on the roof and called to the driver, "Here it is."

Desmond opened the door before the carriage had come to a full stop and jumped down. He stood waiting for her, hands jammed into his pockets. He nodded toward a narrow alleyway between two houses. "It's up the stairs."

Thisbe followed him up the two flights of stairs to a door high in the outside wall. He opened the door and went inside.

"You leave it unlocked?" Thisbe asked in surprise.

"I've nothing to steal."

She walked into a small, oddly shaped room with a peaked ceiling that sloped on both sides down to a short wall. It had clearly once been an attic. Next to the door was a single window letting in a dim light, clearly limited by the taller building beside it. The place was small and spare, with only a few pieces of plain furniture, none of them new. But it was meticulously clean and had a certain quaint appeal.

Thisbe glanced around the room. Books were scattered across a small table. His comb and brush, along with shaving paraphernalia, sat on the chest beside a washbasin, a small mirror above it. A muffler was draped over the back of a chair. It felt very awkward to stand here in this private place of Desmond's. She was pushing in where she didn't belong, where she wasn't wanted.

It was obvious that Annie Blue's Eye was nowhere to be seen, and that there was little place to hide it. Desmond ostentatiously opened each of the dresser drawers and shoved the clothes to the side to show that the Eye was not there. When he closed the last one, he turned to her, arms crossed, eyebrows raised.

Thisbe swallowed. It hurt to see this harder, colder

Desmond. She walked to the window, just to give herself something to do. Looking out, she said, "I haven't said anything to Katie. Nor to my mother or anyone but you. Nor would I accuse Katie without any proof or a chance to defend herself." She forced herself to look at him. "I'm not acting like an aristocrat. I suspect her because of her connection to you, not because she's from a lower class."

"Really?" Desmond moved closer. "I think that's *exactly* why you accused her. Why you assumed I had taken it. You know there are several others who want it, yet you came straight to me. What about Carson? Wouldn't you have taken his word as a gentleman when he said he didn't steal the Eye? Would you have accused Carson as quickly, as harshly, as you did me?"

"No! Because I didn't love Carson." Tears sprang into Thisbe's eyes, and she started for the door. She would *not* let him see her cry.

"Thisbe…" Desmond's voice lost its hard edge. He caught her arm, stepping in front of her. "Thisbe, look at me." He tilted up her chin and cupped her cheek, his thumb sliding across it to wipe away an errant tear. "I'm sorry. I'm so sorry that I caused you any pain. If I could go back and change it all, I would. But I can't. The best I could do was tell you the truth, even though I knew it would cost me your affection. And I am telling you the truth now. I did not steal the Eye."

It was an almost physical pain to be this close to him— to hear his voice, to feel his skin upon her cheek, to look into the dark depths of his eyes. With all her heart, Thisbe wanted to believe him. She wanted to melt into his arms and feel his lips on hers, to put her faith in him. But she was wiser now. She knew to think rather than feel. She took a step back, breaking their connection.

She would use her head. And her head suspected he

was probably telling the truth. Her anger and hurt had colored her judgment. She had wanted Desmond to be the culprit. But, looking at it logically, it would be a foolish thing for him to steal the Eye right after she'd shown it to him, and Desmond was not foolish. Nor would he be unwise enough to stay in the city, working at the same place, where she could so easily find him. When she told him it had been stolen, the shock on his face had been very real.

"Very well," Thisbe said. She wasn't ready to trust him, but if he hadn't stolen it, she could use his help. If he had, he'd obviously hidden the thing, and perhaps she could get a clue from him as to where. "I'm willing to go forward on that premise."

There was a tinge of disappointment in his eyes, but he only nodded and said, "Obviously the others in my group are the main suspects. Mr. Wallace, Professor Gordon and Carson. One of the others could have done it, I suppose, but..." He shook his head. "They haven't displayed as much interest. I'd put them last."

"I presume you told all of them about the Eye," Thisbe ventured.

The guilt on Desmond's face was answer enough. "I'm sorry. I told them that the dowager duchess wouldn't let us study it. So, yes, they knew for certain that it was real and that your grandmother did indeed possess it. I suppose I should have told them it didn't exist, but that didn't even occur to me. I couldn't lie to Professor Gordon. The man has been ridiculed so much, I couldn't bear not to let him know that he'd been right about the Eye all these years." He dragged his fingers back through his hair. "Clearly I am a failure at deception."

He had done well enough at it with her. Thisbe bit

back the words; they would only show her hurt. "I take it you described the Eye to him."

"Only in general terms. I said it was an optical device, a lens with prisms. That's all, and I said nothing about where it was located. Indeed, I told Gordon many times how impossible it would be to find and steal something out of that house. I assumed he would continue to try to convince your grandmother, but I couldn't believe that anyone would steal it."

"Clearly someone did. Professor Gordon seems the likeliest."

Desmond sighed. "I'd hate to think he would go that far, but he did seem almost desperate. He thinks he can prove his theories are right if he has the Eye, and he wants so badly to be accepted by his peers again. We must talk to him. He'll be at the laboratory."

"First, we should return home and take our carriage. It will make the ride more pleasant." And much safer not to be in such close proximity to Desmond.

Gordon was not at the laboratory. Neither was anyone else, so they were able to search the cabinets. Two were locked, but Desmond found the key in one of Gordon's desk drawers. Disappointingly, they contained nothing but supplies and equipment.

"I didn't really think he would hide it there," Desmond said. "More likely he'd want to keep it close to him, away from prying eyes."

They returned to the street, where her driver patiently waited, and Desmond directed him to Professor Gordon's flat. Inside the coach, they sat across from each other in awkward silence. Thisbe decided that it was hardly any better to sit across from Desmond than next to him, for now she could look at him, see every feature that her heart had missed: the shape of his lip, the little curl at the nape of his neck, where his hair met his collar, his long, slender fingers. He was without his gloves again; the man needed a keeper.

She turned her head away. Better to keep her eyes on the window.

"How is your family?" Desmond asked abruptly. Thisbe glanced over to find him steadfastly studying his hands. "The twins? Are they well?"

"The twins are as they always are. Healthy as horses and leading everyone on a merry chase."

A faint smile curved his lips and he glanced up. "And your sisters? I suppose your family must hate me now."

Thisbe shrugged. "The Morelands don't traffic much in hate. Disappointed, perhaps."

He nodded, his eyes sad. "I am very sorry for that."

Thisbe was determined not to be swayed by sympathy, but after a moment, she said, "Olivia stood up for you. A bit."

The corner of his mouth quirked, and good humor briefly glinted in his eyes. "A champion for lost causes, I see."

"She has a kind heart." Thisbe returned her gaze to the window. Every look at him weakened her resolve. "Ah. We're stopping. We must be here."

They stepped out onto the cobblestone street and started toward the building, but before they reached it, the door opened and a man emerged.

"Carson!"

Carson stopped, looking equally startled. "Desmond." His eyes were curious as his gaze slid over to Thisbe, but he said only, "Miss Moreland."

"What are you doing here?" Desmond asked, frowning.

The other man raised his eyebrows slightly at Desmond's

abrupt tone. "Looking for the professor, as I imagine you are. He's not at the laboratory, so I thought I'd try here, but no luck. Perhaps he's in class or the library."

Desmond's eyes narrowed, and he walked around Carson to enter the building. Carson watched Desmond's back for a moment, then pivoted to Thisbe. "He seems a bit...distrusting."

"Yes. As I have learned to be."

"Ah. I see." He paused. "I must say, I was surprised to see you and Desmond together."

"Well, needs must."

"My, but we are cryptic today." Carson's eyes danced. "Dare I venture a guess why?"

"Yes, why don't you?" Thisbe's gaze was level. Carson was just below Gordon and his patron on Thisbe's list of suspects. However flippant he might be, he must be as interested in the Eye as the rest of them, and he was the only one in the group besides Desmond who had sought to make her a friend.

Carson studied her. "Frankly, I'm not sure, though I confess I am growing more curious by the moment. Something to do with the Eye, I presume. The dowager duchess has relented? Somehow that seems unlikely. Harrison has managed to work his way back into your good graces and you've let him use the Eye? From your frosty manner, I think not." His eyes widened suddenly. "It's missing. That's it, isn't it? Someone stole Annie Blue's Eye."

"You leaped to that conclusion quickly."

"It seemed the only logical explanation left. I'm right, aren't I? I can see it in your eyes."

Desmond returned. "He doesn't answer his door."

"I suggest we try the university next," Carson offered,

"We?" Desmond directed a black look at his colleague. "I don't recall anyone inviting you along."

"That's why I invited myself." Carson lifted in hands in a placatory gesture. "What's the harm? I know why you're looking for him, and I can help."

"You told him?" Desmond asked Thisbe.

"I guessed it," Carson said. "Come, come, Desmond. No need to be piggish about it. Three heads are better than two, after all."

"I am the one you need to ask," Thisbe pointed out. "And you might as well come. At least I'll know you aren't running off to tell some accomplice about it." And it would be easier, surely, if she was not alone with Desmond.

"There you go." Carson grinned. He made a sweeping gesture toward the carriage. "Well? View halloo, children. We'd best be after our quarry."

CHAPTER TWENTY-ONE

CARSON *WOULD* MANAGE to insert himself into it. It only made sense, as Thisbe had said, to keep an eye on Carson, but the man was a veritable fly in the ointment for this single chance to be alone with Thisbe. And wasn't that a sorry state of affairs, to hunger so for Thisbe that even her icy, decidedly unfriendly company was something to treasure?

The past week had been such a cavalcade of misery that even her castigating him hadn't completely drowned out Desmond's pleasure in seeing Thisbe. When he looked up and saw her sweeping into his workshop, her color high, her eyes brilliant, his first emotion was pure joy. It had been immediately followed, of course, by the certainty that she was furious. Guilt, indignation and anger had bubbled in him, mingling with pleasure and a peculiar hope—after all, there must be some feeling for him still inside her to invoke such fury.

She was beautiful even when she wouldn't smile, her voice welcome to his ears, though it sliced at him. And even as he'd lashed out at her for acting like an aristocrat, his bitterness could not dim what he felt for her. She had been so typically Thisbe, defending her actions with reason and honesty, that he'd wanted to kiss her until neither of them could breathe.

However painful it was to be with her, knowing that he had lost her, aware of how badly he had bungled everything, his heart soaked up every moment of it. Now here was Carson, sitting beside him, chattering away like a magpie, teasing Desmond and flirting with Thisbe in that careless way that Desmond would never be able to carry off.

It was futile to brood over it, however, and Desmond knew that he should set his mind to accomplishing the one thing that might find favor in Thisbe's eyes. He must locate that wretched Eye and restore it to her grandmother. For himself, aside from a bit of guilt that his actions had in all likelihood set the thief on his course, Desmond didn't care a whit about the Eye. He had little liking for the dowager duchess; he doubted that the instrument actually worked; and frankly, at this moment he didn't really care whether or not it did. Nor was he feeling any warmth for his colleagues, at least one of whom was apparently a thief.

But one thing he would like, very much, was to see Thisbe's eyes light with pleasure, to have her smile at him warmly. He wanted to prove to her that he had not stolen the Eye, and perhaps giving it back would go some small way to showing her that he had never used her to get the thing.

Desmond had no hope that he could win her back; he'd lost her love, and he'd lost her trust. He doubted that either of those could really be mended. Then there was the inconvenient fact that he somehow spelled doom for Thisbe. Even if those obstacles could be surmounted, he would never be a suitable husband. He had no name of any note, no hope of fame or fortune.

No, his goal was much smaller than that and, hopefully, more achievable. If he could win back some of the regard she had once had for him, enough at least for friendship, if he could remove the loathing for him in her eyes, that would be enough.

Which was a lie, of course. It wouldn't be enough. It would never be enough. It wouldn't satisfy his hunger, his longing to kiss her again, to hold her in his arms, to feel the shiver of pleasure run through her when he caressed her.

But it would at least be far better than the emptiness he had now.

Thisbe's presence at the school garnered some attention. Women had been admitted to the university only this year, and the sight of a female was still something of an oddity. Thisbe ignored the stares, and Desmond's scowl at the gawkers soon sent them on their way.

Professor Gordon's minuscule office was dark and locked, no student waiting to see him. After equally fruitless trips to several lecture halls, they turned to the library, an immense place filled with countless nooks and crannies for sitting and reading.

"Best to split up," Carson suggested. "We can cover more territory."

Desmond jumped at the opportunity to rid them of Carson's presence. "Yes, good idea. Thisbe and I will take this side."

Carson's amused glance told him he understood Desmond's real interest in dividing the work, but he said nothing and strolled away.

"That was rather rude," Thisbe said as they walked away. "Not to mention high-handed. What if I had preferred to accompany Carson?"

"I presumed you'd want to keep your eye on me, given that I'm such a villain," Desmond replied.

"I'd like to keep an eye on both of you," she retorted.

"But Carson was right—it would take us a great deal more time if we remained together."

A glare and a "shh" from a nearby student sent them on their way more quietly. They searched every floor, asking each patron—to the annoyance of a large number of them—whether they had seen Professor Gordon that day. Most didn't know the man, and the ones who recognized the name had not seen him recently.

When Carson rejoined them, he reported a similar lack of success. "He's fled."

"You don't know that," Desmond protested.

"I know he's not at home, he's not at the laboratory and he's not here." Carson ticked off his points on his fingers.

"It's understandable that you don't want your friend to be a thief," Thisbe told Desmond, her voice more gentle than it had been any other time today. "But it doesn't look good that he's nowhere to be found."

"People go places other than home and work."

"Gordon?" Carson raised a skeptical eyebrow.

"Point taken," Desmond admitted.

"He has to be somewhere," Thisbe said. "He cannot simply vanish. We must—"

"Wallace," Desmond said.

"He's also someone to look into," Carson agreed. "But first—"

"No. I mean, Professor Gordon could have gone to Wallace's house. Wallace has been pressing him about the Eye. I think the professor would have been eager to show the Eye to his patron."

"Yes. And if Wallace stole it, he'd want Gordon to examine it. Conduct some experiment with it." Thisbe smiled at Desmond, and for an instant, everything seemed as it had been, their conversation easy.

Then Carson spoke, and the moment was gone.

Thisbe's smile dropped away, and her body stiffened a little. Clearly she had remembered that she was supposed to despise Desmond.

The visit to Wallace's house proved equally fruitless. No one answered their knock, and the windows were shuttered, with no bit of light showing.

"He's bolted, too," Carson said, turning away. "What's your plan now?"

"I don't know that I have one," Thisbe admitted as they gathered at the carriage.

"I think we're done for the day," Desmond said. He didn't want to discuss the subject with Carson. The sooner they could rid themselves of the man, the better. "It's getting dark, and we've run out of options."

To his surprise, Thisbe didn't protest. "Yes, perhaps you are right. I must talk this over with my grandmother. Please, I beg you, both of you, don't let out word of this theft." She looked searchingly at Carson, then Desmond.

"Of course," Carson replied. "I won't say a word. If I can be of any further help to you, I hope you will not hesitate to call me."

"Thank you. I will remember."

"Good day, then." Carson nodded in farewell. "Harrison? I'm headed for the laboratory. You?"

"No. I believe I'll go home." With Carson hanging there, waiting for him, Desmond could do little other than depart. The man was a complete hindrance. Desmond glanced at Thisbe and could read nothing in her face.

"Good day, then." Thisbe settled the matter by taking her leave of the men and getting into her carriage.

The two men walked off. For once, Carson provided none of his usual light chatter, and Desmond was too sunken in gloom to say anything. He had intended to remain with Thisbe, but Carson had neatly blocked him there. He should have come up with something more clever to separate Carson from the group.

At the cross street, Desmond parted from his colleague, setting off in the general direction of his home. At the next corner he glanced back and, seeing that Carson was no longer in sight, he turned again. If he wanted to talk to Thisbe, he would have to call at Thisbe's house and hope she would admit him, though it seemed unlikely.

A carriage rumbled up the street and came to a stop beside him. Desmond glanced over. It was the Moreland coach, and Thisbe was opening the door. A happiness far greater than was reasonable flooded him. Perhaps there was still hope for him after all.

"I THOUGHT WE could walk—Broughton House isn't far," Thisbe said, stepping out of the carriage. Desmond looked faintly surprised, and she realized that a stroll was not something one would typically do with a person she disliked. She quickly explained, "We need to talk. We'll have more time if we walk." She felt herself blushing and broke off to tell the coachmen to return to Broughton House.

"Good. I wanted to talk without Carson about," Desmond agreed as they started down the street.

"I did, as well. I was about to suggest stopping myself. Carson was helpful, but I didn't want to admit him to our plans."

"Do we have plans?" Desmond's mouth quirked up on one side.

"No," Thisbe admitted, quelling the flutter in her abdomen that his half smile always brought. "I don't know where else to go or what to do."

Desmond nodded. "I wonder…"

"What?" Thisbe asked. She knew that look on his face. "What are you thinking?"

"I'm thinking that Carson left us too easily. I would have expected him to protest or come up with reasons to stay."

"The way he did this afternoon when we went to the university," Thisbe agreed.

"The question is why, when he was so eager to be with us before, was he so willing to leave now?" Desmond asked.

"Perhaps he simply wanted you gone, as you did him," she suggested.

"Possibly. If so, he may turn up on your doorstep soon. That was my intention."

It shouldn't have pleased Thisbe so much that Desmond hadn't wanted to part from her. "Did you think I wouldn't come around to get you?"

"Yes," Desmond answered simply. "I'm not one of your favorite people at the moment."

Thisbe didn't want to get drawn down that path again. "Why do you think he wanted to get away from us?"

"One possibility is that Carson is the thief. He seems a much more likely candidate for breaking into your house than a portly, sedentary man of middle years such as Professor Gordon. And why was he hanging about Gordon's flat when we went there? Did you notice that he never really answered my question?"

Thisbe nodded. "Yes, I saw that. And you're right—Professor Gordon doesn't seem the sort to break into Broughton House. Neither does a gentleman of Mr. Wallace's position. But if Carson is the thief, why did he join us?"

"To throw us off. To fix it in our heads that the culprit is Gordon or Wallace." He shrugged. "Or he could be entirely innocent of the theft and helped us search as a kindness, then merely wanted to get home for his supper."

"But you don't believe that."

Desmond shrugged. "I'm not sure. I can't help but be suspicious of him. At the beginning, when we first learned that the duchess wouldn't let us study the Eye, Carson was the one who brought up stealing it."

"I see." Thisbe tried to ignore the pang in her chest at this reminder of Desmond's betrayal.

"On the other hand, Carson is prone to jests and sarcastic remarks, and I'm not sure he means them. He has this way of talking…"

"As if everything is ironical—as if he's amused and cynical all at the same time."

"Exactly." Desmond flashed her a grin. "It makes it hard to figure him out."

"What if…Carson has a partner," Thisbe mused. "Carson was keeping us on a false trail, giving the other man time to go to ground with the Eye. Once that was accomplished, Carson was eager to join his partner."

"So he could be in league with Gordon or Wallace. Or maybe a conspiracy of all of them."

"Another possibility is that Carson had nothing to do with the theft, but he wants the Eye himself," Thisbe continued. "So he helped us, hoping he'd get a clue."

"That's it." Excitement threaded Desmond's voice, and he turned to her. "Perhaps he realized where the thief might have hidden the Eye. He covered half the library by himself. What if he met someone who knew where Gordon went and he didn't tell us?"

"He set off to find Gordon without any interference from us." Thisbe caught Desmond's enthusiasm. "We must go back and see if we can find who talked to him." She turned to look in the direction of the university.

"I think it's too late," Desmond said. The afternoon had turned to dusk, with evening falling rapidly, as it did in winter. The purplish sky was deepening to black, and along the street, the gas streetlights were already on.

"Oh." Thisbe's voice fell. "Yes, of course. Whoever he talked to would be gone by the time we arrived."

"It doesn't matter. We can revisit the library tomorrow morning. If he did find someone there, it's quite possible the man could be there again. Or there might be someone we didn't talk to today who could give us the information we want."

"Yes. Of course. That's a better plan." They started toward Thisbe's house again, their pace picking up. "That will give us time to think about everything. I'll talk to Grandmother about Mr. Wallace, see if she knows whether he has a house in the country he might have gone to. She knows an amazing amount about everyone."

As they walked, they made plans for meeting at the library the following morning. It was a little disturbing how much Thisbe's heart lightened at the prospect of continuing their search the next day. That was dangerous.

She should keep her distance, maintain the proper perspective. It would be foolish to rely on her growing belief that Desmond had not stolen her grandmother's artifact. After all, the reasons for Carson joining their search applied to Desmond, as well. He could merely be trying to mislead or distract her.

There had been many times today when everything had seemed the way it had before, when she felt the thrill, the satisfaction, of their minds running along the same path. Was she allowing that ease, that familiarity, to sway her? She could not let herself be fooled by him again. It would be reckless to trust him, to let herself dream once more.

Before long Broughton House loomed up before them. Thisbe stopped at the passageway that led to the side door and turned to Desmond. The glow of the streetlamp fell across his face, highlighting his deep, dark eyes, his mobile mouth, the line of his cheekbones. What was he thinking? What did he feel? Regret? Sorrow? Satisfaction at a job well-done?

"Thisbe…" He moved closer, lowering his head a little to gaze into her eyes. "I want to explain."

"Desmond…please. Don't. I cannot—"

"I'm not asking you to forgive me. But I want to tell you the truth. I cannot bear that you go on thinking I set out to use you, that I didn't really feel what I did for you. I didn't engineer meeting you. I had no idea who you were when I saw you at that lecture. I learned later that Wallace had approached the dowager duchess about getting the Eye, but I didn't know that Moreland was the duchess's family name or that you were her granddaughter. I know it sounds too great a coincidence, but coincidences do happen. I sat down beside you on purpose, but it was because you were so beautiful. I was drawn to you, but not because you were the dowager duchess's granddaughter."

Thisbe drew a shaky breath. "Even if I accept that explanation, at some point you *knew* who I was, yet you continued to deceive me. You used me to gain entrance to my home so that you could find the Eye."

"I didn't give a damn about the Eye. I don't know how to convince you of that, but it's the truth. What I felt for you, the things I said to you, had nothing to do with Annie Blue's Eye. When I realized that it was your grandmother who owned the Eye, I told Professor Gordon I wouldn't do it. You know that I never asked you about it or attempted to persuade you to help me."

"If you'd only told me…"

"I didn't dare. I was too afraid of losing you. I didn't want to see the disappointment and distrust in your eyes. I didn't want you to look at me the way you do now. It seemed to me that if you knew, it would taint everything."

"If you were so concerned about losing me, then why did you leave me?" Thisbe clamped her mouth shut, ashamed of the note of longing and hurt in her voice.

"For the reasons I told you. As long as you were with me, you were in danger."

"Because of Grandmother's prediction?" Thisbe asked scornfully.

"Yes. I didn't want to believe it at first. I told myself it was nonsense. But when they threatened you, I realized that the duchess was right—I endangered you."

"Threatened me? Just a moment. Who threatened me? What are you talking about?"

"Mr. Wallace. Or, rather, some ruffian whom I assume worked for Wallace. He implied that something would happen to you if I didn't steal the Eye for them. Do you remember that day when you were knocked into the street?"

"Yes. But that was an accident."

"That man who grabbed your arm and kept you from falling was the man who had threatened to hurt you the day before. He engineered that fall to show me what he could do."

"Desmond." Thisbe shook her head. "I can't take all this in. It's so absurd. Like something out of one of Olivia's novels."

He took her by the arms, his gaze intent on hers. "It happened. It was real. I couldn't let anything happen to you. I had to break all ties with you. I had to show them that they couldn't reach me through you. To prove I had lost whatever favor I had with your family."

"Why didn't you tell me this then?"

"I should have. It would doubtless have been an effective way to remove whatever affection you had for me." He sighed. "I was weak. I couldn't bear for you to think so little of me." He reached up to cup his hand against her cheek. "If I couldn't be with you, at least I could remain untarnished in your memories. But, of course, that wasn't possible."

"Desmond…" Tears swam in her eyes, blurring the image of his face.

"No, don't cry," he murmured, wiping a tear from her cheek. "I never wanted to cause you any pain. If I could do anything to take it away, I would." He lowered his head and kissed her lips softly. "Thisbe, I'm sorry. So sorry. It would have been better for you if you'd never met me. I'd take it all away if I could."

"No," Thisbe said fiercely. "I don't want that. I'd never want to not know you. To not remember…"

Impulsively, she stretched up to kiss him. His arms wrapped around her like steel bands, and his lips sank into hers.

CHAPTER TWENTY-TWO

IT WAS INTOXICATING. Exhilarating. Heartbreaking. Suddenly every nerve ending was alive, every sense awakened. The air cold all around them, the heat searing inside her. The feel of him, the scent of him, the taste of him, all achingly familiar and so long missed, dizzied her.

Their lips parted only to reunite, his arms falling away only to slide beneath her mantle. Thisbe's hands clutched the lapels of his coat as she pressed herself up into him. She had never before felt such heat, such throbbing need. She wanted to feel his skin against hers, his mouth on her body, his hands on her flesh.

Constricted by their clothing, they caressed and kissed, lost for a few minutes in a passion blind to everything else. Desmond shuddered, a low moan escaping him, and he broke from her. He stared at her for a long moment, his eyes stark. Then, with an inarticulate growl, he turned and rushed away into the night.

THISBE RAN UP the back stairs to her room to compose herself before she could face anyone in her family. Her cheeks were flushed, her lips soft and reddened, and her breath came far too rapidly. And those were just the outer signs. Inside her, heat burned low in her abdomen, and every nerve in her body tingled. Even after she had outwardly pulled herself together, her mind kept returning to their brief encounter, remembering each touch, each kiss, and she melted inside all over again.

Despite everything Desmond had done, she still wanted him. But she could not allow that to make any difference. After all, she loved chocolate, too, but that didn't mean it was good to stuff herself with it. And love was far more treacherous than chocolate.

Kissing him had been wrong. Foolish. She should never have done it, and it was imperative that she not allow it to happen again. She shouldn't even meet him tomorrow at the library. Looking at him, talking to him, even laughing—everything about him tempted her.

But how could she not use his help in her search for Gordon and Wallace? She must find the men, and Desmond knew far more about them than she did. It was only logical to combine her efforts with his again. And, really...she was a grown woman, intelligent and disciplined. Surely she could control her worst impulses; she would simply have to take more care. But as she drifted off to sleep, a nagging voice in the back of her mind whispered that she was only making excuses...

THE FIRE ROARED UPWARD, and all around her the crowd cheered. As they watched the figure standing still amidst the blaze, a storm blew in. Heavy gray clouds scudded across the sky, and thunder rumbled in the distance. The wind swirled, bending the flames away and sending sparks shooting into the air. It seemed almost as if the wind protected the woman from the pyre, and for a wild moment, Thisbe thought the heavens were about to open and send down a deluge to extinguish the burning logs. But there was no rain. And in the next instant, the wind tossed the flames onto the woman's skirts.

The fire raced up her clothes. Within seconds, she

*was engulfed. Flames swirled around her and her fiery
strands of hair danced on the wind. But, impossibly,
Anne's face showed no sign of pain, only a deep, abid-
ing rage. There was another clap of thunder, and lightning shot across the sky.*

*Anne's eyes were as bright and fierce as the light-
ning. She raised her bound hands and pointed straight
at Thisbe. "Thou shalt obey me. There is no escape—
thou owest me."*

*Thisbe stared at her, rooted to the spot, her chest
flooded with fear. The air around her was charged, her
hair standing up on her arms. She tried to speak, to deny
the other woman's words, but no sound came out.*

*Anne raised her arms, turned her face up to the heav-
ens and cried, "Come, Samael, I await thee. I call on
thee, oh, Gabriel, oh, Dumah. Hear thy daughter's plea.
By treachery am I slain, and I look to thee for vengeance.
Come thou, Barachiel and Harut, to my bidding. Come,
Michael. Come, Kushiel. Come, Azrael and Abaddon.
Grant me thy strength." She lowered her gaze and her
bound hands to Thisbe. "I bind thee to me. By all the
saints above and the demons below, I bind thee. A life
for a life. Thou art mine..."*

THISBE CAME AWAKE with a start, as she always did after
one of these nightmares, her heart pounding and gasping
for air. The faint scent of lightning hung in the air, her
scalp still prickled and the hair on her arms was raised.

She lay there for a few minutes, waiting for her heart
and lungs to return to normal. She wasn't sure that her
mind and emotions could. Anne Ballew had cursed her?
Bound Thisbe to her? What did that mean? And how
could she possible owe her anything? The woman had
died three centuries before Thisbe was born.

Thisbe groaned. This was ridiculous—as if she could make sense of the outlandish words in a dream! If she kept this up, she really was going to go mad.

Well, that had murdered sleep as effectively as Macbeth. Thisbe got out of bed, wrapped her dressing gown around her and went to the window. Dawn was breaking. She might as well get ready for the day. And she wanted to speak to her uncle before she left to meet Desmond.

She was lucky enough to find Bellard at the breakfast table, eating in companionable silence with her father. Thisbe waited until her father and great-uncle had finished their meal before she asked, "Do either of you know anything about the names of angels and such?"

"Angels?" Her father blinked. "Well, the Christian era is a bit past my time of expertise, but, let me see, there's Jophiel. Isn't he the one who drove Adam and Eve from the Garden?"

"I was thinking more of Michael and Gabriel. Abaddon."

"Well, I believe Gabriel was a messenger," the duke said. "Rather like the role of Hermes in the Greek pantheon."

"Ah, but in the Muslim religion, he's considered the angel of destruction," Uncle Bellard pointed out.

"Is that so?" the duke said, turning to his uncle, intrigued, as he always was, by any academic discussion.

"Yes. Now, Michael, interestingly, is regarded as the angel of mercy by Muslims, but in Christian faiths, or at least some of them, he is the angel of death."

"Naturally," Thisbe muttered.

"Now, who else, dear? I don't believe I'm familiar with that last one you said," Uncle Bellard went on.

"Have you taken up a new area of study?" her father asked. "Religions?"

"No, it was just a dream I had. Someone said their names."

Her great-uncle sent her a shrewd look. "Ah, I see. Were those all the names that were mentioned?"

"No, there were others. Azrael, Dumah…" Thisbe related all the rest of the names Anne Ballew had called upon. She remembered them vividly.

"Odd dream," the duke commented. "I've heard of Azrael. He's the angel of retribution."

"And death," Bellard added.

"Another angel of death?" Thisbe remarked.

"Mmm, I believe death figures prominently in several of them. Samael is connected to death somehow as well, though I cannot remember exactly how." The small man popped up from his seat. "Wait a moment. I know just where…" His expression turned vague, and he hurried out of the room.

"I didn't mean for him to go to any trouble," Thisbe said guiltily.

"Nonsense." The duke waved off her concern. "Nothing Uncle Bellard loves like research. Keeps him young, in my opinion."

Proving her father's words, the old man was soon back, carrying two tomes and beaming. "Such a fascinating topic, Thisbe. I could get lost in this for days."

"And probably will," her father said with a chuckle.

"Too true, dear boy. Now…" Bellard opened both the books on the table. "Samael's connection was that he was the one who collected souls. Abaddon is another angel of destruction. His name is Apollyon in Greek."

"Ah, yes, of course!" The duke nodded. "I should have known that."

"And here we have punishment—that's Kushiel. Dumah's domain is vindication." Bellard sent Thisbe a significant look. "Barachiel is considered chief of the guardian angels, and his domain is blessings. And lightning. This one is intriguing." He turned to the other book. "I could not find it except in Islam. Harut came to Babel, along with Marut, and taught man magic. Sorcery."

"Goodness," the duke said. "Your dream sounds rather disturbing."

"It definitely was," Thisbe agreed. She sat back in her chair as the two men began to delve further into the books. Anne Ballew was growing more frightening by the day. Thisbe must find the Eye. There was clearly more involved here than recovering one of her grandmother's possessions. She felt certain that somehow the Eye was the key to resolving her nightmares.

Even after the time spent in discussion with her father and Uncle Bellard, she was ready long before she was scheduled to meet Desmond at the library. Too impatient to sit still, she decided to arrive early and wait for him inside the carriage, and when she saw him walking toward her with that familiar long-legged stride, looking so…*himself*, her heart leaped in her chest.

This was not a good way to begin. She schooled her expression as best she could—impassivity was not one of her skills—and stepped out of the vehicle before Desmond could reach it. Taking his hand to step down was not a good idea.

She said nothing about the night before, and luckily Desmond appeared as reluctant as she to bring up the matter. They walked to the library in an awkward silence. Once inside, they made their way through the library, earning a number of disapproving looks along the way. By the time they had finished, the awkwardness between them had disappeared, but they learned nothing about Professor Gordon's whereabouts.

They tried Gordon's office again, but found it just as dark and locked as the day before. An older gentleman dressed in the robes of a professor emerged from the room next door, and looked disapprovingly at them. "Are you looking for Gordon, as well?"

"Yes." Desmond walked forward eagerly. "Do you know where he is?"

"Everyone seems to be excessively interested in him these days. As I told the others, he's gone to visit his sister. She's ill."

"The others? Who else asked about him?" Thisbe asked.

The man frowned at her. "I've no idea of their names. How would I know everyone who comes to Gordon's door? Students, I suppose. Someone involved in his wretched experiment."

"Do you know where his sister lives?" Thisbe took another tack, earning her a second scowl from the professor.

"I say, that's rather an impertinence. Students chasing him down at his sick sister's home! There's no respect anymore. I told them it was a mistake to let females read for the examinations. Opened the gates to all sorts of—"

"Thank you, sir," Desmond inserted before Thisbe could respond, taking her arm and pulling her away.

"That man!" she fumed. "It's typical of the sort of narrow-minded, antiquated, so-called teachers at universities. It's no wonder they turn out so many students reading for perfectly useless fields, yet pay scant attention to something important. Something up-to-date."

"Yes, yes, I know that they should have more courses in chemistry and physics," Desmond said, trying, without much success, to suppress his grin. "But it would be a waste of our time to carry on the argument."

"I know. No one will ever be able to change that locked

mind of his. And you're right—our time is better spent on planning our next step. We can go back to Broughton House, and—"

Desmond's eyebrows shot up. "Your home? I doubt your family would welcome my presence."

Thisbe waved off his worries. "It's probably better that you not run in to Grandmother. But as for the others... Mother is certain the effects of social inequality are to blame for your misdeeds. Uncle Bellard hasn't yet realized you're no longer around. And Olivia is rather on your side."

He followed her into the carriage. "I notice you didn't mention your other siblings or your father."

Thisbe shrugged. "They are a bit more protective, but we want to avoid Kyria, anyway, as there are bound to be gentlemen hanging about her. Papa is happily fussing with some new artifacts. And my brothers will be out of the house most of the day doing last-minute things for Theo's trip. Reed came down from Oxford to see him off." Unconsciously, she sighed. "Theo's leaving for Southampton tomorrow afternoon, and the next day he'll set sail for Brazil."

"You will miss him."

Thisbe nodded. "It isn't as if he's around a great deal, but I always know he's not completely out of reach. But the Amazon... He'll be gone for months and months. He's never gone that far away before."

It was easy to talk with Desmond, just as it used to be. Unlike her voluble family, he didn't jump in immediately with plans or opinions, but listened, was calm and intelligent and understanding. Which, come to think of it, was probably why he had been so popular with her relatives. It was nice to have a calm center in the middle of the Moreland vortex.

When they walked into the house, Thisbe heard voices coming from the sultan room, one of which was her grandmother's. She made an abrupt right turn into the formal drawing room. "Let's sit in here with Old Eldric. It's quieter."

"Old who?" Desmond glanced around the stately room.

"The first duke." Thisbe pointed to the portrait over the fireplace. "One of the ghosts Grandmother claims to talk to."

Desmond studied the portrait. "If I were able to speak to spirits, I don't think I'd choose him."

Thisbe laughed. "Nor me. It's cold in here, I'm afraid—we never use it. I'll ring for Smeggars to lay a fire in here."

"No need. I can do it." Desmond squatted down by the enormous fireplace and began to arrange coals on the grate. "Do you suppose Gordon really went to his sister's?"

"Does he even have one?"

"Yes, that much at least is true. She lives in Chelmsford. But it's rather suspicious, don't you think, that his sister should fall ill and require his presence at precisely the same time the Eye disappears?"

"Very much so. However, it doesn't mean that he *didn't* go to visit her. This would be a good time for him to get out of the city. Or he could hide the thing at his sister's and return, so that any search of his rooms would turn up nothing."

"Unfortunately, he could also have hidden the Eye anywhere in the city," Desmond pointed out as he lit the fire.

There was the sound of footsteps and male voices in the hall. Theo and Reed. Thisbe sighed and turned toward the door just as Theo poked his head into the room.

"I say, Thiz, why are you in here?" His gaze went past her to Desmond, still crouched by the fireplace, and he scowled. "What the devil is *he* doing here?"

DESMOND SUPPRESSED A sigh and rose to his feet. He wasn't looking forward to more bruises from Thisbe's brother. Desmond had always been able to hold his own with the lads in the village, but Theo Moreland was another matter altogether. Not only was Theo apparently some sort of school champion in the "gentlemanly art" of boxing, but Desmond also couldn't help but feel that the other man was on the right side of the matter. Besides, Desmond was already on thin ice with Thisbe, especially after grabbing and kissing her last night. Hitting her beloved twin was certainly no way to mend things. As if Theo weren't bad enough, Thisbe's other brother came up behind Theo.

"Theo." Thisbe rose to her feet. "Don't you dare start a brawl in here."

"I won't." Theo strode into the room, Reed following. "I plan to haul him outside."

"Oh, for heaven's sake. Don't be so primitive. Reed... control him."

"That's easier said than done," Reed commented, but he gripped his brother's arm. "She's right, Theo. You'll bring Mother and Grandmother down on your head if you don't watch out."

"Oh, leave off. I'm not going to hit him," Theo said in disgust and jerked his arm from Reed's grasp, turning to Thisbe. "But I cannot fathom why you would take up with this scoundrel again."

"I am not 'taking up' with him again. I am trying to recover Grandmother's possession."

Desmond noticed Thisbe didn't dispute that he was a scoundrel.

"Which *he* stole," Theo reminded her. "It's a damned stupid thing, anyway. Annie's blue eye? What the devil's that?"

"Annie Blue's Eye," Thisbe corrected. "It's part of a legend, and it may be stupid, but you know how Grandmother feels about it. Besides, I don't believe Desmond took it. We're trying to figure out who did and how to get it back."

"What legend?" Theo asked.

"Who stole it?" Reed queried. Her brothers sat down, their suspicious expressions turning to interest.

"Desmond, you tell them," Thisbe said. "You know it much better than I."

Desmond launched into his tale, certain that Thisbe's brothers would scoff at the story of Anne Ballew and the instrument she invented, but they listened intently. Clearly, any Moreland found it difficult to pass up a mystery.

When Desmond finished, Reed said, "Your tutor sounds a bit off his head to me, but I'd put my money on the patron taking this Eye."

"Why is this Wallace fellow so obsessed with the thing, anyway?" Theo asked. "I understand that your professor thinks he'll win back his tattered reputation, but what does Wallace have to gain from it?"

"Fame, I suppose," Thisbe offered. "Maybe some acceptance in scientific circles."

Theo looked skeptical. "Sponsoring their experiments is enough to make him popular with scientists. He must want something more than that if he's willing to steal an object from a duke's house."

"I believed he was eager to move up the social ladder,"

Thisbe said. "But now I see that his interest in meeting Grandmother may have been due only to the Eye."

"He'd like to enter a more exclusive circle," Desmond agreed. "But he's been fascinated by the spiritual world since his wife died. I think that's why he's looking for the Eye."

"He wants to talk to his dead wife?" Reed asked. "Very well. I can understand one becoming obsessed with that."

Theo snorted. "That's because you're a bloody romantic."

"Ha! Who is it that's always coming to the rescue of some damsel in distress?" Reed countered.

"Boys, please," Thisbe interjected, staving off an argument.

Desmond covered a smile at the way Thisbe addressed the two men like children. But, now that he thought about it, though Theo was but three or so years younger than Desmond himself and Reed only two years behind Theo, the two of them seemed far younger than he. Certainly younger than he felt.

However large they were, however intelligent, wealthy and titled, the two of them had been raised in privilege, sheltered from most of the harshness of the world. They had never faced adversity or heartache, never come up against a thing they could not do, a barrier they were unable to cross. They were not yet the men they would become.

This new understanding subtly altered his view of her brothers. Fond as Desmond had become of the Morelands, he had felt no bond with these two. It wasn't just that he had been around them less. The truth was he hadn't thought of them as actual people; he'd just viewed them as members of the aristocracy, to be regarded with wariness, vague enmity and a certain contempt. He had made an effort to avoid them rather than come to know them. And, perhaps, deep down he had been a little jealous of the close ties between Theo and Thisbe.

Thisbe went on crisply, "Back to the matter at hand—Desmond and I are considering whether we should pursue Mr. Wallace or Mr. Gordon. They're both mysteriously missing."

"Together, you think?" Theo asked.

"It could be," Thisbe agreed. "But even if they're in league with each other, they might have gone their separate ways, and we don't know which one has possession of the Eye."

"The patron's more likely to have it," Theo said. "He's the one paying for it."

Reed nodded. "They're either together or Wallace has it. He's not likely to show up at Gordon's sister's house, with or without Gordon. If they've gone to ground, I'd warrant it's at Wallace's. Does he have a manor house? A shooting lodge?"

"I don't know." Thisbe sighed. "I asked Grandmother last night, but she knows nothing about the man."

"That must have vexed her." Theo grinned. "But I'm sure she'll soon find out."

"Still, it may take some time for her tentacles to spread that far. Smeggars is after the information, too, but even servant gossip can be slow."

Desmond, who had remained quiet amidst the Moreland chatter, spoke up somewhat tentatively. "It occurs to me…we've already established that it's not likely that either Gordon or Wallace actually broke into the house and stole the Eye. Yes?"

"Either one would have hired a professional," Thisbe agreed.

"Wouldn't it be likely that Wallace would again hire the same man who threatened you?" Desmond went on.

"What? Threatened Thisbe?" Theo leaned forward. "What do you mean? Who threatened you, Thiz?"

"No one actually threatened me," Thisbe assured him. "He tried to coerce Desmond by saying he would hurt me if Desmond didn't get the Eye for him."

So Thisbe believed him about that. Desmond's spirits picked up. "He told me he wasn't a thief, but he would have been the one Wallace went to, and I'd bet that he decided he was a robber after all when Wallace offered him money. Or he hired one. Unfortunately, I doubt he still has the Eye—he would have turned it over to Wallace."

"I'd still like to talk to him," Theo said grimly.

"Now, *him* you're welcome to knock about," Thisbe interjected.

"My thought was, he might know where Wallace has taken it," Desmond added.

"So what we need to do is find this fellow," Theo said.

"How?" Thisbe asked practically. "Desmond, do you know his name?"

"No," he admitted.

"Well, we'll scour the disreputable taverns until we find him." Theo rose to his feet.

"That should take some time," Reed commented drily, but he stood up, as well.

"I'm going with you," Desmond said with quiet determination, also rising.

Theo frowned at him. "We don't ne—"

Desmond met his gaze levelly. "*I'm* the one who knows what he looks like."

Theo's scowl deepened, but Reed said lightly, "Don't be an ass, Theo."

"Oh, all right."

"Wait a moment. You're not going without me," Thisbe said.

All three men swung to her. "No."

She rolled her eyes. "This is *my* quest, and if you think you're going to cut me out, you'd best think again."

"You're not going," Theo said flatly.

"It's too dangerous," Reed added.

Desmond said mildly, "You'll stick out like a light-house in that sort of place, Thisbe. Remember how it was at the university? Just think what attention you'd garner in a tavern of ruffians. It would ruin any chance of anyone talking to us."

Thisbe set her jaw, glaring at Desmond for a moment, but then sighed, deflated. "I suppose you're right." She added crossly, "But you must promise to come back and tell me as soon as you find out anything."

"Of course."

"And be careful." She looked at her brothers. "You, too. Don't do anything stupid."

"Why do you look at me when you say that?" Theo laughed. "You didn't tell *him* not to be stupid." He jerked his thumb toward Desmond.

"I don't have to tell Desmond," she retorted.

Theo and Reed left to put on their coats and order the carriage brought round, leaving Thisbe and Desmond alone. Thisbe put her hand on his arm. "You will take care, won't you? Not do anything rash?"

"I promise."

"And keep Theo and Reed safe?"

He raised his eyebrows. "I wouldn't think they'd listen to me."

"Maybe not. Theo is the kind who likes to run toward danger, not away. Reed is more practical, but he'll do anything Theo does. He can't resist the challenge. But they will listen to reason." She smiled and knocked her knuckles lightly against her head. "You just have to get through that Moreland bullheadedness."

"You're not bullheaded." Desmond moved closer. "You're beautifully unafraid and passionate."

Thisbe's green eyes pulled him in. He wanted to kiss her again, even though it would be irredeemably foolish. The echo of footsteps in the hallway broke his trance, and Desmond released her hand, stepping away.

Thisbe followed the men into the hallway. "How are you planning to find this man? You have no idea who he is or what places he frequents."

"True." Reed grinned. "Fortunately, I know someone who will."

CHAPTER TWENTY-THREE

DESMOND FOLLOWED THE other men out of the house and into the waiting carriage. In his opinion, their carriage would stick out as much as Thisbe would, but he said nothing. As long as Thisbe was safely uninvolved, it didn't matter how little chance they had of succeeding. At least he was doing something, and there was the possibility, however slight, that they might come across Wallace's man.

Theo took the seat across from Desmond, and Reed sat beside him—the better, Desmond supposed, to keep him under control, though he couldn't imagine what they thought he might do.

"How did you do that?" Reed asked. He was the friendlier, or at least the less hostile, of Thisbe's brothers.

"Do what?"

"Persuade Thisbe not to come with us."

"Why wouldn't she agree?" Desmond shrugged. "It was logical. Thisbe always listens to reason."

Theo snorted. "Clearly, you didn't grow up with her."

"Well, no," Desmond admitted.

Theo drummed his fingers on his knee for a few moments, then said, "Did this man really threaten to harm Thisbe?"

"Yes, of course. I don't remember his exact words, but his meaning was clear. The next day, Thisbe fell on the street, and this man was right there. He said she should be more careful, that she might have fallen in front of a carriage."

"Bloody bastard."

"You're saying that's why you stole the Eye?"

"I *didn't* steal it. I can see what Thisbe meant about Moreland bullheadedness." Perhaps it was not the wisest thing to say, but Desmond was growing increasingly weary of being accused of theft. "But that was why I stopped calling on Thisbe. I wanted them to believe that they had no control over me that way." He looked at Theo. "Your visit to my workshop did a pretty thorough job of convincing them."

"Happy to oblige." Theo sighed and leaned back in his seat. "Though I suppose I should apologize if you were trying to protect Thisbe. It's just... I hate for Thisbe to be unhappy."

"So do I," Desmond replied simply. "I never wanted to cause Thisbe distress. But I wanted even less to expose her to physical harm. Perhaps there was some other way, but I couldn't think of one."

Both men continued to study him. Their steady, assessing gazes reminded Desmond of the rather disconcerting stare with which the young twins sometimes regarded one, as if they could see things inside you that no one else could. The Moreland men, he thought, were an odd lot. Well, the women were, too, he supposed. But they were tremendously hard not to like. Even these two.

"I know I'm not the sort of man you'd want for your sister. I've no title or money. I don't expect you to approve of me, but you're dead wrong if you think I used Thisbe for my own ends." Desmond wasn't sure why it was important to him that they believe him, but somehow it was. "I did not pursue her because of the Eye. Obviously she was a lady, but I never dreamed she was the granddaughter of the dowager duchess. I admit I was wrong not to tell Thisbe about the Eye and our interest in it from the moment I realized who she was. But I was afraid of losing her. I was a fool. Haven't you ever acted the fool over a woman?"

Theo snorted and looked at Reed, his eyes dancing. "Remember that tavern girl in Little Biddenton? You always were a soft touch."

Reed's cheeks turned red, but he smiled. "And what of the don's daughter at Oxford?"

"Don't remind me." Theo's smile faded as he turned to Desmond. "Men have always been fools over women at one time or another. I don't care unless it touches one of my sisters. I don't give a damn whether you're poor as a church mouse or rich as Croesus, and titles are nothing but chains. Maybe I'm inclined to believe you didn't set out to hurt Thisbe. But you deal wrongly with her again, and I'll snap you like a twig."

"I understand."

"Sorry to interrupt your threats of violence, Theo, but we're here." Reed nodded toward the window.

The carriage had stopped before a gray stone building. "An orphanage? Your expert in criminals works in an orphanage?"

"No. He's a resident." Reed opened the carriage door and climbed out.

Theo, seeing Desmond's surprise, said, "Mother's not the only one trying to save the world. Tom Quick's a pickpocket who made the mistake of trying to nab Reed's wallet one day. Lad's quick, not just with his hands, so Reed decided to put him in Mother's orphanage and send him to school."

"Instead of sending him to jail."

Theo nodded. "As I said, Reed's a soft touch."

From what Desmond had seen of the Morelands, there wasn't a one of them who wasn't a soft touch. Except the dowager duchess, of course.

As soon as he walked into the building, Desmond realized that this orphanage was not like any other he'd ever seen. The walls were not a drab gray, but a pleasant light blue, and there were no pervasive scents of ammonia, gruel or sweat.

A woman bustled forward to greet them, exclaiming, "Lord Raine. Lord Moreland. What a delight to see you. Is the duchess with you today?"

"No, just us, Mrs. Wadley. I wanted to visit Tom Quick. Is he in class?"

"Classes are done for the day. He's doing his chores, so I'm sure he'll be happy to be pulled away."

She settled them in a small room and went off at her same quick pace. Desmond was curious to see the boy Reed had befriended. He supposed he must adjust his view of the Moreland men again.

A few minutes later, Mrs. Wadley returned with a lad whom Desmond deemed to be no more than eight or nine years old. He was dressed in neat, fresh clothes, his blond hair combed; he would have looked like any child the same age if it had not been for his blue eyes, which were watchful and calculating. He wore a cocky expression, but Desmond could see the wariness behind it.

"Sir." His eyes went first to Reed, then over to Theo and Desmond.

"Go on, Tom, make your bow, the way Mrs. Timmons taught you," Mrs. Wadley urged.

The boy's chin jutted out for a moment, but he executed a neat bow.

"There! Very good." Mrs. Wadley's voice rang with delight.

"If we could speak with Tom alone, Mrs. Wadley…"

"Yes, yes, of course." The woman whipped out of the room, closing the door behind her.

"How are you doing, Tom?" Reed asked. "You want to sit?" He gestured toward an ottoman.

This offer seemed to relax the boy, for he plopped down on the round leather seat, the defiant tilt to his chin dropping. "I'm a'right. Mrs. Timmons's got me in the next year's grammar. Says I'm a helluva reader. Better wif numbers, though."

Tom had a curious accent, his words slipping into deep cockney now and then, while others were carefully correct. Learning to speak like a gentleman, Desmond thought, as he himself had.

"Somehow I doubt those were Mrs. Timmons's exact words," Reid commented. "But I'm glad you're progressing."

"I figure I can get more skimmin' from the till than liftin' wallets."

A pained expression crossed Reed's face. "The goal was for you to get an education so that you could make a better living *legally*."

The boy grinned, his blue eyes twinkling. "Just jokin' with you, guv'nor. I'm not lookin' to wind up wif…with my neck stretched." He looked over at Desmond curiously. "'Oo… I mean, who's he?" He expelled his *h*'s forcefully. "Not a nob like you."

"Mr. Harrison is a friend of my sister's. He's trying to find someone, and I thought you might be able to help us."

"Yeah? How's that?" Tom's attention was fully caught now, his eyes bright with intelligence.

"A fellow came by to threaten him," Reed explained.

"What for?"

"It's a far too long and complicated story," Reed told him. "I'm not sure I understand it entirely myself. But the thing is we want to locate the ruffian who threatened him. I thought this might be within your area of expertise."

"Expertise," Tom repeated. Desmond could almost see him rolling the word over in his mind and storing it away. "Something I'd know, right?"

"Exactly."

"Sure. I know 'em all. The O'Tooles and the Cooper lot, those Scots boys—you don't wanna be dealing with them, I'll tell you."

"He didn't sound Scottish," Desmond said. "In fact, now that I think of it, he didn't have much of an accent."

"A toff?" Tom asked.

"No. But I'd say not someone from Seven Dials, either. He wore a suit rather like mine and a bowler—he didn't look like a ruffian. Blond hair, light-colored eyes, blue or gray, I'm not sure. Tall."

"Tall as you?"

"No. Not that tall—nor as tall as, um…" Desmond gestured toward Theo. He didn't know the man's title— what had Mrs. Wadley called him? He went on hastily, "More like Lord Moreland, perhaps a bit shorter. But wider." He held out his hands to indicate the man's girth. "Not fat, either, just big."

"A punisher, sounds like," Tom said knowledgeably, nodding.

"I believe he works for Mr. Zachary Wallace."

"What owns the warehouses? I mean, *who* owns the warehouses."

"I don't know," Desmond said, surprised. "It's odd— I've never really thought about how he makes his money." He thought. "I believe Carson once said Wallace was in shipping."

"Aye, that'd be them. They're down at the docks."

"Is his business involved in something illegal?" Theo asked.

"I don't know, sir. But he 'ires big blokes to guard them. Everybody knows to leave 'em alone."

Desmond glanced at the other two men. "It sounds fairly likely."

"Can you think of anyone else it could be, Tom?" Reed asked.

"Well…there's Gentleman Jack." Tom frowned. "But you don't want to muck about with that one, guv. He kills folks. Kills 'em and makes it look like it weren't murder. But he don't dress like him." Tom pointed at Desmond. "He's fancy, like. Dresses like you, sir, only flashier. Top hat and cane and all that. Not that big, neither. No." He shook his head decisively. "It ain't him. You orter stay away."

"We won't go near him, no need to worry," Reed assured him.

"I ain't worried. It's just… Stick a fork in you, and I'll be tossed out then, won't I?" He flashed his cocksure grin again, but Desmond thought he looked a trifle pale underneath.

"Can you recall anything else about the warehouses or their owner, Tom?"

He shook his head. "It had writin' on it, like. Only I couldn't read it back then. Oh! Next to the writing, there's a drawing of a pig."

"A pig?"

Tom nodded. "Big hog. Only he has these horns going out like this." He shot his fingers out from beside his mouth. "Mean-looking."

"Tusks," Theo said. "It's a wild boar."

"Was it red?" Desmond asked, his voice rising in excitement, and Tom nodded in reply. "Wallace has a coat of arms hanging above his fireplace. I doubt it's real. But it features a red boar."

"That's it, then." A slow smile crept across Reed's face, and for the first time, Desmond thought that Reed could be as intimidating as his brother. "We've got him."

"Not quite," Desmond reminded him. "We still don't know where to find him."

"That'd be down by the docks," Tom said confidently. "Those blokes hang about the Double Roses or that tavern beneath a bawdy house—it's called, um, well, I'm not sure it has a name. It's 'neath Madam Tansy's place. Then there's the Bell and Anchor."

Reed raised an eyebrow. "They must drink a good deal."

Tom shrugged. "Sometimes they get tossed out of one or the other. Anyway, they're all pretty close to each other. I'll show you." He jumped to his feet.

"I am not taking you on a tour of seedy taverns," Reed said drily.

"But how else are you going to find them?" Tom protested. "*I* know how to stay out of trouble." His tone indicated his doubts that the same could be said for the three of them. "You need me. I know folks like them. He'll do." He nodded toward Desmond. "But you two?" He shook his head. "You'll never get anywhere dressed like that. And soon as you open your mouths, they'll know you don't belong."

Reed sighed. "Just what do you propose we do?"

"I can get you fixed up so's your own mum won't know you. I used to fix up the beggars, didn't I? I can do the talking while you keep quiet. Maybe him—" He swung toward Desmond. "Can you talk different? More like a regular chap?"

"I can't talk like you." Desmond's voice slipped into the tones of his youth. "But I can be a bloke up from Dorset, now."

"Righto." Tom grinned. "He'll do well enough. But he still ain't a local."

"You don't think a child will be noticeable in a tavern?" Theo asked.

"Not me. They'll just figure I'm practicing my trade." He wiggled his fingers. "I could pretend to pick your pocket and—"

"Let's just keep it simple, shall we?" Theo looked over at his brother. "Where's the harm? It's nothing Tom hasn't seen before—it won't shock him or shake his moral foundation."

"No reason to put him back into the life," Reed protested.

"I won't run away, if that's what you're thinking," Tom added. "It's not so bad here."

"Oh, for…" Reed sighed. "Very well. But you'll stay in the carriage. I'm not putting you in danger, whatever you say."

Under Tom's guidance, they visited a vendor's cart piled high with articles of clothing, coming away with rough jackets, trousers and caps to replace their own. Even Desmond's plain serge jacket had to be exchanged for something with a patched sleeve.

The shopping spree was followed by a meal at an inn, where Tom put away an astonishing amount of food for a lad his size, keeping up his impertinent chatter all the while. Then, finally, fed and dressed in their worst, they took their carriage to the docks, stopping at some distance from their first two destinations, which stood across the road from each other. Hands in pockets, heads down in the cold, they tromped along the street to the Bell and

Anchor. Its sign was barely visible in the evening gloom, all the paint having long worn off it, but after missing it once, they turned into the tavern on a second try. Small, dark and cramped, the room was not the most pleasing of prospects, but at least it was half-empty, the evening's drinking having barely begun.

The ale Desmond ordered for them turned out to be barely drinkable, and as the evening wore on, they managed to pour as much into a nearby spittoon as they drank themselves. Gradually the place filled up. It was annoyingly dark and smoke hazed the air, making it difficult to distinguish the features of the other customers. More than once Desmond made his way to the tap so that he could get a closer look at a face.

"How long do you think we should wait before we try one of the others?" Reed asked.

"Feels like we've already been here half the night."

"A little over an hour," Desmond countered, keeping his gaze on the door. It opened and a small form slipped in. "Um, your lad just came in."

"What?" Reed turned to look and saw Tom making his way toward them. "Damn."

"Guv." The boy tipped his hat.

"Didn't I tell you to wait in the carriage?"

"Aye, but I thought you'd want to know I saw three of them warehouse blokes going into the Double Roses. There was another big man with them, only he wasn't wearing the uniform. He took off his bowler, and I saw his hair in the light. It's blond."

"Let's go." Theo stood up. "Much more of this swill, and my stomach will revolt."

Tom led them along the street and through the door of the tavern. It was larger than the other one and noisier, though equally filled with smoke. Tom sidled up to Desmond and whispered, "That's them against that wall." He nodded discreetly toward a table where several men sat. Three were dressed in dark uniforms. "Those lumps in their pockets are cudgels."

Desmond nodded and wound his way through the crowd, not looking toward the table in question as he circled it at a distance. Behind him, Reed and Theo separated, closing in on the same spot from different directions. Desmond moved closer. The man's face was turned away—he was talking to one of his companions. He laughed and turned back, his gaze falling on Desmond.

The man stiffened, recognizing Desmond at the same instant Desmond identified him. Desmond started forward. From the corner of his eye, he could see the Morelands do the same. With a roar, their quarry jumped up, overturning the table and sending mugs and ale flying, and ran for the door. Desmond started after him, but the man's companions had all surged to their feet, as well. They were cursing, and looking around, blocking his way.

But as Desmond shoved his way through the men, Theo stepped into the fleeing man's path and knocked him down. The man Desmond had thrust aside turned with a snarl and swung at him. Desmond ducked and came up to hit him in the gut. Reed charged into the fray, and Tom jumped onto a chair to break a glass of ale over another guard's head.

In an instant the room plunged into chaos.

CHAPTER TWENTY-FOUR

THISBE PACED UP and down in front of the fireplace. Aside from her father and great-uncle, all the men she loved were in danger, and as the evening wore on, she cursed her decision not to accompany them. Desmond had tricked her into it with logic—which only went to show how wily the man was. She wasn't sure that she could trust Desmond, but she knew that her heart would break if anything happened to him.

Thisbe did not care to examine that whole line of thinking. It was confusing and irrational. However, she was certain that in moments like these, she should go with her heart rather than her head.

"It's been hours. Where could they be?"

"I'm sure they're having a grand time chasing this fellow all around the East End. What they will accomplish is another matter entirely," her grandmother replied witheringly. She was seated on one of the many uncomfortable chairs in the formal drawing room, back ramrod straight and cane planted on the floor in front of her, her hands wrapped around its neck. She reminded Thisbe of a knight resting on his sword.

It would not have been Thisbe's preference to have her grandmother's company as she waited for the men to come home, but she had to admit that the dowager duchess's indomitable confidence helped to steady her own frayed nerves.

"Perhaps we should—" Thisbe began, breaking off at the sudden clatter in the entryway, followed by a footman's startled exclamation.

She started forward, but before she could reach the door, her brothers and Desmond reeled through the door, followed by a disheveled boy. Thisbe gasped at their appearance, and her grandmother said, "Well, you are a sorry sight indeed."

The duchess was right. Reed was limping, half-supported by Theo, and Desmond swayed as he stood. Their rough, ill-fitting clothes—which they had not been wearing when they left the house this afternoon—were ripped and covered in grime, and their hair was equally disordered and dirty. Dried blood ran down the side of Theo's face and his hair was matted with it; Reed's cheek was red and one eye was beginning to swell; and Desmond had a lump on his forehead and a cut on his swollen jaw. All of them sported scrapes and the beginnings of bruises, and they reeked of ale.

"Desmond!" Thisbe cried out and started toward him, then stopped. Drawing a deep breath, she went on more calmly, "What happened to you?"

"And how did you manage to acquire a street urchin?" Cornelia raised her lorgnette and focused her gaze on the boy.

"That's Tom Quick, Grandmother," Reed said, his words a trifle slurred. "I am sending him to school."

"Mmm. I would have thought the aim would have been to *improve* him."

"Yes, well..." Reed swung toward the boy, and his sudden movement made both him and Theo stagger.

"You're drunk!" Thisbe exclaimed.

"No, not drunk." Theo dismissed her words with an airy wave of his hand. "We had to blend in, you see."

"You smell like the inside of a barrel."

"Oh, that." Desmond lifted the lapel of his jacket and sniffed. "Someone tried to crown me with a mug, and it spilled all over me."

"Master Theo!" Smeggars rushed through the door, and in his agitation he slipped back to their childhood names. "And Master Reed. What have you done now?"

As he fussed over them, a maid entered with a basket of supplies, followed by another with a pitcher and a washbowl, with the twins' nurse bringing up the rear.

"Hallo, Katie," Desmond said cheerfully.

"Hallo, yourself." She looked over the men with an assessing eye. "Ah, well, not so bad." She turned to Thisbe. "No need to worry, miss. I'll fix 'em up, right as rain. Used to patch up my own boys often enough, didn't I?"

"That should stand you in good stead with Alex and Con," the dowager duchess commented.

"Aye, my lady. They're going to be corkers, right enough." Katie grinned at Cornelia. "Best sit down, gentlemen. This may take a bit."

As she set to work cleaning and doctoring their wounds, Theo began a recital of their evening, punctuated by comments from his companions, ending with a description of the fight. "So then this other chap jumped me from behind before I could pick the villain up off the floor—"

"Desmond cracked the man with a cudgel he took off the other ruffian," Reed interrupted, a faint note of pride in his voice. "But then one of the guards tackled him, and I had to go after that fellow."

"I kicked 'im in the shins," Tom inserted.

"So you did." Reed frowned faintly. "I suppose we should have taken you back to the orphanage."

"That's all right," the boy assured him. "I can get one of them breakfasts like I had 'ere last time."

"He's right. A bit of food would do nicely now," Theo commented. "Now, Thiz, don't growl."

"I'm not." Thisbe bit off her words. "Much as I am enjoying hearing all about you three brawling in a dock-side tavern, it would be nice to learn the result of your adventures. Did you find out anything from this man you went to find?"

"Oh. Well." Theo glanced at his brother, then Desmond. "As to that…"

"He slipped out in the middle of the fracas," Desmond admitted.

"Men!" Cornelia said with disgust, rapping her cane on the floor and standing up. "Absolutely useless, the lot of them. It's clear, Thisbe, that you and I will have to take care of the matter."

THISBE WAS AT breakfast the next morning when the dowager duchess walked into the dining room. "Grandmother. I'm surprised to see you up so early." The dowager duchess usually had only tea and toast in her room before she began the long process of her toilette, coming down for a full breakfast much later.

"We should make an early start of it," Cornelia replied.

"Start of what?"

"Finding out what the boys did not."

"You really mean that?" Thisbe stared at her.

"Of course I meant it. I said it, didn't I? We'd have gone last night except that the boys would have made a fuss. No doubt they left the place in such a shambles we wouldn't have been able to get any information, anyway. Better to start fresh this morning."

A smile spread across Thisbe's face. "You're right. We'll show them what women can accomplish."

It took some time to start off, as her grandmother did

not believe in "gulping her food—bad for the digestion," and it took the duchess a lengthy time to don hat, gloves and fur muff, as well as change her cloak twice. There was a further delay when it was discovered that Alex and Con had climbed up to hide inside the baggage compartment of the carriage—their presence revealed by their giggles—and had to be returned to their nurse.

The coachman looked startled when the dowager duchess directed him to drive to the Double Roses tavern, but he knew better than to question Cornelia, and the carriage rolled off.

"It's rather early for tavern customers," Thisbe ventured mildly. "And surely he wouldn't be so daring as to return to the same place, anyway, knowing that we are searching for him."

"One should never underestimate the stupidity of others," the duchess told her. "However, I don't expect to find him there. It's the barkeep I plan to talk to."

The docks were bustling at this time of the day, but the nearby street where the Double Roses stood was almost deserted. The area, which by night was undoubtedly disreputable enough, looked even more wretched by the light of day. Refuse lined the edges of the street. Cobblestones had been worn away or pried up, leaving an obstacle course for the carriage. The buildings were dirty, their signs faded, shutters missing, and over it all was a stench that came partly from its nearness to the Thames and partly from causes Thisbe thought it best not to consider.

When the carriage rattled to a stop and Thompkins scrambled down to open the door, he wore a worried frown. "Ma'am, this doesn't look the sort of place for a lady."

"I'm sure it's not." Cornelia climbed out. Thisbe paused

to grab the spare umbrella from beneath the seat and followed her grandmother.

Thompkins trailed along unhappily. "I best go inside
with you. I'll get me whip."

"Nonsense. You must stay with the horses. They are far
more likely to appeal to a thief than two mere women."

Thisbe refrained from pointing out that when one of
those mere women wore diamonds on her fingers, throat
and earlobes, thieves were apt to be interested. She followed her grandmother through the door of the tavern and
stopped beside her, surveying the wreckage of the room.
Tables and chairs lay overturned and broken among great
puddles of ale that had not yet soaked into the floor, and
the whole place reeked of cheap alcohol. Pieces of glass
and pottery littered the room, along with the few mugs
and glasses that were still intact. Even most of the metal
tankards were dented.

The place was empty save for a sullen-looking boy
pushing a broom. At their entrance he stopped, his jaw
dropping. "Cor..."

The dowager duchess raised her eyebrows, and when
he said nothing further, she said, "Mind your manners,
boy. Where is the proud owner of this establishment?"

At her words, a man stood up from behind the bar, his
eyes as wide and round as the boy's. "Blimey."

"How eloquent," the dowager duchess said acidly.

"Um." The barkeep bobbed a little bow. "Ma'am. I—
We're no' open yet."

"I am not here to partake of your wares. I am here for
information. I'm looking for a man, a regular patron of
yours. He is the one, I believe, who started the carnage
here last night."

"Grieves?" He goggled.

"I presume. Thisbe, describe the man."

"Big and blond. He was with some guards from the warehouse."

"That'd be him," the boy interjected. "Thick as thieves, they are."

The other man, seemingly having gathered his wits about him, frowned at the lad. "'Oi! Shut your bone-box. We're no' blowers here."

"You told 'er 'is name!" the boy protested.

"Aye, well, I was surprised, wan't I?"

"This man, Grieves, must have an address," Thisbe said.

"Not tellin' you where 'e kips." The man crossed his arms defiantly.

"Then I suppose you aren't interested in this." The duchess extracted a gold coin from her reticule and held it up. "*Pony*, I believe is the vulgar term for it." She turned toward the boy. "Perhaps you might be more willing."

Before the lad could say anything, the barkeep said, "'E stays at Dot's crib, next to that crimping shop."

"I'd need something a bit more particular than that," Cornelia said. "An address, for instance."

This idea seemed to flummox the man, so Thisbe added helpfully, "The name of the street? The number?"

The other two looked at each other and finally the man said, "It don't have a blinkin' name. That little lane where the Blue Ox is."

"Off Water Street," the boy added helpfully and pointed to his right. "Ain't no number."

Thisbe suppressed a sigh. "I presume Dot is a woman, and her crib must be her house. Is that right?"

"'Course." The boy looked at her as if she were daft.

"Describe it, then, so we can find it."

He did, at such length and in so much cant, that Thisbe had difficulty following it all, but when he had finished, she provided a summary. "It's a narrow house beside one with a red door. It has a window on each floor, but only the top window still has shutters on it. Is that right?"

"Bang up," he agreed and came forward to take the coin the duchess held out, but the older man was surprisingly quick and beat him to it.

"This better be correct," the duchess warned, favoring both with the iron-hard gaze that her servants and family justifiably feared. "If he doesn't live there, I shall send the police to this establishment to investigate the brawl which took place here last night, in which my grandsons were most grievously injured." Then, with a jingle of her reticule, she softened a trifle and said, "But if that is his home, there's another one of these in it for you."

Both men nodded eagerly. "No gammon, honor bright."

"I thought those men were English," the duchess said to Thisbe as they returned to the carriage.

"They are."

"Then they ought to talk like Englishmen. What in heaven's name is a crimping shop?"

"That one I know—Theo once told me. It's a cheap sort of boardinghouse where they frequently press sailors into the navy. And my guess is that 'blowers' means people who betray their colleagues."

"How odd. Well, tell the coachman where to go, and let's be on our way."

It took only a few minutes, a dead end and two wrong turns to find the narrow house missing two shutters. Cornelia rapped on the door with her cane, and when a thin woman with a glare that outdid even the duchess's answered the knock, she once again offered coins for information. They climbed the stairs to the next floor.

The man who opened the door was large and blond, and sported a black eye and swollen nose. He, too, gaped at the sight of two ladies on his doorstep, and the duchess took advantage of his surprise to walk past him into the room.

"Here, now," he protested belatedly, turning around. "You got no right to waltz in here."

Cornelia didn't deign to address his complaint. "Mr. Grieves, I presume? I am here for the name of your employer."

He rolled his eyes, less intimidated than the tavern owner. "Might as well leave, then." His gaze slid over to Thisbe, and he grinned. "*You* can stay, though. I'll show you a grand time."

"I believe not," Thisbe replied. "The one thing I want from you is who hired you to steal the Eye."

"I don't know what you're talking about."

Her grandmother pulled out a coin purse and shook it. "Does this increase your understanding?"

His eyes narrowed. "I lose customers if I shop them to the peelers."

"The police are not involved in this. Just me." Cornelia added a few coins to her hand.

"I could just take that from you, you know," he told her.

"Perhaps…if you'd like to spend the next few years in prison," Cornelia responded. "You know who I am, and you know what the law would do to you. Far easier to sell your information." Taking his shrug for assent, she said, "Who was it?"

He rubbed his fingers together, and with a dramatic sigh, the duchess added another bill. "This will have to do. It's all I have with me."

"It was that little chubby bloke. The one who's trying to hunt ghosts."

"Professor Gordon?" Thisbe asked in surprise. "I thought you worked for Mr. Wallace."

"I do. I work for whoever pays me. This professor fellow's the one wanted me to take that silly quizzing glass. Not, you understand, that I took it."

"Of course not. You hired someone else."

"No—that'd be thievery." Clearly he enjoyed playing his game.

Thisbe sighed. "Did you give it to Gordon?"

"I would have if I'd taken it." He grinned.

"Where has Gordon gone?"

"I don't know. Don't care."

"Does Mr. Wallace have another house? Did he go there?"

"I thought you wanted only one thing."

"It turns out I didn't," Thisbe replied. "Where does Mr. Wallace go when he leaves London?"

"Don't know. Never asked. He never took me with him."

"You have a singular lack of curiosity."

"Safest that way, I've found."

"I must say, you are providing very little return for our money," Thisbe said sourly.

"Told you I didn't know about it."

It was clear they would get nothing else out of him, so Thisbe and the dowager duchess returned to their carriage.

"There now," Cornelia said as she settled into her seat. "We've found out who has it. Now we must get it back." She leveled a stern gaze at her granddaughter. "We have a duty. We owe it to our ancestors."

The duchess's echoing of the words from Thisbe's dream the other night sent a tingle through her. "Grandmother…" She wasn't sure why she felt the sudden need to confide in her grandmother; it was scarcely the sort of relationship they had. Perhaps it was their shared mission today. Or perhaps it was the fact that only her grandmother would find her words believable. "I have been having a dream lately. About a woman. There's a fire and—"

Her grandmother grabbed Thisbe's arm. "You saw her? Anne came to you in a dream?"

"She looked like the portrait of Anne Ballew in Uncle Bellard's book," Thisbe admitted. "But I don't believe in such things."

"What you choose to believe doesn't change what happened."

"Have you ever had a dream like that?"

"No." Cornelia sighed. "But she is known to come to our family at times. It's rare, but my grandmother said that her mother dreamed of Anne. No doubt this theft of her Eye has raised Anne's spirit. That is why she came to you—it is you who must find it." She nodded, pleased with the explanation for her own lack of a vision of Anne. "Did she speak to you?"

"That was what made me think of it. She said that I 'owed' her something. I'm not sure what."

"Naturally. It makes perfect sense. You are the one whom the Eye calls. I was so sure it was Olivia…but that doesn't matter now."

"But it doesn't call to me. When you showed it to me, I didn't feel any tie to it. Not even a tingle."

"No doubt it was blocked by that boy's presence." Cornelia used her favorite term for Desmond. "He is somehow connected." Thisbe thought it was better not to mention Desmond's aunt's belief that he was Anne's descendant. The duchess went on, "I think you must have his help, however dangerous it is for you to be around him. You must be very careful."

"Grandmother, you don't really believe that you can see into the future, do you?"

"Of course not." Cornelia raised her eyebrows. "Don't be silly. I didn't see the future. I saw the curse of death on him."

"Curses aren't real. That's absurd."

"It's absurd to ignore the truth," the dowager duchess retorted, and her eyes suddenly flamed with a fire that was, frankly, unsettling. "I saw it written on him as well as I can see your face. I see it still. One of his kind will kill one of ours. He is bound by it, just as you are bound. I don't know how or when, but sooner or later you will die because of him."

CHAPTER TWENTY-FIVE

AFTER THAT DIRE PRONOUNCEMENT, Thisbe and her grand-mother returned home in silence. Thisbe would have liked to be alone for a few minutes to think, but her brothers and Desmond were in the hall, tossing a ball about with the twins, talking and laughing as Con and Alex shrieked and ran after the balls. The three of them looked almost as disreputable as they had the evening before. Their clothes, at least, were clean now and their hair combed—though Desmond's thick mane, of course, tended to flop every which way.

However, their bruises had had time to develop and their cuts and scrapes to begin healing, so that now their faces bloomed with black and blue, accented here and there by scabs. She supposed it was a better look than blood. At least this time Desmond didn't have a black eye.

The twins spotted Thisbe and the duchess and ran toward them, jabbering, and the men all turned, as well.

"Ladies," Reed greeted them.

"We were wondering where you'd gone," Theo added. "Desmond came, and we were laying plans to find Wallace's thug."

"I can see," Thisbe replied drily, rising from hugging the twins.

"No need," the duchess said airily, removing her gloves with an unconcerned air. "His name is Grieves, and we've spoken with him."

The men gaped at them, then began to talk in a torrent of words almost as jumbled as the twins' babbling.

"What—"

"You never—"

"How did—"

Finally Theo overrode everyone else. "Don't tell me you went to that tavern!"

"Then we won't," Thisbe replied, occupying herself with handing over her outerwear to the waiting footman. It was satisfying to see all three men's jaws drop.

"You can't be serious. With those ruffians about?" Reed protested. Desmond, Thisbe noted, was wise enough to say nothing, though he looked equally horrified.

"Actually, the area is quite empty at this time of day," Cornelia informed him. "Much easier to ask the landlord who the man is and where he lives."

"He told you?"

"Yes, of course. As did Mr. Grieves."

"But how did you make him do that?" Theo exclaimed.

"I have found, my dear," his grandmother replied, "that money is generally more persuasive than fists."

"You paid him?"

"Yes, of course. He was clearly a man for hire."

"He doesn't have the Eye," Thisbe added. "He gave it to—" she hesitated, her eyes going to Desmond "—Mr. Gordon."

"So the professor does have it," Reed mused. "Interesting."

Desmond didn't say anything, but he didn't need to. His expression spoke clearly enough. He reached over and picked up the ball, holding out his other hand to the twins. "Come on, lads, we'd best get you back upstairs."

Reed joined him, swooping up Alex while Desmond took Con.

"Well, that's that," Cornelia announced. "I believe I shall take a rest. These little excursions take so much out of one."

"One would think," Theo muttered, hands on his hips as he watched the dowager duchess climb the stairs. He swung back to Thisbe. "I cannot believe you went with her to the docks."

"I could hardly allow her to go alone, could I? And, I must point out, we succeeded."

"I suppose it shouldn't surprise me that Grandmother was able to wring it out of him. She's always terrified me." He began to stroll down the hall toward the sitting room, and Thisbe joined him.

"I must say, you and Reed are certainly thick as thieves with Desmond," she told him sardonically.

He shrugged. "I was wrong about him, I think. He's someone we can trust."

"Because he's willing to get into a tavern brawl with you?"

"No…well, yes, a little. He had my back. And he… Thiz, what he told us… I think he loves you."

"Oh, really?" She raised one eyebrow.

"He told us you were always reasonable," he quipped with a grin. "You'd have to be blinded by love to believe that."

"Ha! Maybe he just recognizes reason more clearly than you."

"He should have told you who he was, but it's easier to say that than to do it when you think you'll lose someone you love. Tell me, would you have told him your father was a duke if you thought he'd leave you for it?"

"He did leave me." Thisbe avoided the question.

"I can't blame him for wanting to protect you. I should cancel my trip and stay here to help you."

"Don't be silly. I am perfectly fine. They have the Eye, so there is no need to threaten me any longer. Grandmother and I have already dealt with the only dangerous person involved in this affair. Are you saying that I cannot deal with one aging scientist?"

Theo held up his hands in a warding-off gesture. "I value my life too much to ever say that. It's just… I feel as if I'm deserting you."

"You're not. I refuse to let you ruin an expedition you've been wishing to do for years. You better get on that train to Southampton this afternoon."

"All right. I will. But Reed—"

"Must return to school," she said, finishing his thought. "You say you trust Desmond, and he will be with me. Now, go upstairs and pack. If I know you, you haven't finished that yet."

He smiled and swept her into a short, fierce hug. "Love you, Thiz. I'll send you something from the Amazon."

"You better write."

He laughed as he turned and walked away. "Now, that is less certain."

Thisbe watched as he strode down the hall, a lump rising in her throat. She had meant everything she said to him; what she hadn't said was how much she would miss him.

"I CANNOT BELIEVE it's Professor Gordon." Those were the first words out of Desmond's mouth when he joined Thisbe in the sultan room a few minutes later.

"Why would Grieves lie?"

"Because he's a criminal?"

"But why not say it was Wallace? It makes no difference to him which man it was, surely."

"It could," Desmond said stubbornly. "He might protect Wallace so the man would continue to hire him. Wallace could hardly do that from Newgate."

"Still, it seems foolish to not look for Professor Gordon."

Desmond let out a gusty sigh and sank down onto a chair. "I'm sorry. Of course we must search for him." He set his elbows on his knees and leaned his head on his hands. "It's not that I cannot believe he took the Eye. He was desperate to get it, and to his way of thinking, it didn't really belong to your grandmother. It was Anne Ballew's and belonged to science. But if he hired Grieves to do that, then it means he also sent Grieves to coerce me into taking it. It was he who told Grieves to threaten you."

"Not necessarily." Thisbe fought the urge to go to comfort him. "Wallace could have hired him for that coercion, and Gordon for the theft. He said that he worked for anyone who would pay him, and I believe that. He's not a man with loyalty."

"Thank you for offering me that sop." Desmond raised his head and half smiled at her. "But you're right—the logical course is to look for Gordon first. Should we go back over the same ground? See if we can find someone else who might know where he went? A neighbor, perhaps. We didn't knock on all the other doors at his lodgings yesterday."

"Nor did we go to his sister's home," Thisbe pointed out. "He could have taken the Eye and gone there, after all. At least she might have a better idea where he might run."

"I don't think we can overlook the possibility that he might have taken it to Wallace," Desmond said.

"True. Their joint absence is suspicious. Well, we must choose one and start with it."

"It's almost noon," Desmond said. "I'm not sure there's time to go to Chelmsford and return."

"Then let's save it for tomorrow. We can set out early in the morning."

Desmond sighed. "That leaves us with the undoubtedly fruitless option of retracing our steps."

They returned to the university, making another tour of the library and Gordon's office and lecture halls, but they turned up no information about Gordon, other than an indignant tirade from one of his students: "He's missed two straight sessions now. What use is it to hire a tutor if he disappears on a whim? I ask you."

They went to the laboratory next, where they found only Benjamin. He, it appeared, had talked to no one, including Gordon and his other coworkers.

"Neither Albert nor Carson?" Desmond asked.

"No. No one's been here but me for the third day now," the man replied plaintively, then frowned. "Wait. Why aren't you at the shop? A chap from there came by yesterday, brought some of your instruments." He gestured toward the table, where Desmond's kit sat. "What is going on?"

"That's what I intend to find out." Desmond turned away, not looking at Thisbe. "We should go." He strode out of the room.

"Desmond…" Thisbe caught up with him as he stepped outside. He didn't answer, just opened the carriage door for her to get in. "He let you go, didn't he? The owner of the shop. It was because of me, wasn't it? Because I barged in there the other day."

Desmond shrugged and cast her a wry smile. "He

thought I had become something of a disturbance in the shop."

"Oh, Desmond… I'm sorry. I didn't think… I was so angry and…" Her voice trailed off. She hadn't even thought about the fact that Desmond had spent all his time the past few days helping her search for the Eye. It had been thoughtless of her. Snobbish, even—in her sphere, no one was employed. She laid her hand on his arm. "I'm sorry. I will go talk to the man, explain that—"

"No!" He jerked his arm from her grasp. His usually soft brown eyes were suddenly hard, even fiery. "I don't want you to do anything for me."

His anger shocked Thisbe, and she pulled back, hurt by his rejection. In the next moment, it came to her: he had said he never intended to use her for anything. He was proving it by refusing her help, even though she had freely offered. No, it was more than that, deeper— he wasn't just trying to prove his worthiness to her; he simply *was* a worthy man. He didn't use people. Like his honesty or kindness or love of knowledge, it was an integral part of him, bred deep in his bones and blood. When she refused to believe that, it had been a denial of him in every way.

He had shrugged off her lie of omission in not telling him her name because he knew her, knew how little that lie was a part of her. She, however, had not had the same innate faith in him. If he had hurt her, she realized now that she had hurt him, too.

"Desmond, I'm sorry," she said, and he glanced at her, puzzled.

"Sorry about what?"

"About, well, everything."

His eyes widened, but before he could speak, their carriage pulled to a stop in front of Mr. Gordon's building.

Thisbe, suddenly shy and uncertain, opened the door and scrambled out, forestalling any response.

Desmond caught up with her before she reached the outer door, but he seemed no more eager to talk than Thisbe was. He trotted up the stairs and pounded on the nearest door. "Let's try the landlord."

After a long pause, a rail-thin man opened the door and peered out at them. His eyes were sharp, as was his nose, and the deep line between his eyebrows gave him the look of a permanent frown. "What do you want?" His eyes narrowed as he regarded Thisbe. "Who are you? Why are you coming round here?"

"I am Lady Thisbe Moreland," Thisbe said crisply, deciding that this was a moment that called for a display of power. "My father is the Duke of Broughton."

"I got nothing to do with no duke."

"No doubt. But one of your tenants does. Mr. Gordon on the floor above? Did he tell you where he was going? How long he would be gone?"

"No. Like I told the others, I don't know nothing about him." He started to close the door, but Desmond braced his hand against it, holding it open.

"The others? There've been other people trying to reach the professor?"

"Said so, didn't I?"

"Who were they? How many?" Thisbe asked.

"I don't know. I don't keep track of everybody that comes here, banging on doors."

"What did you tell them?" Desmond persisted.

"Same as I told you. I don't know where he went. I don't keep track of *him*, neither."

"I need to get into his flat," Desmond said. "I work for him, and he was supposed to, um, lend me a book. But he's disappeared and, ah, I really must have that book. For a class."

Desmond was dismal at lying. She should have realized immediately that he was telling her the truth. It was surprising, really, that he'd managed to conceal his interest in the Eye as long as he had.

"A book, eh?" the landlord snorted.

"He has stolen something from my grandmother." Thisbe decided to take charge of the conversation. Desmond was simply too nice. Adopting her grandmother's tone, she went on, "It would be far easier for you to let us in so we can see whether the duchess's possession is in his flat. Otherwise, my father will have to send the police to search the place. I suspect they might want to inspect the entire building…you know, as a favor to the duke."

"I've done nothing wrong," the man replied sulkily.

"Haven't you?" She crooked one eyebrow disdainfully. Most people had some secret they wanted to hide. Especially a landlord. "I suppose the police will have to decide that. Do you own this building or manage it for someone else? Someone who might discover that you've been keeping a little of his rent money for yourself."

"I never—"

"Or charge for unnecessary repairs." She tried to think of more of her mother's list of grievances against landlords. Unfortunately, the ways in which they took advantage of their renters were usually legal. "You seem a reasonable man. Surely, it is within your rights to enter a tenant's flat when you deem it necessary."

"Aye…"

"It seems necessary here, don't you think?" Following the dowager duchess's advice, she reached into her pocket and brandished a coin.

"Very well," he grumbled, but his eyes brightened and

he was quick to take the coin from her fingers. "Come along, then." He reached inside his flat, took a key from a hook and started up the stairs.

Gordon's flat was small and, unsurprisingly, over-flowing with books and supplies. It took little time to discover that it didn't contain Anne Ballew's Eye. But Thisbe hadn't expected it to be there. Gordon would keep his prize close to him. She hoped to find some clue as to where the man had gone.

While Desmond checked in cabinets and drawers, she went to the man's desk. There was a locked drawer, but she easily found the key in one of the other draw-ers and opened it. There were a number of other papers inside, but a quick scan of them showed nothing of in-terest. After relocking the drawer, she shuffled through the items on his desk.

A folded notepaper with a broken seal caught her eye, and she opened it. Her eyes went immediately to the sig-nature. "Desmond."

At the tone in her voice, he turned and hurried to her side. She held out the note and read aloud. "'I look forward to speaking with you tomorrow afternoon.'" Thisbe tapped the signature.

"'Alfred Symington,'" he said and shrugged.

"That's Uncle Bellard's friend. The one who wrote about Anne Ballew."

CHAPTER TWENTY-SIX

"ALFRED SYMINGTON?" Uncle Bellard said in response to Thisbe's query. "I wouldn't call him a friend, precisely. I met him only once, at Denberry's house. But we have corresponded now and then." He surveyed his bookshelves. "Now, where did I put that book of his?"

"You lent it to me, Uncle."

"Ah, well. Excellent." He beamed and turned to Desmond. "I haven't seen you about much recently. I hope Cornelia didn't frighten you away. You may always escape up here, you know."

"Thank you." Desmond smiled at the small man. "I've been rather busy lately."

"Are you chasing this Eye of Cornelia's, too? Of course, you would be interested in Anne Ballew—you are from Dorset, too, as I remember. I'm sure Symington would love to pick your brain. He's most interested in local legends."

"That's good," Thisbe said. "We would like to talk to Mr. Symington, too. Do you know where he lives?"

"Oh, yes, yes. Let me see…" He began to search his desk until he found a thin leather-bound notebook. "There we are." He flipped through the pages. "Ah, yes, I thought it wasn't far. Tottenham Borough, near Seven Sisters Road." He held out the book to Thisbe. "I should have remembered that. Apt place for him to live, with all the legends about those trees."

"Legends?"

"They 'flourish but do not grow,' isn't it?" Desmond said.

Bellard nodded, pleased at his understanding. "Oh! I don't believe you've seen my new set of hussars. I just got them in." He went happily over to a table, Desmond following. "I've decided to lay out the Battle of Balaclava. That charge, of course, was a terrible mistake—blamed it on Nolan, but my thought is it was Lord Cardigan at fault. He's always been a fool." He gestured at the table, sweeping his arm toward "the thin red line" and pointing at future placements of cannons.

Desmond nodded thoughtfully and agreed, but as he and Thisbe walked back down the hall, he murmured, "Who is Lord Cardigan? A relative?"

Thisbe chuckled. "I think he's the one who led the Charge of the Light Brigade."

"Ah." His brow cleared. "'Into the Valley of Death' and so on. I thought Balaclava was some sort of musical instrument."

Thisbe giggled. "I thought it was a pastry, myself. No one knows nearly enough to keep up with Uncle Bellard—it's best just to nod. You are very nice to him."

"How could anyone not be?"

"There are those who can," she said darkly. She paused as they neared the stairs and turned to him. "Seven Sisters tomorrow?"

He nodded. "It seems the likeliest place for Gordon to go. With their mutual interest in Anne Ballew, they're likely to be friends. If we're lucky, he's staying with Mr. Symington."

"Or Mr. Symington knows where he went or what he's planning to do." Thisbe fell silent. She wished Desmond would stay, but she couldn't think of anything to delay his leaving. "I—I appreciate your help with this."

"I will always help you. You must know that." His eyes were dark and warm. He leaned forward, his hand coming up, and Thisbe thought breathlessly that he was about to kiss her. But he drew back a step, his hand dropping. "Besides, I am to blame for it going missing. I should have realized what Professor Gordon might do. Stopped him."

"How could you have done that? Perhaps it's time we stop casting blame—ourselves and each other. I—" Impulsively, she stretched up to kiss him, her lips light and soft on his. She heard his quick intake of breath, and his hands went to her waist.

"Thisbe…" His fingers tightened, his eyes going to her mouth. "You don't know how much I want to kiss you right now."

"Perhaps you should show me." Her lips curved up.

At that moment there was the sound of footsteps on the stairs. For one of the few times in her life, Thisbe wished everyone in her family was far away. Desmond stepped back, letting his breath out in a whoosh, and turned toward the stairs just as Olivia came into view.

"Oh." She stopped, her eyes going apologetically to Thisbe. "I, um, think I forgot something." She began to turn back.

But Desmond was already greeting her sister, the moment gone. "Hallo, Livvy." To Thisbe, he said, "Tomorrow morning, then."

Thisbe nodded, and Olivia added, "Come for breakfast. Grandmother never comes down that early."

Desmond chuckled. "Ha. With my luck she'll make an exception." He gave Olivia's braid a playful tug and trotted down the stairs.

"I'm sorry," Olivia said. "I didn't know."

"Of course not. You didn't do anything wrong. Desmond was about to leave, anyway."

"Yes, but… I don't know… You looked as if maybe you aren't mad at him anymore."

"Maybe I'm not." Thisbe grinned. "We'll see what happens."

She went to her bedroom and pulled out Mr. Symington's book, turning to his biography of Anne Ballew. The familiar face gazed out at her. There was pride in the look, even a touch of arrogance. Had she thought her intelligence would keep her safe? Allow her to succeed where most women would not even dare to go? If so, she had certainly paid for not recognizing the strength of inbred prejudices against women and class, indeed, against any ideas that challenged accepted beliefs.

What was the meaning of her dreams? Why did this woman's vision populate them? However nonsensical it seemed to place any value in dreams or to see them as signs or portents, Thisbe could not dismiss her experiences. She was not, after all, a woman given to flights of fantasy nor one easily influenced. There must be some reason she continued to have these vivid nightmares.

Thisbe decided to approach the matter scientifically. The dreams must come from one of two sources. They were either imaginings that sprang from her own thoughts and feelings, or they came from outside herself, which meant that someone or something was capable of invading her sleeping mind, an idea that was frankly horrifying.

Thisbe decided to concentrate on the first possibility. What could be lodged in her brain that came out only in this form of expression? Picking up a pencil and piece of paper, she sat down at her desk and began to make a list. What had been in the dreams? Fire, a woman who might or might not be Anne Ballew, pain, fear.

Her image of Anne wanted her to save someone. Her child? She had said something like that. That last dream, she had said Thisbe owed her and that Thisbe was hers.

The idea that Thisbe belonged to her was the most easily explained; her grandmother claimed they were Anne Ballew's descendants. But what did Thisbe owe Anne Ballew? Finding the Eye? Perhaps what had to be saved was not someone but something—the Eye. This interpretation made sense. The Eye had been greatly on Thisbe's mind the past fortnight. It wasn't unusual to have nightmares about something that worried one. So she'd dreamed about Anne Ballew begging her to save the Eye.

The problem with that was that Thisbe had dreamed about Anne before she even knew the Eye existed. Before she knew Anne Ballew existed. She had dreamed of fire before she knew the woman was burned at the stake.

Thisbe tossed down the pencil on the desk in disgust. So much for reason and the idea that the dreams came from her own worries. That left the alternative: the long-dead Anne Ballew had come back to haunt Thisbe's dreams because she wanted Thisbe to recover Anne's invention.

It struck Thisbe that she had not had the dream until her grandmother had come to visit. Could it be that the Eye was somehow causing her dreams? She wasn't sure whether it was more frightening to think that Anne Ballew's spirit was invading her dreams, or that the Eye itself was capable of doing so. Frankly, both seemed ludicrous.

She considered her grandmother's statement this morning that Desmond was also somehow connected to the Eye. Thisbe couldn't hold back a shiver at the memory of the dowager duchess's words: "One of his kind will kill one of ours. He is bound by it, just as you are bound."

What was his "kind"? What was hers? Why were they both bound? In her last dream, Anne had said, "I bind thee," which fit her grandmother's statement. But bind her to what? How?

Desmond had said his aunt believed he was descended from Anne Ballew. It seemed to Thisbe that being from Dorset was exceedingly thin proof that Anne was his ancestor. But then, there was no proof that Thisbe and her grandmother were Anne's descendants, either, other than that they possessed the Eye.

Perhaps Desmond was the one who was Anne's offspring and Thisbe was not. Perhaps they were both her descendants, cousins in the eighteenth degree or some such thing. Or perhaps neither of them were descended from Anne Ballew, and this was all utter lunacy.

With an impatient shake of her head, Thisbe stood up and left her room. Enough of this. She was going down to have supper with her family…who, in comparison to these thoughts, seemed remarkably sane.

SHE WAS FROZEN. *The bitter cold swirled all around her, pulling her down into its dark center. There was nothing beneath her, only an unending icy abyss. Thisbe struggled to breathe, her heartbeat loud in her ears. She must escape or she would die. She was certain of it, but she was unable to move, unable to think. She was helpless and alone, deserted by everyone.*

But, no, that was wrong. The woman was there, too, as lost and alone as Thisbe. The fire was gone from Anne Ballew now, as well as all life. Her face was drained of color. Hoarfrost clung to her hair and clothes. Anne's eyes were closed, her hands folded on her chest, posed for the grave.

Dead. Alone. Condemned.

Thisbe shuddered. Was this to be her fate, as well? To drift unfeeling and unknown through all eternity? Was this Anne's vengeance?

Anne's eyes flew open, milky white with death. "The fault is thine!"

"No, I've done nothing," Thisbe whispered, but the words died in her throat. It was her fault. She should see; she should know. What good was all her knowledge when she could not understand?

Anne Ballew floated toward her, and though her eyes were opaque, unseeing, they were fixed on Thisbe.

"No, no..." Panicked, Thisbe tried to move back, but she could not.

"Thou must. I will have justice." Anne Ballew flung out her arm, and her corpselike hand reached for Thisbe...

THISBE STRUGGLED TO open her eyes. She was huddled in a ball, shivering; the bedclothes wrapped tightly around her were not enough to warm her. She had been dreaming again. What had once consumed her with fire now froze her to the marrow.

She shuddered before logic returned to her. Obviously, the fire must have gone out. Thisbe turned her head toward the fireplace. It still burned, the coals glowing, lending the palest of light to the dark room. And there, standing between Thisbe and the fireplace, was Anne Ballew.

The cold that swept Thisbe now went far beyond the physical. This was no dream, but a real woman. One of flesh and bone, silhouetted by the light behind her.

There was none of the fierce thirst for vengeance that she had seen on Anne Ballew's face in the past. She was a woman in anguish, her face contorted, her dark eyes pleading.

"Save him, I beg of thee," she whispered. "Save him. It is too powerful. It will destroy him. Blood of my blood, bone of my bone. Please, you must, you must—"

With a wordless cry, the woman was gone. Thisbe lay for a moment, unmoving. Anne Ballew had been in Thisbe's room; the woman had spoken to her. It was utterly unbelievable, yet Thisbe knew it was true.

"Desmond!" With a jerk, Thisbe flung aside her covers and jumped out of bed. The apparition had been talking about Desmond. She was as certain as she was terrified. Anne wasn't talking about the Eye; she was clearly talking about a man—"blood of my blood, bone of my bone." Desmond must be Anne's descendant.

Thisbe couldn't sit here quaking. She had to save him. Jamming her feet into the first pair of half boots she found, she didn't bother with stockings or changing clothes. She just threw her dressing gown around her and belted it, then covered it all with her cloak.

She slipped down the staircase to the side door, then eased it open and stepped out into the cold night air. Pulling her hood up over her head, Thisbe began to run. It was dark and fog hung over the city, the only light the fuzzy glow of streetlamps. In the distance the bell of a clock tower chimed once. She hurried through the night, her heart pounding, her mind skittering wildly about.

A hansom cab drove slowly down the street, and Thisbe ran out to hail it. The driver looked at her strangely, but Thisbe paid no attention; there was no room in her for anything other than the panic surging in her chest. She didn't know what the danger was—something to do with the Eye, she presumed—but the very vagueness of Anne's warning made it all the more terrifying.

She shifted impatiently on the seat as the cab rolled through the streets, their pace unbearably slow. As they drew closer to Desmond's home, the streetlamps grew fewer and fewer, leaving great stretches of darkness. When the horse clip-clopped to a stop, Thisbe scrambled out of the carriage and peered up at Desmond's building. There was no light in any of the windows; the narrow alleyway leading to his stairs was a great well of shadows. The sight only added to her foreboding.

Thisbe thrust some coins into the driver's hand, then hurried into the alleyway and up the stairs. She arrived at Desmond's door, out of breath, and rapped sharply. She tried to keep her voice low. "Desmond! Desmond, it's I. Are you all right? Open the door."

She didn't pause for an answer, but opened the door and rushed inside, calling his name again.

"Thisbe?" Desmond said groggily as he sat up. He pushed back his mop of hair and stared at her in confusion. "What's wrong?" Now alarm infused his voice, and he stood up, but Thisbe was across the room before he took a step, throwing herself against him.

"Desmond! Oh, Desmond! Are you all right?" She wrapped her arms around him, clinging to him, her fears tumbling out in a jumbled, incoherent stream.

"Of course I am." He put his arms around her, kissing the top of her head. "I'm fine. What is it? What happened? I can't understand you."

"She said— I was so afraid. I thought you were—" Thisbe lifted her head and looked up into his eyes. Her hands framed his face. "I couldn't bear it if anything happened to you." She kissed his lips, his cheeks—soft scattered touches of relief—and her hands dropped to his shoulders.

She felt his skin turn warmer beneath her hands, and she was suddenly, breathtakingly, aware of his bare torso. It was equally clear that his long, lean body was naked all the way up and down. Desmond's arms tightened, pressing her into his body, and his mouth found hers. Thisbe flung her arms around his neck, returning his kiss with all the passion that had been simmering in her from the moment she met him.

Desmond was safe; he was hers; and she kissed him as if she were claiming him once and for always. He made a low noise, his fingertips digging into her cloak, and their kiss deepened. Thisbe wanted to spill out all her feelings for him, but the emotions that swirled in her were too strong, too inchoate to be spoken, so she gave them to him in her kiss.

Desmond's hands roamed over her, but he was hampered by her cloak. Thisbe jerked at the ties of the mantle and shrugged it off. Now he caressed her freely. His hands slid around to her front and went still as they found the sash of her dressing gown. His body tightened, heat surging in him, and Thisbe knew Desmond had realized she was dressed in nothing but her nightclothes. After an instant's hesitation, he tugged the bow apart and his fingers glided beneath the robe.

Thisbe quivered at the touch of his fingers through the cloth of her nightgown, and everything in her ached to feel them against her bare skin. She wanted… Oh, God, she wanted so much. Taking a step backward, she dropped her dressing gown on the floor and pushed off her loosely buttoned shoes. She reached down and began to pull up her nightgown.

Desmond stood still, his eyes glittering and his chest

rising and falling in rapid breaths as he watched her drag
the loose shift up her body and over her head. His words
were a ragged whisper: "Thisbe, we shouldn't."

She shook her head, reaching out to him. "No. Don't
say it. I want this. Desmond, I want you."

He pulled her to him, and all words were gone between
them, all speech and thought and hesitation vanished in
the flame of their desire.

CHAPTER TWENTY-SEVEN

THISBE SLID HER hands across Desmond's back, learning the feel of his bare skin, warm and smooth beneath her fingers. She followed the contours of his body, curving over the pad of muscle, trailing up the bony outcropping of his spine.

This was what she wanted, what she had ached for and dreamed of. To touch him, to feel the shudder of his response, the flare of heat within him that matched her own. Sensations bombarded her, almost too much to take in, stoking the fire that burned deep in her abdomen. It dazed and dazzled her, but one thing she was certain of: this was, in every way, right.

Kissing and caressing, they tumbled onto his bed. Desmond rolled onto his side, and Thisbe missed having his flesh pressed to hers, but now his hand was free to explore her body as they continued to kiss, and that, she found, was another delight altogether. He started at the top, gliding down over her throat to dip into the tender hollow at the base, then traced her collarbone and slid down to the soft swell of her breasts.

He teased his fingertips around the edge of one of her breasts, and trailed, light as a feather, over the orb. His mouth was avid on hers as his hand encompassed her breast. All too soon, he moved on, but the spread of his fingers across her stomach was almost equally arousing. Her body tightened in anticipation as he arrowed down to his obvious goal. At last his fingers slipped between her legs, and, amazingly, that was only the beginning of deeper, fiercer delights.

As his slender, agile fingers brought these new, intense sensations, he broke off his kiss and moved his mouth to her breasts. The pleasure was overwhelming. Thisbe let out a moan, her fingers digging into the sheet beneath. It was too much; surely, she could not stand this. But she found she could. And could want even more.

Desmond covered her, taking his weight on his arms, and Thisbe widened her legs, welcoming him. She was a learned woman; she knew what happened next. But nothing could have prepared her for the actuality—the new and strange feel of his flesh pushing into her, and the urgent, compelling need to take him into the very depths of her being. There was a flash of pain, overridden by the all-compelling force of her hunger, and finally the indescribable satisfaction as he filled her.

He began to move within her, his motion slow and rhythmic, and Thisbe moaned at the pleasure that built in her with every stroke. She tightened in anticipation. Finally, a low cry burst out of him as he shuddered, and an unexpected, shattering pleasure swept through Thisbe. She clung to Desmond as he collapsed against her, and they lay together, intertwined and replete. This, she knew, was all the world to her.

DESMOND CRADLED THISBE in his arms. He felt as if everything inside him, including his brain, had been wiped clean. Stunned, satisfied and drained, he floated in a haze of pleasure, and for a few long minutes, he let himself luxuriate in it. If he could only have this…

But this, of course, was the one thing he could never have. Desmond was too practical a man, too aware of the realities of the world, to hold on to a fantasy for long. He let out a sigh, pushing his hand back through his hair. "I'm sorry. I shouldn't have—"

"You regret this?" Thisbe asked, rising up on her elbow to stare down at him. Her hair fell all around her, silky black and alluringly mussed, and her lips were soft and dark from their kisses. The covers slid down her arm, revealing her bare shoulders and breasts, and she looked so desirable that his just-slaked thirst for her surged back in full.

Her tone was wounded, and Desmond quickly assured her, "No. Of course I don't regret this." He reached up to stroke his hand down her arm. "I could never regret this. It was… I'm no good with words, but it was the most wonderful thing that's ever happened to me."

"I think your words are good enough." She smiled and eased back down, her hand resting on his chest. "I never imagined what it would be like," she went on. "But I suppose you knew already. You have done it before."

"Not exactly."

"Really?" She raised up again to look into his face.

Desmond felt a blush rising in his cheeks. "Well, I mean… I had my studies and work, and I couldn't really afford to spend my money on Haymarket ware when there were books to be bought and tutors to pay. And, anyway, that seems rather sad, somehow. There have been girls I liked and, we, um, well, we did a bit of… But I couldn't risk getting any of them with child, not when I didn't feel for them what one should. I'm not all that old, you know," he declared, a little defensively.

Thisbe smiled and bent to brush her lips against his. "I'm glad."

"Also, I am somewhat shy," he admitted.

"I noticed." She kissed him again, more lingeringly,

and his blood began to heat in his veins. He slid his fingers into her hair as their kiss deepened. Everything in him ached for her.

With a groan, Desmond wrenched away and stood up, grabbing his trousers and donning them, as if they could miraculously shield him from his desire. "No. We can't."

"Why not?" That was Thisbe, of course—direct and without hesitation.

"There are any number of reasons." Why must he argue against the very thing he most desired? But he had to control this; he had to be cautious. Because Thisbe was fearless. She would rush in no matter what the odds, no matter what the obstacles. "For one thing, if we keep on, you could get pregnant."

"I see." Thisbe pulled up her knees and crossed her arms on them, clearly settling in for a discussion, just as if he weren't half-naked and she completely so, under the blanket. "You don't feel for me what one should to marry."

"No!" he said in alarm. "It's not that. Do you think I don't want to marry you? That I wouldn't be ecstatic to have a reason for you to marry me?"

"It certainly appears that way."

"*You* are the one who would be hurt, your reputation damaged. You know there would be a scandal even if we married—a babe arriving early. I can't do that to you."

"And we know how much I worry about scandal."

"Maybe you don't care, but I care about people maligning you. I care that you would be forced to tie yourself to me."

"Me? Forced?" She raised her eyebrows in disbelief. "I think it's more the other way around."

"Even if we didn't have to marry, there's the disparity

in our classes." He fell back on another argument. "Your family tied to mine?"

"Desmond, you cannot be so blind as to think my mother or father would care a whit that you aren't an aristocrat."

He had to tell her, even though his insides quailed at the thought.

"It isn't just that I'm not the son of a gentleman." He took a breath and plunged in. "I'm the son of a thief. My father isn't dead. He's a felon."

Thisbe gaped at him. "A felon? But you said—"

"I know. I know." Desmond turned away with a groan. "Another way I deceived you. You asked me if he was dead, and—"

"And you said that he was gone, too."

"Yes, but the truth was that where he had gone was the penal colony in Australia. I'm sorry, Thisbe. I'm so sorry, I should have told you. It was wrong, and I've felt wretched, but I couldn't summon the courage to tell you. You already thought I'd used you get that damnable Eye. And then, when you thought I had *stolen* it…"

Thisbe nodded. "I can see why you would be reluctant." She leaned forward, her voice earnest. "But, Desmond, I can hardly get angry about that sort of shading the truth when I did exactly the same by telling you my name was Moreland but not adding that I was Broughton's daughter. It's certainly not such a lie that I wouldn't marry you."

"Thisbe!" He had to laugh. "Only you would equate omitting that you're a duke's daughter with my not confessing I'm a thief's son. Don't you see? It's not the deception—though I do regret that immensely—it's the fact that no one, not even your family, would want a man like that for an in-law."

"Really, Desmond, how dare you?" Thisbe said hotly. "How can you imply that my family would be so judgmental, so narrow-minded, as to brand you with your father's misdeeds?"

"I didn't mean that," he protested.

"What did you mean?"

"Well, I…" He floundered.

"My family likes *you*, Desmond, and they want me to be happy. None of them would care a whit about who your father is."

"Your grandmother would."

"No one whose opinion mattered to me," Thisbe amended.

"I have no money. Hell, I haven't a job any longer. If I did, it wouldn't support a wife, even if she were not accustomed to luxury."

"But that's silly." Thisbe laughed. "Money is the last thing we need worry about. Papa has lots of it, so much he cannot possibly throw it all away on his pots and statues. We can live in any of the houses."

"Any?" He gaped at her. "How many are there?"

"I don't know. There's the house in Bath, where Grandmother lives, and a fishing lodge in Scotland, though no one ever goes there except Theo and Reed when they want to have some boys' outing. The Irish estate, which we never use because Mother disapproves of the subjugation of Ireland. And there's Broughton Park, of course, the seat of the Morelands. It's much larger than the London house."

"Larger?" he asked weakly. At every turn, some new evidence of the gulf between them showed up.

"Yes, we could have a whole wing to ourselves at the park. You'd have a laboratory. You could share mine or have one of your own if you liked. You wouldn't have to make kaleidoscopes—you could spend your time on the things you truly want to study. But if you didn't want to live with my family, Papa would let us have any of the others we wanted. Or we could find somewhere that is ours—*I* have money now. Papa's lawyer set up some sort of fund for all of us children, and since I'm over turned twenty-one, so—"

"Thisbe…" He thrust both hands into his hair, tugging at it, as he so often did when arguing with Thisbe. "It's not your family—they're delightful. It would be wonderful to live with them and have a laboratory and everything I wanted. But I cannot batten on your family like that. I won't attach myself to you like a leech."

"Is it because I accused you of using me?" Thisbe asked. "I don't believe that anymore. I understand what you did and, anyway, I think I said that mostly because I was hurt. I wouldn't think you are any of those things."

"Others would." He sighed. "Besides, it's more than any of those things, and you know it." He walked over and sat down on the bed beside her, taking her hand. "I am a danger to you."

"But don't you see? There's no danger any longer. Now that Gordon has the Eye, there's no reason to threaten me."

"It's not only Gordon and the Eye. It's *me*. I know you scoff at your grandmother's warning, but I cannot ignore it that easily. If I am a danger to you, I—"

"Maybe *you're* the one in danger," Thisbe argued.

"What? Why would I be in danger? Wait. When you came here tonight, you said…" In truth, he couldn't remember what she had said. He had bolted straight from sleep into a waking dream of Thisbe in his arms, and her words had been only extraneous gibberish floating about. "You were scared. What happened?"

Thisbe looked sheepish, an expression he'd never seen on her. "What if your aunt's story wasn't a legend? What if you really are descended from Anne Ballew?"

"What?" That had been the last thing he had expected her to say. "Why would you think that?"

"You don't know that she was not your ancestor, do you?"

"No, but that's true of just about everyone in the world. Being from Dorset doesn't make one her descendant. Nobody even knows if she had children."

"But isn't it more likely that she did have children? She was an alchemist, not a nun, and she was an attractive woman. Her coloring was the same as yours."

Desmond stared. "Thisbe...this isn't like you. It's very slender evidence to base anything on. Why are you—"

"Very well." Looking even more embarrassed, Thisbe slipped out of bed and pulled on her nightgown and wrapper again. Apparently, she, like him, viewed her clothing as defense. "I had a dream tonight. I've been having them for some time now. Ever since I met you."

"You dreamed that I was Anne Ballew's son?"

"Yes... No... Well, not exactly." She took in a deep breath and went on in a rush, "I've been dreaming about Anne Ballew. The woman in my dream is the woman in the portrait in Uncle Bellard's book."

"Well, if you saw her portrait, it's likely—"

"No," Thisbe interrupted, her tone adamant. "I didn't picture her in the dream because I'd seen her in the book. I dreamed about her long before I read it. Before I'd even heard of Anne Ballew or the Eye. There was fire—I felt it. She pleaded with me to save someone. She said I owed it to her. She said she bound me."

"She said this in your dream tonight?"

"She's said it over the course of them. I've had a number

of them, and they've grown more vivid. They've changed from hot to bone-chilling cold." She raised her hands as he started to speak. "I know it's ridiculous. You cannot give me any reason why none of this is real that I have not already told myself. I don't believe in mystical things or speaking to the dead."

"I know. So why do you believe these dreams are real?"

"They're odd—they're intense. They're not like any dream I've ever had. She looks exactly like that woman in the book, and there's the fire. Tonight she told me that I must 'save him.' She said it would destroy you."

"She said me specifically?"

"No, but how many 'hims' are involved in this thing? Who among them is rumored to be descended from her? She called him 'blood of my blood. Bone of my bone.' And, Desmond…I didn't see her in a dream. Tonight she was standing in my room."

"You talked to Anne Ballew?"

"*She* talked to *me*. I said nothing because I was scared out of my wits."

"Just a moment. You were communing with Anne Ballew's ghost tonight, but *my* believing in an omen is ludicrous?"

Thisbe had the grace to look abashed, though she protested, "I saw Anne Ballew with my own eyes, whereas your premonition is from my grandmother, who doesn't want me to be with you."

"Because I'll cause your death!"

"If you a had title in front of your name, I suspect her premonition would change drastically," Thisbe retorted. "Oh, the devil. I don't know what I believe anymore. Maybe my grandmother is mad as a hatter, and I am, too, and neither you nor I have the slightest thing to do with

Anne Ballew. Or maybe Grandmother has been telling the truth all these years, and she can commune with Old Eldric and any number of spirits. Maybe she didn't misinterpret what she saw, and her premonition is accurate. None of that matters because I don't care."

"Thisbe—"

"I don't. It's my life, and I am willing to take the risk."

"I know you are." Desmond went to her and cupped her face with his hands. "You're fearless." He bent to kiss her gently. "But I am not. I cannot bear to think of anything hurting you. I couldn't stand to live any longer if I was the cause of your death."

Tears swam in Thisbe's eyes, and she pulled away. "Do you think I don't feel the same for you? Love makes one a coward." Thisbe walked away, then turned back. "You know...she didn't say you would cause my death. She said your *love* would. We could be together if you stopped loving me."

Desmond gazed at her, his heart leaden. "But *that* is something I can never do."

CHAPTER TWENTY-EIGHT

THISBE AND DESMOND took the train to Alfred Symington's the following morning and were knocking on his door before noon. Thisbe glanced over at Desmond, who was standing beside her on the doorstep. He had been quiet today, and she knew he was agonizing over the night before.

He had enjoyed it; she was certain of that. They had made love again, desperate and hungry in the face of their uncertain future, and Thisbe had found, astonishingly, that she could feel even more than she had before. Desmond insisted on seeing her home. When they parted at the side door of her home, he kissed her long and hard, leaving no doubt that he desired her. Every time he looked at her on the ride to Seven Sisters, Thisbe saw warmth in his eyes. But she also saw his worry and guilt, the dread that being with him would harm Thisbe, the self-castigation for giving in to his own needs.

He was convinced he must protect her. Thisbe understood that. When she believed him in trouble the night before, her only thought had been to save him. But she was unwilling to accept that they must suffer the fate her grandmother predicted.

She had to admit that the dowager duchess's premonition and Desmond's fear that he bore a mark of death seemed less preposterous to her now that she had seen Anne Ballew standing beside her fireplace. But she refused to believe that she had no choice in the matter. What use were omens unless one could do something to change the outcome?

She simply had to work out how to do so. The first step was recovering the Eye and eliminating that danger for either of them, which was why they were here interviewing Mr. Symington this morning.

Thisbe wanted to reach over and smooth the line from Desmond's forehead. He made everything too hard for himself. He'd struggled all his life; he had no experience with anything being easy, no confidence that life would work out the way he wanted.

As if feeling her gaze, Desmond glanced over at her, and his lips curved up in a warm, rather self-satisfied smile before he remembered that he was violating his own rules and tried to change his expression from that of a lover to one of a friend. She wondered if he knew that he was largely unsuccessful at it.

"Do you think he's not home?" he said now. "I thought your uncle sent him a message yesterday evening."

"He did. Perhaps you should knock again."

He did so, and a moment later the door was flung open, revealing a tall, patrician-looking man with dark brown hair punctuated by dramatic sweeps of silver at each temple. Thisbe had not really thought about what Alfred Symington would look like, but it wasn't this. She'd more or less expected a man much like her great-uncle— stooped, bespectacled and abstracted—not someone who looked like a gentleman about to step out to his club.

"Come in, come in," he boomed, making an expansive gesture toward the inside of his cottage. "Had you knocked before? I was reading and didn't hear you until my housekeeper called down." He glanced up at an exasperated-looking woman standing at the top of the stairs, dust cloth in hand. With a shake of her head, she turned and stalked out of sight.

Symington led them into the parlor. "Please, sit down. Shall I ring for tea?"

Remembering the expression on the housekeeper's face, Thisbe shook her head. "No, thank you."

"I am honored to meet Lord Moreland's niece. Such a scholar! I so enjoy our correspondence. Of course, his interests are divergent from mine." He gave her a small self-deprecating smile. "But his comments are always so instructive."

Thisbe introduced Desmond, then added, "Mr. Harrison works for Professor Gordon."

"Ah!" Symington nodded. "I spoke to Mr. Gordon just the other day. Lord Moreland mentioned that you, too, are interested in learning about Anne Ballew and her legendary Eye."

"Yes. I read your book that featured her," Thisbe said.

"Did you?" Symington asked with delight. "How good of you."

"I found it very informative. I was surprised that you were able to find her portrait."

"Indeed!" he enthused. "It was unusual at that time for a woman of her station to have a portrait, much less for it to have survived for so many years. It was, I believe, wrapped up and stuck in a trunk. I'm not sure if it was purposely hidden or merely forgotten, or even if, fearing she was a witch, they were afraid of the power it might hold and thought to contain it thusly. Very superstitious people, you know."

"How did you come by it?"

"I learned of it from a friend. Another historian, Walter Cummings, saw it in a small museum and wrote me about it, knowing my interest. A family discovered it in their attic and gave it to the museum fifty years ago."

"But you are certain it is a portrait of her?"

"There was a note wrapped up with it, identifying her, and, actually, her name was painted on the back at the top. It fits the written descriptions of her—a 'comely woman of dark hair and piercing eyes.' But what makes it even more certain is the pin."

"The pin?"

"Yes, you may not have noticed but she is wearing a brooch. Here, I'll show you." He jumped up and hurried out of the room, returning with his book in his hand. He opened the volume to the portrait and held it out to them, tapping Anne Ballew's shoulder. "There it is. It's clearer in the actual portrait. The pin is highly unusual—a rendering of the mizmaze at—"

"Leigh," Desmond said, finishing the man's sentence.

"Why, yes." Symington looked at him in surprise. "Quite so."

"I'm lost. What is a mizmaze?" Thisbe asked.

"A turf maze," Symington explained. "An intricate labyrinth of raised turf. The best preserved is on Breamore Down in Hampshire, but some think the one at Leigh is the oldest."

"It's been overrun for many years now," Desmond explained. "But that is the purported pattern."

"Anne wore such a brooch always. It was one of her accuser's proofs of her witch-hood—the Leigh mizmaze was also known as Witches Corner, you see. Dorset is rife with superstitions and legends about witchcraft. Anne Ballew was merely the most famous. She was rumored to be a necromancer. They believed she could see the dead and speak with them. But not only that, she could make them come to life again. It was what made her so feared…and envied. It was a time of hysteria about heretics. Easy enough to be adjudged doing the devil's work and end up at the stake."

"What about the instrument she made, the Eye?" Desmond prompted.

"Ah, yes, the infamous Eye. It was supposedly how she was able to raise the dead. As the tale goes, Anne sold her soul to the devil to obtain the knowledge to create the Eye. It's hard to distinguish how much of the story is from Anne's time and how much was added to it in later retellings. There have been differing renditions. I have heard the legend in many places, not only Dorset—London and Hampshire, even the north. I assumed the Eye was apocryphal, frankly, given the extravagance of the tales. I could hardly believe my eyes when Gordon brought it in."

"He showed it to you?" Desmond asked, sitting forward.

Symington nodded. "Had it wrapped in green velvet inside a beautifully carved box."

That sounded like her grandmother's Eye—more proof, if they needed any, that it was Gordon who stole the instrument. "Did you try it?"

"Oh, yes." Symington chuckled. "I felt sure it wouldn't work, but I couldn't resist looking through it. It distorts everything. Poor Gordon was most distraught because it didn't work. He wondered if it was a counterfeit, a copy. He thought I might be able to help him, being knowledgeable about Anne Ballew." He nodded toward Desmond. "But, of course, working with him, you know all about that."

"Were you able to put his mind at rest?" Thisbe asked.

"Sadly, no. I'm afraid my answer distressed him even more. The legend says no one can use the thing successfully besides one of Anne's blood. Others see only a mess."

"Her blood?" Thisbe glanced at Desmond. "Did she have descendants?"

"I've no idea. She had a family, but no one knows what happened to them. One would assume they fled. Changed their name, perhaps. I would have. I suppose they went home to Dorset—it would have been too dangerous for them in London. But they could have struck out for someplace new, perhaps farther away—Cornwall or Northumberland. Impossible to tell."

"What did Mr. Gordon say when you told him?" Thisbe asked.

"Don't you know?" Symington raised his eyebrows and turned to Desmond. "I would have assumed he told you."

"No. That's why we're here. We don't know what happened to him. No one has seen the professor for days. He's not at the university nor his laboratory nor his home," Desmond replied, managing, Thisbe noted, not to tell an outright lie.

"Oh, my. He said he had to tell…someone. I thought it would be the people at his laboratory."

"Did he say a name? Or where he was going?"

"No, neither. Let me think." Symington furrowed his brow. "He became quite agitated when I told him. I was alarmed—he looked as if he might fall down in a fit. He jumped and paced a bit, muttering to himself. I was at a loss for what to say. He said something like 'I have to tell him' or 'he must know.' Then he rushed out the door without even taking his leave." Symington seemed more astounded by that than he had been about seeing the legendary Eye.

"Do you remember which day he came to see you?" Desmond asked.

"It must have been Wednesday—I remember because I have bell ringing rehearsal every Wednesday, and I was a bit afraid his visit might run into that."

"But it didn't, I assume, since he left so abruptly."

"That's right. It wasn't quite teatime when he departed."

They continued to chat politely for a few minutes before they, too, took their leave, though Thisbe would have liked to rush off as quickly as Mr. Gordon had. As soon as they were out the door, Thisbe turned to Desmond and said, "He was going to see Wallace, don't you think? Who else would he feel he must tell about it?"

"I don't know. I suppose he could have some other partner in the crime—perhaps one of the other men at the laboratory. Carson, for instance."

"You just don't like Carson."

"That's not true. I like Carson. I just…" Desmond stuck his hands in his pockets, studying his feet. "I just don't like him around you." He sighed. "I'm sorry. I know it's very dog-in-the-manger of me, but I can't help it."

Thisbe smiled. "I don't mind." She linked her arm through his, then leaned close and whispered, "I think I wouldn't like to have some female scientist working at your laboratory, either. So if that's horrid, we'll be horrid together."

"I'd like that." A look of longing flickered in Desmond's eyes for an instant, then was gone. Desmond cleared his throat. "I agree that Professor Gordon went off to tell Wallace. If the Eye has been useless to Gordon—which I suspect it is for anyone. Not being Anne's descendant is merely a handy excuse—then Wallace already knows that Gordon has failed or will soon know it. The odds are—"

"He'll cut off Professor Gordon's funding," Thisbe said, finishing his thought.

"Exactly. But if Gordon could offer him a reason for the failure other than that it simply doesn't work, Wallace might continue to supply the professor with money while Gordon searches for a descendant of Anne Ballew to operate the Eye."

"He has you."

"I doubt he thinks I'm her descendant. *I* don't think I'm her descendant. You're the one she's been visiting. It would seem more likely that *you* are the heir to her powers." Desmond frowned. "In fact…they might think that very thing. After all, the Eye was in the possession of your family."

"They'd be out of luck there, given that they've stolen the Eye from us."

"That only means they might resort to force. You're still in danger."

"My grandmother is the one who claims to be able to use the thing."

Desmond's lips twitched up at the corners. "I'd take the dowager duchess over any opponent. But I think even she would surrender if your safety was at stake."

"Well, whatever danger there is, all we have to do to end it is recover the Eye. Now that we know Gordon has it in his possession and he's gone off to tell Wallace, all we have to do is find out where his estate is."

"I have an idea how to do that."

"How?"

"We know what time Gordon would have returned to the train station. As agitated as he was, he might have taken a train to Wallace's instead of returning home. After all, he clearly is trying to avoid his usual haunts. I'm going to ask the ticket agent what he bought."

"You think he will remember Gordon?"

He shrugged. "It's worth a try. It's a small place, not like Paddington, so my guess is they only have one or two ticket agents. Not that many people go through the station, and they might notice someone who isn't local. He's fairly noticeable—a rotund middle-aged man with red hair."

Desmond's theory proved right, for in the midst of Desmond's description of date, time and physical appearance, the agent began to nod. "Aye, I remember him right enough."

"Do you remember his destination?"

The man nodded. "Went to London."

"Oh." Desmond sighed.

"That's why I remembered him," the man went on. "He came up and asked about a ticket north, but he bought a ticket to London."

"North?" Desmond asked.

"Do you remember where in the north?" Thisbe quickly said.

"Aye, I'll think of it in a second. Was past Manchester." He tapped his forefinger against his lips. "Ha! Preston!" He beamed. "That's it."

"Preston still leaves a good deal missing," Desmond pointed out on the train home. "Is Wallace's home *in* Preston? Or is that just the closest one can get by train?"

"It gives Smeggars and Grandmother much more to work with. Now they'll know whom to ask. And even if they don't, when we get to Preston, we can ask about. I suspect someone will know of Mr. Wallace. A wealthy widower never goes unnoticed."

Thisbe was proven to be correct. Within two hours of relaying the news to the butler, Smeggars entered the room where Thisbe and Desmond were discussing their findings with Olivia and Uncle Bellard, and announced, somewhat smugly, "Mr. Wallace's country estate is Groveton Manor, a rather splendid house just east of Preston."

"Thank you, Smeggars. You are a jewel."

Smeggars almost let a smile escape. "I took the liberty of inquiring as to the train schedules to Preston. It leaves rather late in the day, as it is an all-night journey, and one must change trains in Manchester. Would you like me to make the arrangements?"

"Yes. For tomorrow evening," Thisbe told him. Desmond had checked the train schedules when they came back to Paddington earlier, but they agreed not to buy tickets until they had more information from Smeggars or her grandmother. "For Mr. Harrison and myself."

"As you wish. Separate compartments, of course."

"Of course," Thisbe responded blandly, though she had little intention of using both. After Smeggars bowed and left, she turned to Desmond. "Though the train doesn't leave until evening, perhaps we should meet earlier to, um—" she cast about for a reason "—discuss matters."

He nodded. "We should probably make another round of searching the usual places. After all, we don't know for certain that he has gone to see Mr. Wallace."

Thisbe was pleased that Desmond seemed as eager as she to extend their time together. But all too soon, he rose to take his leave. Thisbe wanted to say an intimate goodbye to him, but it was impossible in this setting, with her uncle and sister there. If she walked with him to the front door, they would be in full view of Smeggars or a footman. Following him outside would be odd, and, anyway, they would be in full view of the street, which even in the darkness was lit by the lamps beside the door.

So she walked with him downstairs to the large entry

hall, where a footman jumped to get Desmond's coat. After giving him her hand and offering a formal goodbye, she turned away and walked quickly to the music room. There, she darted across the room to a smaller door on the other side, which emptied into the narrow back hall, and to the side door of the house.

Desmond, with his long strides, was already walking past the pathway beside the house, and Thisbe called his name softly and ran toward him. He turned to look down the alleyway, already dim in the evening light.

"Thisbe!" He loped over to her. "What are you doing? And without a coat on!"

He started to take off his own jacket to give her, but Thisbe shook her head. "No, don't. I'm fine."

Desmond opened his coat and wrapped the sides around her, enclosing her in his arms. Thisbe, curling her arms around him beneath the coat, decided that this was a very fine way to get warm.

"I wanted to say a proper goodbye to you," she told him and stretched up to kiss him.

After a long moment, Desmond broke their kiss and said, "We shouldn't." But even as he said it, he was bending his head to kiss her again. Finally, with a groan, he released her and stepped back. "I must leave or—" He shook his head. "I shall see you tomorrow."

As he moved back, Thisbe started to offer to slip out of the house tonight and go to him, as she had yesterday, but she held back the words. She would not throw herself at him, no matter how much she wanted to. She held back, too, the words of love and longing that burned inside her. Desmond must come to the decision that he loved her enough to risk everything; she could not push him into it.

Desmond took another reluctant step backward, but

then he rushed forward, closing the space between them in a single stride. He wrapped his arms around her, lifting her up into his kiss. With another step, they were up against the wall of the house. His body pressed into hers, and Thisbe reveled in the evidence of just how much he wanted her. Clearly, his reluctance didn't spring from lack of desire.

He kissed her lips, her face, her throat, then murmured, "I cannot bear to leave you." He straightened, gazing down into her face. "Every minute I'm with you makes it harder to leave."

"I know." Thisbe reached up to caress his hair. "I feel the same."

"Thisbe…" He leaned his forehead against hers, his eyes closing, his voice harsh with longing and pain. "I'm a bastard to hold on to you. I am the weakest of men."

She would have protested his words, but he kissed her again, hard and quick, then swung away and loped off into the night. Thisbe watched him go. The problem wasn't his weakness. The problem was his strength.

Fortunately, persistence was her best quality.

SHE WAS FLOATING in a cold and terrible void, darkness closing around her. The dream was familiar now, but that made it no less frightening. She had no sense of time or space, no sense of anything except the penetrating cold.

"Save him." The voice was harsh, straining. "It is thy duty. Thou art bound for all time."

Thisbe opened her eyes to see Anne Ballew, clouded by smoke, flames licking at her feet. She was not standing before the fireplace. She was inside it; she was of the fire. Thisbe's throat closed; she felt a terrible weight on her chest.

"I created the evil, and I stand eternally condemned,"

the vision rasped out, stretching her hands toward Thisbe, her eyes no longer black but dancing with flames. "But he is innocent."

"Who?" Thisbe asked, forcing out the word.

"My child...my son..."

"Desmond?" Every word required great effort.

"It consumes his will. His mind. It will eat his soul, piece by piece, until there is none left in him. Thou must save him."

Each time Thisbe spoke, it sapped her strength; she could feel herself weakening, failing. Desperately, she finally asked, "How?"

Anne Ballew flung out her arms to the side, her entire body fiery, sparks spilling into the air around her as her image began to dissolve at the edges. Her words came out in a scream: "Thou shalt die."

CHAPTER TWENTY-NINE

THISBE GASPED, the air rushing into her lungs, and sat up. There was no sign of Anne Ballew. Nor were there any sparks littering the room. The house was hushed and still around her—no cries of alarm from sleepers awakened by a scream, no sound of feet running to investigate. Clearly, she had been the only one to witness it. Thisbe wasn't even sure whether she had been awake or dreaming.

But she remembered the important thing clearly. *Thou shalt die.*

She didn't spring from the bed to run to Desmond as she had the night before. Whatever danger her nightmare visitor threatened, it was broad and vague, not a call to arms. Consuming his mind and will—that sounded ongoing and more subtle than an immediate attack.

What danger was Anne Ballew warning her about? Rising, Thisbe wrapped her dressing gown around her and went to the fireplace to stab the coals with the poker and rouse the flames. She was still freezing. Indeed, she felt as if she might never be warm again. After feeding the fire a few more lumps of coal from the hod beside the fireplace, she pulled the cover from the bed and wrapped herself in it, then curled up in a chair beside the fire.

Anne Ballew said she had created evil; surely she must mean her Eye. It followed that the Eye was what threatened Desmond. The other day Anne had claimed it called to him; tonight she said it drained his will and mind. But Thisbe had seen no sign of either thing in Desmond. He seemed the same as always and motivated more by a desire to help her than any need to have the device.

Could Anne have meant Gordon? Or Wallace? They certainly satisfied the obsession aspect. The apparition had never actually said Desmond's name, only "he" and "him." But if Gordon were Anne's heir, he would have been able to use the Eye, which he had told Mr. Symington he could not. That left Zachary Wallace.

Then there were the woman's final words of doom to consider. Did Anne mean that Thisbe had to die in order for Anne's descendant to be saved? If so, that fit with her grandmother's premonition that Desmond was a danger for Thisbe. That would indicate it was Desmond who was in danger. Perhaps the indications of obsession in Desmond were too subtle for Thisbe to notice. After all, Kyria often told Thisbe that she utterly missed the nuances of flirtation.

Whether the man who must be saved was Wallace or Desmond, why would Thisbe have to sacrifice herself in order to save him? If it meant saving Desmond, then, of course, she would do it. She was not, however, particularly moved to sacrifice her own life for Zachary Wallace's.

But how would her death free Desmond from the influence of the Eye? Couldn't it be accomplished without anyone having to die? Thisbe could restore the status quo by finding the Eye and returning it to her grandmother. It seemed to her that it would resolve the issue. But if that would end the danger, why was Anne Ballew plaguing her about it? Thisbe already intended to retrieve the Eye.

Perhaps Anne's words hadn't been an indication of

how Thisbe could save Anne's kin, but a threat of what would happen to her if she didn't.

Still pondering the issue, Thisbe began to brush out her hair. According to the clock on the mantel, it was almost dawn. She might as well get dressed and go down to breakfast. She was eager to discuss her nightmare with Desmond, and dressing and eating would at least pass the time while she waited for him.

Even her toilette and a lengthy breakfast—made longer by her father and her great-uncle carrying on a discussion of the Peloponnesian War—did not last long enough for Desmond to arrive. Thisbe whiled away more time checking over the traveling bag the maid had packed, then distracted herself for a few minutes with one of Olivia's novels, and finally simply sat in the red salon and watched the minutes tick by on the grandfather clock.

Desmond was late. It was not an unusual occurrence, as he tended to become wrapped up in things, so at first Thisbe was not bothered by his tardiness. After twenty minutes, she began to pace the room. Desmond wasn't usually late when it came to *her*. An hour passed. She checked with the footman twice, but there had been no message from Desmond.

Of course, they weren't doing anything important that day, and he did have to pack and… Oh, bother, it couldn't take him this long to throw a few clothes in a bag. Thisbe rang for the carriage.

She fidgeted all the way to Desmond's flat, telling herself it was foolish to feel this coldness growing in her chest. She would discover that he had overslept or… well, something else that was perfectly innocuous. When they reached his flat, she ran up the stairs and pounded on the door, waiting for only a few seconds before she flung it open. The room was empty. That spot in her chest turned to ice.

Thisbe tried the laboratory next, but found it locked tight, and no one answered her knock. She even visited the optical shop, where Desmond had worked earlier, but the owner shook his head when she asked about him.

She returned home. Perhaps Desmond had come while she was out crazily running about searching for him. He would explain why he was late, and they would have a chuckle over it, and everything would be all right.

But when she walked into the house, the footman informed her that Mr. Harrison had not come to call. He looked at her with some concern. No doubt he thought she was about to faint. Because that was exactly how she felt. Thisbe plopped down on the bench in the entry hall. She could no longer deny it.

Desmond had vanished.

DESMOND OPENED HIS eyes slowly. The world was spinning and his jaw hurt. He was lying in a very cramped space on a hard floor that bounced and rumbled and smelled of dust. He felt as if he were about to retch.

Swallowing back the bile, he closed his eyes again. He was much too sleepy to think. He would do that later. The next thing he knew he was jolted awake by a bounce of the carriage. That was it; he was in a carriage. On the floor. What the devil had happened?

He'd drunk a good deal last night with Thisbe's brothers and they'd wound up in a brawl. No, wait, that wasn't last night. That was the day before…or maybe the day before that. Why was it so difficult to think? He moved his jaw tentatively.

He had a vague memory of a huge hand smashing into his face. Again! Naturally it would land on a spot that was already sore. He hadn't been in a fight since he was a lad, and now he'd had three of them in the space of a few weeks. Maybe Thisbe was right; being with her was dangerous for *him*.

The thought amused him, and his mind cleared a little. Last night hadn't really been a fight. Desmond recalled waking up with a start to see a large dark form looming over his bed. He'd jumped up, but a fist was already connecting with his jaw. He'd fallen, and his head had come up against the wall. That explained the ache on the back of his skull, as well.

Next, there was something being poured into his mouth, making him choke and cough. A man hovered over him, tilting a bottle into his mouth. Desmond recognized that face. It was Wallace's "punisher," as the boy had called him: Grieves. He'd squirmed, trying to escape, closing his throat in resistance, but the man had pinned him down with his knee and leaned heavily on him.

"Drink, you whoreson, drink," Grieves had growled, and pinched Desmond's nostrils together, forcing him to swallow.

What happened after that? The memories rolled slowly on. More darkness, then a vague stumbling consciousness when someone hauled him out of the carriage and ordered him to relieve himself by the side of the road. And hadn't that been humiliating? Hands tied, watched by strangers as he clumsily unbuttoned his trousers. But he'd had to, hadn't he, or would have had to face an even more humiliating result?

Then he made a groggy attempt to escape, jerking his arm from Grieves's hold and trying to run. It had resulted in nothing but staggering a few feet and a tumble to the ground, much to Grieves's amusement. Two men had hauled him up, one on each side, and had thrown him back in the carriage. But there had been a third man, hadn't there? Standing back in the darkness, out of the light of the carriage lamps.

Another abortive attempt to refuse the liquid in the bottle, followed by unconsciousness. And now this slow ascent into awareness. He wondered vaguely how much damage blows and large doses of laudanum would do to one's head.

The muscles of his legs were cramping, for the space between the carriage seats was far too small for his long frame. As if that weren't enough, there was another person in the carriage with him, his feet taking up some of the space.

Desmond kept his eyes closed and tried to ignore the pain in his legs. He needed to regain more control of his brain and body before he let them know he was awake. He wouldn't have much time to act before they dosed him again. But in the end, as the pain turned to numbness, Desmond had to move. If his legs became utterly numb, they'd be of no use to him, anyway. He shifted—not an easy thing to do in these tight quarters—and gradually twisted around to face the man sitting behind him. Desmond expected to find Grieves there, waiting with a fist or a bottle to render him unconscious again. But it was, in fact, worse.

"Professor Gordon!" Desmond felt sick at his stomach. His mentor had been the third man in the shadows, watching Desmond's abduction, the manhandling and drugging of him, and done nothing to help him. No, more than that—he must have been the one to engineer the kidnapping. Grieves wouldn't have acted on his own.

"Yes." The older man let out a gusty sigh. "I'm so glad you're all right. I worried that he had given you too much. Here, let me help you."

Gordon grasped Desmond's arm and helped pull him up onto the other seat. Desmond would have preferred to refuse his assistance, but the truth was, he wasn't sure he could do it by himself. His legs and feet felt like blocks of wood.

Desmond scrunched into the corner, stretching out his legs as far as he could, and regarded his former teacher balefully. "How could you do this?"

"Dear boy, I'm so sorry. I hated to resort to such extremes, but I knew you wouldn't agree. You disapprove of our taking back the Eye, and—"

"Taking it back? You mean stealing it."

Gordon sighed. "I feared you would see it that way."

"What other way is there?"

"Advancing science. Removing an obstruction so we can expand our knowledge of the universe. This is far more important than the possession of property. I do hope you'll realize that. The Eye belongs with us."

"This is a pointless argument," Desmond said in disgust. "Why is it necessary to kidnap me? You already have the Eye."

"Yes. But, dear boy, we must have you to use it."

CHAPTER THIRTY

THISBE'S FIRST HEARTBREAKING thought was that everything these past few days had been a sham. It had a brutally practical logic to it: Desmond wanted the Eye and used her to help him find it after Gordon stole it. Once he'd achieved his goal, he had cast her aside. He never loved her. That magical night in his room meant nothing to him.

But…no. She didn't believe any of that. Whatever sense it made, she knew in her heart that it wasn't true. That night with him *had* been magical. Desmond was as dazzled, as awed, as she. What she saw in his eyes, felt in his touch, tasted in his kiss, was real. She trusted Desmond. She *knew* Desmond. He was a good, honest man, a loyal man. He wouldn't have run away.

If Desmond had gone to find Gordon without her, he had a good reason. He believed he was shielding her from harm. Or, if Thisbe's visions of Anne Ballew were true, the Eye was working on him—stealing his will and mind, as Anne put it, and making him act in a way he wouldn't normally.

There was another possibility, which was the one that worried her: Gordon and Wallace had taken Desmond against his will. Perhaps they knew that Desmond was Anne Ballew's descendant. If they'd tracked down the Eye to her grandmother's possession, what was to say they hadn't traced Anne Ballew's heirs to the present, as well? Now that they'd learned that only the alchemist's relatives could use the Eye, they wanted Desmond to operate the instrument for them.

Maybe Gordon hadn't taken off for Wallace's home as soon as he returned to London, but instead had stayed to kidnap Desmond. He wouldn't be able to do that himself, but he could have used that thug Grieves again.

They wouldn't harm him. Surely they wouldn't harm him if they needed him to use the Eye. Thisbe tried to hold on to the idea, but she was too realistic not to realize that if Desmond would not help them, they would coerce him. She didn't like to think of what awful thing that might involve.

And if he gave in to their coercion, it could be even more disastrous for him. Anne Ballew had warned it would destroy her "child." Perhaps the reason there had been no sign that Desmond was affected by the Eye was because he hadn't actually touched it. If he held it, if he looked through it, it might overcome him and leave him an empty shell. Or turn him into a horrid person. Or subject him to hatred and death, as it had done to Anne herself. Everything Thisbe could think of was equally catastrophic.

This was the reason Anne had invaded Thisbe's dreams. Perhaps Thisbe's visions were nonsense, but Thisbe understood now how Desmond felt about her grandmother's prediction—any chance, no matter how small, that Desmond would be destroyed by the Eye was too much to risk.

She had to save Desmond. She had to keep him from using the Eye.

The problem was doing it. The train didn't depart for several hours. She was tempted to take the carriage to Preston, but the truth was that in the end the train would be faster. But she must do something in the meantime; she could not bear to sit about and wait.

She decided to take another tour of Desmond's haunts. It was, after all, possible that she had missed him. Worse, he and Gordon could be somewhere in the city instead of Wallace's. If she rushed off to the north of England, she could be doing exactly the wrong thing. She needed to look for any clue that might tell her where they were before she committed herself to action.

Thisbe went again to Desmond's flat. This time she walked through the small room, looking into each drawer and cabinet. A fabric traveling bag stood in one corner, and she found some of his clothes in it. He'd clearly started packing for their departure, but hadn't taken it when he left. There were no trousers or shirt folded neatly on the chair by his bed, as there had been the other night, and no suit jacket hung on the back.

His coat hung from the hook by the door, his hat beside it. Desmond was prone to mislaying his hat or gloves, but he was less likely to leave behind a coat. He had, of course, done so that day she met him, but he'd been very pressed for time then. What would have made him run out so hastily this morning? His only appointment was with her. Everything pointed toward the probability that he had not left voluntarily. Unfortunately, nothing hinted at where he'd gone.

Thisbe sat down on the side of his bed. She felt better there, almost as if Desmond were with her. She picked up his pillow and held it close. It smelled like him, which comforted her even as it made her heart ache.

This was getting her nowhere. She must move on. Thisbe set down the pillow and stood up. It was then that she saw the small dark spot on the wall. She leaned closer. It was the color of dried blood. Her heart began to pound.

Thisbe fought for calm. She must keep her head or she would be of no use at all. The spot was little, and it was the only one. Thisbe examined all around the bed and could see no other sign of blood. That spot could have been there for a long time, for all she knew. The other night when she was here, it had been dark, and she didn't spend her time studying the wall.

There was no reason to panic. She must move on in a logical manner. There was no need to try again at the optical shop. If Desmond had gone there, the owner would have told him she had come by looking for him. The laboratory seemed the most likely place for Gordon to take Desmond to test the Eye. Its locked state this morning now seemed suspicious.

She found the place still locked and dark. Thisbe wished she could see inside, but the only window was too grimy to see anything through it. She wished she knew how to pick a lock. Perhaps there was some way she could break it. Her mind went to Reed's protégé. Tom Quick could get the door open in a trice.

"Thisbe."

Thisbe whipped around at the sound of her name. "Carson."

"May I be of any assistance?" Carson trotted down the stairs.

"I was looking for Desmond."

"Mislaid him, eh?" He smiled in his unflappable way. "Looks like no one's here. But we can see." He pulled a key from his pocket and bent to open the door.

The room was indeed empty, as well as cold. Thisbe's hopes wilted. It was clear Desmond wasn't here.

"What about the other room?" Thisbe pointed to the door on the opposite wall.

"The supply room? I doubt he would be in there."

Carson opened the door, revealing the same stacks of supplies and equipment that she'd seen when she and Desmond searched it a few days ago.

"Thank you. I'll let you get to work." She turned away. Where else could she go? Her choices were growing more limited by the moment.

"Wait." Carson followed Thisbe to the door. "Is something amiss? You seem a bit distraught."

Thisbe forced a smile. "No, everything is— I mean— It's just…"

He frowned. "Now I'm certain something's wrong. Is it Desmond? Has something happened to him?"

"I don't know." Though Thisbe's voice was low, her words were almost a cry. "We were going to— He was supposed to come to my house this morning, and he didn't arrive. I can't find him anywhere."

"Is this to do with the Eye? Professor Gordon?"

"Yes. Probably. Perhaps. I'm sorry. I must go."

"Let me help you. We'll look together." He trailed after her to the outside stairs. "If I know Desmond, he's probably reading at the library and doesn't realize the time. We should visit the reading room at the British Museum. Or the university. Have you tried to his shop?"

"He's not there. And I can't imagine that he went to the library today."

"Is he still trying to find the professor? Could he have gone after him?"

"Yes, perhaps."

"I'll close the laboratory and come with you."

Thisbe was tempted to tell Carson the whole story. He seemed sincerely concerned, and it wouldn't be amiss to have another pair of hands if she found Desmond in trouble—especially if those hands could make better fists than her own.

But she remembered Desmond's doubts about Carson, his reluctance to let the other man accompany them on their search. In all likelihood, Desmond's concerns were foolish and sprang from jealousy. Still…he knew Carson better than she did; indeed, she scarcely knew the man at all. Like the rest of them, Carson was eager to see the Eye. Desmond had said he was the first to suggest stealing it. What if Carson was in league with his professor? He could be the man Gordon had rushed off to talk to the other day.

"No, there's no need for you to do that," she told him. "You have work to do."

"I don't mind setting it aside."

She shook her head with finality. "Honestly, I can't think of anywhere else to look. I'll just return to the house and wait for him. No doubt he got distracted, as you said, and he will soon rush in, full of apologies." She smiled, doing her best to infuse her words with light amusement, and started up the stairs without waiting for a response.

"Promise you will come for me if Desmond doesn't appear," Carson called, coming up a few steps.

"Yes, of course. Thank you. Goodbye." She turned to her carriage, where Thompkins stood waiting. She murmured the address of Professor Gordon's flat to her driver as he gave her a hand up into the carriage. She took care not to glance back at Carson. If he was watching her, she didn't want to do anything that appeared furtive.

Gordon's landlord, remembering the coins she had given him the other day, let her into the professor's flat without protest. She found nothing, which she had expected; a room with neighbors all around seemed an unlikely place to hold anyone prisoner. But the trip was not entirely a waste, for the landlord was happy to inform her that Gordon had returned to his flat.

"Not long after you left the other day, it were. I would have let you know, miss, but I didn't know how."

"Has he been here ever since?"

"He nipped in and out a few times, stayed the night and yesterday he left. Carrying a bag." He paused to emphasize the significance of his words. "I watched, you know, just in case you might come back. Got in a carriage, and that was the last I've seen of him."

"What time of day was that?"

"Not sure. It was dark, right enough. I couldn't see the coach too well."

"Was anyone with him?"

"Not in his flat, no. There was a chap driving the carriage, but all I could see was his back. 'Nother fellow beside him on the driver's seat."

"Was one of them a large man?"

The landlord registered surprise. "Oh, aye, he was a big one, sure enough. Not the driver, but the other one."

So Gordon had left in a carriage with two men, one of them most likely Grieves. Thisbe wished now that her grandmother had brought charges against the man. Gordon wasn't taking a hack to Paddington; hansoms had only a single driver. The professor was making a journey by coach—understandable if one was planning to kidnap a person. And why else would he have Grieves with him but to overcome Desmond, something the middle-aged scientist could not do alone?

"Thank you. You've been very helpful." Thisbe handed him a larger coin than before. "If he comes back, send word to me at Broughton House. Anyone there will do."

Thisbe returned to her carriage. As she climbed in, the back of her neck prickled. She glanced behind her. Unsurprisingly, the landlord was standing at his window, watching her. That was good; a nosy man was exactly whom she needed at Gordon's home.

She returned to the house, certain now that Gordon had forced Desmond to go with him. She was equally sure that the likeliest destination for the carriage was Wallace's estate in the north. She took some comfort in the fact that she would make better time by train than they would in the carriage. It would help to make up a little for the long head start they had on her.

She wished Theo had stayed at home; she would feel confident facing down the three men if she had her twin by her side. She would have enlisted Reed, but he was back in Oxford since Hilary term had begun; she couldn't waste the time to fetch him. Again she thought of Carson and again discarded the idea.

It was up to her.

At home, Thisbe took Olivia aside and explained exactly what had happened. If the landlord did try to send her a message, there must be someone in the house who knew where Thisbe was and what she was doing. Also, though she didn't want to dwell on the thought, there was always the possibility that everything would go awry and she, too, would need rescuing.

It would probably be safe to tell Kyria as well, but Olivia was the least likely to try to dissuade Thisbe. For all her bookish shyness, Olivia possessed the heart of an adventurer. Thisbe could not tell the rest of the family. Even her permissive parents would balk at her setting off on her own to rescue Desmond from kidnappers. Better to let them think that Desmond was accompanying her on a journey to retrieve the Eye.

Next, Thisbe went upstairs to find a weapon. Hopefully there would be no need for it, but she believed in being prepared for all eventualities. Theo had a revolver, but he would have taken that with him, and in any case, it was too large and noticeable to carry about. Nor did she know how to use it. But he also had several knives.

He had taken his best one with him on his journey, and, of course, the scimitar he had purchased in the Levant last year was out of the question, as was the claymore. Nor did she feel entirely comfortable with a large camping knife. Fortunately, there were also a number of penknives in his desk drawer, and Thisbe settled on one with a sharp blade that folded up to be easily concealed in her pocket. Lastly, she went to the billiards room and picked up couple of the small hard balls to put in her reticule. Thus armed, she set out.

The trip north was uneventful, though Thisbe was so on edge that she started at shadows. Once, catching a flicker of movement out of the corner of her eye, she whirled around, only to see a young man running to board a different train. She was struck time and again with an uneasy tingling at the back of her neck, not only walking through Paddington, but also in the early morning in Manchester, where she changed trains. Each time she glanced all around, but she could not find anyone watching her.

It was only her nerves. Why would anyone be following her? They had already taken Desmond; it would be of little use to grab her, as well. She doubted that any of the men would look upon her as a threat. Being underestimated was an advantage of being a woman as much as an annoyance.

Alone in her compartment, she was free of that uneasiness, but she could not relax enough to read or do anything but stare blindly out the window, worrying about Desmond. It was equally difficult to sleep that night; every time she managed to fall asleep, she was plagued by worrisome dreams. When morning came, she was bleary-eyed.

However, when the train arrived in Preston in the pale predawn light, she was instantly alert. She left the train and no longer glanced around uneasily. Intent on her goal, she marched over to store her baggage at the claims office. Then, penknife in her pocket and a reticule containing billiard balls, money and smelling salts—should Desmond be unconscious—she set out to find the man she loved.

CHAPTER THIRTY-ONE

"I AM *NOT* related to Anne Ballew." Desmond glared at his mentor. "We've already gone through this. I told you last night before you knocked me out again. And if you keep pouring that bloody laudanum down my throat, my mind will soon be so scrambled I wouldn't be able to help you, anyway." He transferred his glare to Grieves, who stood beside Gordon, arms folded.

"No, no, no, dear boy," Gordon protested and turned to scowl at Grieves. "He wouldn't have slept for almost twelve hours if you hadn't given him so much."

The truth was Desmond had pretended to remain asleep for an hour after he'd awakened. A few minutes ago, when Grieves hauled him downstairs, Desmond had feigned an exaggerated grogginess even though he felt quite alert, even edgy. He wasn't sure how this ruse would help, but his only path now was to stall and obfuscate as much as he could, and wait for some chance to get away.

At the moment, that seemed unlikely. His hands were still tied, and the end of the rope was lashed to one post of the heavy, straight chair in which he sat. It made it awkward to turn toward the third man in the room, but he twisted around to address him now. "Mr. Wallace, this is absurd. I can't see anything more with the Eye than any of you. Anne Ballew was not my ancestor."

"Oh, but she was," Gordon assured him. "We've done our research. It wasn't only talking to your aunt."

"My aunt?" Desmond let out a groan, closing his eyes. "Those are folktales."

"More than that, far more than that. Mr. Wallace traced Anne's husband's movements from London back to Dorset after the tragedy. The family went into hiding, changed their name and moved to Cumby-on-Mallow."

"Where my mother grew up."

"Exactly. There is a gap in the 1600s of a generation or two, but I'm certain that line contin—"

"You'd already done all this before you met me." Desmond stared in disbelief. Perhaps his mind was moving more slowly than he thought; it took him a moment to realize the rest of the implications. "That's why you took me on, isn't? You thought I'd have the Eye or be able to lead you to it." Amazingly, even though he'd already learned Gordon's nature, it hurt to learn the truth. He had never been the one that Gordon chose to tutor. It had been Anne Ballew's heir.

"I hoped you could," Gordon admitted. "But that's not the only reason I chose to tutor you. You're incredibly bright."

"I'm beginning to doubt that," Desmond muttered.

"A hard worker. I've come to regard you with great affection. You're practically a son to me."

"A son? You abducted me!" Desmond's voice rose. He was finding it more difficult by the moment to remain calm and clearheaded. Anger and impatience welled in him.

"That's a harsh way to put it."

"How else could I put it?" Desmond drew a breath, pulling his voice back to reasonable calm. He needed to win this argument, not infuriate these fanatics. He could not allow them to push him into a rage. "Gentlemen, I fear this is pointless. I shan't be able to use the

Eye. I seriously doubt that *anyone* can." Except perhaps someone in Thisbe's line, but *that* thought was one to avoid at all costs. "If you will but think about it, Professor, you'll see that your proof is suspect. You said they changed their name. Can you prove that? Can you prove that the Ballew name didn't simply die out naturally in that community? Or migrate? You took a flying leap across several generations. That's not research—that's wishful thinking."

"You're wrong." Wallace's voice was fierce. "The research is correct. I found the Eye, didn't I, despite its changing hands?"

"Yes, you did," Desmond said, continuing his easy-going tone. "Perhaps I'm wrong about the research. But even if you are right and I am descended from Anne Ballew, doesn't it seem unlikely that her powers would remain in her descendants? The talent she had has surely been watered down to almost nothing now."

"There's one way to find out, isn't there?" Wallace strode to a cabinet and unlocked it, pulling out the carved wooden box Desmond had seen in the dowager duchess's sitting room. Desmond stiffened at the sight of it; something hard and sharp pierced his chest.

"The Eye." Desmond watched Wallace set the container on a small table and reverently remove the Eye, holding it up. Desmond's breath quickened. The dawn light through the windows sent rainbows arcing from the glass, so beautiful Desmond couldn't take his eyes from it. He remembered when the dowager duchess revealed it to him and Thisbe in London, how lovely it had been, but it could not compare to this exquisite dance of color and light. He wished that Thisbe could see it now. He wished… His heart squeezed in his chest.

"Look at it." Wallace carried the Eye over to Desmond.

"This small instrument carries all the power in the world. Can you not feel it? Don't you want to see what it offers? A world beyond our wildest dreams."

Desmond struggled to keep his face a blank. The truth was that something tugged at him deep inside, pulling him toward the Eye. He yearned to hold it in his hand and admire it. To look deep into its depths and see…everything that lay beyond. The truth, the meaning, the all-encompassing wisdom of the ages.

The need to discover had always been with him, but this was something more. Something different. This was a visceral thrum in his belly, an ache. He wanted to grab the Eye from Wallace's hand. The man didn't deserve it, wasn't worthy even to touch it. The Eye belonged to *him*.

THE THOUGHT STRUCK him like a slap in the face, knocking him out of his bizarre trance. Good Lord, was the thing actually creeping into him, seeking to control him? He thought of Thisbe's dreams, her fear that the Eye would overwhelm him.

Well, *that* was not going to happen. Maybe it wasn't all a hoax; maybe the thing really did have power. But he was not about to let anything take over his mind and will. Nor was he willing to give these men the satisfaction of seeing how much the Eye tempted him. He brought the thought of Thisbe into his mind and focused on her image—her firm mouth, her resolute chin, the love and trust in her green eyes when she looked at him.

Desmond shrugged. "It's a quizzing glass." He went on in a coolly analytical tone, "Rather large, with some interesting facets. Elegant carving on the handle." It afforded him a good deal of pleasure to see outrage flood Wallace's face.

"You're a fool." Wallace jerked away the glass and returned it to the box.

"No doubt," Desmond agreed, ignoring the fierce spurt of loss and regret. "Clearly, I'm not the one who should operate it. The best thing is to untie my hands and send me on my way, and we will all forget this incident. I shan't bring charges against you for kidnapping, and…"

"You will do as I say!" Wallace erupted, his face flooding with red. Gordon took a nervous step backward.

"I won't." It was easier now, with the Eye out of his sight, though he still felt that edgy, impatient pull.

"You have to!"

Grieves stepped forward and backhanded Desmond, making his head ring, but at least it was a blow that didn't knock him out. "He'll do it. A bit more of this, and he'll be begging to."

"You think beating me unconscious will enable me to use the Eye?" Desmond directed his gaze at Wallace.

Grieves raised his hand threateningly, but Wallace snapped, "No. Don't be a fool. Step back, Grieves."

Gordon hastened to join the conversation, smiling in a benign way. "There's no need for animosity here. I'm sure Desmond will come to his senses. Just imagine the fame, my boy, the respect in the scientific community. Think of the knowledge."

"Think of the money," Wallace added harshly. "That's what matters. I'll pay you. Five hundred guineas. That's more money than you've ever seen, I warrant."

"I won't do it."

"Yes, you will." Wallace smiled thinly. "Eventually. You sit there and think about it. Think about what that amount of money can do for you. And think about the fact that it's the only way you're getting out of here."

"You cannot keep me here forever."

"I'll be happy to end your visit if you like," Grieves replied, grinning.

"The Morelands know where I am," Desmond pointed out.

"Ha!" Wallace scoffed. "You're a fool if you think people like that will stir themselves to help you."

"They know you have the Eye, as well." It occurred to Desmond, too late, that he shouldn't have reminded them about Thisbe's family. It might occur to Wallace that the owner of the Eye was the likeliest person to be descended from Anne Ballew, and the last thing he wanted was for Wallace to go after Thisbe. Quickly, he did his best to divert them from the possibility that the Eye had been passed down through Anne's descendants. "The dowager duchess's great-grandfather bought the Eye, and, however little right she has to it, that woman holds on to what she possesses. You want to go up against her? I wouldn't advise it. The Duchess of Broughton will hunt you down like a wolf on a rabbit."

Wallace sneered. "I am hardly frightened by the prospect of a doddering old woman's wrath."

Desmond snorted. "Then you're the fool here."

"You'll feel differently after you've spent some time thinking about your choices." Wallace nodded to the other men. "Gentlemen. Let's leave Mr. Harrison to contemplate his future."

Desmond sagged against the back of the chair after they walked out of the room. It was tiring keeping up this pretense of sangfroid. He didn't feel cool or calm or reasonable. What he felt was an overpowering need to get out of this place.

That blasted Eye was too strong, too dangerous. He'd resisted its pull today, but he didn't want to be put to the test again. He hadn't felt its power when the duchess showed it to them before. He had wanted to examine the thing, to test it, but no more than he usually desired to understand things. But today… Maybe Thisbe's fear regarding the Eye had infected him, but he didn't want to experience that compulsion again. He no longer desired to see what the glass might show. He feared it.

What would happen when Wallace realized he wouldn't get what he wanted from Desmond? He could scarcely allow Desmond to tell everyone Wallace had kidnapped him. The only way to get rid of that possibility was to get rid of Desmond.

And what about Thisbe? She was bound to come after him—he felt a little qualm, thinking she might believe he had voluntarily left her, but surely she knew him better than that. In any case, whatever she thought regarding Desmond, Thisbe suspected the Eye was here, and she would come for that. The idea of Thisbe winding up in Wallace's clutches made it even more imperative that he get out of here now.

Twisting, Desmond worked at untying the rope from the chair. It was incredibly difficult to unfasten the tight knot with his wrists bound. The chair was heavy; he didn't think it would be possible to break the back from it. Perhaps there was something in the room he could use to cut the rope. He glanced around the room for a letter opener or scissors—anything with a sharp edge. Could he manage to get a coal out of the fire and burn through it? Use the fireplace poker as a lever to break the chair?

He stood up. It was bloody awkward, as the short length of the rope would not allow him to stand straight, but he grasped the chair and began to pull it. Hearing a noise in the hall outside the room, he turned quickly.

"Thisbe!"

"Desmond!" Thisbe rushed across the room to Desmond. They'd tied him to a chair. Fury rose in her.

"No. Get out. Get out."

"That's hardly the greeting I'd hoped for," Thisbe said drily and pulled Theo's knife from her pocket.

Desmond's eyes widened. "You're armed?"

"Only with Theo's penknife. I'm afraid it won't do much damage, but it was the easiest to hide." She sawed through the rope. "Oh! Look at your wrists. They're bleeding."

"I was trying to get loose." He sounded faintly apologetic. "What are you doing here? How did you get in?"

"I found a window unlocked," she explained. "I've been creeping about the house looking for you. There!" The knife finally cut through the last fibers, and she pulled off the rope. "Here, you take the knife. I have another weapon." She held up her reticule, which only made him look confused, but there was no time to explain.

"Here! I say!"

They whirled around to see Professor Gordon standing in the doorway. As one, Thisbe and Desmond charged him, and the older man stumbled back into the corridor. But as they turned to run, Zachary Wallace popped out of a door down the hall and started toward them.

"This way!" Thisbe whirled to run in the other direction, but stopped when she realized Desmond had gone straight at Wallace. Desmond punched Wallace, first in the stomach, then on the chin, and the other man folded.

Professor Gordon, recovering from his stumble, grabbed Thisbe's arm, and she swung her reticule at him. She intended to hit his head but he dodged surprisingly quickly, and her blow landed on his shoulder.

Letting out a yowl, Gordon dropped her arm and grabbed his shoulder.

"What do you have in there?" Desmond asked in astonishment.

"Billiard balls."

He began to laugh, then took her hand, and they started again toward the front door. Wallace struggled to his feet, facing them. Desmond unfolded the knife, his eyes and voice cold in a way Thisbe had never witnessed before. "Really? You want to try that? I believe I have the reach on you."

"And I have the gun on you," a voice behind them said. Thisbe and Desmond froze and pivoted slowly to see Grieves standing in the hallway behind them, grinning, a revolver in his hand. He strolled forward, keeping the weapon trained on Thisbe. "Now. Drop the knife."

Desmond opened his hand and let it fall to the floor.

"And that bag!" Gordon pointed at the reticule in Thisbe's hand, then returned to rubbing his shoulder. With a sigh, Thisbe dropped the purse.

"Now." Mr. Wallace straightened his jacket. "Perhaps we can have a reasonable discussion."

Thisbe glanced at Desmond, and he shrugged. "I hope you told the authorities where you were going."

"Of course," Thisbe replied coolly. "Grandmother is even now haranguing the prime minister—Mother, more practically, is doing the same at Scotland Yard. Worse for this lot, though, is that Reed and Theo are already on their way here." She doubted that these men would know that Theo was crossing the Atlantic at this moment, but hopefully Desmond would get the message that she was lying through her teeth.

"Mmm. Bad luck for you," Desmond told Grieves. "Thisbe's twin has a wicked temper."

"Theo's very protective of me." Thisbe looked up at Desmond, feeling wonderfully in tune with him. Despite their predicament, she couldn't keep from smiling and taking his hand.

"Here, now, stop that." Grieves frowned suspiciously. "Move on." He waggled the gun in the direction of the room they'd just left. "Back in there."

"You do realize, Mr. Grieves," Thisbe said conversationally, "I could pay you a great deal more than Mr. Wallace. Release us, and I will double whatever he's promised to give you."

Grieves grinned. "That's tempting. But if I let you go, how do I know you'll pay me?"

"Grieves…" Wallace said warningly.

"You have my word," Thisbe said. That, of course, would mean nothing to a man like Grieves. "I'll give you these earrings as a token to ensure my payment."

"I can take those from you, anyhow," Grieves replied. "You. Harrison, get in there. Missy, you stay here." He came forward and grasped Thisbe's arm, his gun touching the back of her skull. He sent a challenging look at Desmond.

Desmond regarded him stonily, but turned and walked back into the room they'd just left, followed by Wallace and Gordon. Grieves directed Desmond toward the bookcase and pushed Thisbe down into the chair Desmond had occupied before, letting go of her arm but keeping his gun aimed at her head.

"Now, to the matter at hand." Wallace removed the box from the cabinet and reverently took out the Eye.

"I told you I'm not going to use it." Desmond crossed his arms.

"Ah, but that was before we had this young lady with us." Wallace smiled triumphantly. "I believe you may be more amenable now."

"Desmond, don't." Alarm shot through Thisbe. "You can't. It's too dangerous."

"Dangerous? No, no," Gordon said, tut-tutting. "There's no danger. All he has—"

"Excuse me, Mr. Gordon," Thisbe said crisply. "But you don't know anything. Not about the Eye. Not about Desmond or Anne Ballew. And least of all about me." She stood up, looming over the shorter man, and Grieves, huffing out a muffled laugh, didn't stop her. With a steely gaze worthy of Old Eldric himself, she went on, "My grandmother chews up little men like you and spits them out. She knows everyone of importance up to and including the Queen. You think your name is sullied in the scientific world now? Wait until the dowager duchess is through with you."

Gordon gaped at her, his mouth opening and closing like a fish. Thisbe swung away from him dismissively and addressed Wallace. "And you. You're already guilty of thievery and kidnapping. Do you really mean to add murder to that list? Just to get a glimpse beyond the grave? There's no need—if you kill me, you'll see it for yourself soon enough."

"Shut up, you stupid girl!" Wallace erupted. "It's not about seeing spirits. I don't want to *see* my wife. I want her back." He shook the Eye at her. "You've no idea what this can do. He can raise the dead with it. He'll make her whole again! Alive!" His eyes were lit with an unholy fire as he raised the Eye like a holy vessel before Desmond. "Do it! Her life for my wife's."

"No, Desmond!" Thisbe moved forward. Grieves and Gordon simply stared, riveted by the scene unfolding before them.

"You're mad," Desmond told him flatly.

"Am I? Maybe so. But that's how you know I'll do what I say."

"If you kill me, you'll have nothing," Thisbe said. "It's a ridiculous threat."

"That's why I won't do it quickly. You'll die a slice at a time." Wallace tossed the Eye at Desmond and grabbed Thisbe's arm, jerking her forward. Wrapping one arm around her, he pulled against him, his other hand at her throat.

A sharp pain and a trickle of moisture down her neck told Thisbe that the hand at her throat held a knife. Desmond, the odd instrument in his hand, stared at Thisbe and Wallace, his face several shades paler. Wallace's knifepoint prodded her again.

"Stop!" Desmond shouted. "I'll do it. I'll do it." He raised the glass to his eye and stared into it, frozen.

"No!" Thisbe screamed, throwing back her head and smashing Wallace in the nose. She jumped, grabbed the Eye from Desmond's paralyzed grip and flung it across the room.

A shot rang out, and everyone whirled. Carson Dunbridge stood in the doorway, a smoking pistol in his hand. "Well, Desmond, for such a dull chap, you certainly do get into a lot of trouble."

CHAPTER THIRTY-TWO

FOR A MOMENT everyone in the room was still, gaping at Carson, who now aimed his gun at Grieves. Even Wallace stopped in his rush toward the Eye.

"Carson. Thank God," Desmond said, a bit of color returning to his face.

"Thisbe, you'd best get that Eye before Mr. Wallace starts after it again. And you, the chap with the gun, put it down on the floor and kick it over to Desmond. Gently now."

Grieves did as Carson bid, and Thisbe rushed to pick up the Eye. It was strangely hot, and a vision flashed through her mind—a gloved hand reaching into a fire. She went still, her eyes widening, but the Eye turned searing, and she shoved it into the box and closed it. She glanced over at Desmond. He looked almost as usual now. Had that shocked look on his face come from fear for her, or fear of what he'd seen in the Eye? He'd seemed peculiarly stiff, almost frozen, when she ripped it from his hand. Had he felt what she did?

Putting her questions away for another, quieter time, she set the box on the desk and went to help Desmond tie the hands of the other men. The first problem was finding enough bindings to wrap around three sets of wrists. Thisbe had sliced through the rope that had been around Desmond's wrists. Picking up her abandoned penknife—these folding knives were remarkably handy; she would have to start carrying one in her pocket—she sliced off the bellpull and the tiebacks for the draperies.

"What shall we do with these three?" Thisbe asked as she returned with her makeshift ropes.

"Lock them in the cellar," Carson suggested.

"Carson!" Gordon said, shocked. "It's winter. There's no heat down there."

"Not the finest of accommodations," Desmond agreed. "But the servants will hear you after a time and let you out."

"Are there any servants?" Thisbe asked. "You'd think one of them would have been curious by now."

"They're not here," Gordon said, looking more alarmed by the moment. "No one will hear us until tomorrow."

"We'll tell the authorities all about it," Thisbe promised. "No doubt they will take you out to put you in jail."

"Jail!" Gordon's eyes bugged. "I say, that's a bit extreme."

"No doubt kidnapping, theft and murder are quite ordinary."

"He wouldn't have *killed* you," Gordon argued.

"Only because it wouldn't have suited his purposes." Thisbe wrapped the pull cord around the professor's wrists.

In the end, they wound up herding the miscreants into the cellar with blankets, water and candles, and locked the door. As soon as Carson turned the key in the door, Thisbe launched herself into Desmond's arms and kissed him, until finally Carson's discreet throat clearing recalled them to the present situation.

Thisbe picked up the box, Desmond grabbed a coat off the hook by the door and they started toward town.

"In retrospect, one of us should have hired a carriage," Carson commented as they trudged along.

Thisbe began to laugh, and soon they were all roaring, the tension of the past few hours pouring out. Finally, they quieted and started forward again. Desmond took Thisbe's hand as they walked, and they all recounted their individual tales of the past day. Desmond described what he remembered from the kidnapping, his story punctuated by Thisbe's exclamations of outrage.

Thisbe told Desmond about her frantic search for him, and when she reached the conversation she'd had with Carson in the laboratory, she turned to him and said accusingly, "You followed me, didn't you?" Carson's grin was answer enough. "I knew I saw someone!"

"You tested my skills, I must say," Carson said. "But Desmond would have had my head if I let you go off on your own, and I knew you'd only send me away if I joined you. It was clear you didn't trust me."

"I'm sorry."

"No need." He waved away the apology. "You're probably wise." He glanced toward the box Thisbe held cradled to her chest. "That seems to be a powerful lure."

"You're not looking at it," Thisbe told him firmly. "None of us are going to look at it. It's dangerous. I'm taking it right back to Grandmother, who apparently is insensitive enough to not be disturbed by it."

"Were you disturbed by it?" Carson asked curiously.

Thisbe shrugged. "It seemed warm, which is odd."

"What about you, Desmond?" Carson went on. "Tell me. Does it work?"

"No." Desmond shook his head. "Not at all. It was merely a lot of jumbled, faceted views of the room. Nothing magical or mysterious."

"What are we going to do about that lot?" Carson jerked his head in the direction of Wallace's house.

"Turn them in to the authorities," Thisbe replied. "What else would we do?"

Desmond grimaced and exchanged a glance with Carson.

"What?" Thisbe said. "Why did you look at each other like that?"

"You have more faith in the authorities than I," Desmond told her. "Wallace is known in this town—a wealthy, respected man. We are three strangers. And I—" He glanced down at his shirt and trousers, torn here and there and stained with dirt, Gordon's too-large coat hanging over them. "I look as though I've been lying on the floor of a carriage all night. They don't know that your father is a duke, and how can you prove it?"

"You think they won't believe us."

"Would you?"

Thisbe was forced to agree. "Probably not."

"Even if they did believe us, I suspect Gordon and Wallace wouldn't receive any punishment," Carson offered. "They'll put it all on Grieves, who actually performed the abduction and the theft, and he will be the only one to go to prison."

"I wouldn't mind that," Thisbe muttered. After a moment of silence, she went on, "But we can't let them go without any sort of consequences."

"Given your grandmother's web of gossips, they'll be punished," Desmond said. "Wallace will be socially ruined in London. Gordon won't dare show his face in the scientific community."

Thisbe studied him. "You don't want Gordon to be punished, do you? Even after what he's done to you!"

"I know—it's not reasonable. But...however wrong his

motives were, he did help me a great deal. I can't bring myself to wish him imprisoned." Desmond shrugged.

"I could," Thisbe retorted.

"Ah, but that's how you can tell our Desmond isn't an aristocrat," Carson told her lightly. "He lacks that requisite hardness of heart."

"Grieves walks away without any damage," Thisbe grumbled.

"A man like Grieves will wind up in jail sooner or later," Desmond said. "Or dead in the gutter."

The walk back into the city seemed much farther than it had when Thisbe made it earlier, fueled by fear and anger, but eventually they reached the edge of town. Prosaically, their first stop was a tavern, and all of them agreed they were starving.

Thisbe looked around the place with great interest, and Desmond said with some amusement, "This is the first time you've been in a tavern, isn't it?"

"Not quite. I went into the Double Roses with Grandmother the other day." She ignored Carson's startled look. "But this is the first one I've seen with customers. It's quite interesting. It's a lot cleaner and better appointed than the other tavern. Oh, would you two stop looking at each other and smirking? It's most annoying. It's scarcely *my* fault women aren't wanted in taverns."

"It's not that." Desmond squeezed her hand. "It's your reaction to the place."

"Most women I know would find it 'low and distasteful' rather than 'interesting.'" Carson pulled out a chair for her at one of the tables.

"Nor is it my fault that you know boring women. Now, if you two are done laughing at me, what should I do with this?" Thisbe set the box on the table. "It looks rather odd sitting here."

"There." Carson covered it with his hat.

The hat looked odd as well, but at least Thisbe didn't have to look at the box, which made her deeply uneasy. Now that she'd touched the Eye, she understood the danger better. She was more certain than ever that she needed to keep the Eye out of Desmond's hands.

He seemed quite placid in the Eye's presence—indeed, she and Carson were more fidgety than he. But she couldn't stop thinking of Desmond's unmoving shock when he looked into the glass. They needed to get the Eye back in her grandmother's hands as soon as possible.

But when they reached the train station, they discovered that they had missed the last train south. The next train to Manchester would not arrive until the next morning. Thisbe sighed. "There's nothing for it but to find an inn. The town is large enough they may have one that's comfortable. Fortunately, *some* of us weren't kidnapped and were able to bring money with them."

She knew that Desmond would have been hard-pressed to pay for a room and the ticket home, anyway, but she was pleased to come up with an excuse that wouldn't embarrass him. She led them to the baggage office and retrieved her sturdy fabric bag. She opened the case and pulled out a coin purse. "I've plenty for the inn and tickets for all of us." She looked at Carson. "I'll warrant you didn't carry much with you, either."

"I didn't have time to go home and fill my pockets," Carson agreed. "Since you are so flush, I think we need to do something about him." He nodded toward Desmond. "No respectable inn will look favorably on his attire."

"True." Thisbe studied Desmond's ripped, dirty clothes and the peculiar look of his coat, which was both much too large in its girth and ludicrously short in the arms and hem. "We can probably all do with some freshening up in the lavatory here, and then we'll find you some decent clothing."

It was a relief to put the Eye away in her bag. Thisbe shoved it down to the very bottom, covering it with her clothes. Desmond reached down to pick up the case, but she grabbed it. She wasn't about to let Desmond be so close to the Eye the rest of the day.

His eyebrows shot up, as did Carson's. "Surely you don't think I'm going to *steal* it."

"Of course not. But I promised my grandmother I wouldn't let it out of my possession." It was a bit horrifying how easily lies seemed to be coming from her now, but she didn't want to discuss the real reason for her anxiety in front of Carson. He had helped them immensely and she trusted him, more or less, but the fewer people who knew about Desmond's heritage, the better.

With her face and hands washed and hair repinned, Thisbe felt much more herself, and Desmond managed to brush much of the dust from his clothes and fingercomb his hair into some degree of order. A few questions led them to a cart selling used clothes. Thisbe found that there was something quite intimate in helping Desmond choose what to wear—reaching up to try a hat on his head or holding a shirt up to his chest—and it sparked a heat in Desmond's eyes that sent tingles all the way through her.

Once or twice Thisbe noticed Carson glancing at them speculatively. It was clear that he suspected their true relationship—how could he not when they had shared that kiss right in front of him? She could only hope Carson would keep his suspicions to himself. Much as she wanted Desmond, she didn't want it to be because he believed he'd ruined her reputation.

In the end they managed to come up with a pair of

trousers that were only a bit too short, as well as a shirt, stockings and an ascot. The coat would cover his lack of a waistcoat or jacket. They returned to their former source of information, a hack driver, for the name of an inn he termed "decent 'nuff for a lady."

When the driver deposited them at the yard of the inn, Carson hung back as they started toward the door. "I've been thinking," he told them. "I don't believe I'll stay here tonight."

"What? But…what are you going to do?" Thisbe asked, startled.

"My family home isn't far. I'm from the Lake District. It occurrs to me that I could hire a horse and ride there." He glanced up at the sky. "Long as this day seemed, we started early, and there's still daylight left. I can reach home—or at least close enough to find my way in the dark."

"But…" Desmond trailed off.

"Are you certain?" Thisbe asked. She had the suspicion that Carson was giving them the opportunity to be alone tonight, and she couldn't help but be grateful for his tact.

He nodded. "Of course. It's all turned out rather well, hasn't it?" Carson smiled and reached out to shake Desmond's hand.

"Thank you," Desmond replied. "I'm sorry if I've been distrusting."

"Quite understandable." Carson smiled, his gaze flickering over to Thisbe. He doffed his hat to her. "Miss Moreland. It's been quite an experience."

"Indeed. Thank you."

Thisbe and Desmond gazed after Carson as he walked toward the stables. "Do you think he knows?" Desmond asked. "I mean, that you and I—"

"Yes," she said simply. "It's my opinion he's being gentlemanly. Leaving us free to pretend to be husband and wife."

"Thisbe...I don't think that's a good idea."

"Don't you?" She smiled up into his eyes. "What's wrong with it?"

"Don't. When you look at me like that, I can't think straight."

"You think too much." She moved closer.

"Thisbe..." He leaned closer, his nostrils widening as if breathing in the scent of her. "How do you always manage to smell like lavender? Even now."

She laughed lightly. "It's on my handkerchief." Thisbe had dampened it to wipe a smudge from her cheek earlier, then tucked it into her cleavage, and she reached in now to pull it out.

"Good God." His voice turned husky; his eyes darkened. He curled his hand around the cloth—whether hiding it from himself or taking it, Thisbe wasn't sure. "Thisbe...I have to talk to you."

"Then let's get a room and talk in private."

CHAPTER THIRTY-THREE

DESMOND NODDED, uncertain he could say anything intelligible at the moment. Desire slammed through him like a fist, adding to the already roiling mix of love and pain that had swirled in him since he'd looked into the Eye. He clenched his hand around her handkerchief and shoved it into his pocket. He would keep it forever.

It was foolish to give in to Thisbe's suggestion. Reckless. Irresponsible. However determined he was to do what was right, being alone with Thisbe in a room with a bed was all too likely to end with him doing the opposite. But he wasn't strong enough to deny himself this last chance to be with her.

Desmond didn't speak, didn't dare even look at Thisbe as they followed the innkeeper up the stairs, afraid that merely the way he looked at her would tell the innkeeper how illicit their relationship was. Once inside the room, the sight of the bed was another blow to his control, as was the snick of the key turning in the lock.

Desmond went to the window, stalling. He couldn't bear to do this. He had to. He swung around and blurted out, "We can't— I have to— I lied before."

Thisbe lifted her eyebrows. "When?"

"To Carson, when he asked if I'd seen anything through the Eye. I told him no, but that wasn't true." He hesitated.

Thisbe looked at him with trepidation. "Desmond, you're scaring me. What did you see?"

"I saw you!" He knew again the paralyzing terror, the hopeless, wrenching despair that had gripped him when he held up the Eye to his sight. Desmond forced out his next words. "I saw you dead."

"That was an illusion. A vision isn't reality."

"It was," he almost shouted. Taking a deep breath, he moderated his voice. "It was true, Thisbe. I'm certain of it. You were on the ground, and you weren't breathing. Your lips were blue. You were cold as ice." He saw the shiver that ran through her, and he nodded. "Yes. Like you were in your nightmare."

Desmond could see that even Thisbe was shaken. Still, she insisted, "That was nothing but a dream."

"It was nothing but a dream that told you the Eye would destroy me."

"I wasn't certain," she protested. "It was just that ignoring it was too—"

"Too great a risk to take," Desmond said, finishing for her. "Thisbe, the Eye *did* destroy me—to see you lifeless and know I was the cause of it."

They gazed at each other helplessly for a moment. Tears welled in Thisbe's eyes. "You really believe this, don't you?"

"I do. I don't know if I'm Anne Ballew's descendant or if I am some sort of monster who attracts death or if life is simply misery, but I am sure of one thing. Your grandmother was right. I will cause your death."

It seemed as if he could actually feel his heart cracking in his chest as he gazed at her. Desmond wanted to memorize her face, stamp the look and feel of her into his brain. He wanted to hold her inside him always, no matter what the pain. It didn't surprise him that he could not have her; that was the way of life. But, God, how he hated whatever had given him this fate. Hated it even more that it ripped open Thisbe, too.

Thisbe straightened, and her eyes took on that glorious light that never failed to devastate him. "If I am to lose you, then let us have this one last night together."

He went to her, pulling her into his arms and bending to kiss her. He would not regret this; he would not fight it. Two nights. For them there would never be more than the night in his flat and this. So little for so much love. But he would take this night; he would seize this one moment and make it last a lifetime.

They kissed and caressed, moving slowly, seeking the utmost pleasure from each movement, each sensation. Before, they had come together in darkness, enveloped in taste and scent and touch. Now they made love by the light of day, and the sight of her dazzled him.

Desmond slipped off Thisbe's clothes a piece at a time, revealing her smooth white flesh in aching, thrilling increments. Her skin was soft as satin beneath his fingertips, sweet upon his lips and tongue, and now he saw the full beauty of her pearl-white skin, the long slender stretch of her legs, the fullness of her breasts, tipped by dark pink nipples.

The extent of her loveliness enveloped him, filled his head and heart. He kissed her mouth, her breasts, her back, unwilling to leave any part of her body unknown to him, his own body tightening and pulsing in response. Need built in him, almost painful in its intensity, but firmly he suppressed it, savoring the escalation of desire.

Amazingly, Thisbe seemed to find equal pleasure in him. She tugged up his shirt, sliding her hands beneath it, and Desmond eagerly stripped off his clothes. Each stroke of her hand, every movement of her mouth over his flesh, made him quiver. Her fingertips trailed across his skin, exploring the ridges of his ribs, the curve of his buttocks, the hard line of his thigh. Thisbe's breath quickened, her body warming as she roamed his body. The evidence of her arousal sent his own passion surging.

And when she slipped her hand between his legs, he shuddered, almost undone by the rush of pleasure. They sank onto the bed, too hungry now to be gentle, too driven by their need to wait. Desmond pulled her beneath him, and she opened to him.

And slowly he slid into her. Memory could not match the exquisite pleasure of her body closing tight and hot around him. Thrusting and retreating, he stoked the fire inside. Every movement, every sound Thisbe made, pushed him higher, deeper, and when he felt the shudder of her completion, he could hold back his own no longer.

He shook under the force of it, drowning in the wonder of release, the sweetness of coming home. In this moment he was part of her and she of him, joined in a way that shattered and renewed them. "Thisbe, my love. My love."

THISBE STOOD AT the window, gazing out into the gathering darkness. Desmond had left moments ago, thoughtfully allowing her a chance to dress in privacy. She was grateful, not because she was uncomfortable at being naked under his gaze—indeed, the thought of it stirred her. But it had given her the opportunity to give way to her tears.

She had cried for the love of him and the loss of him. She understood now how Desmond felt, the fear of harm to another that was greater than any fear for self. He meant his vow, and she would not plague him to break it.

Thisbe would make this night something to treasure, to hold in her heart forever. She would wipe away the evidence of her tears, then take advantage of the luxury of an indoor bath that the inn surprisingly offered its guests. They would go down to dinner and afterward they would make love again and hold each other throughout the night. And that would have to be enough.

In the course of two months, her life, her world, her very being had changed. She knew now that there were forces that science could not explain, that logic could not conquer emotions. She understood that acceptance could require more courage than fighting, and parting could be an act of love greater than staying.

Thisbe doubted that she would ever reach the point where she wouldn't prefer fighting to giving in. But perhaps she could reach acceptance. She leaned her forehead against the cold windowpane.

Oh, who was she trying to fool?

She would never quit. Yes, she understood; yes, she would give Desmond the freedom to do what he thought he must. She wouldn't give in to the urge to argue or persuade or tempt him. But she knew she would never stop searching for a solution. She would find a way to change this fate that Desmond had accepted. After all, she was a Moreland.

IT WAS WORSE this time, far worse. The fear more piercing, the pain sharper, the cold so intense it burned her. "Save him. Save him. He cannot resist."

A figure stood on a stony ledge, his arms outstretched, wind tugging at his hair and shirt. She couldn't see his face, only his black silhouette against a fiery sunset. Storm clouds massed above them, and rain streamed down, blurring her view. Thunder crashed above them, and lightning raced down, striking the large rock behind the man with a blinding flash.

Smoke puffed up from the stone, and sparks danced

in the air. Thisbe watched, frozen in place, as the wind caught the smoke and swirled it around the man, growing thicker and blacker. Darkness streaming to him from all directions, enveloping him in its sinister embrace.

"Go," the voice rasped in her ear. "The Eye tears him apart."

The swirling darkness drifted away, revealing a hellish scene: two dark figures struggling, outlined by the blaze of the falling sun.

"Save him. Your debt to pay."

She tried to run, struggling for breath, her feet leaden, the cold penetrating every fiber of her being. She would never reach him in time.

"You must. You must. Yours for mine. Life for a life."

A knife flashed. Thisbe screamed, throwing herself forward...

"THISBE? LOVE, WAKE UP." Desmond's arms were around her, lifting her and cradling her against his chest.

"Desmond!" Thisbe clung to him. "He killed you!"

"I'm not dead, love. I'm right here."

She was racked by shivers, even with Desmond's warmth all around her. "I know. But it was horrible. I was so scared."

"None of it was real. There's no need to be afraid any longer—the danger has passed."

"No. It's not over. I know it's not over. I should have gone to the police, made them lock up those wicked men. They will try again—I know it."

"Tell me what happened." He smoothed his hand comfortingly over her back.

"He stabbed you."

"Who stabbed me?"

"I don't know." She shook her head and sat back to

look at him. "I couldn't tell. The sun was blinding—all I could see was your outline against the light. It could have been Wallace. Grieves? I don't know. But I knew the other one was you. He had a knife and he stabbed you. I couldn't reach you. I ran as hard as I can, but I couldn't move. Oh, Desmond!"

She threw her arms around him again, her cheek against his chest, soaking in the warmth of his chest, the reassuring thump of his heart. He was here, and he was alive. There was still time to change it. "It's the Eye. I'm certain of it. She said it's tearing you apart."

"Thisbe, look at me. I'm fine."

"Yes, for now." She slid out of his arms and returned with her traveling bag. "I know what I saw. I'm not insane."

"Of course not."

"She told me I must save you." Thisbe was thinking well enough now that she held back the rest of Anne Ballew's words. The idea of "a life for a life" would set Desmond against the idea. "It's the Eye. It's evil. There's only one thing to do." She dug through her clothes and pulled out the box. "I have to destroy it."

"But your grandmother will be apoplectic."

"I don't care. I have to destroy it." She fumbled with the fastening of the box and pulled it open.

The box was empty.

FOR A LONG MOMENT, they simply stared at the plush green velvet lining. Finally, unhelpfully, Thisbe said, "It's gone."

"But what— How—"

They looked at each other, the thought registering at the same time. "Carson!"

"He stole it!" Thisbe slammed the box shut. "No wonder he left quickly."

Desmond cursed, swinging out of bed and beginning to dress in sharp, angry motions. "How could I have been so stupid? He was after it the whole time. That's why he followed you. That's why he was so eager to help."

"He must have sneaked it out of the box when I wasn't paying attention."

"There were a dozen times he could have done it. At the train station, at the tavern. The cart when we were looking through the clothes—neither of us was paying attention. He could have done it at the very beginning. We were tying up Wallace and the others while he held the gun on them. I never looked over to see what else he might be doing."

"I checked three times to make sure the box was still in the bag," Thisbe said in disgust. "Why did I never think to open it?"

"No use worrying over it now." Desmond tossed the box back in the bag and began gathering their other belongings while Thisbe dressed. "We have to get it back."

Thisbe's fingers stilled on her buttons. "Desmond… that must have been Carson who was fighting you in my dream. I should have realized—he was too tall to be Wallace and too slender to be Grieves. It's Carson who stabbed you." Suddenly all impetus to recover her grandmother's possession vanished. "Let him keep the Eye."

"You said you needed to get rid of it, and you can't do that unless you get it back."

"What if that is how the Eye will destroy you? Maybe that was her warning—to stay away from the fight."

"She said the Eye would tear her child apart, didn't she? That 'he can't resist it.' That doesn't sound like getting stabbed in a fight."

"She said it would 'take you over,'" Thisbe admitted somewhat reluctantly.

"And you said the way to stop that was to destroy the Eye, which means we must get it back from Carson."

"But I can't let him kill you!" Thisbe cried. "You don't know that will be the outcome. Did you actually see me die?"

"I saw him plunge the knife. I couldn't reach you. I knew—"

"You *assumed*. Our fate isn't written in stone. What you saw was a possibility. If we know what might happen, I can protect myself from it."

"You're a fine one to be talking about changing one's fate!" Thisbe stormed, planting her hands on her hips.

"Look." He went to her, taking her hands in his. "Anne Ballew came to you for a reason. She wants you to change the outcome. She believes you can end the evil she created. If you are her descendant—"

"But I'm not. I'm positive."

"Then why was it in your family's possession? Why are you so connected to it? To her?"

"Because I am her *enemy*."

"What?"

"I think it was my ancestor who brought the charge of witchcraft against her. I saw him in my first dreams, standing beyond the fire, watching her death, unmoved. No, worse than unmoved—gratified. I think he wanted the Eye for himself, wanted Anne's power. So he orchestrated her death and took the Eye. That is how it came to be passed down from generation to generation in Grandmother's family."

"Are you certain?"

"Not in any way I can prove. But some of the things Grandmother said about it indicate that. 'One of his kind, one of ours.'" Carefully, Thisbe excised the idea of paying for one life with another. "In my visions, Anne told me that I owed it to her, that she had bound me. Yesterday, when I grabbed the Eye from your hand, it burned me. I saw a man's hand in a thick, old-fashioned glove reach into flames and grab the Eye. And in that instant, I knew what had happened. My ancestor killed Anne for the Eye, an evil act to gain the evil she had created."

"Then that is why you will be the one to end it," Desmond said with finality. "Can't you see the perfect symmetry? She created the evil—your ancestor compounded the wrong by killing her to get it. Now you must rid the world of it."

Desmond was right. She had to end it. Thisbe knew it in the same way she knew her connection to the Eye. This was Anne Ballew's curse on Thisbe's ancestor and all his line. *I bind thee.* The debt that must be paid. *Yours for mine. A life for a life.*

Thisbe must destroy the Eye and the evil that infused it so that the nightmarish scene she'd witnessed in her sleep would not come to pass. She would ward off Desmond's death. And if the price for his life was her own, she would pay it.

CHAPTER THIRTY-FOUR

"How will we find him?" Thisbe asked as they hurried down the stairs. "All Carson said—*if* he was telling the truth—was that his family estate was in the Lake District."

"That's why it's a good thing that he invited me to visit him once," Desmond replied. "It's near Grasmere. I can find it from the village."

There were no more horses to hire, but there was a light carriage, and the innkeeper assured them the team was fresh and fast. It was warmer, too, than riding on horseback in the wintry air. When they started out, Thisbe's stomach roiled, but oddly, as they drew closer to their destination, her nerves calmed, a steady resolve forming inside her.

She and Desmond talked little. What was there to say? That she loved him above all else? That their lives hung in the balance?

It was late afternoon by the time they reached Grasmere. A few miles beyond it, Desmond directed their driver to turn off. The lane curved around a tor that thrust up from the ground like the prow of a ship. Nestled beneath the stark cliff was a deep, dark tarn.

Facing this harshly beautiful view was a gray stone manor house, set like a jewel among a cluster of trees. They left the carriage ready to face their adversary, only to be told, rather anticlimactically, that Carson was not at home.

"He didn't come here?" Thisbe asked the butler at the door, then turned toward Desmond in dismay.

"Oh, no, he's at the manor, miss. He is simply, um, out at the moment." The butler peered more closely at Desmond. "Sir!" Oddly, his face flooded with relief. "I'm sorry, sir, I didn't recognize you right off."

Desmond smiled. "I'm surprised you remembered me at all. It's been several years since I was here."

"Yes, but Mr. Dunbridge comes home so rarely since his father passed on. Please, come in, let me show you to the drawing room. I'm Willoughby, sir. I'm terribly sorry that Mr. Dunbridge isn't here to greet you. He didn't tell us he was expecting visitors."

"He didn't know we were coming," Desmond told him. "We were in Grasmere and decided to drop in."

"We should have sent round a note first," Thisbe added. "But Desmond has told me so much about this lovely home, I greatly wanted to see it. I'm sorry to put you to any trouble."

"Oh, no, miss, no trouble at all. I'm so glad—I'm sure Mr. Dunbridge will be happy to see you." The butler's troubled expression belied his words.

"Do you know if Carson will return soon?" Desmond asked. "Or where he went? We could join him."

"Yes, that is… Well." Willoughby began to wring his hands and finally he blurted out, "I'm worried, sir. I wouldn't say anything, but I know you're a friend of Mr. Dunbridge, and, well—"

"What's wrong?" Desmond asked cutting through his excuses. "Has something happened to Carson?"

"No, it's just, well…" He took a deep breath and apparently decided to cast aside his butlerish inhibitions.

"He rode in late last night, long after dark. We'd had no idea he was coming, and I hadn't made up his room. He had no baggage with him, and he…simply wasn't his usual self. He seemed most agitated, and he was carrying around a *quizzing glass*, of all things. He wouldn't set it down or let me put it up for him."

"Did he say why he came here?"

"No! Nothing that made any sense. He kept talking about some woman named Anne, and he went into his father's office and rummaged about in it. Then he grew quite angry when he couldn't find something, which you know is not like him at all."

"No, it's not. What was he looking for?"

"I don't know, sir. He asked where I'd packed away his father's things and when I told him the attic, he went up there and came down with an old metal box. He locked himself in his father's office the rest of the night and today, as well. He refused anything to eat or drink. He was, well…" Willoughby lowered his voice to a discreet whisper. "He was rather rude, really. And his manners are always faultless."

"I fear something is troubling him greatly," Desmond told the man. "The truth is that's why we came here. We need to talk to him."

"Yes, yes, please do. He hasn't been gone long. He just walked out. Without even putting on his greatcoat! He was rather…unsteady, and I think perhaps he had been sampling his father's brandy all this time."

"He was foxed?"

"Well, I wouldn't say that, sir—Mr. Dunbridge can carry his liquor, as you know. But he was not himself. He was still carrying that odd quizzing glass, and—and…" The butler took a sharp little breath. "He had a dagger in his other hand."

"Where did he go?" Desmond gripped the man's arm. "Which direction?"

"Up, sir." Willoughby pointed to the front door. "He went up the tor."

DESMOND'S LONG LEGS ate up the ground more quickly than Thisbe's, and he was soon far ahead of her. He circled back a time or two to help her over a rougher patch, but Thisbe could see that he ached to run ahead. She would have waved him on, for she didn't really need his aid, but she couldn't forget the struggling men in her dream, silhouetted against the sunset. The sun was even now hovering on the horizon.

Thisbe glanced up. The sky had been clear when they arrived, but now dark clouds were gathering above them. Heart in her throat, she hurried after Desmond. He was several feet ahead of her when they emerged on the flatter top of the tor.

He stopped abruptly, and Thisbe, coming up behind him, saw why. Carson stood on a low flat rock at the edge of the tor, behind him only an empty fall to the tarn below. His arms were spread wide. In one hand he held a small dagger, and in the other, the Eye.

Exactly as she had pictured in her dream. "My God," Thisbe murmured. "It's him! Carson is Annie Blue's 'child.'"

She saw it with blinding clarity now. It was no wonder Desmond hadn't been affected by the Eye, yet Carson had turned jittery. It was Carson who was under the spell of the Eye and him that Anne Ballew had entreated Thisbe to save.

Carson wore no coat, as the butler had told them, and his shirt hung open down the front. A long line of red slanted across his bare chest. Thisbe realized, shocked, that the red line was blood. The sky was even darker now, and the wind rose, tugging at the open sides of Carson's shirt and whipping his hair. He looked utterly wild.

Thisbe glanced at Desmond, unsure what to do. Carson was too close to the edge of the cliff for safety; if they rushed him, he might stumble off. Indeed, given his frenzied expression, she wouldn't put it past him to leap out into the air as if he could fly. Even a shout might startle him into falling.

Before they could do anything, Carson spotted them. "Desmond! Thisbe!" He laughed, and the madness in his voice sent shivers down Thisbe's spine. He gave them a salute with his dagger. The gesture made him sway a little, and Thisbe's heart jumped into her throat. "I wondered when you'd find out. Sorry." Carson shook his head. "I hated to deceive you, you know. I always liked you, Dez."

"And I liked you. I'm still your friend, Carson. Why don't you come down here, and we'll talk?"

"No." Carson's voice was buoyant, and he grinned. "Can't do that. I've no friends now." He pointed the Eye at them. "Only power."

"Carson, what you see through that lens isn't real. It's deceptive. An illusion."

"That's because *you* aren't her child. You're a good chap, but they were stupid to think you were her descendant. *I* am her son. I have her diary." He pointed the knife at a slender leather-bound book on the rock beside him, then raised the dagger before him like an emblem. "I carry her athame."

"I know you are her descendant," Thisbe told him. "Anne Ballew came to me in my dreams. She warned me that the Eye would destroy you. She begged me to save you."

"Now, now." Carson wagged the athame in playful scolding. "No lying."

"It's not a lie. I dreamed about her time after time. She told me the Eye was evil. She said I must save her child. I just didn't understand—I didn't realize it was you. But now I see."

"Don't lie!" Carson shouted, his light manner dissolving into fury. Thunder rolled, and lightning streaked across the sky. It began to rain. He raised the Eye, sending flashes of color all over the area. "The Eye will never hurt me. It *belongs* to me."

"No one disputes that it's yours, Carson," Desmond said in a placating tone. He had moved cautiously forward while Thisbe held Carson's attention, and he took another slow step as he spoke. "I'll gladly relinquish all pretension to being Anne Ballew's heir. The Eye rightfully is yours. But what use is it to you?"

"It holds her power," Carson raged. "Don't you understand?"

The air crackled with energy. Thisbe felt the hair on her arms rise. Somehow the juxtaposition of the rainbows of light and the almost electric surge of power made the scene even more fearsome. Ignoring her own fright, Thisbe moved quietly to the side, taking advantage of Carson's focus on Desmond to remove herself from Carson's line of vision.

"Not really," Desmond admitted. "Seeing the spirits of the dead doesn't seem—"

"Don't play the fool, Desmond." Carson laughed. "You're no good at it. It's not seeing the dead. It's raising them."

"Necromancy? That's what Wallace wanted, too—he was determined to bring his wife back, but why do you—"

"Don't be a fool. I'm going to use it to raise *her*!" Tiny blue-white sparks danced in the air around him, and the air around them grew even more electric.

"Anne Ballew?" Desmond stared.

Thisbe was on Carson's left and much nearer to him now. Desmond, too, had moved closer. Carson was too wrapped up in his words to notice how much ground Desmond had covered.

"I'll have Anne Ballew's knowledge. I'll have her power! I'll have everything our family's been denied all these years. The riches, the land, the adulation. I won't be on the fringes—I won't be the laughingstock my father was."

Desmond, looking alarmed, took a long step forward and reached out.

"Stop!" Carson pointed the knife at Desmond. "Don't come up here."

The energy in the air dissipated a little. But, no, Thisbe realized, it hadn't lessened; it had simply moved, coalescing around Carson and Desmond. Desmond's hair whipped in the wind as wildly as Carson's, and the prismatic dance of color created by the Eye now encompassed only them. Thisbe's eyes widened. Carson could control its power? Or, worse, it could control Carson?

"Why not?" Desmond said as casually as if they were standing on a street corner, even though Thisbe was sure he must have felt the change in the air.

Carson laughed. "I know you, and you'll try to stop me."

"Why would I do that? I'm just trying to understand. You know me—I always want to learn the 'why' of everything."

"You do. You do. That's why you're the best of us. But I—" Carson flourished the athame. "I have the power."

"How is that?" Desmond continued his incremental movement forward. "Surely it takes more than being of her bloodline."

"Of course it does. But you see, *I* know how."

Desmond was getting too near Carson. Thisbe remembered the struggle in her dream too well. The last thing she wanted was for Desmond to get within Carson's reach. She wanted to cry out to him to step back, but she could not give away her position. Carson seemed to have forgotten about her entirely.

Don't get close, she urged Desmond in her mind. *Just stay where you are, and I'll have him. I have a plan.*

She didn't intend to take down Carson. All she had to do was snatch the Eye from his hand. The knife was in his right hand, as one would naturally hold it. The Eye was in his left, the weaker hand, and he kept waving it about like a handkerchief as he talked. In just a few more feet, she could run at him. He'd turn, no doubt, to face the attack, but instead of attacking, Thisbe would grab the Eye before Carson realized her true goal. She would run, hopefully before Carson could stab her. And Desmond would never be at risk.

"How do you use the Eye?" Desmond asked, still in his harmlessly curious voice.

"It takes blood. My blood. Her blood. It's all in there." He gestured again toward the thin book on the rock. "Her family escaped with her journal—her enemies didn't find that. We changed our name, but we kept our secrets. Her formula. My blood." Carson sliced another line of red down his chest. Thisbe winced, but Carson didn't seem to feel the pain.

"So, um, do you need to cut a certain pattern?" Desmond asked. "That must be rather difficult to handle by oneself. Step down, and I can help you." He reached out his hand.

"No!" Carson roared, his eyes blazing brighter. "I know what you want. You'll take my blood and use it for yourself."

The energy from Carson to Desmond grew even stronger, changing into a tighter, thicker figure that encased only them. Even through the rain, Thisbe could see tiny flashes of blue-white light popping up among the steadier flow of colors. Thisbe had no idea what that meant, but she was certain it couldn't be good. And why hadn't she seen any of this in her dream?

"No, no," Desmond said soothingly. "I won't. I can't use the Eye, not even with your blood. You know that—I'm not her kin. I just want to help."

"You don't! You're like them. Wallace. Gordon." Carson spat out the names. "They stole my birthright. It's *my* sacrifice." Suddenly Carson jumped down from the rock ledge to face Desmond, one hand curled around his dagger, the other pointing the Eye threateningly at Desmond. "It's *my* power."

Thisbe sucked in a breath. The line of energy between the two men was concentrated into a flow of brilliant light that consumed the bands of color. But, she realized, as the power had strengthened in its narrowed path, the energy it had cast over the whole area had dwindled. And Carson had changed his position; by stepping down from the rock, he had put the Eye within easier reach for her.

As she took a cautious step forward, she realized that the scene before her was not the same as it had been in her dream. The two men were no longer silhouetted against the sun on the low rock. She stood even with them rather than below. Her perspective was entirely different. Desmond was right: she could change what happened. She already had. She could make everything right. Thisbe crept forward, keeping a careful eye on the men.

"Yes, the power is yours. Entirely yours," Desmond said calmly. "I only want to help you."

"Don't try to stop me," Carson told him. "You don't know what the Eye can do. I don't want to hurt you. You feel how it's holding you back? I can do more. I can drain the very life from you."

Thisbe froze in horror. This… Yes, this was what the Eye was capable of. Desmond, however, didn't look frightened. He shook his head and took a step toward Carson. Astonishment flashed across Carson's face.

"Stop! I compel you!" Carson held his ground, his face fierce. Above them lightning lit up the sky and thunder roared. Carson was clearly concentrating all his will into the Eye.

Thisbe darted forward. Carson heard her approach at the last minute and whipped around, but Thisbe was already reaching for the Eye. She tore it away, but the force of her pull sent her staggering back and she fell. Carson came after her, dagger raised. Thisbe rolled away just as Desmond leaped forward. He grabbed Carson's arm and hauled him back.

Thisbe struggled to her feet, the Eye clutched in her hand, and saw before her the very outcome she had feared: Carson and Desmond grappling for control of the athame. Desmond held Carson's knife hand motionless at the top of its downward arc, but Carson's strength was that of a madman. Desmond had to use both hands to stave off the dagger, so he could not block the blows from Carson's other fist. Blood was streaming down Desmond's face.

"No!" Thisbe screamed and launched herself forward. Clasping her hands together around the Eye, she swung it upward at Carson's head with all her might. Carson flailed out, shoving away Thisbe. She fell back, hitting the large flat rock, and skidded across its rain-slick surface. Suddenly there was nothing beneath her legs. Desperately she scrabbled for purchase, but her fingers slid across the smooth, wet surface. She heard Desmond scream her name as the world fell out from under her.

CHAPTER THIRTY-FIVE

"THISBE!" DESMOND'S HEART froze in his chest. He shoved aside Carson and ran to the edge of the cliff, the splash in the water below resounding in his ears. There was no sign of Thisbe in the dark tarn, only the widening circles where she had entered the water.

The rocky ledge on which he stood jutted out over the water; there was no way down the cliff on this side. Behind him, Carson was staggering to his feet, but Desmond didn't even glance at him, just whirled and ran to right side of the tor, where a rocky scree sloped down to the water. It was not a sheer drop as it was under the ledge, but it was shorter and steeper than the way they had come up.

Desmond tore down it in a slipping, sliding run, once tumbling head over heels and rolling several feet before he was able to scramble up and run again. He took the last few feet to the tarn's edge in a single leap.

She wasn't there. Oh, God, she wasn't there. He searched the water for any sign of Thisbe, jerking off his shoes as he did so. There it was—the spread of dark hair on the surface. He dove into the water. The icy cold was a slam to his heart, but he didn't pause as he sliced through the water. He had learned to swim in a river, battling currents, and he was a strong swimmer, but the cold of the water sapped his strength.

He couldn't find her. Could no longer see her hair

floating on the surface. He stopped and frantically looked all around. Something grazed his foot. He plunged downward into the dark water, his hands groping around him. His fingers touched fabric, and he grabbed it. Pulling with all his strength, he kicked to the surface. He breached the water, carrying Thisbe's body with him, and sucked in a lungful of air. Treading water, he managed to get Thisbe's face above the surface and his arm around her.

She was limp against him, offering no assistance as he struck out for the shore. Desmond prayed he was swimming in the right direction. The setting sun was gone now, the world darkening around them. It would be disastrous if he'd turned in the wrong direction and was swimming toward the center of the lake. He kicked, using one arm to stroke backward, his other holding Thisbe up out of the water. The cold was enervating, dragging at his muscles, and Thisbe's sodden skirts and petticoats weighed them down. Numbly, he continued.

Suddenly, as he reached forward in his stroke, his fingers hit dirt. He'd reached the shore. Desmond crawled from the water, pulling Thisbe up onto the shore beside him. He hadn't even the breath to say her name as he bent over her. Her face was pale, her lips almost blue. It was the vision he'd seen in the Eye: Thisbe pale and dead on the ground.

"No!" He pressed his fingers against her neck. There was no pulse. "No! Damn it, Thisbe, no."

He refused to let her die. Bending Thisbe over his arm, he slapped her back. Water drained from her mouth, but her chest didn't move. He hit her harder. Nothing. He'd read… His frozen brain struggled to remember.

After laying her on her back, he pushed on her chest, pushed again and again. Bending, he placed his lips against hers and breathed into her mouth. He pushed on her chest. He breathed; he pushed. Forcing his air into her. Demanding that she live.

Thisbe jerked. She began to cough violently, rolling onto her side. Desmond sat back on his heels, shaking with relief. If he'd had the energy, he would have laughed. He would have cried. But all he could do was sit there, gulping in air and soaking in the knowledge that Thisbe was alive.

The rattle of rocks drew Desmond's attention to the scree he'd just descended. Carson was stumbling down it. The dirt that coated his body, mixing with the blood on his chest, was mute testimony that Carson had taken a tumble or two on his way down. Wearily, Desmond watched Carson reach flat ground and start toward him.

"Didn't mean—" Carson panted as he came to a stop and fell to his knees a few feet away from Desmond. His eyes went to Thisbe. "I'm sorry— I didn't— Oh, God, is she—"

"She's alive." Desmond thrust down the desire to go after the man with his fists.

Carson nodded, but his attention was no longer on Thisbe or Desmond. He was examining the ground all around him, twisting and turning and sweeping aside dirt and pebbles. "Where is it?" He looked up, and Desmond saw that Carson's eyes were still crazed. "Where is it?" Carson repeated frantically. "Give me the Eye!"

"Oh, for— It's gone." Desmond pushed to his feet. He'd had enough of this. He was cold to the bone and he needed to get Thisbe back inside the warm house. He gestured toward the black tarn behind him. "It's at the bottom of the lake."

"No!" Carson screamed and ran toward the water.

"You bloody idiot." Desmond smashed his fist into

Carson's jaw, and Carson went down. Still, he scrambled to rise. "Stop! Would you stop? It's gone."

"No, it's not." Thisbe's voice behind them was so shredded it was hardly recognizable.

Desmond whirled around. Thisbe was the color of death and shaking, but she had risen to her knees behind him. She drew the Eye from the pocket of her sodden skirt and held it aloft. "I have it."

She set the Eye on a rock beside her. Scooping up a smaller rock, she smashed it down on the Eye. Light flashed, and the very earth seemed to tremble beneath their feet. Carson let out a strangled cry, and the wild light in his eyes died.

Thisbe crumpled to the ground.

SHE WAS UNIMAGINABLY COLD. Thisbe looked around for Anne Ballew. She had just seen her a few moments ago, standing in the darkness, soft sparks of light cascading over her. For the first time, Thisbe saw Anne smile. But she was gone now. There was nothing but blackness and the cold that soaked clear through to Thisbe's bones.

But, no, there was a voice. Thisbe knew that voice; she'd heard it before in the darkness, pulling at her. Now she was wrapped in warmth, blessed heat seeping into her. "Thisbe, love, come back," the voice kept saying, the words a breath across her cheek, a rumble against her back.

It was clear, she thought with some annoyance, that he was not going to let her rest...

THISBE OPENED HER heavy eyes. Desmond cradled her tightly, his arms encircling her and his leg thrown over hers. A mountain of blankets weighed them down. "Desmond?"

"Thank God." Desmond's voice trembled almost as much as she did. "I thought you were gone. I thought it had broken you." He squeezed her even more tightly to him, and repeated, "Thank God."

His voice was hoarse, and he buried his face in her hair. Was he crying? It seemed very strange.

It was difficult to think; her mind seemed to float away. Still, Thisbe knew she should say something in response. "I'm cold."

He chuckled now, kissing her cheek. "I know, love, I know. You'll be warm soon."

The next time she awoke, she was still cold, but it was more normal now, just a feeling of being chilled, as when one had stayed outside too long. She shuddered.

"Thisbe?" Desmond's arms around her loosened, and he rose up to look down into her face. "How do you feel?"

"Sore." She realized that the coldness before had concealed the fact that every bone and muscle in her body ached. She coughed. "And my lungs burn."

"Of course they do. I'm sorry." He smoothed back her hair from her face, gazing at her in the oddest way, as if he hadn't seen her in years. "I don't think anything's broken, though." He slipped out of the bed, and she saw that his face was red, his shirt damp with sweat. He must have been unbearably hot under the pile of covers with her. "I'll run down and get you a cup of soup. I don't want to ask Willoughby to bring it. He seems to be the only one working here." He started toward the door, then hesitated. "But everything's safe—you'll be fine here."

Thisbe blinked. "Of course I will."

She closed her eyes again. It was pleasant here. But who was Willoughby? For that matter, where was she? On the edge of sleep, she let her mind drift, thoughts and memories slowly filtering back in. She was remembering now, but it seemed too great an effort to think.

The sound of Desmond entering the room awakened her, and she shoved herself up to a sitting position, her aching body protesting. She felt as if she'd been beaten—which, she supposed, she had, even though it was a tarn that flattened her.

Desmond hurried to her side and helped her sit up. She took the soup he offered and began to eat as he stuffed pillows behind her back, pulled the covers up around her and generally fussed over her. Then he brought a chair over to her bedside and sat down, watching her as if every bite she took was fascinating.

"Who's Willoughby?" she asked when her stomach was sated enough she was no longer gulping down the soup.

"The butler here."

"Oh, yes, now I remember. We're still at Carson's house? I would have thought he tossed us out."

"Carson's not in much position to be tossing anything," Desmond replied. "Do you remember what happened?"

She nodded. "I remember almost everything until I went sailing off the tor. After that, it's a bit of a blur. I don't remember hitting the lake, but I must have landed in the water instead of on the ground or I'd be in much worse shape." Thisbe took another sip of the soup, thinking. "Then I remember darkness and cold. I thought I saw Anne Ballew again, but that was probably a dream I had while I was asleep. And then..." She frowned. "I remember light and the ground seemed to move."

"It did," he confirmed. "When you destroyed the Eye."

"Did I? I wish I remembered that. How did I destroy it?"

"Crushed it to bits with a rock. It's nothing but ground

glass now and a twisted scrap of metal, which I melted in the fireplace. There's a burn mark on the rock where you destroyed it."

"What happened to Carson? You sounded as if he was ill or…" Thisbe trailed off. Perhaps she had smashed Carson's mind, as well.

"He's not sick, though he bloody well should have caught pneumonia, capering about out there in the rain in his shirtsleeves. Willoughby says Carson's just been sitting, staring into the fire." He shrugged. "He stopped me in the hallway as I was coming back here."

"Carson? Are you serious? Why?"

"He wanted to apologize."

"Well, I would think he should have done that to me," Thisbe retorted.

Desmond laughed. "I told him that. But I believe he's too ashamed to face you yet."

"What did he say?"

"How sorry he was. How he wasn't himself. How he never meant to hurt you. He seems to feel pretty wretched about the whole thing." He sighed. "There wasn't a single wry quip in all he said. I've never seen him so…exposed."

"Do you believe him?" Thisbe asked.

"I think it's true that he didn't know what he was doing. He was 'possessed' by the Eye somehow. I have been envious of Carson, jealous, suspicious, but I don't think he's a bad person deep down. He was a friend to me long before he thought we could lead him to the Eye."

"So you forgave him?"

Desmond snorted. "I'm not that kindhearted. However accidental it was that he knocked you down, the fact is, he *killed* you."

"Yes, well, he tried to stab you, and that wasn't accidental at all," Thisbe said with some heat.

"Trust you to be more upset about what he tried to do to me than what he actually did to you." Desmond smiled and lifted her hand to kiss it. "I told him I couldn't give him absolution. I think that would have to come from you. Right now, I find it a little hard to care what happens with Carson."

Thisbe was silent for a moment again, thinking. "Something puzzles me about all this."

"Only one thing?" Desmond laughed.

"Well, one thing at this particular moment." She smiled and squeezed his hand. It felt so wonderful, so right, to be with him like this, free of restraints or worry. "Carson was Anne Ballew's descendant. That's clear from his having the journal and that knife and all."

He nodded. "I think that's safe to assume."

"Then why were you able to see the vision of me dead?"

"I'm not sure. I've been thinking about that and... the thing is, we don't really know that Anne Ballew had only one child."

"You're right." Thisbe straightened, intrigued. "I should have thought of that. Even if she had only one child, that child very well may have had more than one and those children had children—there could be a number of people who are Anne's descendants." She paused, considering the idea. "Do you think that's why the Eye couldn't stop you? Carson certainly thought it should. He looked astonished when you kept coming toward him."

"Perhaps. Or maybe he didn't use it properly—or that power was just a myth."

"But then why didn't you feel its allure? Why didn't it 'call' you as it did Carson?"

"It did 'call' me," Desmond confessed. "When Wallace showed the bloody thing to me before you arrived,

I wanted so badly to take it. All I could think of was how much I could learn, how much knowledge it held. I wanted it so much, it scared me."

"But you didn't take it until he forced you."

"No. It was too seductive, too strong. I wasn't about to let anything control me like that. That's why I refused to take it until he threatened you." He raised her hand to his lips and kissed it. "It was far easier to refuse when you were there."

"Me? Why?"

He shrugged. "I just didn't feel such a pull. I didn't feel it when your grandmother showed it to us, either."

"Really? How odd."

"I think your power must have been stronger than it." He smiled at Thisbe.

"Or perhaps it was our love that was more powerful," Thisbe said.

He leaned in to kiss her, and the conversation was put aside for the moment. When Desmond raised his head, he said, "You should sleep."

Thisbe shook her head. "I'm fine—I'm feeling stronger by the moment. And I've done nothing but sleep for— How long has it been?"

"It's been a day now."

"A day!"

He nodded. "I was getting worried… Hell, I was terrified. You didn't die—or, rather, you did, but you came back to life, but I feared your mind was gone. That you would be nothing but a shell."

"Stop. Go back. I 'came back to life'? What does that mean?"

"When I pulled you from the water, you weren't breathing. But the Swiss discovered a century ago that if you forced your own air into someone's lungs, sometimes he would begin breathing again on his own."

"That's what you did for me?" Thisbe gazed at him, wide-eyed.

He nodded. "I read an article not too long ago about pushing the water out of one's lungs and he suggested that pushing the air *out* of your lungs, as well as in, would more closely simulate breathing. I was afraid I'd break your ribs, but I was desperate. Your lips were blue. You looked…"

"The way you saw me through the Eye."

He nodded.

"Grandmother's prediction came true, after all. Our love led to my death. What we didn't know was that your love would be bring me back."

Desmond leaned forward suddenly, setting aside her cup and taking both her hands in his. "Thisbe, I am such an idiot. Which, of course, probably comes as no surprise to you." He lifted her hands to kiss them. "I should have trusted you, trusted myself. What I told you the other day, that we aren't bound by an inflexible destiny, that we can reshape our fate into something better—that is the truth of the matter. It's what I believe. But I was afraid to believe that you could actually love me."

"How could I not love you?" Thisbe caressed his face.

"There are many reasons, but I'm not foolish enough to point them out." Desmond smiled. "It makes no sense, but I wanted a future with you so much that believing I could have it terrified me."

"I understand."

"Do you? I'm not sure *I* do. All I know is that yesterday, when I saw you go off that ledge, all I could think was that I would not let you die. Whatever I had to do, I would. The only thing I couldn't do was sit back and allow it to happen. Our lives are what we make of them. They're what we do with what we're given. I had been given the most precious gift possible in your love, and I'd been too scared, too stupid, too blind, to take it."

Tears filled Thisbe's eyes. "Then you'll marry me?"

Desmond grinned. "I'm the one who's supposed to ask you."

"I never do what I'm supposed to," Thisbe retorted. Wrapping her arms around his neck, she kissed him. When at last she pulled back, she said, "So will you? Marry me?"

"Of course I will."

"And all those qualms about being thought an adventurer?"

"Why should I care what other people think? All I care about is you," he told her. "And if that means living in an enormous house with your delightful family, and being waited on by servants, and researching exactly what I want in our own private laboratory…well, those are hardships I shall simply have to bear."

Thisbe laughed and pushed back the covers, no longer cold at all. After swinging her leg over his, she straddled him and hooked her arms loosely around his neck. "Then perhaps you might show me how glad you are that I didn't die."

His mouth softened, his eyes darkening. "Are you sure you feel well enough?"

"Desmond, dearest, I'll always feel well enough for you." Thisbe moved in to kiss him, bearing him back down on the bed.

THEY RETURNED TO London the following day. Unsurprisingly, when they related their story to the family, the dowager duchess rose from her chair like a vengeful goddess.

"You destroyed Anne Ballew's Eye? Really, Thisbe, I sent you to find the thing, not ruin it." Her gaze swiveled to Desmond. "No doubt that was your idea."

"No, Grandmother, I am the one who made that decision. I smashed it to bits." Thisbe ignored her grandmother's gasp and plowed ahead. "All Desmond did was *save my life*."

"Of course, that is the most important thing," the duchess said, though her tone left some doubt as to her words. "But it does seem to me that one could have achieved both things. It's an heirloom—our ancestor entrusted it to us. Anne Ballew gave us our gift."

Thisbe's eyes flashed. "Anne Ballew wasn't—"

Seeing the expression on Thisbe's face, Desmond interrupted, stepping forward. "Anne Ballew wasn't in favor of saving the Eye. As you know, she appeared to Thisbe in her dreams and specifically told her to destroy it."

"I'm not at all sure you heard her correctly, Thisbe," Cornelia said.

Desmond went on in an admiring tone, "You have the ability, ma'am, even without the Eye. You don't need it. Look at how accurate your prediction was. Thisbe did die because of our love."

"Of course I was right…despite what all the disbelievers said." The duchess looked pointedly around the room at the other members of the family.

"You were completely vindicated," Desmond agreed.

Cornelia preened. "Not that I needed any vindication. I have always known my gift was powerful."

"The Eye was too powerful for people who don't share your gift to use. And, as we've seen, it can easily fall into the wrong hands. I'm sure you'll agree that it's better that they not have the opportunity."

"Perhaps you're right," Thisbe's grandmother admitted, looking somewhat mollified. She followed the statement with a piercing look. "And now, I suppose, you'll want to marry my granddaughter."

"Yes, ma'am, I intend to ask her father for her hand."

Cornelia heaved a sigh. "You are hardly the suitor I would have picked for my granddaughter, but Thisbe seems peculiarly set on you. And one cannot but be grateful that you kept her from drowning. I grant you my permission," she said with a regal nod. "Provided, of course, you wait to have the banns read, like decent people, instead of rushing off with a special license." She sent a withering look at her son and his wife.

Desmond's interview with Thisbe's father was a far easier matter. When Desmond asked for his daughter's hand, the duke said, "I don't suppose I have any say in the matter. But it was kind of you to ask." He leaned forward, his usually vague gaze intent. "The only question I have for you is…do you love her?"

"That's an easy requirement, sir. I love Thisbe with all my heart. I've loved her from the moment I saw her."

The duke smiled and sat back. "That's something I'm familiar with."

THISBE AND DESMOND were married three weeks later. Surprising everyone, Cornelia went to call on Zachary Wallace. Surprising no one but Desmond, after her visit Mr. Wallace was inspired to bestow an unconditional research grant on Desmond.

When Desmond went to thank Cornelia, the duchess fixed him with her steely gaze, and said, "My daughter-in-law assures me that you object to the notion that Thisbe's fortune becomes yours the moment you marry her—possibly the only subject on which Emmeline and I agree. But we cannot have you penniless. You must have the wherewithal to buy Thisbe presents and purchase your books or whatnot. This seemed the obvious solution. You can scarcely maintain that you haven't earned whatever that man pays you. Mr. Wallace, of course, realized the advantages of my not bringing charges against him, and he was happy to agree to that arrangement." Cornelia's lips curved up at the memory of another battle won. "And now, one hopes, you will buy yourself some proper attire for the wedding and a ring appropriate to Thisbe's station."

Desmond bought the clothes, but the wedding ring he gave Thisbe—and the one she preferred—was the simple gold band his mother had worn.

The wedding took place at Broughton House with scarcely a hitch. The duke was only a few minutes late, and though Desmond forgot his tiepin, that was easily solved by borrowing one from Reed. The twins performed admirably, carrying the rings on their small square pillows without a single jump or skip and not once tossing the pillows or hitting one another with them until after the ceremony. Kyria and Olivia kept Thisbe's nerves at bay all morning. And the dowager duchess and Great-Aunt Hermione, who had traveled up from Bath for the occasion, had only one small tiff.

Thisbe and Desmond said their vows. He kissed the bride. Emmeline dabbed away tears, and Kyria and Olivia cried even as they declared the wedding perfect. Reed shook Desmond's hand and said with a grin, "Welcome to the family. I hope you have steady nerves."

The celebration was small and typically Moreland, with a great deal of talking and laughter and spontaneous outbursts of song from Aunt Penelope, who had arrived from Paris with champagne and a wedding dress made by Worth. The twins dodged in and out in a game of chase with Lady Rochester's barking spaniel. On the other side of the room, there was dancing, with a string quartet providing the music.

Thisbe danced with Reed and her father and Uncle Bellard, who, despite his shy nature, was a nimble dancer. Most of all, she danced with Desmond. He hadn't the skill of her great-uncle or Reed, but she fit his arms perfectly, and Thisbe could look into his deep brown eyes and dream of all the lovely things the future held.

Later, Thisbe took Desmond's hand and pulled him from the party. He raised his eyebrows in question as he followed her out the door. "Where are we going?"

"I want to show you something."

"That sounds tantalizing."

His slow smile sent a dart of desire through her. It was amazing, really, how she seemed to want him more each day. "It's not what you think," she told him in a prim voice and followed her words with a teasing sideways glance. "But perhaps something else might follow."

She took him through the long gallery and up a set of stairs. At one end of the short hallway stood a closed door, and a corridor intersected the other.

"I've never been here," Desmond said, looking around. "I don't think I shall ever learn where everything is."

"That's because we don't open this wing unless we have a very large number of guests." Thisbe opened the door, revealing yet another hall. "Come. Let me show you."

They went to a large, sunny room at the far end of the hall. Several tables bore various scientific equipment from microscopes to Bunsen burners to burette titration systems to—Desmond's eyes lit in appreciation—a colorimeter. There were also closed cabinets and open shelves filled with beakers, pipettes, jars of chemicals, and other supplies.

"It's our laboratory," Thisbe said, sweeping her arm around the room. "Smeggars set it up. There's a sitting room and a bedroom right down the hall. We have our own private wing. We can even close that outer door to keep out the twins."

Desmond laughed. "Good luck with that."

"Isn't this lovely?"

"It is." He moved closer, putting his hands on her hips. "So are you."

She linked her hands behind his neck. "It's our own little home. You'll be happy here, won't you?"

Desmond's brown eyes were warm and intense as he gazed at her. "Thisbe, wherever you are is my home. I love you."

"And I love you."

"Then that's all that matters," he said and pulled her into his arms.

* * * * *

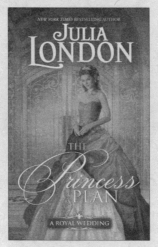